Standing Orders

Matador
9 Priory Business Park,
Wistow Road, Kibworth Beauchamp,
Leicestershire. LE8 0RX
Tel: 0116 279 2299
Email: books@troubador.co.uk
Web: www.troubador.co.uk/matador
Twitter: @matadorbooks

ISBN 978 1785893 209

British Library Cataloguing in Publication Data.
A catalogue record for this book is available from the British Library.

Printed and bound by CPI Group (UK) Ltd, Croydon, CR0 4YY
Typeset in 11pt Aldine401 BT by Troubador Publishing Ltd, Leicester, UK

Matador is an imprint of Troubador Publishing Ltd

Dedicated to my wife, Rosemary in the year of our Silver Wedding Anniversary.

PROLOGUE

Three-year-old Onaedo was chasing a cockerel around the courtyard into the shadows, while her mother watched with wonder and pride through the open kitchen window. 'Maki' Nkowo wiped the excess suds from her hands and shook them into the orange bowl. The washing-up was finished and she called to her daughter.

'Don't go out of the courtyard, little one. *Papa* will be here soon.' She knew Onaedo liked to make an occasion of her father's return home after work.

Maki folded the dishcloth and padded it down gently beside the sink, before moving a pile of documents to one side. As she slipped her ring back onto her wedding finger, she smiled to herself. Removing her jewellery to do the washing-up was not really necessary but every time she put the ring back on, it was a reminder of her special day. Simple moments were important after so many childhood days of fear and heartache.

'Careful you do not fall, Onaedo.' Placing both hands on the sill, she peered down on her daughter who was playing just below the window. As Maki straightened, she raised her eyes to the fading sky, relishing the early evening air. She loved the scent from the palm oil plantation on the eastern plateau slopes, drifting across the scrub and announcing a fresh radiance to the Nigerian village of Uminwani.

The cockerel throttled an urgent plea for help as Onaedo's hands almost made contact with his feathers. 'Come inside now, my daughter. You must leave the poor creature alone and wash your hands. It is almost time to eat.' If Dilibe was not home soon, they would have to start without him. Onaedo stopped, while a relieved rooster looked over his shoulder and began to strut around the courtyard confidently once more. The little girl skipped towards the call and disappeared from view to make her way into the house by the back door, while her mother quickly moved the documents onto the top of the refrigerator.

'Good girl. Now stand on the stool beside the sink and wash your hands.' With her mother by her side, the child climbed onto the small wooden platform and did as she was told. Once dried and inspected, Onaedo challenged her mother to play their game.

'Will you catch me, *Mama*?' Onaedo was preparing to leap from the stool, flapping her arms like the cornered rooster in the courtyard.

Maki stood in front of her daughter. 'Alright, but be careful. ..After three… Are you ready my little chicken?… one … two.. threeee.' With that compelling invitation, the little girl jumped safely into her mother's welcoming arms.

'Can we go and look for *Papa's* car coming now, please *Mama*?' asked Onaedo.

'Yes, but wait a moment, I just need to take something with me.' While her daughter twisted her face into a puzzled expression, Maki turned around and collected the important papers from the top of the fridge.

Together, mother and daughter then moved purposefully to the front of the house and sat outside. The porch was Maki's favourite part of their home, where she could indulge her most enjoyable pastime. She loved the peace, sitting on the wicker chairs and resting in the shade, away from the fading heat. From there, they had a good view of the open countryside. More importantly for Onaedo, the main dusty road into the village wound its way along the side of the plateau, about a mile away. She could see cars coming well before they reached Uminwani. Onaedo settled into her seat, holding her picture book and thumbing the corners of the pages, while occasionally peering into the distance. Maki took advantage of the quiet moment to examine once more, the documents she had been working on.

Onaedo's father was Dr. Dilibe Nkowo, the local doctor for the region. He had married Maki four years earlier in 2001, after she had returned to Uminwani. They wanted to stay in the Village to help improve the quality of life for others. Like most people in this part of South-East Nigeria, they were Igbo and both had survived the Civil War that ravaged the land in the late 1960s. Their village was a small community of about two thousand inhabitants, where most people knew each other and were connected in some way. The Nkowo family were highly regarded in Uminwani and their status was well deserved.

Feeling guilty about working when she could have been playing with her little girl, Maki broke the silence. 'Can you see *Papa's* car, Onaedo?' He was later than usual and Maki was feeling concerned. The child gripped the arms of Dilibe's chair tightly and pulled herself up, in response to her mother's question. Once more she peered into the distance.

'Not yet, *Mama*.'

Onaedo continued to act as 'look-out', while her anxious mother put some of the papers under the glass paper-weight, on the small table. They included the timetable she had devised for the following day. She read her notes quietly to herself, keeping half-an-eye on her daughter, who was still exploring the scenes in her book and frequently peering into the distance. Maki was not nervous about having to make an important speech or meeting high-ranking dignitaries, two events that would feature in tomorrow's plans. Her emotions were heightened by the anticipation of meeting once again, the man who had made everything possible.

Suddenly, a dirty, white Volkswagen Beetle was spotted and Onaedo burst into life. 'Here it is! Here comes *Papa's* car, *Mama*!' She started to wave her arms vigorously, in the hope of spotting some sort of signal from the vehicle. Without thinking of the consequences, the little girl attempted to stand on the chair but was told to sit properly by her mother. Onaedo's gesturing was rewarded when the headlights were switched on-and-off, three times as a matter of routine. 'He's coming, he's coming!'

'Right. Come inside with me, my darling and help me to finish setting the table for our meal. Your father will be here soon and he will be hungry.'

Maki took her daughter's tiny hand and returned to the kitchen, where she removed three knives, forks and spoons from the drawer beside the sink. She knew she should have already completed the preparation for the family's evening meal. Wiping her brow with the back of her hand, she turned to Onaedo. 'The plates are on the table, Onaedo. Do you remember where we put the cutlery?' She held the items in front of her daughter to reinforce the meaning of the word, *cutlery*.

'Yes, *Mama*.'

'Good. Then come with me and show me, my darling.'

As she controlled the excitement of her father's imminent arrival, her mother watched carefully while Onaedo placed the cutlery onto the dining room table with the precision of a surgeon. Maki wondered if she would also become a doctor, like herself and Dilibe. The thought of having a daughter as beautiful and precious as Onaedo had been impossible during Maki's own childhood years. Yet, here she was – their most prized treasure. The name 'Onaedo' was chosen because it means 'priceless gift,' in the Igbo language. Thanks to Maki's friend, there was growing hope in her heart, something that had taken so much to achieve. Maki could not wait for their meeting.

Suddenly, the door at the front of the house opened and Dilibe called to his family. His wife approached the sound of his voice but she was rapidly overtaken by a smaller pair of legs.

'I am home everyone. Where are my two beautiful girls?' Just as he finished his question, his knee was assaulted by a hug from Onaedo, who ran straight into him. 'Whoah, there Onaedo. You almost knocked me over.' Watching the little girl's unbounded excitement at her father's arrival was something Maki never took for granted.

Dilibe bent down and with one swift scooping action, lifted Onaedo upwards. Like many doting *Papas* before him, he briefly let go of his daughter on the upswing so she almost hit her head on the ceiling, before he caught her firmly on the way down. Onaedo chuckled like the innocent she was, while Dilibe kissed her firmly on the cheek, before placing her on solid ground once more.

'Be careful, my husband. Do not get her too excited. ' Maki found it difficult to relax, even after more than thirty years.

'She is fine. Stop fretting *'ezi nwunye'*. Have you not worried enough in your life?' Although *'ezi nwunye'* means 'good wife', Dilibe had used the term so often it had virtually become his partner's alias.

'Yes, but I only feel safe when I am with you, my brave *onyeagha*.' She would sometimes respond with pet names of her own and refer to him as 'warrior,' when poking fun. 'Now go and wash before you have your food, my husband.'

'Mmm. I am not sure I am a warrior, just yet,' he responded with a smile.

After kissing Maki quickly on the lips, Dilibe collected Onaedo once more in his arms and the three of them wandered from the front of the house, along the passage to the door of the dining room where the table had been set by Onaedo and her *Mama*.

'I set the table today *Papa*,' declared an enthusiastic Onaedo.

'Yes, you were a very good helper but first allow *Papa* to go and wash his hands and freshen-up while we get the food,' commanded Maki. Dilibe then disappeared upstairs, intending to change and organise himself as quickly as possible. Meanwhile, Onaedo and her mother took the final items from the small kitchen to the dining room. The little girl was allowed to carry the serving utensils, enabling her mother to wear oven gloves and transport the hot pot with both hands. Maki had cooked some of Dilibe's favourite dishes and the smell of her home cooking filled the house as it was transported along the passage. She knew he would not take long in the bathroom : he could not resist the tempting aroma of her yam porridge with vegetables and breadfruit.

As the family sat together around the walnut table with its pristine white cover, Onaedo recounted her chicken-hunting strategies and both parents listened with feigned interest. The dining room, like the rest of the house, was small and functional. Its ceiling fan whirred slowly to provide the slightest hint of a cooling draught. Their good jobs meant the couple were free from some of the financial pressures experienced by others in Uminwani. The cream-coloured walls were drab but Maki always made sure the house was clean. After enjoying their food together as a family, the clattering sound of Onaedo's spoon coming to rest noisily in her bowl, signalled the end of the meal.

Maki frowned disapprovingly at Onaedo before turning to her husband. 'You go and play with your daughter. I will see to the clearing of the plates,' declared *'ezi nwunye'* as she rose from her seat.

'No, I will help you and then we shall sit together,' he insisted. Maki knew she was lucky to have such a considerate husband. Dilibe gathered their plates into a single pile, extending his fingers on both sides of the stack, before heading to the kitchen with a full load.

Once all the dirty dishes had been cleared from the table, Maki scraped the remnants of their meal into the kitchen bin. As she did so, she inwardly balked at her actions. Not that many years ago, she would have considered these scraps a feast. Her memories were always lurking.

The three of them set about their tasks: Maki washed the dishes, while her husband dried them. Onaedo was allowed to put some of the unbreakable items back into the low green cupboards. She soon got bored and retired to a hard chair in the corner of the kitchen. Onaedo curled into a ball and began looking at her picture book. After a couple of minutes of rare silence, Maki looked over her shoulder to check what her daughter was doing. She could see that Onaedo was now in her own world, exploring the fascination of the animal pictures in her book. Maki gently elbowed her husband, who suddenly stopped wiping a plate and focussed on the subject of his wife's attention. They looked at each other and shared the intimate moment together.

Soon everything was tidy, the evening chores were completed and they had an opportunity to unwind as a family. The three of them returned to the front of the house, where Dilibe was allowed to reclaim his seat on the porch. Onaedo sat on his lap, with her book open. They explored its contents, while Maki sat beside them, with her own thoughts, staring into the distance. She listened with inner content to the trill of some wild guinea fowl and the caw of a scaly francolin as they broke the still evening's silence. The birds' calls brought a unique late symphony to the Village as the blood-orange sun began to draw its silhouettes around the buildings. The ping call of a wood dove from a nearby woodland made a late contribution to the twilight concert.

The beauty of the evening was intoxicating, when Maki suddenly awoke from her glazed daydream. 'Why don't we go for a short walk together, to the edge of the Village? It is a beautiful evening.' Dilibe shuffled in his seat. His wife knew what that meant: he was tired. Perhaps the suggestion was not a good idea. She could always tell when he was worn out, his body language was easy to read. Dilibe rarely talked about his own work or the demands of his day. He preferred to leave tales of diarrhoea, vomiting and inoculations at the front door. Occasionally, if a patient died that day, he would feel the need to unburden his thoughts.

Onaedo came to her parents' aid with a massive yawn. Maki had lost track of the day's lateness. 'Time for your bed missy, I think, declared her mother. Go upstairs, little one and put on your nightdress. I will come to tuck you in and then read you a story.'

'Can *Papa* read me a story tonight?' pleaded Onaedo.

'Not tonight. Perhaps tomorrow. *Papa* has had a busy day.' Dilibe did not protest. 'Now give your father a goodnight kiss and make sure you are in bed when I come upstairs.' After a loving embrace from Dilibe, Onaedo trudged wearily from the porch to her room, with a scruffy stuffed hippo dangling from her limp arm, while she sucked the thumb of her other hand. Watching her daughter trudge up the bare wooden stairway, Maki thought that perhaps the strutting rooster had outlasted his tormentor and won the race with the little girl, after all.

Maki turned back to explore the porch view once more, before sneaking a sideways look at her husband. His silence and untouched glass of lemon juice told her all she needed to know. She could see Dilibe's eyes begin to close so she left him alone and went upstairs to supervise her daughter's evening ritual. Onaedo was already in bed when Maki entered the petite, white-walled room. She collected the little girl's lime-green dress and undergarments from the floor, along with the tiny red open-toe sandals, which marked the trail to her bed.

Onaedo was lying on her back, with only her head showing above the bed-sheets. The same moon-eyes that Maki used to see in her own reflection, were asking for a story. As her mother sat on the edge of the bed, she took one of the three colourful books beside the small green lamp, resting on the adjacent low, brown chest and began to read aloud. Slowly and gently, her soothing voice coaxed Onaedo into a land of dreams.

After a final arrangement of the bedsheets and planting a gentle kiss on her sleeping daughter's forehead, Maki returned downstairs, where Dilibe was dozing. Approaching from behind, she placed her hands on his shoulders, causing him to almost jump out of his chair. Maki felt guilty about waking him. She should have remembered he had started to fall asleep before she had attended to their daughter. 'Sorry, my darling. I did not mean to disturb you.' She bent over and placed a kiss on his cheek. He patted her hand resting on his shoulder, before sitting up and rubbing his eyes. The sun was beginning to set and Maki noticed one or two lights in adjacent houses being switched on. She took a refreshing sip from Dilibe's glass, before offering him the tumbler.

Maki took her papers once more and sighed as she sat, examining their content. She shuffled the top pages and then looked under her chair for something. Her shoulders became more relaxed when she finally saw the rogue sheet. Stretching her fingers in an effort to pick it up, Maki managed to free it from under the leg of the table. Gingerly she dusted it off with a gentle blow and positioned it back to its rightful place, aware of being observed.

'Everything alright, my darling?' inquired Dilibe, who was stretching both his legs under the table.

'Fine, my husband,' she lied. The misplaced sheet of paper was her only house-copy of the arrival times of the guests the following day. Maki would have had some serious re-thinking to do if it had gone missing. She tapped the papers onto the table to tidy the edges. For a moment she was concerned that she had taken-on too much recently. In some ways she would be glad when Onaedo started school and she could return to work. She stretched her arm across the table, hoping Dilibe would take her hand. Her husband obliged without a second thought.

'You are not worrying about tomorrow I hope?' he asked, sympathetically, while gently squeezing his wife's fingers.

'No, I am happy with the arrangements. My speech is complete and I am looking forward to the opening of the Community Centre and seeing my friend. It will be a good day.' Maki knew tomorrow was going to be a very big occasion for her community and it was mainly the result of her efforts. She would be the main player in the scenes which would unfold in the next twenty-four hours. Maki had come a long way.

She returned a squeeze to her husband's hand and sat motionless in the beautiful dying light, appreciating the peace. The sound of the chirping crickets suddenly stopped as a bullfrog croaked its mating call in the fading light. A twig snapped from a garden across the way, while a neighbour gathered wood for a fire. Dilibe and Maki sat silently, content in each other's company. No dialogue was necessary between them. They had both experienced a time when the noise of a Civil War was foremost and threatening. On this particular evening, the absence of gunfire meant the soothing sound of silence was even more enjoyable.

When a cry of '*Mama*' disturbed their peace, Maki momentarily felt disappointed this precious time was interrupted. Angry at her own selfishness she quickly followed the cry, to see Onaedo sitting –up in bed, rubbing her eyes. Knowing exactly what to do, she hugged her daughter, before helping her to settle once more.

'Do not worry, little one. *Mama* is here. Nothing can harm you.' Maki remembered how nightmares had threatened her own childhood innocence. Brutal experiences at the hands of vicious soldiers during a savage conflict, were hard to divest. She was an adult before her horrendous memories no longer interfered with her night-time peace. Not for her, the threat of being chased by a giant cockerel in a courtyard as it had been in Onaedo's dream. She was grateful that her daughter had avoided those terrifying experiences prompted by the reality of war.

As Maki lay beside her precious child, gently stroking Onaedo's hair and humming a soothing lullaby, she remembered the first time anyone had successfully tamed her own demons. Sister Mary at St Jerome's Mission had taught her how to feel safe over many nights. Gradually, the Nun had ushered away the fears and night-time monsters with similar, lilting melodies.

Lying intimately with Onaedo, she recalled those days more than thirty years ago. The end of the Civil War in 1970 was a different era, made easier by her friend. Her thoughts harkened back to that time while she guarded her daughter.

She remembered the bullying soldier who pointed a gun at her as she hid behind a tree. That moment of numbing terror was not easily forgotten. Maki sat silently and pondered those days, which even now occasionally crept from the shadows of fear.

PART ONE

I

T om Kettlewell was sitting impatiently alongside another student, waiting for his Monday morning seminar with Dr Herbert. He uncrossed his legs and bent from the waist to look at the floor, resting his folded arms on his thighs, before blowing a sigh. The chair was hard and uncomfortable, something he did not notice when the discussion was in full flow. Just as he was counting the number of tiles on the floor, he thought he detected movement. It was almost time and 'Doc' was not usually late. Then, with typical predictability, a shadow appeared through the glass panel in the door, heralding his arrival. A wispy-haired suit entered the room precisely at the designated hour. The dishevelled old man got straight down to business and handed the two envelope files containing the marked assignments to their respective owners. A third undergraduate had not turned up for the seminar.

'Where's Mr Fisk?' inquired the Lecturer. The other two shrugged their shoulders in unison. 'Doc' became a little disoriented. 'Just read my comments on your assignments for a few minutes please gentlemen. I need to return to my office. I've left something behind. I won't be long.'

Tom surreptitiously slid his assignment out of the covered folder that was protected under his elbow, feeling like a self-conscious spy. He did not want the other student sitting next to him to see his grade and was pleased to squint a red circle surrounding the letter 'A' at the top of the page. He made no attempt to try and read any of Doc's comments, choosing to cosset his achievement later, in private. The other undergraduate was less reticent.

'What did you get, Tom?' asked Eric. They were both Maths students, in their final year at Sheffield University. It was their second seminar of the Michaelmas Term in 1969 and the grades from this assignment contributed towards their final degree marks. These assessments were important.

Tom felt like a matador thrusting the final sword into a bull's neck, as he savoured his response. 'I got an A. What about you?' *Have some of that, you nosey bastard,* he thought.

'What again! Another A! You jammy git. I only got a B. You've got to be on for a first, now,' Eric declared enviously.

Tom knew he was right. He had a real chance of a First Class Honours Degree if he continued along the lines of his first two years, although he preferred not to talk about his ability. He did not want to tempt fate. Tom Kettlewell came from a working-class family in the town of Consett in the North East and had welcomed the chance to abandon the blazer, flannels and tie of Grace Darling Grammar School for the uniform of a student breathing the revolutionary air hanging over a university campus in the late 1960s. His self-indulgence involved long black hair, sideburns and eighteen-inch, flared, corduroy trousers.

'Doc' Herbert returned to resume the seminar. Tom fixed his sapphire eyes on the target, hoping for some sign of recognition of his achievement but the tutor made no further reference to the assignments. The extensive written critique at the bottom of each piece of work would have to suffice. There was no time to waste. Doc could not delay any further, the cross-examination of his charges on the finer points of *Recursion Theory,* in the barren, brown interrogation cell of a room. However, these regular seminars were not dry and pointless academic exercises to Tom ; he was one of the few undergraduates genuinely excited by the unseen potential in numbers. The opportunity for discussion on this particular theory presented a chance for him to shine once again because he knew how it could be used to develop his area of specialism – computers. For Tom, time in seminars did not drag, fear of questions did not threaten nor was the unknown intimidating. To the contrary, the exchange of views was frequently a thrilling experience.

At the end of the discussion, Doc reminded the two students of the time of their next appointment as he looked down at the dates in his diary. Tom clipped his briefcase closed, got up and nodded in Doc's direction as he left the room but the Lecturer was examining some papers on his desk and failed to recognise his student's plea for attention. Tom disappointedly tucked the work under his arm and made his way out, walking along the corridor with Eric, who was still expressing his envy at the 'A' grade. Tom stopped to read the departmental noticeboard at the bottom of the stairs and allowed Eric to continue on his way. As he scanned a poster about a *Maths Society's* meeting, he became aware of Doc passing behind him and sensed a pause. He half-turned and Doc gently squeezed the undergraduate's elbow, before whispering in his ear, 'Well done, Tom. Keep it up.' These six simple words gave Tom all the attention he needed. They represented respect from someone he admired. As he left the Maths Faculty building to make his way to the Refectory, he knew he would enjoy his lunchtime cottage pie and chips.

After an afternoon lecture, Tom headed towards the Library to start preparing for his next assignment, so freely given by Doc at the end of the seminar. He would normally have returned to his place in Trippet Lane but his work took precedence. Tom liked this time of day on Campus. Most students had returned to a Hall of Residence or their digs and simply evaporated. Only the isolates like him, were snugly ensconced in the act of study, before being thrown out by the shrill of the Library's closing bell. He deposited his things on a table in the centre of the large room and opened two textbooks, before placing a *Biro* pen on top of one of them, to make it appear as if he had been there some time. Content at having established his territory, he walked purposefully to the stacked shelves at the side, where he proceeded to browse the books and track down the references he needed.

Tom's studying ended after about four hours of semi-productive work. He left the Library and walked past the red-brick Civil Engineering building to the offices of the Students Union. His destination was the University Bar, which was busy in anticipation of the following day's demonstration against the South African Rugby Tour. The atmosphere was boisterous. There were about seven or eight groups of undergraduates standing by the pumps and most of the tables were taken. He bought himself a pint of McEwan's *Tartan* and glided through a group of anonymous, denim-clad students, before finding a seat next to his mate Kelvin.

Tom knew Kelvin from the *Politics Society* meetings they both attended. Kelvin was a popular figure at the University and played for the First XV rugby team but also mixed with many of the key figures from the other sports. It was unusual to have a sportsman involved in the political aspects of student life because the 'jocks' were usually a close-knit group who simply wanted to chase a ball around a field. However, Kelvin came from a solicitor's family and was cut from superior cloth. His white hair and ashen moustache made him appear as a sickly figure but that was misleading. He was a powerful athlete, who played as a flanker and took no prisoners on the rugby field. Kelvin was fearless and honest and Tom knew he could be a major threat in any future contest for the post of President of the Students Union if they both ever decided to stand for the post.

They inevitably chatted about the following day's Anti-Apartheid demonstration. Kelvin was exploring the room with his eyes throughout their discussion. He was confident with his own body image and always on the look-out for attractive girls. After about a quarter of Tom's beer had disappeared from his glass, someone standing at the Bar suddenly turned to face the drinking assembly and shouted, 'Apartheid!'

Returning as a single voice came the loud response, 'Out!' Kelvin raised his fist in salute.

This exchange occurred twice, before the conclusion, 'OUT, OUT, OUT!'

There was further chanting ...'What do we want?'

'Freedom!'

'When do we want it?'

'Now!'

The senior barman called out to the throng. 'Stop that chanting, you lot or I'll close the Bar.' His instruction was ignored. There was no attempt to tone down the noise so at that point the shutters above the counter were slammed closed authoritatively. The serving of beer was concluded for the evening. Someone dropped a glass in protest and the alarming sound caused the re-appearance of the barman. 'Any further disturbance and the Bar will not re-open tomorrow.' This threat was sufficient deterrent and some grumbling students started to head towards the exits in order to decant to some of the nearby City pubs.

Tom swotted Kelvin on his shoulder, with a wrist-flick. 'See you tomorrow, Kel,' who nodded in response. Tom was not bothered about going to any more pubs. He headed somewhere more appealing.

II

He woke at about seven o'clock and glided out of bed, naked. Tom walked down the small hallway, yawning and scratching himself before eventually finding the toilet. On his return, he could see Felicity lying on her stomach with her head buried into the heart of a luxurious pillow. She was totally naked with one leg hanging outside the sheet, balancing on the edge of the bed. Her other leg was extended and although it was fully covered by a single blanket, Tom explored its three-dimensional shape with lascivious curiosity. Felicity's long brown hair fell-off her shoulder and down her back, like the tentacles of an octopus. He stood for longer than he needed, admiring her nakedness and inwardly congratulating himself on the night's activities. Felicity was in a solid, deep sleep and he wondered if he should nestle beside her.

Felicity Stroud had graduated with a First Class Honours Degree in English in 1968 and then stood as a postgraduate for the position of President of the Students Union. Her natural eloquence, confidence and pert breasts were enough to carry her to a resounding victory, following a successful campaign. Tom found the strength of her personality and the attraction of her rich lips to be very alluring. The pair had been an item since the student body first vented its opposition to the South African Rugby Tour, a few weeks earlier. They had worked closely together during the organisation of the rally .

Tom sat on the edge of the bed and reached for his boxer briefs, before starting to get fully dressed. His loins told him to initiate another session but his conscience was directing him to the Library. He had an assignment to complete and he needed to work. As he got up from the bed to put on his jeans, Felicity began to stir.

'Where are you going?' She pleaded directly into the pillow as if speaking with a mouthful of food.

'I need to make an early start. Things to do.' Tom wanted to begin addressing his assignment. He was ever the conscientious worker.

'Am I not one of them?' Felicity asked, as she turned over onto her back under the bedclothes, supporting her head with her arm and exposing a tantalising amount of breast. Tom could see she was making a play for him.

'Later, perhaps.' Part of him could not believe he was turning down her offer. He was torn between his conscience and his instincts.

'I'm not used to being rejected.' With that, she threw back the sheets to reveal her full, well-toned, naked body. Tom looked at her and knew he could not resist. Suddenly, he did not care about his conscience.

A couple of hours later, Tom left Felicity's flat, feeling some relief at being away from her for a while : sometimes she could be overpowering. He decided to return to his flat and deposit his stuff, before heading to the student march. As he walked back to his place in Trippet Lane, he recalled the first time he was attracted to Felicity. It was following a political meeting of student activists, when the idea of a protest march against Apartheid was being considered. She had led the discussion and he remembered her as an extremely eloquent and highly-driven brunette, with long hair tied into a ponytail for the purposes of the meeting. A former pupil of an expensive private school on England's south coast, she had 'moved North' where she perceived her contribution to the class struggle would be greatest. This unnerved Tom; he knew that his own credentials in the battle against the bourgeoisie were impeccable but Ms Stroud was a product of a different upbringing. She was attempting to betray her own class, for reasons Tom could not fathom. Nevertheless, he considered her to be a forceful asset to 'the cause'.

After the meeting, they went to the University Bar and it was clear there was some chemistry between them. Felicity was blunt about where their chat was going. 'You're more than welcome to come back to my flat. I've got a place in Rossington Road, near Endcliffe Park. Do you know it?' she asked him, precociously.

Tom shrugged to indicate he did not know that part of the City. In reality he was thinking *'Christ, how many students have a flat in that area!'* He lived in a room and shared a bathroom with three other students in Trippet Lane, a less salubrious part of Sheffield in 1969. Endcliffe Park was out of the price range for most undergraduates at the time. Felicity did not seem to share the same financial constraints as most other students.

Naively, Tom had responded, 'Shall we walk or catch the 'bus?' In that moment, he knew he had projected himself as weak and immature. His social maturity came nowhere near his intellectual strength and his self-consciousness showed.

'No, I've got my car with me. One of the perks of being President of the Students' Union is I have a parking sticker for the Campus. I'm in the top car park, so it won't take us long. I'll go and get it and drive around to meet you by the steps at the main entrance. Ok ?' She seemed to have everything planned the way she wanted. Tom admired her for that.

While they travelled to her place in a blue Triumph Herald, Tom had glanced down to explore the car's interior and noticed Felicity's dress had caught on the handbrake, exposing her inner thigh. She seemed to be unaware of her *faux pas*, although he wondered for a moment if she had done it deliberately. He was not surprised to observe that she was also wearing an ankle bracelet. They pulled-up to a black- panelled front door and the car was left on the street, before they entered the house and went upstairs to her flat.

Tom was just beginning to recall the first time they had sex together, when his fantasy was brought to a halt. He had arrived back at the flaked-red, iron gate that marked the entrance to his place in Trippet Lane. After going upstairs to the flat, he entered the kitchen and made himself a coffee before moving to his bedroom. When he finished changing his clothes, he lay on his bed and looked at a cobweb in the corner of his ceiling, trying to spot the spider responsible for the construction, without success. With his hands behind his head he indulged his thoughts once more, enjoying the peace, before he began to fall asleep. Twenty minutes later, he woke with a start and after realising the time, he quickly jumped off his bed. He was in danger of being late for the rally so he grabbed his coat and set off on the familiar walk back to Campus. This time, he walked purposefully and quickly. As Tom approached the University, he heard singing and chanting, which become louder as he got nearer. A lot of the students were sitting on the steps in front of College House, while the majority were gathered in the nearby Quad. The large rectangular space was full of fired-up undergraduates, ready for a confrontation. The acoustics were amplified in the relatively confined area, adding further heat to the rising temperature of the occasion. When he turned the corner, he almost gasped at the number of students who had amassed at the starting point.

It was good day for a protest march, a typically dry, crisp autumn afternoon, the last Wednesday of November 1969. There were placards everywhere, expressing views against the Rugby Tour, with some of the slogans directed at the political issue of Apartheid itself. One placard that caught Tom's eye showed a picture of a white South African police officer beating a black worker, while the slogan underneath read, *"If you could see their national sport, you might be less keen to see their rugby"*. In her role as Student President, Felicity was already in position. She was at the front of the crowd with a megaphone, shouting instructions and trying to establish some sort of order. Finally, she exerted her authority and after demanding silence, the crowd settled. The still air was broken by the loudspeaker's amplified crackling which preceded Felicity's voice.

'Right everybody. Firstly, thanks for turning out this afternoon and showing your support. Just to remind you, we will be marching along West Street and Leopold Street towards the Town Hall. We have been informed that the Police are in force at the bottom of Leopold Street and will try to prevent us from getting to present our petition to the Council. We don't intend to let them stop us. Am I right?' The call was answered by a chorus of yelling and arm waving.

'Right! Let's march brothers and sisters!' The thick mass of dark, winter clothing then began to move-off in high spirits, heading towards Sheffield Town Hall and looking like a sports stadium emptying after a big match. The students poured towards their destination, approximately a mile from College House. The throng filled the width of the road and stretched for about a hundred yards. There must have been about a thousand students and supporters on the march. As they wound their way through the streets, bemused pedestrians going about their daily business, watched with interest. Some of the observers called out in support, while others were less sympathetic. *'Get back to the Library, you lazy buggers'* and *'You're a waste of taxpayers' money'* were a couple of the more audible, derogatory comments. The majority of innocent bystanders simply watched in amazement at the size of the moving mass.

The principal banner at the front of the demonstration read, *'Boycott*

Apartheid' in large red letters. The slogan was held by six students, who carried it at waist height. Those walking behind the main sign carried individual placards and occasionally responded to the megaphone's invitation to chant reminders to the public about the reason for the protest. Tom was approximately three rows back from the front of the march. The leaders were clearly impressed by the turn-out and waved their arms like conductors in an orchestra, suddenly demanding *fortissimo*.

As they reached Leopold Square, there was a blue wall waiting in front of the Town Hall. Police Officers, three-deep were standing, arms linked, prepared for a confrontation. The protestors were about a hundred yards from the human barrier when a large group of people suddenly joined the march from both sides of the street. The mob did not look like they were from the University. They quickly crossed over and merged with the students near the front. Tom recognised a couple of them and noticed a flash of red hair under a pair of raised fists. There was no mistaking this idiot : it was the odd-ball students knew as 'Red Reg'.

'Reg', was a shabbily dressed fanatic, who could be seen every Monday and Friday at the main entrance of the Campus selling the newspaper of the *Trotsky Socialists Party*. He had never attended University but was always hanging around, especially when something important was going on. Nobody knew whether his real name was Reg or not, it was simply his term of reference. Rumours and myths about him had circulated among the undergraduates for years. One claimed that he had been in jail a few times for violent behaviour. Whether this was true or not, it did not matter: he was a person best avoided.

Tom became concerned at his presence. He sensed danger. A number of the additional horde of newcomers were standing immediately behind Kelvin, who was now in the front row. They seemed to energise the chanting and arm waving. An echoing noise wafted down the street as the Police Superintendent in charge of the official forces, tried to send instructions to the students via a bullhorn, ordering them to go no further. The orders were lost in the cacophony of noise that engulfed the street, especially when Felicity started to counter-instruct her forces, using her own loudhailer.

The students' Plan A was to storm the Town Hall building, invade the chambers and make a mass protest to Councillors about their failure to officially object to the South African sporting presence. Realistically, they did not think this was going to happen. It was clear from the number of Police at the rally that the plan would fail. The back-up scheme was for Felicity and a few members from the Students' Union to make representations to the Mayor and inform him of the sizeable petition against Apartheid that had been produced by all the people of the City. If the Police did not allow such a representation, students would demonstrate peacefully by sitting-down on the road in protest, and refuse to move. There were not enough police vans or cells to move everyone and traffic would be brought to a halt. At least, that was the theory.

As the march approached the Police cordon, the atmosphere was still congenial. A few of the officers even returned smiles at the inevitable face-off with the students, whose chanting front line was stationary, about ten feet away. Things suddenly changed when a glass bottle containing liquid fire sailed over the heads of those at the front of the rally. It came from where 'Red Reg' and his associates were gathered. Almost simultaneously, there was a surge from behind, careering some students into the blue line. More bottles were thrown and a policeman's trousers were caught alight by the splash of flames from a shattered glass petrol bomb. An inevitable physical confrontation ensued. Someone at the interface knocked-off a police officer's hat, which was the prelude to pandemonium. Tom felt helpless and his body was passed through the crowd as if he had been fired from a missile.

He saw Kelvin and a girl grappling with a policeman, who had clearly become angry at the change of mood. The copper was about to hit Kelvin with a truncheon when the female student grabbed his arm. They both fell to the floor, two yards away from where Tom was now flapping around. The girl tried to stand but the bobby was holding on to her arm as another policeman bent down to help his colleague. It looked as if they were going to arrest her. Tom took the initiative. He charged into the first copper who was now getting to his feet. This caused a collision with the second policeman and for a split second the girl was free. Tom grabbed her arm and pulled her back into the safety of the crowd.

'Quick!' he said with unsurprising urgency, 'Let's get out of here while we can.' Tom positioned himself between the female student and the line of police and headed back to where most of the other protestors were shouting and waving their fists at the fracas that was taking place in front of them. With one hand under her arm, Tom manhandled her to a position of safety and they retreated to a side-street, away from the action. A bus pulled into a stop nearby, the couple boarded it and made their escape complete. Away from the maelstrom, Tom took stock of the situation as they settled into their seats.

'That was a close one,' he declared with an audible gasp, swotting his jacket with his right hand. 'I'm Tom by the way.'

'You're not kidding. We almost got ourselves arrested there. And I'm Emma' she blurted , before relief broke into a huge smile, lighting-up her face. Tom looked at her, somewhat confused and broke into a grin of his own.

After a short ride, they got off the bus without paying before the conductress approached them for their fare. The pair then began to stroll back to Campus and found themselves close to Tom's flat. He brought it to Emma's attention. 'I can make you a cup of coffee if you like. It might help calm us both down a bit. If you want to .. that is.' Tom was surprised when she accepted because he thought it too soon to become that friendly. When they entered, the place was empty and Tom made a laughable attempt to tidy-up, scurrying ahead of Emma. He was picking-up various items still lying on the floor as he walked in front of her. 'Sorry about the mess. But hey, what can you do? Four single blokes, sharing a hovel is not the best place to bring someone to impress them.'

Emma was a very attractive girl with short brown hair and a stunning figure, covered mainly by the trousers she always wore. The only trouble was that it made the curvatures of her beautiful buttock cheeks look even more appealing to the many male eyes that watched her carry her tray of food to the Refectory tables, every lunchtime. Her brown sparkling eyes were an even greater attribute than her rear and they nearly always betrayed her feelings. Emma's appearance had not escaped Tom's notice.

She sat down, while Tom left the room to make coffee. He filled the kettle and set about tidying the kitchen, moving dirty pans into the washing-up bowl, straightening chairs and moving erratic books. Meanwhile, Emma perused the small lounge and looked around the room, wearing a wry smile at the evidence of male chaos. There was a two-seater settee and non-matching armchair, with a patched-up arm-rest. Newspapers, books and old magazines littered the floor. In the corner, there was something resembling a large bean bag, next to one of the record player's speakers. Then her eyes fixed on something lying on the coffee table. There were papers with a leaflet relating to a charity called, *'Support an African Child'*. She could see an accompanying letter addressed to Tom and a scruffy-looking picture half-sticking out of the adjacent envelope. This caught her interest. She was aware that she should not read Tom's mail but curiosity gained the upper hand. The letter was handwritten in beautifully neat script and Emma began to read its contents, while she could hear Tom thrashing around in the kitchen.

Dear Mr Kettlewell,

I am writing to you to tell you about the progress of the child you are sponsoring with us. Her name is Amaka Onyali and we think she is about five or six years old. She was brought to us at the St. Jerome Mission after her parents and family were killed during the war in Biafra. She was very ill and frightened when she was first brought to us. She survived living in an International Red Cross refugee camp before being brought here to our Mission.

After much care, she has finally started to smile and last month she spoke to us for the first time. With God's grace and your support she will make a good recovery.

I think she is a very intelligent child and I have sent you a picture that she has made for you.

Thank you very much for the money you send for her. It means that she is safe and will continue to be cared for by us at the Mission where we will see that she has a good education.

I will write again in the future about her progress.

Yours sincerely,

Sister Mary Uloma

The simplicity of the letter hit Emma hard and she was taken-aback by Tom's act of generosity. She unfolded the other sheet from the envelope. It felt a bit like blotting paper and revealed a child's picture. There was a yellow blob surrounded by blue, which she presumed was meant to be the sun in a clear sky. Six people were at the bottom of the drawing, standing outside a brown house. Emma held her index finger and thumb to her mouth in semi-disbelief. Suddenly she was engulfed by a feeling of warmth towards Tom and failed to hear him approaching.

The door burst open with a noisy thud as Tom kicked its lower panel, entering with a cup of coffee in each hand. 'Caught you!' he said triumphantly.

Emma felt her face flush with embarrassment. 'Oh, sorry. I didn't mean to …' She had been caught in the act.

'Yes you did. Don't give me that' he said jokingly. 'What are you looking at anyway ?' he asked with a total absence of accusation. Emma held up the drawing. 'Oh, that. It's a picture drawn for me by the child who I have apparently been helping to support in Nigeria.'

Emma took the sketch carefully in both hands and turned it around to admire its simplicity, once more. She smiled as she considered its innocence. 'It's sweet.'

Tom put down the cups of coffee and took the sheets from her. He returned them to the coffee table and while offering one of the mugs to Emma, he spilled some of the hot drink onto one of his cuffs. He quickly put down the mug and shook his wrist as if it was on fire, trying desperately not to swear as Emma started to giggle. Quickly, he changed the subject. 'The demonstration should certainly make the newspapers after that mini riot. No doubt the press will have a field day writing about irresponsible students.' Secretly, he hoped Emma would be impressed on learning that he donated money to a charity dedicated to supporting children in Africa. As Emma took a sip of her drink, Tom relaxed into the armchair and started to pick at the patch on the arm-rest. Emma felt the heat withdraw from her face and their conversation returned to an even keel.

The sound of people's voices outside entered their world and when Tom looked out of the window, he could see groups of students walking along the street. He accurately surmised they were returning from the march. 'Looks like the rally is over. Everybody seems to be making their way back to the Campus.'

'I suppose I'd better go back as well,' said Emma, with a tinge of disappointment.

'You don't have to.' At that moment their eyes engaged and they were both aware of the slightly veiled implication of Tom's invitation to stay. He partly wanted to hear Emma say that she did not want to go, while also hoping for the release of a refusal. Intimacy between them would only have caused complications.

'No, I'll be on my way. Your flatmates might be back any moment. And you should return to the Campus as well. You're on the Anti-Apartheid Committee, remember? You need to know how it finished and there may be things to do, especially if anyone was arrested.' He had suspected that whatever her response, he would have felt some regret when they separated. Their meeting under such bizarre circumstances had left him feeling confused.

Together, they set off walking back to the Campus from Tom's flat. It was clear they would arrive back to the University at the same time as the majority of students. Tom tried to pick-up on how the march had finished by listening to conversations as they overtook the small groups in front of them. There seemed to be a mixture of excitement and concern. Apparently, some of the students had been arrested and taken to the Station in police vans. Rumours were circulating that Felicity was one of those apprehended.

III

The rumour about Felicity's arrest was confirmed when Tom and Emma arrived on-site. A couple of the President's minions were running around the Student Union Office, frantically trying to look efficient. Tom was not sure what they were doing. He was more convinced they were trying to avoid doing anything. No one had attempted to take control of the situation so he sprang into action. 'Has anyone phoned the Police Station to find out what has actually happened?' There was a look of bewilderment on the female faces. Tom raised his arms as if to say 'Hallelujah' but his exclamation was more of a growl. One call to Directory Enquiries produced the number for the Station and another enabled him to speak to the Duty Sergeant.

'Hello, my name is Tom Kettlewell and I'm representing Miss Felicity Stroud, who I believe has been arrested on the student march, this afternoon. Can you please confirm that she is in custody?' He tried to sound as officious as possible.

'Hang on for a moment, please.' The Sergeant rested the phone's receiver on his desk. Tom could hear voices through the handset but could not establish what they were saying. After a few minutes trying to eavesdrop, the officer returned and picked-up the phone. 'I have been informed that none of those currently held in custody have requested legal representation. What did you say your name was?'

'Never mind.' At that point, Tom put down the receiver. He saw no good reason to disclose his name when there was so much uncertainty. Suddenly, he did not feel so brave.

At that moment, Kelvin walked into the office and Tom was shocked by his eye injury. 'Hi, Kelvin. …Christ! What's happened to you? Are you alright? That needs to be looked at mate.' Tom's concern was genuine. Kelvin was sporting a large red bump just above his left eye. He was angry and shaken.

'One of the Pigs smacked me with a truncheon, when that big push happened. Me and Emma were shoved straight into a copper but Emma stopped the bastard from hitting me. That was just before you pulled her away, I think Tom. As soon as I got back to my feet, some other Pig hit me instead. I'll be alright though. I've had worse playing rugby.' Tom was surprised that Kelvin mentioned Emma by name. There was little indication at the demonstration they were friends.

Tom quickly described Felicity's predicament. He agreed a course of action with Kelvin. Tom would go with Hazel, one of Felicity's friends from the Student's Union, to the Police Station and provide whatever assistance was needed. Kelvin's part involved going to the Refectory and explaining to the returning Students what had happened to their President. He would also take the opportunity to thank everyone for supporting the demonstration.

As Tom got into the passenger seat of Hazel's black 1963 Morris 1000, he suddenly realised that he had lost contact with Emma, at some point. She was with him when he arrived at the Students Union Office but when he got off the phone to the Police Station, she was nowhere to be seen. He was annoyed at himself for allowing that to happen but there were more pressing needs.

Kelvin entered the Refectory where there was a large audience waiting. Most of the students had returned to their own place after the *demo*, rather than go back to the University. Nonetheless, there was still quite a gathering in the Refectory. As those sitting near the doors saw Kelvin enter, they gave a large cheer. Others looked-up and joined-in. They could see that he was sporting a battle injury and his imposing physique and friendly demeanour were greatly appreciated.

Kelvin usually gave his best speeches at half-time in the changing room but he also did well on this occasion. Projecting to a few hundred attentive faces, he thanked everyone who had supported the rally and declared triumphantly that the afternoon had been a huge success. There was no doubt that the size and nature of the demonstration would be reported in the media and might even make the National Evening News. They had accomplished their goal and made the Establishment aware they could not avoid public opinion and especially those who were prepared to take action. The only downside was that some students appeared to be in custody. He reported that Tom was at the Police Station trying to sort-out a way through the chaos. This was greeted with loud applause. Finally, with a rallying call he called out one final time, 'APARTHEID!' The predictable reply came thundering back from those gathered. Even students who were taking their early evening meal, put down their cutlery to join in. After the final 'OUT, OUT , OUT' there was another round of applause, followed by the sound of chairs scraping against the varnished floor as people rose to filter away and resume their usual routine.

IV

Tom arrived at West Bar Police Station, where he was presented with a chaotic scene. As he made his way to the main, ground floor entrance, he could see that under the archway, at the back of the station in the vehicle pound, there were three empty *Black Maria* vans, all with their side-doors fully open. One of them still had a blue light flashing on its roof. Tom estimated that each van could hold about eight people, accommodating four, handcuffed prisoners. There were two local newspaper reporters waiting outside the entrance, no doubt in the hope of making tomorrow's first edition. Approaching to within ten yards of the building, the main glass doors suddenly opened, followed by a cacophony of noise and ensuing chaos. A group of students burst forth into the courtyard and Felicity was among them. Some of the students hurled abuse over their shoulders, hoping that the Police could not make-out the insults they were shouting. The reporters headed for one of the male students who was still bloodied from his earlier battles.

Tom called-out. 'Felicity, over here. Quick!' He was not sure if she heard his call. Felicity looked around, a little bemused, before breaking into a smile when she spotted Tom and Hazel. She moved swiftly over to the pair and gave an almighty embrace to Tom. 'You ok?' he asked reassuringly. As they separated from their clinch, Tom glanced over Felicity's shoulder and could see the battle-scarred student pointing in their direction. The reporters turned and locked onto Felicity's gaze.

'Come on. Let's get out of here before the vultures arrive.' None of them argued.

Breaking into a trot and then a sprint, the threesome escaped around the corner, out of sight of the reporters. As they passed another group of the students, Felicity called out to them. 'Come and see me in the Union Office, tomorrow everybody. We'll sort it all out from there.' It was a garbled instruction which they may or may not have heard. Hazel unlocked the back doors from inside her car and Tom and Felicity jumped in. Just as the engine turned over, the reporters caught-up and started banging on the windows. 'Miss Stroud, Miss Stroud what did they charge you with? What did your parents have to say? What's happened?'

'Piss off, you jackals!' Tom was taken aback by Felicity's venom. It was the first time she had resorted to base language in his presence. They both looked out of the rear window as the car pulled away. Felicity added the V-sign for good measure. The pair then slumped back into the seat and there was a short period of silence before Tom tried to ask a question.

Once again, Felicity took the initiative. 'Kiss me properly first, darling and then I'll tell you everything.' Felicity enjoyed exercising control whenever the opportunity presented itself. She was not about to waste it on this occasion. Tom kissed her purposefully while Felicity put her arms around his neck and pulled him closer.

Upon breaking from her embrace, Tom tried to ask the same question again, with rising anxiety. 'Don't tell me you have been charged?'

'Relax darling. Nothing's happened. They let us all go, after some attempt at a telling-off, such as it was. I've had worse scoldings from my Headmistress. I don't know what you saw but all hell broke out at the front of the demo, especially after someone threw a petrol bomb. Some people charged from behind and we were catapulted into the Police line. There was a lot of pushing and shoving and after the bobby's hat was knocked-off, things turned ugly. I was passed back into the Police area like a rag doll and shoved into one of those black vans. They even tried to handcuff me. I mean … really?'

'Then what happened?'

'Well it didn't take long for the van to fill-up with others and we were whisked-off to that God-awful place. Do you know, they put me into one of those cell things? It was terrible. I'm only glad I didn't need to go to the toilet. They actually had a bucket in the corner and you were expected to … you know. I mean – an actual bucket! ' The three of them laughed.

Felicity continued. 'I understand that some others were charged but I don't think they were students. I believe they were known to the Police as regular troublemakers at these sorts of events. Anarchists I suppose. It's all rather exciting don't you think? '

'I could have done without it,' said Tom defensively.

'Liar ! You enjoyed it as much as I did. What happened to you anyway?' Tom avoided the question and shrugged his shoulders in response. By that time they were approaching Endcliffe Park and Felicity leaned forward to address her friend who was behind the steering wheel. 'Thanks for bringing me back from the war, Hazel darling. I don't know what I would have done without you.' Turning to Tom, she continued. 'Are you going to come in Tom, you're welcome to stay.' Hazel glanced into the rear-view mirror to try and catch Tom's response. There was no need as he made his reply audible.

'No, I think I had better get back to *Uni*. What time is it now? …ah, right, it's eight o'clock already. I would like to gauge the students' reaction and somebody needs to show a face around the place I suppose. I think it's probably better if you have an early night. You've had enough excitement for one day.'

'Not quite.' She looked at him provocatively and her implication was obvious. Then she added, 'I suppose you're right, really. I do feel a bit shaken. But I'll leave a door key under the mat, if you change your mind.'

Hazel pulled-up outside the black door, like a seasoned taxi driver. After a peck on the cheek with Tom, Felicity thanked her friend once more and got out of the car. She walked along the path waving casually over her shoulder, without any real sense of purpose. Feeling free to exercise some authority of her own and to prove she was capable of taking the initiative, Hazel spoke. 'I'm going back to the Campus as well Tom. Do you want a lift?' Tom accepted the offer and expressed his gratitude. 'In that case, you might as well get in the front seat.'

Tom was glad she suggested it, otherwise he would have looked like a chauffeur-driven tosser, especially since the car was only an old Morris 1000. It started to drizzle slightly so Hazel activated the windscreen wipers. As they screeched back and fore, Tom attempted to engage in polite conversation with Hazel. 'It seems as if it was a success, today. I suppose we'll get a better idea from the morning papers. Let's hope we get a mention, at least.'

Hazel's ability to converse dried-up as she became engrossed in her driving. She was concentrating fully as conditions worsened with the increased intensity of the rain. Hazel was one of those indistinctive students, who always seemed to be near the action without ever exerting any presence. She was studying politics and in her third year, quite dumpy with thickly-rimmed glasses and short, wavy hair. Her left leg was continually pumping up and down as she engaged the headlight dip-switch next to the clutch.

She dropped-off Tom by the main University entrance. He crouched low on exiting the car to thank her through the passenger window, then quickly tapped on the roof with his hand to indicate she could pull-away. While he turned towards the foyer, he simultaneously lifted the collar on his corduroy jacket in a gesture to keep the rain at bay. Once inside, he brushed himself-down, and shook his hair as he leaned forward before combing himself with the fingers of his left hand, as he had done many times before. He became aware of someone watching him and saw one of the Porters behind the main counter-desk giving him an icy stare. 'Brrrrr. It's turning foul out there,' Tom said, in an attempt to be congenial. The Porter turned away and entered the back room behind the counter, without an acknowledgement.

'*Charming,*' he thought to himself, as he bounded towards the stairs, leading to the Bar, taking two-steps at a time. He could hear the sound of revelry coming through the doors of the College Bar, as far away as the penultimate flight of steps. The place was packed and as he pushed through the crowd, one or two people nodded and offered positive mutterings of approval for the day's success.

Tom got to the Bar and a couple of students who were there before him, stepped back to allow him to order. He felt a glow of satisfaction at the gesture of respect. While waiting for his pint to be poured, he looked over his shoulder to the corner of the room, where the rugby crew were in full flow. He paid for his drink and sauntered through the groups to where they were seated. Tom did not normally seek-out the rugby boys but he knew they were an affable crowd so he thought he might get some accurate feedback from them. Kelvin was holding court and the jokers in the team had already composed a new chant on his behalf. As Tom got closer, they saw him approach and gave a rendition. 'Kelvin's a Cop Killer, 'ello, 'ello!'

Kelvin stood-up and approached Tom, who could see he was 'three sheets to the wind.' Kelvin shook his hand and almost stumbled into an embrace. Some of the bruising on Kelvin's bump had now started to appear and the swelling had dropped to close his left eye. He looked like he had done ten rounds with Henry Cooper. 'Jeez, that looks nasty, mate,' was Tom's gesture at reassurance. Kelvin was face-to-face with Tom and he garbled a drunken inquiry about Felicity.

'Bloody Hell, I forgot to say. I suppose I should make some sort of announcement to let everyone know.' Without answering Kelvin's question directly, Tom turned to face the crowded Bar. He tried clapping his hands to gain their attention but was unsuccessful. He got on a chair, while Kelvin helpfully banged a glass on the table, supported by his team-mates who yelled for silence. Most people turned to see where the noise was coming from and stopped their conversations.

'If I could just have your attention for a minute please, everyone. Thank you … I've just come back from West Bar Police Station. As you may know, some of our friends were forcibly ejected from the demonstration today and prevented from exercising their democratic rights by the Establishment's bully boys in blue.' This was greeted with a hail of boos. 'I am pleased to report that all those students taken to West Bar have now been released without charge.' This was greeted by a raucous cheering. Tom interrupted the noise by further claiming, 'This includes our Union President, Miss Felicity Stroud. So thank you everyone for making today a success.'

At that moment, some of the other students who had also been carted-away in *Black Marias*, entered the Bar. They were some well-known characters in the group and they were easily recognised by the other students present. The cheering increased dramatically and was accompanied by chants of 'He-ros, He-ros!' One of the more colourful individuals in the group raised his fist in the air, in a defiant gesture of power.

Tom returned to his conversation with Kelvin, who was beginning to get less steady on his feet. 'That's good news, Tom. Where is Emma Lawson by the way? I was with her one minute and after a scuffle I looked around and she was gone.'

Tom gestured using a *Gallic* shrug. It was easier than trying to talk. 'Unless she's here in the Bar, she must have gone straight back to her Hall, I suppose. Ok, well cheers for today Kelvin. You played a blinder.' On that note, Tom patted Kelvin on the back, who then turned to sit amongst his rugby playing friends, squeezing into the bench seats with a wriggle. As he moved away, Tom considered Felicity's invitation. It was nearly ten o'clock, not too late by student standards and he contemplated heading for Endcliffe Park. He made his way out of the Bar with a rejuvenated level of determination and knew exactly what he wanted to do and where he was going to spend the night.

It was not long before Tom was lifting a mat to remove the key.

V

After another night of unbridled sex with Felicity, Tom made his way to the Campus. He needed to check on the outcome of a recent computer programme. It meant calling into the Computer Engineering Department at the University to collect his printout. The IBM 704 mainframe occupied a large room in the corner of the site. To students not interested in computers, the room housing the hub of the Department must have seemed like a scene from a 1960s science fiction film. Ten-inch spools, wheeled clockwise and anti-clockwise inside glass-panelled, metal cabinets with perfect synchronicity. A couple of technicians in white coats perused the scene with clipboards, making notes as they peered into the inner working of the master computer.

He crossed the room and went straight to the Department's large wooden pigeon-holes where the printouts were deposited by the operators, once they had been spewed out of the computer. The twelve-inch-wide, 'K'-for-Kettlewell section was almost full of the characteristic, white computer- paper, with perforated edges and punctured, regular holes on each side. When Tom sifted through the concertina folds he was able to raise the printout above his head with both hands, while still retaining a three-inch-high stack on the floor. It looked like he was trying to wallpaper the room as he struggled to read the text. He was not surprised to find the programme had run successfully and he had managed to de-construct the logistics of the tested theorem.

Tom had studied the early computer programming language, *Fortran* while attending grammar school. He had been encouraged to study the subject by Mr Sleeman, the Head of Maths at Grace Darling Grammar School. Colin Sleeman was a dumpy, little man, anonymous to most of the school's teaching staff. However, he was a mathematical wizard. His hooked nose, glasses and bald pate with long side-hair, made him look like an owl, which was ironic because his wisdom set him apart from his peers. What he lacked in charisma was reimbursed by his enormous analytical ability. Tom stood-out immediately as a schoolboy with exceptional ability and Colin Sleeman felt he had the prodigy he had been longing for. When Tom saw numbers, he saw patterns and to a computer programmer that was gold dust. His ability was confirmed when '*Slogger*' Sleeman saw Tom devour old exam papers in his lessons. It came as no surprise when the 1965 Mathematics GCE O-level exam results revealed a Grade 1 pass for Master Kettlewell. Rather than wait for Tom to take guidance on his A-level choices, Mr. Sleeman sent for him one morning and told him straight.

'Look, Tom … *(one of the few occasions 'Slogger' ever referred to any pupil by his Christian name)* … for you there is only one choice for your A-levels. You will study Double Maths and another of your own choosing. I suspect it will be Physics. When you decide on Double Maths I will also take you for extra study in Computers and you can take the new Computer O-level after a year. Take these choices and you will go far my boy, of that I have no doubt. You have a rare gift and I am sure you will get a good degree in the future.'

Tom had a lot of respect for Mr Sleeman. With other people he may have been tempted to say '*Bugger off and leave me to make-up my own mind*' but he knew *Slogger's* intentions were in his best interests. Tom's three A-level 'A' grades, two years later confirmed the accuracy of the prediction. Tom knew he was entering the birth of the computer era and he wanted to make the most of this advantage.

Tom had always been thrilled by the joy of numbers and regarded their endless array of sequences as a challenge to his intellect. He never felt threatened when faced with a difficult set of calculations. They existed to be conquered. Whereas he could see the enjoyment that chess offered some mathematicians, Tom felt more at home with computers. They had a practical value and he believed they were the future. He had devoured the challenges of Pascal and had moved beyond its structural understanding, becoming involved in the development of Wirth's variants under Doc Herbert's tutorage. Tom could even imagine that perhaps one day in the future, a computer would fit on top of a desk, instead of filling a room.

He left the Computer Room with a feeling of buoyancy and proceeded to his lecture. The session on Applied Mathematical Theory was to be delivered by Dr Hounslow, a colleague of Doc Herbert. Unfortunately, 'Hounser' lacked the same clarity of delivery as Doc so Tom was in two-minds about whether to go to the Library instead. He was trying to ensure the printout was securely housed in his tattered brief case, while wrestling with the bag pressed against his knee and was unaware of other students going about their business. Suddenly his attention was caught by a familiar figure on the other side of the walkway, heading towards the Library. It was Emma and he called after her.

'Hello Emma. Sorry, I didn't see you there at first.' Emma turned around and stopped. Her smile told him all he wanted to know as he crossed over and walked towards her. 'You got a lecture ?'

'Oh, hello there. No I'm just on my way to the Library. You ?'

'I was just deciding whether to go to a boring lecture or for a coffee in the little Italian place in Glossop Road that serves great *Cappuccino*. Fancy a cup before you visit the Library? I promise not to spill any on myself this time.' Tom decided to miss his lecture if Emma agreed to join him. Fortunately, she did not take much persuading. Within ten minutes they were in Cavelli's Coffee Shop where the silver machines were hissing-out steam and producing the morning aroma of their special beverages. They found a table in the corner with a window view that looked-out onto the B-road. Tom returned from the counter with two frothy *Cappuccino* coffees and carefully placed them on the table where Emma was sitting.

'*Tah ..daaaa* ! There you are, I knew I could do it. Two unspilt cups of the best coffee in the city. Amazed or what?'

'Mmm. I haven't tasted the coffee yet, so it's too early to tell.'

After a slight pause, Tom decided to address the issue of what happened at the end of their last meeting. Emma must have been wondering about the nature of his relationship with Felicity. 'I'm glad I saw you because I owe you an apology.'

Emma turned from perusing the coffee shop's décor and looked at him directly. 'Apologise? For what?' He sensed her question was guarded.

'For what happened yesterday, when we got back to University after the march. ... You know, having to sort out that business with our Lady President. One minute you were there and the next you were gone.'

Emma took a sip from her cup, 'Oh, that. Don't worry about it. I haven't given it a second thought,' She waved her hand as if swatting away a fly and he could tell she was keeping her emotional distance. She took another sip of coffee, holding the cup in both hands with her elbows pressing on the table. Then, her demeanour seemed to change and she spoke to him with more softness in her voice. 'You working on anything in particular this morning?' He was pleased to get away from the elephant in the room.

Emma's question was an opportunity for Tom to strut. 'Yeah, I've got an important assignment to prepare. It's another one that contributes towards my finals.'

'Oh, right …you're doing Maths aren't you? I've heard your final year is very onerous.' responded Emma genuinely as she turned her cup in its saucer. Her preoccupation with her own academic requirements that morning were her priority and her interest in Tom's studies was only prompted by courtesy.

'What's your essay about?' asked Tom, politely. He was pleased to talk about assignments, something that gave him more solid ground on which to walk. He was examining her eyes as she spoke, pondering where to take this conversation.

'It's about an aspect of the Civil Rights Movement in America and whether segregation is ever justifiable. I hate it when I have to moralise in an essay. It seems so false, set against what is happening in the real world.' Tom could see that she had her feet on the ground, unlike some of the female 'air-heads' at the political meetings he attended.

'I know what you mean,' he responded sympathetically, even though he did *not* know what she meant. Missing the point still further, he added, 'I was watching a bit from a documentary on Biafra the other night, on the *telly*. Did you see it?' Tom felt a need to try and impress. It seemed to go unnoticed.

'I did actually. Those poor children. They're nearly always the main casualties of any war.' This girl seemed to have strong opinions of her own. He was finding it difficult to make progress so he decided to step it up a gear.

'Yeah, and that bloody Prime Minister, Wilson is sending arms to the Government just to make sure no other African colony feels like breaking free to threaten the *status quo*. I used to think those pictures of the emaciated children were due to famine. In reality, it is more like deliberate starvation because the blockade of Biafra means people just can't access the relief that's being sent.'

Emma was undaunted by his attempt at pseudo-intellectual pontification. She seemed to have a view of her own. 'Yes, I don't blame their leader, Ojukwu for inviting Western journalists into Biafra to promote those pictures around the world's media. It's a sick irony that starving kids with matchstick legs have bloated bellies. Those images make a powerful argument for doing something positive. It makes me feel so useless when you see innocent children suffering with kwashiorkor, like that.'

Tom felt like the tables were beginning to turn on him. He was impressed by Emma's apparent knowledge of the situation. It was not everyone who knew the name for the type of malnutrition caused by protein deficiency that was producing so much human devastation in Biafra. In his mind's eye he pictured the heart-rending newsreel shown on a nightly basis and the horrific toll of hunger which had affected so many Biafran children. He was being overpowered by a demure brunette, while it seemed as if he could not leave a mark on her opinions.

Their harmless teasing and flirting became a competition, with each trying to outdo the other. However, Tom did not mind if his lost this particular battle. He sat opposite Emma and felt a level of ease that was new to him. He revealed that he was from the small steel-making town of Consett, near Newcastle where his Mum and Dad still lived. His Dad had been a shop-steward in the local steel-works but quit to look after his mother, who had diabetes. It was clear from the warmth in Tom's voice, that he idolised his father and was close to his mother.

Emma explained that she was from the small village of Digby in Lincolnshire. Her father, Edgar Lawson was an American who had served with the Eighth Air Force in Buckinghamshire, during World War II. He worked on photographic interpretation and assisted on mission planning for the strategic bombing of German cities. While on active service he met Emma's mother, Jean. After the War, Edgar stayed in the UK, married Jean and they ran a small printing business in Lincoln. Emma's interest in her father's birthplace was a major stimulus towards her subject choice of American Studies at University. She hoped that one day, she could capitalise on her dual nationality and live in the USA.

Emma wanted to use her degree to work in politics. Tom admired her ambition.

They laughed at each other's jokes, more than the tales deserved and Tom tried to hide his admiration of Emma's verbal jousting. The pair sat and chatted for more than an hour, ordering an *Espresso* for their second cup. Emma tried to insist on paying for their caffeine rush but it was a challenge that Tom was able to rebuff. When Tom spoke, he subconsciously leaned forward in his seat, stroking his chin with the fingers of his left hand. Emma appeared more relaxed in her chair, occasionally looking out of the window at the distracting traffic. He wondered what she was really thinking about as she listened so attentively to his voice.

Time escaped them and they realised their commitments had been affected. For once, Tom did not really care about his studies. He felt comfortable with Emma and when he looked at her, he experienced something he could not explain. It was an attraction that was unlike the physical desire he felt for Felicity. While he sipped his drink, Tom appreciated being less cautious with this enigmatic young woman.

When they finished their coffee, they got up together, scraping their chairs in unison. The noise caused Tom to stop and lift his under the table, to avoid drawing attention to the truanting pair. As they made their way out, Emma was ahead of Tom, walking to the café's heavily glassed front. A yard from the exit, Tom accelerated to open the door. She thanked him with mock courtesy. 'Why, thank you kind sir.'

They strolled back to the University, walking in small steps. Although Tom was taller than Emma, their height difference was not marked and they looked like a couple who were natural together. For the first time in his life, Tom felt that he wanted his good looks to count for something. Emma seemed to enjoy *his* company too and he instinctively felt she was attracted to him.

'How about going for a drink together sometime ?' asked Tom, surprising himself. He desperately hoped for a positive response. The Felicity conundrum would have to be resolved some other time.

'Yes, that would be nice,' answered Emma, who also seemed to want to pursue the relationship.

By this time, they had virtually arrived back at the University. Tom could not help making comparisons between Emma and Felicity and before he had completed his emotional stocktaking, they entered the busy foyer. Suddenly, they were interrupted by Felicity's familiar voice. '*There* you are darling. I've been looking for you all morning.'

Tom tried to hide his surprise. 'Oh, hi I was just going to …' He was concerned that Felicity might see he was with Emma and any chance of pursuing that relationship would be destroyed. He selfishly wanted to keep his options open.

'Never mind about what you were *just* going to do. We have some business of our own.' Felicity grabbed Tom by his collar and pulled him into a passionate embrace. Whether she suspected anything untoward had taken place was unclear. Perhaps she was simply marking her territory. Instinctively, Tom pushed her away and as he separated from her hold, he looked around anxiously, only to see the back of Emma disappearing into the swell of other students. Once again, it must have seemed to Emma that Tom was complying with Felicity's needs and she was being ignored. Not for the first time in recent days, he was angry at himself. He knew that at some point he was going to have to be decisive, although he wondered if he had the courage.

During the journey in the car to Felicity's flat, Tom said very little and his mind drifted towards thoughts of Emma. He began to reproach himself for the way he had treated her. One minute he was caring and considerate, the next he behaved like a *Neanderthal*. He had always hated the male stereotype who acted badly towards women. He was sexually attracted to Felicity but felt he would have to invest an emotional part of himself if they were to have a relationship and that was something he was reluctant to do. Felicity was alluring in more ways than one and their association un-nerved him in a way he was not yet prepared to countenance. She usually acted with such pretentiousness that Tom wondered what the hell she was playing at. Then he thought for a moment, perhaps that was precisely what she *was* doing – playing some sort of game. The only trouble was that Tom did not know the rules. There was something about Felicity which Tom thought distanced her from forming a meaningful relationship. She did not seem to need anyone and although she was attractive in the short term, Tom could not envisage it would lead to something that would last.

VI

At four o'clock the following afternoon, after working in the Library and attending three lectures, Tom made his way from the Campus towards his place in Trippet Lane. He had arranged to meet Felicity at nine o'clock that evening so he had some down-time and wanted to relax. He needed a bath or at least a good wash before re-engaging with Felicity and he wanted to ensure he got the use of the bathroom before his flatmates.

Tom had only ever had one regular girlfriend before Felicity and that was while he was in the sixth form. They had indulged in 'heavy petting' and he had to wait until University before he enjoyed full sex. Tom had never craved sex the way some of the other students seemed to, although he never turned his back on an opportunity. Usually, he took his chance at some of the Students Union's concerts, when the girls were drunk enough not to care. He did not want them to care. Tom viewed Felicity's availability as a convenience rather than a time to start caring. She seemed to him like a good prospect on paper: attractive, rich, eloquent and intelligent, with seemingly similar goals to himself.

At half-past-eight, he tucked his green *Ben Sherman* shirt into his denim jeans before leaning back to comb his hair, assisted by his bedroom mirror. With one final glance of admiration at his reflection, he clasped his hands together and headed for his evening entertainment. As he approached Felicity's flat, he did not notice that her Triumph was not parked outside. Her anonymous neighbour from the Midland Bank must have left open the communal front door so Tom went inside. He ascended the noisy stairs and glanced at his watch. It was ten minutes past nine. He tapped on the door of Felicity's flat, courteously at first, before increasing the frequency and volume of his knocking. No answer. He went outside to try and spot any semblance of activity but there was none. Clearly, she was not at home and he wondered if she had been delayed or whether he had got the schedules wrong. He went over in his mind the conversation he had with Felicity, when they made the arrangements and was convinced he was correct about the time. There was nothing he could do other than wait outside, like some obedient puppy, something he was not prepared to do. After making his decision to leave, he faked a punch to the door and decided to head for the University Bar.

As he walked beside the Park, a young boy was approaching with his mother, from the opposite direction, dragging a stick across the railings to make the sort of machine gun noise that appeals to most mischievous soldiers. Tom thought it was late for a boy his age to be out and about, though his smart clothes suggested the couple may have been returning from a family visit nearby. Tom swerved-out, away from the railings to allow the pair to proceed unaffected by his presence. Suddenly, he was almost blinded by flashing headlights as a car pulled-in only a few yards in front of him. It was Felicity and she had someone with her in the passenger seat. He could not see if it was a male or female companion due to the glare of the headlights. Felicity wound down her window and beckoned Tom over to the car. He approached, tentatively.

'Sorry, Tom but I bumped into an old friend and she invited me to a party. We're on our way there now. Come if you want, darling.' Felicity was still airing her superiority and maintaining an upper-middle class distance. She was once again issuing orders and he was not willing to succumb to her demands. This time his conscience won the dispute and he declined. He gave a dismissive response of his own by waving his hand across his face.

'Well, if you are sure, I'll see you later. *Ciao* for now, darling.' She leaned out of the car window and blew Tom a kiss, before speeding away in her Triumph Herald, in true Felicity-style. He watched the car disappear loudly down the road and struggled to contain his anger and disappointment; Tom inwardly cursed the friend in the front seat, where he should have been sitting. He was furious and knew that he had been played. It was clear to him that Felicity lived only for the moment. Tom was not sure of the nature of her political convictions and became more certain that she was playing some sort of role for her own personal gratification. Tom knew his own actions came from the heart. He was not even sure that Felicity had one.

VII

Tom avoided Felicity over the next few days, preferring to share another Canteen coffee with Emma, when they bumped into each other again, during a mutual break in their lecture schedules. On Friday evening, he inevitably found himself in the Student Bar, talking to Kelvin, who was wearing his black eye with immense pride. The purple bruising on his face had been given an added brown-yellow mix to accompany his bloodshot sclera. It was a genuine shiner. Although it was the end of the week, the Bar was quiet, reflecting the overspending that had befallen most students on the night of the Anti-Apartheid rally. 'Will you be playing tomorrow, Kelvin or are you going to give it a miss?' inquired Tom, suspecting that he would receive a positive response.

'Nah, the quack has told me to give it another week, just in case the retina is damaged. So I'll just be watching from the touchline. Fancy joining me or will you be chasing your golden degree.'

'Thanks for the invite but you're right. I need to keep on top of my assignments. Fancy another pint ?'

Without waiting for an answer, Tom lifted Kelvin's empty glass and made his way to the pumps. Shortly after placing his order, the door in the corner of the room opened and four female students entered, laughing and making a bit of a noise. Tom recognised Hazel at the head of the group and then he could see Felicity, followed by two others from her entourage. Tom picked up the two, foaming pint glasses and turned to make his way back to Kelvin. He did not see Felicity approach but she placed her hand on his arm to force his attention. Standing close, she pressed her breasts into his body and said, 'Sorry about the other night, darling. You're not still cross with me, are you ?' It was clear from his failure to respond that Tom was irritated. Felicity's three friends were oblivious to the application of her wiles and carried on chatting amongst themselves. 'Come back to my place later and I'll make it up to you.' She followed up her invitation with a peck on the cheek. Tom half-smiled and returned to sit with his friend. Kelvin had spotted the kiss.

'She's got the hots for you, alright, my handsome pal. Going to give her one later ?'

'We'll see,' replied Tom.

Kelvin and Tom were later joined by a few other members of the rugby team, who clearly were not bothered about drinking the night before a match. While the girls filtered to the opposite end of the room, Tom and Kelvin indulged in a few more pints, until closing time. Tom left the Bar first, leaving Kelvin to talk tactics with some of his team-mates. He checked his watch and after his interaction with Felicity, he knew where he was heading.

Tom arrived at his destination just as two young women were leaving through the outer door. While they were occupied with their conversation, he slinked through the open entrance, before the hinge finished engaging. Wanting to avoid being seen by anyone in the building, he crept up the stairs, hoping to give her a surprise. He was successful. As the door opened, her face was one of astonishment.

'Hi, I thought you might have been asleep and wasn't sure if you would still be up,' said Tom in a matter-of-fact way, despite the unusual situation.

'I was just about to go to bed. What time is it?' she asked, brushing her hair back with her fingers and staring into his face.

'About eleven. Is it ok?' asked Tom, hopefully. He was standing with his left foot half-way across the threshold, in an attempt to make a plea for entry. Given the circumstances, there was little else she could do. She crouched past him and pressed her hand into his back, while casting a furtive glance along the upstairs' corridor.

'Oh sorry... yes ... come in quick ... before anyone sees you. Take a seat. Would you like some coffee or something?' There was no reason to speak in a hushed tone but it was caused by the sense of panic she was experiencing.

'No thanks, we seem to drink coffee every time we see each other.' Emma was a little shaken by Tom's surprise visit. 'How did you find me? You've never been here before ... have you?'

Tom felt obliged to respond in a whisper as he stood awkwardly, just inside the room. 'Well, I've been to this hall of residence before but during the day and never like this. I know the Warden can be a bit strict about male visitors at this time of night but I managed to get passed her without being spotted.'

'But how do you know my room number?' Emma had never liked surprises and was not sure how she felt about this one. She stood with both thumbs hooked into the rear pockets of her tight jeans and then turned with her hips, signalling Tom to enter further into her student cell.

He continued the conversation as he brushed past her. 'I bumped into that friend of yours. What's her name ... er...? Cathy, from Bolton. She told me the number of your room. And here I am.'

Emma invited Tom to sit with a casual arm movement and he moved to what was supposed to be a semi-comfortable seat. His choice was limited, given the size of the room. Emma sat at a desk-chair after turning it to face him. Feeling a little out-of-place, he leaned forward and briefly mentioned the nature of his most recent assignment, in order to break the ice. He deliberately avoided mentioning Felicity.

While he was talking, Emma's gaze was fixed on him but her mind was elsewhere. Tom could see that she was guarded and bemused by his sudden appearance. He wanted her to relax as she had done in their previous meetings .When Emma pushed her hair behind her ear, Tom wondered if he had over-stepped the mark. The last thing he wanted to do was frighten her. He then re-considered her offer and accepted the invitation for coffee, trying to avoid watching her every move. Even when she was filling the kettle at the tiny sink, Tom could tell that her thoughts were racing. The fact that he had broken contact with her on two recent, significant occasions must have been playing on her mind, although they had shared some time together since then. She must have been considering the mixed messages he was sending. All the time he was seated, Tom nervously played an imaginary tune on the invisible keyboard resting on his thigh, with the fingers of his right hand.

Emma passed his cup and then slumped into the chair, looking at him intensely. She avoided the temptation to raise her eyebrows but waited for him to break the silence about why he had appeared, unannounced at her room, late at night. He had her attention.

'Something has been bothering me and I wanted to clear the air.' Emma looked at him, without a flicker of emotion. 'I'm sorry that I was rude to you the other day. I didn't know Felicity was going to jump on me like that. It was the second time she got in the way and I should have been more considerate. It was just the way it happened. Anyway, just to let you know – I've finished with her. I wanted to see you.' Emma tried to say something but Tom cut across her and continued. 'I do not want to offend you. I like you too much for that.' He was passed playing games and had decided to go for broke. It was time for the truth.

Emma picked-up a pencil and pressed the desk top gently with each end as she slowly rotated it between her fingers, giving deep thought to what was happening. She turned her head to one side and sucked through her teeth as if to say *'I don't know what to think'*. Just as the end with the rubber made contact with the polished surface, a loud bell gave two sharp rings, startling Tom.

'What the Hell was that?' he asked as if he had been electrocuted.

'The bell is the notice to any non-resident, that it's time to leave the building. The Warden is about to do her rounds.' Tom gestured his hands like a quivering *Al Jolson* and screwed his face in mock fear. Instantly, he became aware of his vein of immaturity.

Nevertheless, time was not on his side. They both recognised that more needed to be said but this was not the occasion. Tom got out of the chair at the same time as Emma rose from her seat at the desk. They moved towards each other and their faces were close for a moment. There was a pause. Tom was not sure what to do. If he was rebuffed at this point, it could signal the end of a relationship before it had even begun. He settled for a consolation prize. 'Will I see you again?'

'You'll see me tomorrow, probably, if you want to,' said Emma, resorting to being cagey once more as she moved to the door.

Tom gave a major throw of the dice, while he anxiously clenched his fist behind his back. 'It's the Christmas Ball, a week today – next Friday at the City Hall. We could go together, if you fancy it?'

Emma raised her eyebrows. 'It's a bit posh for someone with your beliefs isn't it? Won't the black tie and dinner suit compromise your principles?' Tom thought for a moment. He could hardly say to her, 'Of *course they will compromise my principles. I don't want to mix with a bunch of bourgeois twats, swanning about as if they own the place, dressed as penguins.'* Instead, as they shuffled forward together, he simply responded, 'I will enjoy it … if *you* come with me.'

By this time, they were standing together at the door. Emma reached past him and tried to grasp the chrome-plated handle. Tom gently clamped her arm. They were close, once more. She looked at him silently, in half-surprise and half-expectation. Tom pulled her towards him and they kissed. This was more than a goodnight kiss: he wanted to show her that he cared. As their lips parted, they looked at each other. Emma rested an open palm on Tom's chest and then raising her hand, put her index finger to his lips. 'Don't say anything,' she said. 'Let's just leave it like that for now.'

Tom turned his head upward and studied the ceiling before returning to look into Emma's eyes. He gave her a shy smile and allowed her to open the door. Then he left, in silence. Emma closed the door behind him, before turning in one movement to rest against the wall for support. She faced the room, smiling in disbelief and pleasure. She did not know where this journey would lead but she hoped that her instincts would prove to be right.

Tom walked through the corridors and out of the hall of residence with a youthful spring. There had been a point when he thought he would have returned to Felicity's flat that evening but something pulled him towards Emma. What was it, he wondered? He felt it must have been what happened that afternoon of the demonstration, when they first spent some time together. Tom was glad that he had bumped into her friend, Cathy on his way out of the Bar, otherwise he could easily be sharing Felicity's bed. Despite the obvious attractions Felicity offered, he wanted something more.

VIII

The 1969 Student Christmas Ball was due to take place on Friday December 12th at Sheffield City Hall. The term 'Student Christmas Ball' was always a bit of a misnomer because most students did not attend or even consider paying the five pounds for a ticket. It was expensive, elitist and considered part of a culture that any self-respecting student would want to avoid. The Ball was the showpiece for lecturers, their wives and the University's Vice-Chancellor. It involved a three-course meal, a dance band and speeches. Each table comprised ten people, who usually shared a common platform related to some aspect of University life. Those students who did attend the Ball, belonged to a particular sub-group who wanted to be part of an upper-middle-class culture but for Tom's purposes it was ideal. It showed Emma he was willing to go that extra mile.

Tom managed to get tickets for the Mathematics Department's table. Mathematicians at the University were not renowned for their willingness to attend social functions, never mind a public gathering that involved mixing with students. Doc Herbert had been in charge of the Department's ticket allocation and he was unable to muster much support from his colleagues. When Tom approached him to ask about ticket availability, Doc was delighted.

'Yes, Tom my boy. I've got a couple of tickets. In fact, they're going spare, so you can have them for free. I'm only delighted you want to come along.'

'No,' said Tom 'I don't expect them to be free. In fact, I insist on paying for them.' The event might have been a bourgeois function but Tom was not going to be patronised.

'Tell you what Tom. Because you have saved my bacon, just give me a couple of quid for each ticket and we'll call it quits.' Tom gave Doc a five pound note. He considered it an appropriate amount to maintain the

40

upper hand. 'I think that's what it comes to Doc. I'm not very good with division.' They both laughed.

Tom hired his suit from a swish shop located in the City centre. It relied heavily on the University as the mainstay for its business. *Thomas Lee & Co* rented academic gowns, dinner suits and ladies' evening dresses to anyone who was willing to pay the going rate. Tom took longer than usual to dress that evening. He allowed himself a touch of vanity as he admired his appearance in the circular bathroom mirror. Recognising the need for student dignity, he wore an old anorak over the top of his smart jacket, in case any friends spotted him.

Tom had arranged to meet Emma at City Hall's main entrance and arrived with plenty of time to spare. He stood at the top of the steps to shelter from the chilly evening, which became colder when he removed his anorak and held it over his arm. The main guests were greeted under the lobby's impressive pillars as they arrived. Tom moved to the side, not wishing to attract any attention, while his eyes scanned the night to try and spot Emma arriving. He saw a taxi pull-up on the opposite side of the road and recognised her voice as she sorted out the fare with the driver, through his cab window. Emma had her back to Tom as he approached. She turned to move towards the steps and as the taxi pulled away, Tom was facing her, about six feet away.

'Wow!' he said genuinely. 'You look stunning.'

He took her hand and after they had walked about ten yards, the heavens opened and a torrential downpour threatened to soak them both. Tom held his anorak over the two of them, using it like an umbrella. Emma crooked her right arm around Tom's left and pulled him a little closer. They walked quickly up the steps, giggling as they skipped towards the entrance. Once inside, Tom gave his wet coat a good shake and the couple glided through the foyer, heading towards the Ballroom and still holding hands. Before going into the main arena, Tom took Emma's wrap, along with his own coat and queued at the cloakroom's counter for a ticket, while Emma visited the Ladies Room.

As he was waiting in the queue, he felt self-conscious and out of his comfort zone. He was silently whistling an improvised tune and shuffling his feet, hoping not to be recognised. When he became sufficiently courageous, he raised his head and scanned the scene. He could see some of the guests through the double-glass doors at the entrance to the Ballroom but failed to spot anyone he knew. The couple had timed it well, with enough bodies already inside to ensure an anonymous entry. Emma returned from the Ladies Room and smiled at her waiting escort. He gently ushered her forward by placing his hand lightly on her back as they wafted into the glitzy world of penguins and princesses.

Inside the Ballroom, the crowd swelled to a sizeable number and Tom estimated that about two hundred people were already in the room. He counted thirty tables, as well as the main rectangular seating area which accommodated another fifteen. The VIP table was under the Sheffield coat of arms, which displayed the words '*Deo Adjuvante Labor Proficit*' ('With God's help our labour is successful') in bold red carving.

Tom made his way to the bar, dodging through polite groups of dignitaries, who were chatting and smiling, in anticipation of an enjoyable evening at the end of a busy Michaelmas term. He ordered Emma a *Babycham* and avoided ordering a pint for himself, discreetly requesting a bottle of Mackeson stout. He drew attention to himself only when the girl behind the bar asked rather loudly if he wanted a cherry with the *Babycham*. He nodded a response. Then, he turned to explore the crowd and for a moment he thought he saw anonymous, old men's faces staring at him. He knew that some of the lecturers would recognise him and be aware of his political views. They would not want upstarts like him joining their dignified evening.

He glanced around, now desperately looking for a familiar face as he presented Emma her drink, before nervously straightening his dickie-bow and taking a small sip of *Mackies*. He did not see Doc and his wife, Phyllis approaching from behind. Doc was holding a whisky tumbler, while his wife was drinking a dry sherry. Tom offered his hand to his tutor and smiling falsely, pushed open an invisible door with his left arm to introduce Emma. Doc shook hands enthusiastically and nodded as he acknowledged Tom's guest. Watching with silent interest was Doc's wife Phyllis, who was soon given a speaking role. She would not be the first person that evening to throw Tom a curve ball. 'Good, evening, Tom. I've heard a lot about you, from Stanley.'

Tom was just about to ask, '*Who the hell is Stanley?*' when he realised she was talking about Dr Stanley Herbert, her husband.

Phyllis and Doc greeted Emma warmly and Tom was relieved they were in safe company. A man in a red jacket suddenly banged a gavel onto a wooden block, at the main table, causing heads to turn. He invited everyone to take their seats so the function could begin. The University's Vice Chancellor, Dr Eamonn St. John recited grace before the meal. Tom stifled a fit of the giggles during the rendition and desperately tried to distract himself by looking at his shoes, before pretending to blow his nose into a soundproof handkerchief. Fortunately only Emma noticed Tom's odd behaviour.

As they sat down and the general noise level increased after the blessing, Emma asked Tom to explain the joke. He told her that Dr St. John had been standing directly under the letter 'O' on the coat of arms. When he spoke, it looked as if he had a halo over his head and the irony of his angelic surname had caught Tom's funny bone. He felt that word, *immature*, resurrect itself once more. It was not the impression he was trying to create and was glad that Emma said nothing further.

Each of the guests' tables had two bottles of white wine and two bottles of red, positioned between a jug of iced tap water and the shining cutlery. Serving ladies wearing black uniforms and working in groups of three began to scuttle around each seat, starting with the VIP tables. They were an efficient workforce. One woman asked whether the guest wanted soup or melon. If it was the former, she wiped the plate and laid down a soup dish, while her accomplice followed with a ladle. If it was the latter, another server lowered a small plate of fruit. Like a swarm of worker ants, trios of serving ladies covered the room.

While they waited for the higher numbered tables to be served, each group engaged in polite conversation. On Tom's table, one of the senior maths lecturers took it upon himself to serve the wine and proceeded to ask the question, 'Red or white' to each guest seated. The increase in volume caused by the numerous conversations meant that it became more difficult to talk to anyone more than two seats away. Emma and Tom found themselves spread between a Phyllis and Stanley sandwich.

'So what are your plans after graduation, Tom,' asked Phyllis politely. She appeared genuinely interested. He placed his knife on the side-plate, delaying any spreading of the rectangular knob of butter onto his crusty roll. His hands fell from the table, onto the napkin covering the lap of his hired trousers and he turned towards Phyllis.

'I'm not really sure yet. Best to concentrate on getting a degree first and then take it from there.' Tom had never tempted fate by taking life for granted. He had seen too much bad luck in his parents' lives. His mother Betty was struck down with Type 1 diabetes when she was only forty-one, while Dennis Kettlewell had been sacked for simply being a shop-steward.

Doc picked-up on Tom's response as he was breaking his own roll in half. He brushed away some of the crumbs that had fallen onto the cream, linen tablecloth. 'He will be in demand of that I'm sure, Phyllis. If Tom doesn't get a really good degree, I will be amazed. Then everyone will be chasing him.'

As Tom listened to his tutor, he pondered his luck that Doc was on board. Dr Stanley Herbert was clearly Tom's best ally in the fight for a *First*. The direction of their delicate conversation was saved by a visit from the first of the trio-in-black. Tom decided on the soup, while Emma opted for melon. After waiting for everyone to begin eating, Tom picked-up his spoon and was dipping his head towards his round plate when he became conscious of someone looking at him. He gazed across the heads in the room and spotted Felicity in the distance, glaring in his direction. He half-gestured a wave but Felicity did not change her facial expression. After a few uncomfortable seconds, her eyes averted Tom's attempt at acknowledgement. It was clear, she was not happy. To his relief, the rest of the meal, comprising chicken or beef, apple pie or ice cream, passed-off without incident. So did the rest of the evening in the Ballroom, once the speeches had been endured. When the dancing started, Tom had enough sense to keep half an eye on Felicity's movements and to avoid her. He tried to ensure Emma remained blissfully unaware of any danger.

The live music was a good standard so Tom and Emma danced to three of the waltzes played by the large orchestra. Their dancing was passable but they would not have worried anyone on *Come Dancing*. Tom had learned to waltz, or at least to perform a version of the dance, during wet-weather games lessons when he was at school. If the weather was inclement and the grass sports pitches were vulnerable to damage, all the sixth-formers had to report to the Sports Hall for dancing lessons instead of the usual rugby, soccer and hockey. This occurred most commonly during Wednesday afternoons in the winter weeks. The girls loved those lessons, while the boys resorted to being thirteen years of age at the thought of having to put their arms around someone of the opposite sex. When order was established, Mrs Bamber from the Music Department would play the gramophone through a loudspeaker and call out instructions, while the youngsters followed her commands and attempted to dance. Mr Allen and Miss Fleetham, the Heads of Physical Education ensured order was maintained. Tom did not mind missing football as much as some of the others. The waltz was the one dance he was able to experience with his mother before she became incapacitated; it was her favourite.

The evening was winding down when the orchestra finished playing the *Last Waltz*. There was some bewilderment among the remaining guests about where to go next as people turned around, half-expecting some sort of announcement. Instead, the official event finished with a whimper. Tom suggested to Emma that he should retrieve their coats before the cloakroom became too busy. She agreed and stayed to have a final conversation with Stan and Phyllis while Tom exchanged two yellow tickets with the female attendant, for an anorak and Emma's wrap. Standing deep in thought and wondering about taxis, he turned away from the cloakroom desk not paying much attention to the other guests. Going against the tide of the crowd, Tom collided with someone. 'Sorry,' he said politely.

He recognised the voice of the respondent. 'In a rush are you, dear boy?' It was Felicity. She had been drinking and had now cornered her prey. 'Where have you been for the last two weeks, my darling Tom? Anyone would think you were trying to avoid me.' She was spitting venom in his direction.

'Oh, hi Felicity. No, of course not. Just been busy recently. Assignments mostly.' Tom became terrified. No one else had this effect on him. He needed to grow a pair and it needed to be quickly.

'Not too busy for that sweet, little thing over there.' She pointed over Tom's shoulder by raising her chin. 'What's the matter, Tom? Lost your appetite?' Felicity was raising herself out of her basket, ready to bite. Whereas Tom had previously interpreted this behaviour from her as flirtatious, he now sensed it was threatening. He was beginning to realise why Felicity played games. She only liked winning.

'For what?'

'You know what.' She lowered her hand and tried to grab his crotch. Tom pushed it away quickly and forcibly, trying desperately not to be seen.

Finally, he showed some testosterone. 'Look, Felicity. You seem to have your wires crossed. I'm with Emma because I want to be. There never was a you and me. It was nice for a few weeks but now it's over. Let's just move on.' He turned away and headed towards Emma, hoping that by being reasonable, Felicity would be placated. It was a forlorn hope. As he walked out of earshot, Felicity hissed under her breath, 'It's over when I say it's over, Tom Kettlewell.'

Stan and Phyllis were just about to walk towards the exit when Tom caught Doc's eye as he approached with Emma's wrap. They converged and shook hands. 'Thanks for your company this evening, Tom. It was an enjoyable occasion. Much better than the others we've been to. We've said our goodbyes to Emma. She's a lovely girl, Tom. Don't lose that one, my boy.'

Tom waved goodbye in Phyllis' direction but she was not content with such a shallow gesture so she walked towards him. Taking his hand, she pulled him close and gave him a peck on the cheek. 'Nice meeting you, Tom. Good luck with your studies. And thanks again to you both. You make a lovely couple.'

Tom and Emma stepped out into the fresh December air. The rain had stopped and it was a cold, quiet evening. 'Shall I try and get a taxi, Emma? There's probably no buses at this time of night.'

'I'm not bothered. I don't mind walking, if you don't. It's not that far. Let's just walk.' That was the best invitation Tom had received all night. It was the part of the evening he had been hoping for ; he took her hand and they began to amble slowly through the City centre.

There were numerous pools of water from the heavy rain, at points in the pavement, where it had collected in the depressions and cracks. On the dry areas, pieces of grit crunched under foot as the leather soles on Tom's hired patent leather shoes, intermittently collected and deposited the detritus of the day. They walked along a street of shops, Emma's arm wrapped around his, with Tom on the side nearest to the road. He remembered his father telling him that is how all gentlemen should accompany a woman. It was a legacy from the days when a man might have to withdraw his sword, in order to defend a lady's honour. '*Consett had not moved on a great deal,*' he thought to himself as he indulged in a smile.

They strolled in silence, inevitably arriving at a large puddle lying in the middle of their path. While continuing to hold hands, Tom went to the left, and Emma walked to the right of the water. Their arms straightened as they extended going around the small pool but they kept hold of each other, converging on the other side. As they met, their bodies collided. Tom pulled Emma towards him and kissed her, longingly and passionately. He knew she was good for him and could sense a change in himself every time he was with her. She was giving him something to hope for and he needed to ensure he did not make any more mistakes with their relationship.

'Thanks for a lovely evening,' said Emma. 'Not bad for a first date,' she teased.

'So I did impress you after all then?' Tom desperately wanted to hear her say yes. He should have known better. Emma could not be taken for granted.

'That would be telling,' she continued. Although she was playing with him, Tom did not detect any malice in her voice as he had with Felicity. This was harmless fun. The irony was that to Tom, the stakes were much higher. He was beginning to project his life forward and he liked what he saw.

Along the way, they discussed Doc and Phyllis and how happy they seemed together. Tom made no reference to his encounter with Felicity. Their conversation was interrupted intermittently by tempting kisses. It was becoming increasingly difficult to keep their hands off each other. Eventually they reached the main doors of Emma's hall of residence. No one was allowed to enter after midnight without the Warden's permission. It was clear they had no chance of spending the night together in Emma's room. Tom was not going to allow their first time to be in his flat. He did not want anything to undermine such an important occasion. He would rather wait.

Just before Emma pressed the buzzer they kissed once more. Tom tried to speak but before he said anything, Emma held her index finger against his lips as she had when he appeared at her room, that late night. She spoke softly. 'Shhhh .. it's ok. That's not the last time we shall ever kiss. If I could invite you inside, I would. Please believe me. I want us to be together just as much as you do. But I will see you tomorrow and hopefully, the day after that.'

'It's just …'

'I know.' She pressed her finger once more. 'Goodnight.'

'Goodnight.'

With that farewell, the Warden appeared at the door before Emma had a chance to press the buzzer. Tom turned and watched her enter the corridor before disappearing into the lift. He suddenly felt alone, for the first time in his life.

IX

Tom and Emma had arranged to meet at lunchtime in the Refectory. Tom arrived after his hour-long, eleven o'clock lecture, following a visit to the Computer Room, where he collected a printout. He was seated in the Refectory fifteen minutes after they started serving food, aware that Emma had a lecture that finished at twelve-thirty. However, it was important to be in the Refectory first because he wanted to watch her enter. At a quarter-to-one Tom saw Emma at one of the till points, paying for her food. She passed through the check-out and while holding her tray she scanned the tables, looking across the busy Refectory, where a hive of students seemed to be swarming everywhere.

Tom was deliberately sitting in a different part of the hall to his usual spot, by the large bay window. When he saw Emma look across to that area, she seemed disappointed. Tom was pleased, it was the reaction he was hoping for. Rather than watch her continue to struggle, he raised himself from his seat and waved across to attract her attention. Emma's face broke into an enchanting smile and he was hooked.

A couple of boys on the adjacent table examined Emma's slim body as she approached Tom. They were among the many horny students who enjoyed admiring her gorgeous figure. Tom kissed her as she arrived at his new location, before placing her tray on the table. He told a lie about why he could not sit at his usual place in the Refectory. While they ate their lunch together, the conversation turned towards the forthcoming Christmas break.

Tom was not hungry and pushed his plate of half-eaten food to one side, ensuring the crossed knife and fork stayed for the ride. Leaning forward, he told Emma that he intended to return home to Consett at the week-end. Emma listened and nodded in silent acceptance, confirming that she had similar plans, now the end of term was imminent. After taking a penultimate scrape of yoghurt from its plastic pot, she informed Tom that her grandmother would be visiting her family this year. Mrs Lawson was due to fly-in from Portland, Maine in the next couple of days. Emma's Gran had wanted to come over to celebrate *Thanksgiving* in November but she had suffered some minor ailment and postponed the trip. 'Dad told her that in Britain, Christmas is the major turkey-eating season. It'll be great to see Gran again. I only wish we could be together as well.' Tom reached across and kissed her.

After looking around to ensure no one had commented on their intimacy, Emma scooped the white, pliable spoon around the inside of the yoghurt container one last time. 'How are things on the revolutionary front, these days?' she asked in a matter-of-fact way. 'You haven't said much about the Apartheid campaign and things seemed to have calmed down since the demonstration at the Town Hall.' She was right, Tom's studies were now commanding his full attention.

His elbows were resting on the table as his eyes followed the spoon to Emma's lips. 'I think that's inevitable. We made our point and got the media coverage we were after. Hopefully people will now sit-up and listen to the arguments against Apartheid. Who knows, they may even *do* something.' He pushed the salt cellar he was playing with further to the side and gazed around the Refectory, now at its busiest. 'I certainly hope the authorities give serious consideration to the planned South African Cricket Tour next year. We all feel pretty confident that if it goes ahead we can strangle it at birth.'

She handed her unwanted carton and sandwich packaging to a lady in a sky-blue tabard, who suddenly appeared at their table. Emma smiled a thank you, while continuing to address Tom. 'What does our Lady President have to say on the matter… now she's out of the clink?' Tom sensed Emma did not like Felicity much, although naively, he was not sure why.

He shrugged his shoulders in response and aware the Refectory was becoming crowded, Tom suggested they move to the nearby Canteen for a coffee, where it was quieter. When they stood, two tray-carrying students immediately bee-lined for their vacant seats. Emma threw her bag over her shoulder and grabbed Tom's arm in a bustle of familiarity. Soon the courting couple were in the more peaceful environment of the Canteen. Emma grabbed a table, while Tom queued for the coffees.

Tom was annoyed that Christmas was about to disturb their relationship. He did not want to go back to Consett. Settling into a wooden chair, he took a sip from his cup before taking hold of Emma's hand. She broke the silence. 'Tell me more about your Dad. He sounds like quite a man from what you've told me about him so far.'

This was one of Tom's favourite subjects and he seized on the opportunity. 'He is. People in Consett who know him, talk about him with respect. He fought to keep the steelworks open when others wanted to close it. *British Steel* doesn't want to keep it going because they would rather concentrate on other steel plants. The rumours about closure have started to circulate again, only this time no one will fight it the same way that my Dad did. Mark my words, there will be no steelworks in Consett in ten years' time.'

'What sort of a place is Consett? I don't know much about it.' Tom had to remind himself not to regress into his North Eastern accent when talking about home. His mother did not like him to talk that way,

'My old Grandad used to say that Consett was the only place where the crows fly backwards,' he said smiling and slowly stirring his coffee, with a white plastic spoon.

'What? I don't understand.'

'Well there was so much muck and pollution in the air that flying backwards was the only way they could keep the dirt out of their eyes.'

Emma shot him a puzzled look. 'So it's an industrial town is it?' Tom wondered if Emma knew more about the States than she did about her own country. She certainly seemed to know very little about *his* home area.

'Just a little bit. It's a sort of smaller version of Sheffield in some ways. You can see the cooling towers from anywhere nearby. We make steel. We made the steel that was used to build Blackpool Tower. I can remember when I was growing-up thinking that everything in Consett was red. When the works was going full tilt, the air hanging over the Town gave everything a red hue. Even the roads were red because when it rained, the iron oxide in the air was washed out and stained the streets. We even had pink snow, one year.'

'Is that another of your crow-flying-backwards stories?' Even to Emma, this story seemed to be pushing the truth a little too far.

'No honest, it's true. The snow did have a little shade of red when it was lying. As it fell from the sky, it picked-up some of the oxide pollution in the air.' Tom made himself sound convincing.

'Mmm. ... Not sure if I believe you or not on that one. ..It doesn't sound like the nicest place in the world, if I'm honest.' He wanted her to think positively about his home region. It was important to him. He hoped to take her there one day so it was necessary to paint a better picture.

'Well, it's not all dour. We are on the edge of the Pennines, so there is *some* nice scenery. Growing up, the three of us used to go to Derwent Reservoir and have picnics. It has stunning views from the hills, where there are beautiful woods and rivers; on a blue-sky day there's nowhere better. The reservoir is not far away, only about five miles. Some of the views up there are spectacular.'

Emma pushed the empty cups to one side and after a few moments of silence, she declared, 'Well, it's no good sitting here any longer. It's almost two o'clock and they're clearing everything away. We have been sitting here longer than I thought. I need to go back to Hall and get some work sorted.'

They rose from their seats and the chairs scraped their familiar, reassuring noise. As the couple walked past large, glass doors, Tom looked into the Refectory to see piles of abandoned plates with loads of unwanted food on the tables. Ladies dressed in light blue were pushing large trolleys along the aisles next to the tables in order to collect the students' un-returned waste. The female workers piled the dishes into towers, after having first scraped-off the surplus food into plastic bins on the side of their trolleys. Tom pondered the irony of the situation. It was not a very dignified job for any worker but if the students took back their own plates and did the task themselves, it would mean no money for the women. He could not help think that there had to be another way.

Tom and Emma walked back to her hall of residence along some of the streets they had walked the night before. The conversation was light and the closeness was obvious. Eventually they reached the street leading to their destination.

'Will I see you later? I thought we could go out for a drink or something?' asked Tom anxiously.

Emma remained silent and as she let go of his hand, she spun around like *Alice in Wonderland*. 'Why later?' she asked. Tom looked puzzled. They stood motionless, staring at each other, with Tom uncertain of what to say. After an embarrassing pause, Emma took the initiative. She poked his chest with her index finger and then said mockingly, 'Derr – And they say you might get a first-class degree.' He shook his head, still bemused. 'Do I have to spell it out for you? The Warden might do her rounds late at night but not in the middle of the afternoon.' The dawning realisation of what Emma was saying finally struck home. They entered the building together, walked past the unsupervised front-desk and got into the lift before stopping at Emma's floor. She walked ahead and unlocked the entrance to her room. While Tom closed the door, Emma closed the curtains.

It was the moment he had been hoping for.

X

Tom raised his arm and allowed it to free-fall onto the top of the noisy alarm clock beside his bed to stop its infernal, tinny ringing. It only did half the job of waking him up, the cold did the rest. It was dark on this northern, winter morning and it was freezing in his bedroom. His misty breath was condensing as he raised himself from the mattress and swivelled across the bed, before cursing the shock when his bare toes met the wooden floor. Rubbing his hands together like an enthusiastic miser, he wished he had slept in his socks. Some thought was given to switching on the electric fire and retreating under the warm blankets as quickly as possible but that would only have delayed the inevitable. There was no avoiding it, he had to get up and put on his clothes. It was time to return home for the Christmas break.

At that moment, Tom thought that living in a hall of residence was not such a bad idea after all. It would at least be warm, despite the additional expense. He looked around the barren room, trying to locate his jeans and denim shirt, while he put on last night's socks that were still on the floor. The rest of his clothes were elsewhere. He scampered along the corridor and eventually found them in the bathroom, which was even colder than his bedroom. To make things worse, not only was there no hot water, there was no one else in the flat and there was nothing to eat for breakfast. He decided to forget about a shave and a wash, and settled for a rub with a wet flannel, before making his way to *National Express* at Pond Street Station.

Tom was aware his Dad would be waiting for him when his coach arrived in Consett, even though it was only a short drive to their house. When he got off the bus, he knew to look for a royal blue Humber Sceptre, Dennis Kettlewell's pride and joy. His Dad had bought the brand new car from the Humber dealer in Newcastle in 1964. He paid for it using his redundancy money from the steelworks. It was Tom's Mam, Betty who persuaded her husband to buy the vehicle.

Tom had no say in the matter. Although he was only fifteen years-of-age at the time, he tried to side with his Mam's view. 'Go on, Dad. It'll be great. ' This was as forceful as he was prepared to be when trying to persuade his father to change his mind. Nonetheless, Tom was pleased with the outcome when Dennis eventually bought the car. It was another arrow in the quiver of respect Tom had for his Dad. Five years after purchase, the Humber looked as clean and new as it had on day one, due mainly to the pampered polishing, cleaning and waxing his Dad bestowed on his precious possession most Sundays.

After another tiring journey, Tom collected his hold-all from the belly of the bus. It was already dark on a cold, North-Eastern winter afternoon. As he walked out of the bus station, under the big clock commemorating Edward VII's visit to Consett, he looked around. He did not have to wait long before he heard his Dad's familiar, fingerless, top-lipped whistle. It was followed by a call that Tom had heard many times before. 'Ower 'ere, Tommy lad.' His Dad was the only one who called him Tommy. It made his son feel special.

Tom skipped across the road, where his father was leaning against the car, standing with one foot inside the open door. As his son approached, Dennis watched with intense pride, before embracing Tom in a hold more affectionate than any ordinary man-hug. As they parted, he kissed Tom on the side of his temple and gently pushed him to arm's length. While still holding onto his son he spoke admiringly, 'Oh, it's good to see ya, Tommy. Yer look gud onit an'all... Howee, yer mother's on pins.' Tom walked around the front of the Humber and got into the passenger seat, placing his bag between his feet, while his Dad jumped in and turned the ignition key.

As the car moved forward into the queue of traffic, Tom inquired about his mother's general well-being. He listened intently to his Dad's response. 'Oh, she's not too clever, son. She had a couple of toes removed about a month back. The skin ulcers on her feet were playing her up and that diabetic new... er, what's it called again?'

'Neuropathy?'

'Aye that's it. That neuropathy has been given her some jip. She's complained of tingling and her feet feeling numb. Not that she complains a lot, mind.' Tom was agitated that he had been kept in the dark about the effects of his mother's diabetes. Of course, he knew why he had not been told. His Mam, Betty had clearly given instructions to her husband not to say anything. Her directive was all his Dad needed to hear in order to obey.

Dennis engaged careful driver mode and eventually pulled away from the bus station. Whenever he drove through the town centre, his eyes were always fixed firmly on the road, especially when it was dark. Tom turned to his right, swivelling slightly in the seat and studying his father's features closely. 'I'm sorry to hear that she's not been well. Can't wait to see her, though.' The car effortlessly engaged into fourth gear as Tom's scrutiny confirmed that he and his Dad shared the same blue, compelling eyes and single chin, a characteristic of several members of the Kettlewell family. However, Dennis looked drawn and tired. A restful sleep pattern had no doubt escaped both parents, since his Mam's illness took over. His Dad's black hair was thinning on top and going silver at the sides. If his life had been easier and his grooming had been better, Mr Kettlewell Senior would have looked very distinguished. As the traffic lights at the crossroads turned red and the car stopped, Dennis allowed himself a wave to a couple of friends crossing the road. They returned his gesture, in a friendly, familiar manner. Tom's emotional core warmed to see his father being acknowledged by members of the community. They owed him a lot.

Several times during his childhood, Tom could remember people coming to their terraced house in Taylor Street to ask for Dennis's help from the Union, in his role as Shop Steward at Consett Steelworks. Tom would have to move out of the living room to allow some privacy for the discussions. Once, when he was about eight years-old, he hid behind the door to eavesdrop. A woman was crying because her husband had been injured at the Steelworks. He had suffered terrible injuries caused by a splash-back from a smelting pot. He lost his arm and almost his life. British Steel offered pathetic compensation and the woman did not know how she was going to cope. As the Branch Official, Dennis fought the case and took it to the Union's solicitor. The man subsequently received a small pension and significant compensation. It meant he could afford to pay-off his mortgage and have a small amount to live on, without the worry of debt. No wonder Dennis was considered to be a burr under the saddle of the bosses.

When it was Dennis's turn to need help, he received none. Betty was in her early forties when Tom recollected she was first ill. Initially, she was diagnosed with a virus. Shortly afterwards, she started to lose weight. Tom could remember he was always being asked to get a drink for his mother, who was forever in the toilet. She then started to have daily injections of insulin, her heart began to suffer and she could not walk very far. That was the period when Dennis took time off work. In the beginning, the bosses were relieved when *Dennis the Menace* was not around. After a few months, they started to go after him. Although Dennis dragged it out and fought them on every corner, eventually he was made redundant.

It was during those formative years that Dennis began to educate his son in the ways of the world. Tom learned that bosses were the workers' enemy. 'Always had been, always will be.' The bosses did the bidding of the Establishment and that meant forcing the working-class to *toe-the-line*. The rich were determined to hang-on to their inherited wealth, no matter what. Still, there would be no Russian Revolution in this Country. The Union mandarins would be allowed to manage their own class but they would never be allowed to assume real power, according to his Dad.

It was not difficult to trace Tom's own political views back to their source. The shoots of Tom's moral principles owed more to the faith he had in his father than anything he had personally experienced. Tom was close to his Dad and hardly ever challenged him. As the Humber turned-off the main road and moved along the rows of terraced houses, Tom looked at the familiar skyline of cooling towers that had dominated the vista during his youth.

'Ah-ve made a shepherd's pie, if you're hungry Tommy. It won't take long to warm it up. I left yer Mam with her feet up but I dinnit suppose she's nodded-off, with you comin home.'

They pulled-up to the family home. Dennis gently closed the door and locked the car by carefully turning the key. They entered the house and after wiping their feet on the bristly, brown *Welcome* mat, they both turned right into the living room still wearing their top-coats. On his way,

Tom dropped his hold-all without looking down, knowing it contained only clothes. Betty was sitting in one of the three-piece's arm chairs with her feet on the leather pouffe . The radio was playing gently in the background and *Mantovani* was streaming soothingly from 'Melody Fair' on Radio 2. Betty made no attempt to get up when she saw Tom as she knew that her son would understand her condition. Tom approached and bending over his Mam, he put his arms around her and hugged her close.

As he pulled away from the familiar embrace, he could see she had tears in her eyes so he teased her. 'Ah thought you'd be pleased to see me. I didn't think I'd make yer cry,' he said in an attempt to avoid her pain.

Betty laughed and tried to distance the tears. 'Eee. I am pleased to see yer, pet. We both are, aren't we Dennis. Get yer coat off and let's have a look at yer.'

'He nars that, man,' responded her husband, supportive as always.

Tom could see Betty's right slipper was cut away to make room for the bandage that protected her foot. 'Dad told me in the car that you've been in hospital to have a couple of toes removed, Mam?' When speaking to his mother, Tom consciously avoided talking in strong dialect. He wanted her to be aware that her sacrifices had not been wasted.

'Just the little one and the one next to it, hinny. They had started to turn black with poor circulation so before the disease spread they decided to remove them. They're just a little bit sore now ... Dennis, put the kettle on and give our Tom something to eat. This lad must be parched and I bet you would like one an'all. I know *I* would.' Betty would always try and deflect attention away from herself. Her self-effacing nature was just one of the reasons why Tom loved her so much.

As soon as his Dad left the room to make a cup of tea and retrieve the shepherd's pie, Tom lowered his voice and nodding in the direction of the kitchen asked, 'How's *he* been, Mam?'

'You know what he's like, son. He just gets on with things. I don't think I've ever heard him complain his whole life. If he did it would be the end of him. You can see though, he's beginning to look tired. Mind you, it's no wonder after all the things he does.'

'Don't suppose he's going to change now.'

'No, I don't suppose he will ...and I wouldn't want him to, neither.'

After finishing his shepherd's pie and settling into his room, Tom helped his Dad with the washing-up. Tom washed, while Dennis dried to ensure everything was put away correctly. This meant returning the cutlery to their drawer in the white, Wolverine kitchen unit. The round, white anonymous dining plates were housed in the cupboard below. The cups were placed on the home-made mug tree in the corner, under the window, a legacy of Tom's O-level woodwork class with Mr Hinton.

Tom and his Dad spoke in familiar language and their movement around each other had been choreographed over many years in the kitchen together. They were enjoying being in each other's company for the first time in a while. Their topics of conversation covered football and the recent local bereavements of some names Tom might have recognised. He was brought up-to-date with the progress of some of his friends. Cyril Poppy's lad, Harry had joined the Police Cadets and 'Gone over to the other side.' Several of Tom's mates had left the area in the immediate post-school years. A couple had followed their fathers into the steel industry. As they set about their routine, Dennis asked his son, 'What do you fancy doing tonight, Tommy?'

'I'm a bit tired after the journey, Dad. Thought I'd just stay in and watch a bit of telly with you and Mam. Dennis knew Betty would like that. So did Tom.

After *Songs of Praise*, while Betty and Dennis were watching *Paul Temple* on television, Tom asked to use the phone in the hallway. He did not reveal the nature of his call to his parents but simply wanted the comfort of hearing Emma's voice. As he left the lounge, Betty shot her husband a knowing look. It was unusual for Tom to make a telephone call so soon after coming home. While appearing to look at the brown, *Bush* tv set, Betty was actually trying to tune into the pitch of Tom's voice on the phone.

Tom held the receiver tightly and after getting through, he was reassured by the telephone call. Emma told him that her Gran had arrived from America and they were excited about seeing each other again. The whole family was looking forward to Christmas. Aware of the circumstances, Tom ensured their conversation was brief. He said a quiet goodbye, before gently replacing the receiver and galloping upstairs to use the toilet, taking two steps at a time. On returning to the living room, he entered whistling lightly.

'Somebody's in a good mood,' said Betty, impishly.

'Well, it is Christmas,' volunteered Dennis, missing the point completely.

'What's her name, son?'

'Who?' repeated Dennis, compounding his naivety.

'Well, there's something different about our Tom, this time, father. Looks to me like it might even be serious.' Then looking directly at her son, she added, 'Is it?'

'Not really sure. Still early days.' Tom did not return the gaze.

'Thought so,' declared Betty, wriggling into her chair with a sense of triumph.

'Will someone tell me what's going on?' asked Dennis, in desperation.

'Don't yer just love him? Look at him. Look. He's like a fish out of water.' She looked at her husband who was moving his head back and forward between them, open-mouthed. 'Our Tom's got a girlfriend.'

'Oh, right... has he? How do you know that? He's said nowt to me.' Betty laughed mockingly and shook her head, while Tom grabbed him around the shoulders and patted his bald spot.

Together as a family, they watched the Sunday Musical on BBC; it was *White Christmas*, surprising nobody. Around ten o'clock, Betty and Dennis went to bed, leaving Tom free reign to view *Rowan and Martin's Laugh-In* and *Monty Python's Flying Circus*. Quietly, he eventually retired to his room and from the landing he could hear his father snoring. A floorboard creaked, and then he heard, 'Goodnight, son,' from his mother.

'Goodnight, Mam. You alright?' After being reassured that all was fine, he closed his bedroom door and looked forward to his dreams.

XI

There were four days to go before Christmas Day so it was too early to buy the yuletide groceries. After one of his Dad's bacon-butty specials, the three members of the Kettlewell family were sitting around the coal fire together and the *Jimmy Young Programme* was on the radio. 'Fancy a look out, this afternoon, Tommy lad?' asked his Dad. 'Thought we could have a pint in the Station Club and then have a drive up to the Reservoir.'

'Yeah, ok. That'd be good.' Tom knew that a visit to the Workingmen's Club was an opportunity for his Dad to show-off his clever son to his friends in the community. It had become something of a ritual on his return visits. Tommy did not mind. He knew Betty would not want to come and the fuss he would have to endure was a small price to pay for everything his Dad had done for him over the years. Some reflected glory was the least he deserved.

After arriving at Dennis's favourite watering-hole just after opening time, the pair soon had a pint of *Federation Beer* in their hands and were standing at the bar with several other early drinkers. Some of the men recognised Tom and shook his hand, while inquiring after his progress at University. A small group gathered and quickly Tom became the centre of their attention. He did not attempt to respond to the friendly leg-pulling made at his expense and knew it was simply one of the things he had to tolerate whenever he returned home. He thought that perhaps it would have been different if he had been perceived as having a real man's job. Most of the ribbing was made by enthusiastic, middle-aged, male drinkers who were regular revellers at the Club. However, Tom and his Dad quickly became an anonymous presence as more people started to arrive and the place began to fill. Dennis was aware of the comments by his so-called friends and not wanting to prolong his son's discomfort, he placed

61

his empty glass on the table and suggested they leave. Tom did not mind abandoning his unfinished drink and nodded in agreement. Following a loud farewell to the others, they walked past the long counter to the exit nearest the car park and set off for Derwent Reservoir.

It was about two o'clock in the afternoon and there was not a lot of daylight left. Within twenty minutes they were at the Reservoir and Dennis parked in a muddy lay-by, created by a farmer's gate-entrance to a field. During the ride, Tom updated his father about Emma and it was clear that his son had found a spark in his life. Dennis was pleased, although he knew it was always going to happen one day. Tom and Dennis got out of the car and walked back the hundred yards to the road sign which showed the boundary between the counties of Durham and Northumberland. Tom stood abreast of the border with one foot in each county, as he had done on many occasions as a boy.

'Bring back memories, Tommy, lad?' asked Dennis.

'Aye. All good ones, thanks to you and Mam. Come on. Let's walk up to the bridge.' With that, Tom put his arm around his Dad's shoulder in a gesture of warmth. They walked in unison towards the quaint, stone archway over the upper Derwent. From there, they would be able to see back to their car, with the Reservoir's Dam staring boldly back at them. The light was beginning to fade through the dark-grey skies although a few rays of red sunshine were trying to penetrate the clouds. It was a cold, northern December day and snow was in the air, just like old times. The wind was still and the noise of crows filtered the sky. The mood was pure and their conversation was intimate.

'So this is yer graduation year son. What are yer gonna dee with yer degree?' asked Dennis, with genuine interest. This was no harmless question; he wanted to hear a decisive response.

Their walk was almost incidental to the nature of their discussion. 'It depends on how good the degree is, I suppose. My tutor reckons I'm on for a first but we'll have to wait and see.' Talking about himself to his Dad was the only time Tom was prepared to share his inner thoughts. With his father, there was no tempting of fate, only loving honesty.

'And if you get a first?' Dennis asked, with growing pride in his voice, as they continued slowly along the wet lane.

Tom then bent down to up-root a long piece of reed, before swishing it as if whipping a horse. It was a distraction to allow more time for thought. 'I'll have two choices. Either stay on at *Uni* and do a doctorate or go straight into industry.'

Dennis stopped to admire the view and looking around, continued his questioning, 'What sort of industry?' Whatever the response, he knew it would be a 'damn-sight' better than Consett Steelworks.

Tom threw the switch into the hedge and stopped, while Dennis continued a few paces ahead. 'Computers, I think. That's the future. Pretty soon the potential of computers is going to explode onto the industrial scene and they're going to be looking for programming talent. I know that ICC will snap-up anyone who gets a first in Maths. I've been doing options in Computer Programming and I'm quite good at it. My tutor, Doc Herbert has been very encouraging. He thinks anyone going into computers will earn a fortune, in the next ten years.'

Turning back to look at Tom directly, Dennis offered some parental advice. 'Money's not everything, mind son – *Doctor* Thomas Kettlewell has a nice ring to it. Yer mother'll be delighted if yer become a doctor.' He neglected to mention that he would not mind either.

They were now stationary, standing face-to-face in the fading winter daylight. 'We'll have to wait and see. Money gives you power and power gives you control. I could do more damage politically if I had money. It struck me a few weeks back, when I was on the Anti-Apartheid demonstration.'

'What was that?' asked Dennis, genuinely not knowing what his son was referring to.

'You remember when you said the bosses would just let the Union leaders have some power over their members, while they would retain the real power for themselves.' Dennis nodded. 'That's what struck me about the protest march. People at the front of the march were the ones with the gravitas. The rest were just one of the many.'

'There's nothing wrong with being one of the many.' said Dennis, who was really talking about himself.

Tom turned half-away and rolled some stones under his foot, like an agitated stallion. 'I know that, Dad. As long as you're happy with it,' declared Tom indicating his inner frustration at the projection into his future.

'And you're not?' asked Dennis, continuing onward.

'No. If I'm going to make a difference …and I mean a real difference…

I'm going to have to make an impact somewhere. I don't have the acumen to be a crafty political animal. With me, what you see is what you get. That's how you made me and I'm proud of it. Honesty is a virtue but in politics it is second to cunning and other conniving qualities.'

They had reached the bridge and could hear the trickling water more clearly as the roadway opened out. 'So you want to go into politics one day?'

Tom took the first step along the upward curve of the crossing. 'I'm not sure. I just want to make a difference in the world.' This was the nub of Tom's difficulty. He was not sure what he wanted from his future. He sensed he had the potential to be an important figure one day but was uncertain of the direction life would take him. However, Tom did not feel threatened by being able to share this vulnerability with his father, only loved.

His Dad was now at his side and they were standing half-way across the bridge, at the arch's highest point, absorbing nature at work. 'Good luck anyhow, Tommy lad. I'm proud of yer. An honest politician would be a rare thing.' With that, Dennis took a two shilling piece from his pocket and dropped it over the side of the bridge wall, into the cold waters below. It sploshed into a white ripple and the pure water could not hide its presence.

Tom peered over the top and looked into the raw, filtering freshness of the river, about ten feet below. 'What did you do that for, Dad?'

'Two-bob for a wish, son. I hope yer dreams come true.'

Tom turned and smiled. 'I've a good mind to take my shoes off and go and fish that out.' Father and son laughed together in a rare moment of adult companionship.

Dennis faked a boxer's punching routine to his son's chest. 'Come on Tommy, the light is fading. Let's get back to the car. It's getting cold and I don't like leaving yer Mam too long.'

They walked back quickly to the Humber as dusk was beginning to settle in the sky. Suddenly, a rush of wind caught their attention and they both looked across the fields at what was happening above the adjacent woodland. There was a mini murmuration of starlings, darting and waving in the sky like a brown, psychedelic wave. The birds were looking for a place to roost for the night and they made a spectacular sight. They changed shape as if they were part of the same being, looking for somewhere to rest, assessing the scene. Suddenly, a hawk came from nowhere and tried to pick off one of the isolates. As if by intuition, several of the starlings from the main group headed straight for the hawk and in the confusion the bird of prey flew away.

'Look at that, Tommy. Did you see that? See how those starlings had the courage to stop that hawk in its tracks. Magic – well done lads! See … it occurs in nature as well. That's what happens when something ordinary takes its courage from those around it and does extraordinary things.' Just as Tom had felt comfortable confiding his hopes and dreams with his father, Dennis continued with his own intimate, personal thoughts as a natural progression. He stared into the brown countryside stretching before him, admiring its rawness.

He turned to his son. 'I learned a lot of things up here as a young boy, Tommy lad. Up here I'm the same as everyone else. Nobody's slave. That's my favourite view of all. Ower there. Yer kna why?' Without waiting for a response from his son, he continued. 'Coz yer cannit see any roads or any modern buildings, yer cannit hear traffic or smell the furnaces. It's the same view as always has been. It's timeless. Up here, none of yer money or power means anything. You are who you are and that's all that matters. I used to watch the birds and the foxes and other wildlife around these woods as a boy and they didn't even know I was there. I'd pick berries and take them home for yer Grandma to make a dish with.

When I was just nineteen years old I got called-up more or less straight away, in 1940. After a few months training, I joined the 7th Armoured Division as a gunner and was involved in just about every fight in North Africa. They called us Desert Rats coz we were always buried in sand. The guns were blazing all the time. It's wonder I haven't gone deaf as I've been gettin' older. After battling up through Italy, they brought us back so we could fight in Normandy. I saw some terrible things in those times, Tommy lad. To keep myself sane, I used to think of my times up here, the peace and quiet. I used to tell myself ah waz up here when the guns finally stopped.

Being back, now – with you – is like medicine for my soul. It's one of the few places where those images of dead bodies blown to bits and the smell of death and shit everywhere cannit come back.'

For a moment, Dennis had forgotten he was talking to his son. Their intimacy while walking together, had allowed his thoughts free rein and it was as if he was talking to himself. Inner secrets he had buried only ever crept out into the open occasionally when Tommy was growing up. This was another of those times. His son listened in stunned silence to his father's recollections. Tom knew his Dad had experienced a hard life but appreciated that he would never understand just how tough it had been for Dennis. His youth had been sacrificed on a World War, allowing his son the luxury of new opportunities.

Tommy looked at his Dad with enormous admiration and pride. Dennis was a good man.

XII

Early in the New Year, Tom was pleased to return to University and see Emma again. It meant he would not be at home for his Dad's birthday but he wanted to re-engage with his own life. The memory of Christmas quickly faded as he immediately resumed his studies with enthusiasm. It did not take long to re-establish a routine in Sheffield and the weeks in January and February quickly passed. The Spring Term also became a time when Emma and Tom grew very close, as their relationship blossomed. Emma always knew that Tom was ambitious and she encouraged his desire towards a first-class honours degree. Their daytime routine involved attending separate lectures and seminars, before sharing long sessions in the Library. Emma was also making good progress in her course and hoped that she might have a chance of a *Two-one*. Her realism persuaded her that a first-class degree in American Studies was probably beyond her reach, while an Upper Second Class was more achievable.

The couple distanced themselves from student politics, opting to concentrate on their work, although they continued to assist in activities associated with the *Stop the Seventy Tour*. Whenever they did attend meetings in the Students Union, Felicity gave the couple a cool reception. She was still smarting from Tom's rejection and seeing them together rankled her.

Tom enjoyed being in Emma's company and she was not intimidated by his strong personality. Despite her delicate features, she was a determined individual with the potential to make a powerful advocate for justice, one day. She never disclosed her inner feelings and that was just one of the many fascinations that intrigued Tom. Time quickly raced through the remainder of their final year at University and after an agonisingly long Easter break, the exam season was soon calling.

The World's own agenda had also advanced. On May 22nd 1970, the

Cricket Council announced that the impending Cricket Tour by South Africa to England had been cancelled. The many demonstrations against the earlier Rugby Tour had triggered a national reaction against Apartheid and there was no way the more vulnerable cricket matches could be protected from further disruption. The decision was met with joy by all Anti-Apartheid supporters. When the news reached the students in the Bar at Sheffield University, there was genuine excitement as they finally saw a successful outcome to all their efforts. It gave everyone in their ultimate year a fillip, knowing that the following dour weeks of frenetic study for the final exams could be tempered by this success.

Tom visited the Bar on the evening of the announcement, after a session in the Library. He was tired and Emma was doing something else that night so he was alone. He heard the news from a student he knew, while ordering a pint. Then he noticed Felicity break conversation with a group nearby. She had seen him enter the Bar and was making her way over to where he was standing.

'Great news about the Cricket Tour,' she said as she approached him. Felicity was holding a glass of cider in her right hand, with a recently-lit cigarette in the fingers of her left. She pushed back the fringe from her eyes. Tom had rarely seen her smoking before, although he was not surprised, it was all part of her image. He did not comment on it, but hid his eyes behind a raised full glass, as he took a drink. After several weeks of limited contact with Felicity, Tom felt a greater sense of resolve and was no longer intimidated by her. He responded curtly, 'Yes, really good. Though I don't think we can take *all* the credit.'

Felicity laughed, politely. 'No I don't suppose we can. Still, we didn't sit back and do nothing either. We may have been one brick in the wall of resistance but at least we helped build the wall.' She put her hand on his shoulder, with some degree of allure. 'Thanks for everything you did for our own demo, Tom. It didn't go unnoticed or unappreciated. Have you ever thought about going after my position of President next year? You know it's just a one-year post for post-graduates, so I'll be standing down at the end of August. You should think about putting your name forward. Who knows, you might enjoy it.'

'I think Kelvin would be a stronger candidate than me,' responded Tom, although this was a smokescreen comment. He was not sure what he was going to do regarding the Presidency but Felicity was the last person to whom he was going to disclose any personal plans.

Felicity proceeded to reveal some designs of her own, possibly working as a P.A. in her father's law firm. She hoped, or supposed, that he would eventually wangle her a job working as a junior in a minor MP's constituency office. Her preferred option was to take another year out and visit the Antipodes.

As she finished speaking, she leaned across Tom to extinguish her cigarette in an ash-tray on an adjacent table. She brushed past him and he could smell her hair. He knew why he had been attracted to her. She had a strong sense of presence and her sexy good looks combined with her personality comprised a heady cocktail. In another time and on another occasion he could easily have found himself in her bed, once again. Unfortunately, she also had a venomous side to her character and he knew he did not have the emotional maturity to handle her when she became threatening. She was capable of doing damage because she had less of a social conscience than Tom. He could not fathom her motives or understand her lifestyle. Perhaps it was better to simply walk away.

'Well good luck with the preparation for your finals, Tom. I don't envy you. I remember, it was just twelve months ago that I was doing the same thing. Seems like yesterday.' Tom took another drink from his glass rather than send any body signals of his own. Felicity interpreted this as her cue, 'Well …I'd better get back to my friends or they will be accusing me of all sorts of things. I know you'll do well. You're a born winner, like me. Cheers, Tom.' She gave him a kiss on the cheek and then turned away, returning to her friends. Tom looked at her curves, until she was lost among the groups of other drinkers.

XIII

Tom had been revising since April, reflecting the way he had worked over the previous two-and-a-half years. He was satisfied he was on course. The following morning saw his last seminar with Doc Herbert. They were having a post-session discussion about his future. Tom's seminar partner, Eric had already left the room. Doc was sitting on the front of his desk, with one leg bent towards his chest, while he cradled it with both hands. The other foot was resting on the back of a nearby chair and Tom was sitting on a hard plastic seat, listening attentively.

'There's no doubt about it, Tom. I want you to stay on for another couple of years and complete your doctorate. I feel that we could make real progress in the Department and this university could be at the fore with you and Dr Brian Collins developing computer programming over the next ten years and even up to the next millennium. You could be directly involved in devising schemes that would work towards revolutionising the use of computers in the workplace and beyond. I've also heard from the *Prof* that he has been approached by several top firms who want to headhunt the best students as soon as the final degree results are announced.'

This was a deflection from the truth. It was Dr Stanley Herbert who always advised a former colleague about 'ones-to-watch' in the Department. He had already recommended Tom but it was easier to put the responsibility onto the Professor than to be seen as an *agent provocateur*. Given a free choice, Doc wanted Tom to pursue his postgraduate studies, before considering other alternatives. 'There's no doubt in our minds that you will be at the top of that list. It could mean huge financial gains for you. Whatever you decide, all the best Tom. It's been a pleasure working with you. I hope we get the chance to do it again, in the future. Good luck with your exams, in June.' Doc held out his arm and shook Tom's hand with genuine affection.

Emma was waiting for Tom outside the Maths Faculty building. When he came out, she dived for his left arm and held him close, before they strolled towards the Library. The day was the first indication of some summer sun and it felt good to be wearing lighter clothes, once again. They walked together in the brightness but Tom seemed pre-occupied with his thoughts, saying very little and failing to appreciate the setting. Emma was more light-footed and even skipped at one point, causing him to almost laugh. The final year of the American Studies degree was not as onerous as it was in some subjects. It was the second year of the course that was the most difficult, with lots of important assignments and essays counting towards the final degree. Anyone who was due to fail was usually asked to repeat the middle year. That way, everyone passed at some level.

They entered the glass double doors of the Library together, then kissed and diverged into their separate pathways of study. The American Studies section was on the ground floor, while the Mathematics area was on a level below. 'See you about seven, for something to eat?' suggested Tom.

It was at this moment that Emma's shoulders tensed. She had been toying with her thoughts for a few weeks, deciding whether to tell Tom about her important news or opt to wait until after his exams had finished. She did not want to disrupt his studying with a distraction that could throw his concentration off-track. During the Christmas break, Emma's grandmother had invited her to visit Portland in the summer. She knew that she was going to accept the invitation to go to America for a few months. Still, she also knew that Tom would not like it and she did not know how to tell him.

They had already spoken about spending some time together during the summer, while Tom considered his options. She had not anticipated her Gran's invitation, which would give her an opportunity to work in a lawyer's office in Portland and gain valuable experience in Civil Liberties Law. As she had always wanted to spread her wings in the States when she finished University, this would be too good an opportunity to waste. It would also mean spending time away from Tom. Even worse, she would have to leave on the day of his final exam results. She would not be able to celebrate with him as her flight from London was later that evening. Emma's Gran had booked her on one of the new Boeing 747 Jumbo Jet flights from Heathrow to New York. From New York, she would catch a three hour flight to Portland, Maine where her Grandmother would be waiting to drive her across Casco Bay Bridge to her home in South Portland. It should have been an exciting time but it was tainted with the inevitable sadness of leaving Tom and the anxiety of telling him her news.

For the next two weeks on Campus, Tom and Emma met only at meal times. Tom was in study isolation, totally focussed on his finals. When the day of his first exam arrived, he was relieved. He was satisfied with his preparation and now it was all about performance. During the two weeks of the exams, which occurred in the first fortnight of June, he preferred not to see Emma at all. He knew that she would inevitably ask him questions and he did not want to tempt fate by talking about his progress. When the hurricane exam cycle had passed over, he knew he had balanced perfectly the levels of anxiety and confidence. Although he did not want to tell anyone, he felt he had murdered the exam questions.

The final degree results would not be announced until the beginning of July and Mathematics was among the first subjects to be published. The time beforehand was always an interval of anxious relaxation for undergraduates. They had completed their studies and there was nothing more they could do to affect the outcome. It was also an opportunity for Tom and Emma to enjoy more of each other's company. Emma wanted to choose her moment to break her news. One afternoon, they decided to spend some time in Weston Park, opposite the University. The old park was a haven in an otherwise busy city. The pillared entrance, the lake and surrounding greenery created a timeless oasis, where tranquillity reigned. It was a glorious summer's day and the Coldstream Guards were playing a variety of popular tunes on the bandstand. The pair sat far enough away to enjoy the music as a background, without interruption to their own private world. Emma had brought a blanket and they lay on the grass together.

Tom was lying on his back, shielding his eyes from the sun with his left arm raised. Emma decided the moment had arrived. She was kneeling above him and the geometry of the situation seemed to help her decision to be assertive. 'There's something I need to tell you,' she began, her mouth suddenly turning dry.

'Oh, yes? Sounds serious,' though not serious enough for him to change position. He was still relaxed, enjoying their time with each other.

72

'Well you know we have spoken about what we were going to do this summer.' Emma felt the tension rising, as she came to the crux of the matter.

'*Were*, going to do?' At this moment, Tom sat up and looked squarely into her eyes.

'It's just that last Christmas, Gran invited me to visit her in America during the summer. She can arrange it for me to spend the holidays working in a law practice in Portland. One of her friends is a partner in a firm there. I could live with her and gain valuable experience working in a legal office. You know, it is something I've always wanted to do… working on Civil Rights legislation. It's a great opportunity for me.'

'Sounds like it's all arranged.' Tom's face dropped and he retreated to his supine position. It was obvious he was irritated by the news, exactly what Emma was expecting.

'Oh, don't be upset. Be pleased for me. I don't want us to be apart either but there's no alternative if I'm going to get some experience in this field.' She did not feel guilty about making the announcement, she had never kept her ambitions secret. Tom instantly understood that it sounded like a golden opportunity but he did not care. As far as he was concerned, hurt and disappointment cast the same shadow and he was sitting under their tree.

When Emma revealed that her Gran had bought the tickets for a flight on the evening of July 1st, Tom's feelings moved on to anger. 'That's the day my results come out. Great – thanks for the support.' He was in danger of saying something he might regret.

'Well, we won't be together when *my* results come out either. I'm going to have to phone the University from Portland to find out how I got on. It's unfortunate but I can't do anything about the timing of things. Gran booked the flight and has paid for it. She didn't know the significance of the date. I'll be with you on the morning of the results. I don't have to head for the airport until the afternoon. It's an evening flight.'

'So, you can squeeze me in. Thanks.' He had entered the world of an inconsolable, selfish pout. He could only think of how this was affecting him. Tom did not see this was a time for logic, his baser instincts were taking control.

With that, he turned over and closed his eyes, feigning sleep. Emma moved across the blanket to kiss him but Tom was warned of her approach by her shadow as she blocked the sun. He jumped to his feet and the atmosphere between them changed. Tom had regressed to a childish sulk, his principal boyhood strategy whenever he was prevented from getting his own way. Emma had some regrets about her decision to go to America but knew it was going to happen, whether Tom liked it or not.

Tom collected the blanket in one sweep as he suddenly jumped to his feet, almost causing Emma to topple. Not bothering to fold it properly he threw the tartan cloth over his shoulder, picked up his pullover and stormed towards the park gates. They walked back the short distance to the University in silence with Emma trying to keep pace. She had never seen him like this before, although she always had a feeling he was capable of spoilt behaviour. When they arrived at the foyer, Emma was uncertain what the next step should be. She looked directly at him and already knowing the answer, asked 'Will I see you later?'

'I'm not sure. I promised I would help Geoff celebrate the end of his exams tonight. The Economics boys have finished later than everybody else.' Although this was factually correct, Tom had not made any previous plans to accompany his flatmate, Geoffrey Miller on his big night-out.

Emma took the initiative and stepping towards him, she kissed him goodbye. Tom's response was less passionate than usual. While Emma stood alone in a state of bewilderment, Tom did a U-turn and left the building through the main doors. There was no further contact between them, that evening.

The following morning, Emma left her Hall and walked despondently to the Campus. She went to the Library and explored some of Tom's familiar haunts, looking for him. It was to no avail. After almost two hours, she was feeling even more dejected so decided to go for an early lunch in the Refectory. It was a familiar meal: orange juice, sandwich and a yoghurt. She was not hungry and did not even open two of the items, preferring only the drink. As she waited, looking at every new face entering the hall via the till, she moved her food containers back and fore on the table, like pieces on a draughts board. She slumped forward, supporting her head under her chin, her elbows on the table. If she sat there long enough, surely she would spot Tom. After finally finishing her yoghurt, Emma saw Geoffrey Miller enter the Hall. She sprung from her chair and approached him. 'Hi Geoffrey. Have you seen Tom?' She tried to mask the level of anxiety in her voice.

'No, I haven't seen him since last night. He cut away from the pub and headed back to the flat before last orders. When I got up a couple of hours ago I saw Trevor in the kitchen and he told me that Tom was up early to catch a bus home. Everything alright?'

'Yes, fine. He did tell me that he might be going home,' she lied. Emma feared the worst.

Someone in the Refectory caught Geoff's eye and he left Emma without looking back or attempting a farewell. She was pleased that he did not try to engage her in further conversation. She was upset and close to breaking into tears. Emma had never considered Tom to be cruel. She knew he was a determined young man, probably more used to getting his way than was healthy for him but this was a callous act. He may have been upset about her decision to abandon their plans for the summer but logically he should have been able to see it was the right choice to go to the States. Emma suddenly felt that she did not know him at all.

That evening, she gave some thought to visiting Consett, or ringing Tom to confront him about their future together. After careful consideration, she decided not to go there. It would have been a sign of weakness if she had allowed *his* actions to dictate her own. In addition, Emma was not sure how he would react. It could result in the end of their relationship permanently. She decided to let him lick his wounds and when he returned to Sheffield for his degree results, she would attempt to repair their relationship. In her opinion, it was not an insurmountable problem.

Tom made his own way from Consett bus station and explained his return home by telling his parents that he wanted to take stock before his results were announced. They were pleased to see him and did not detect a problem, attributing any moodiness to anxiety about the future. Tom told Dennis and Betty that he would return to Sheffield the day before his results were announced. In the meantime, he waited to see whether Emma would telephone him at home. It was up to her, as far as he was concerned.

Tom spent his days walking in the countryside around Consett, thinking about his options. He really liked the idea of being called Doctor

Kettlewell one day but he also hankered after a better life and having real money in his pocket for the first time. His choice was simple, industry and money or academia and prestige. For the remainder of his last visit home as an undergraduate, Tom licked his imaginary, emotional wounds. He missed Emma and longed for their intimate moments together but she had not phoned. This gave him the armoured resilience he needed to bury those pleasant memories.

On June 30th, after saying goodbye to his Mam and Dad, Tom caught the afternoon bus back to Sheffield from Consett bus station. He knew that in the next few days he would make a critical decision about his future. He was not to know that his decision would involve something totally unexpected.

XIV

Tom had deliberately booked the last bus back to Sheffield, knowing he would have a greater chance of avoiding Emma. He did not want to see her again until she returned from America. Perhaps, they could start again, one day. She had made her decision without discussing anything with him and had even kept the whole situation a secret. This was hardly the basis for a lifelong relationship. They needed to start again after the summer. He was right, she was wrong.

Tom got back to his flat to find Geoffrey sitting in the kitchen and wondered for a moment if his flatmate ever left the place. He seemed a permanent fixture with a book in his hand, his feet on a chair and a dishevelled appearance, reminiscent of Guy Fawkes on a bonfire. There was no greeting from Geoff, who spoke without averting his eyes from the page. 'That bird you've been knocking around with, has been looking for you. She's been here a few times to ask whether you're back yet. She came around a couple of hours ago. You're back for your results, right?' Tom nodded, while Geoff continued to focus on the book.

As Tom turned towards the kitchen door to head for his room, he smiled to himself. Despite their limited contact he would miss these intriguing interactions with the Economics student. They were unique and if witnessed by a third person could almost be described as comical. Geoffrey was sure to be one memory anchored into Tom's reminisces about his undergraduate days. He had conducted about a dozen conversations with Geoff during the course of the year. They all seemed to be meaningless necessities, discussing daily banalities, with limited face-to-face contact. Nevertheless, Tom could remember virtually all of them and despite everything, he liked his friend and would miss him.

Tom was not sure where he would be living after graduation. If he decided to continue studying for his doctorate, he could command a room in a hall of residence as a postgraduate. Most *post-grads* did not avail themselves of that facility because they considered themselves above other students and did not want to share the same pastoral regime. If he studied for his *Ph.D.*, he could use the extra grant money for a better place than the dump he had been living in during his final degree year. Of course, he could still decide to work for a computer firm and move away from Sheffield completely. It would all be dictated by tomorrow's events.

Tom did not leave his room that evening, deciding to stay in the flat and read *'Far From the Madding Crowd'* which he had started, while travelling back on the bus from Sheffield. He had not seen the film in the cinema during the late sixties but had been impressed by the iconic posters adorning the hoarding boards. Someone had told him that he looked a little like the actor *Terence Stamp* so he thought he would satisfy his curiosity by reading the book. Tom had previously enjoyed the *'Mayor of Casterbridge'* and wondered whether he was a secret romantic. He preferred to think he was like Thomas Hardy, a critic of the society in which he lived. Time and subject matter may have separated Kettlewell and Hardy but they shared the same disparaging view about life around them.

Tom woke at six o'clock the following morning, knowing he would not be able to go back to sleep. This was going to be a big day. He would get his results and hopefully avoid Emma. There should be something to celebrate, even if it was only an Upper Second. Success would give him the perfect excuse to go out and get legless. Emma had hurt him.

Tom moved silently into the kitchen to make himself an early morning cup of coffee. This was one occasion when he was glad he preferred a strong brand because he never felt more in need of a heavy-duty drink. While the kettle boiled, he propped himself against the sink and surveyed the room. It was clear that Geoff was the last one to leave the kitchen: the chairs were in exactly the same position as when Tom last saw him. From the clutter, it also looked like one of the other flatmates had made himself a late snack and had not bothered to wash-up. It would not have been Geoffrey. Despite appearances, he was more considerate. The mess looked like the remnants of beans-on-toast and Tom had no intention of clearing away the abandoned dirty plate, cutlery and pan. He took his coffee back to his room, where he lay on the bed, in silent contemplation.

After watching the clock drag its way around to seven-thirty, it was time. The results were due to be posted on the Faculty Department's notice board at nine o'clock. Tom was aware this was an attempt to divert student attention away from the actual plan. In reality, one of the lecturers would pin the proclamation of results onto the board early, probably at about eight-thirty. The tutor could then make a getaway before being overcome by the inevitable scrummage of anxious third-year students clamouring to see their names on the sheet.

When Tom entered the old oak doors of the red brick Faculty building, there were about half a dozen students already there. Some were fist pumping, others looked slightly stunned as they became aware of the outcome of three years of effort. The results had been posted. Tom approached with a dry lump in his throat. Despite his outer confidence, he was suddenly aware of his vulnerability. Eric, from his seminar group approached, wearing a huge grin of relief.

'Congratulations, Tom. There are only two firsts and you got one of them. Well done!' Eric suddenly realised that he should not have disclosed Tom's results but he was lost in the glory of his own *two-one* for a moment.

Tom felt a mixture of joy and disappointment at not being able to discover the outcome for himself so did not inquire after Eric's grade. At that moment, one of the other students called across to a group who were approaching the building, 'They're up!' This was the signal for the panic that everyone had expected when they got out of bed that morning. Suddenly, the approaching group of young men and women abandoned any sense of decorum and all broke into a run. Tom saw the herd stampeding towards him through the glass doors and quickly darted over to the board, to confirm what he hoped was true. Then he saw the prize, in black and white. The sheet was headed 'Sheffield University Mathematics Degrees Awarded 1970 *Magnum Cum Laude*'. There were two names listed under the column with the heading, First *Class Honours*: Alison Clara Howard and Thomas Dennis Victor Kettlewell. Tom found it difficult to focus through the mist in his eyes but he had done it: the key was in the lock. He stood to the side of the notice board to enable the winners of the race to look for their names on the list. As he did so, he saw a beaming Doc approach with his arm extended in a warm welcome of congratulations.

'I couldn't be more pleased for you and your family, my boy. I hope that means you will be returning for your doctorate?' Although Tom had obviously been anxious, Doc had known for some time that the result was never in doubt.

'Thanks, Doc…er … I'm not sure what it means at the moment. I'm still in shock, I think.' Tom put one hand on top of his head, like an animated silver-back.

'Absolutely – I understand… Look, I expect you'll want to tell your parents the good news and you're going to need some time just to let things sink in. I'll be in my office upstairs until about two o'clock. Pop in when you're ready and we'll have a chat. I'm just going to hang around here for an hour or so, giving my congratulations and offering support to students as they come in. I don't suppose you've seen Alison Howard anywhere, have you?' Tom shook his head. 'She must be on her way. I'd like to congratulate her as well. No doubt I'll hear that piercing shriek of excitement of hers, when she sees her name in the *Firsts'* column. Anyway, see you later?'

Tom nodded, 'Sure thing, thanks Doc… and thanks for everything you've done for me over the last three years. I couldn't have done it without your support.'

Suddenly, Tom felt alone and confused. Although it was a moment of intense exhilaration there was also a feeling of pointlessness because he could not share the joy of the occasion with someone he loved. When he attempted to leave the building, he was stopped three times to engage in brief, frenetic conversations with clusters of his peers but the whole episode was surreal. After offering congratulations to his contemporaries, Tom was finally able to exit the Maths Block. All around, there was a lot of backslapping and whooping taking place. A group of four girls were in close proximity, three of them trying to console a weeping friend. Tom headed for the Students' Union area, where the row of public telephones was housed. No doubt, it would be everyone's first port of call as students wanted to relay their news to anxious parents. However, he needed to get across to the phones quickly, while there were still some unoccupied booths. He walked out of the building and was about to descend the wide steps, when he was stopped in his tracks. Emma was sitting on the wall opposite the entrance, waiting for him. Tom felt a deep sensation stir within his being.

He knew he could not ignore her and just seeing her tugged at his emotions. He wanted to talk to her. He had wanted to talk to her every day for the last two weeks but his stupid pride got in the way. Emma pushed herself off the wall and walked over to him. 'Congratulations,' she said warmly, accompanying her smile with a hug and a kiss, almost on Tom's lips.

His emotions were now in overdrive and he was totally confused. Tom accepted Emma's embrace and held on to her a little longer than usual, hoping she would pick up on his extra closeness. 'Thanks, how did you know?'

'I saw Phyllis Herbert over by the staff car park. She had just dropped-off Doc. *She* told me,' said Emma, trying to indicate how much she had missed him and hoping it was not too late.

'I was just going to rush across to the phones and tell Mam and Dad. They are bound to be wondering. Come with me, if you like.' As he turned, Emma stopped him and put her hands on his arms, forcing him towards her. 'I've missed you,' she said, almost breaking down.

Tom could hold-on no longer and he kissed her the way he should have kissed her two weeks earlier. In that instant, he could only think of how stupid and immature he had been. He could see the tears in Emma's eyes and he hated himself for doubting her commitment. She was right about going to Portland. It was too good an opportunity and he should have seen beyond his own selfishness. He was annoyed at his weakness. He took her hand and together they walked over to the telephone area. They were passed by several students walking or running in the opposite direction. 'How long have you got?' inquired Tom. He knew she was soon due to leave and catch her flight.

'Only about a couple of hours before I need to set off. I've left my packed suitcase with the Warden back at Hall. We were told to clear out our rooms before the end of this week. I'm due to catch the one o'clock train to King's Cross and then I have to catch a bus to Heathrow. My flight takes off just before seven o'clock tonight. Don't ask me what time I get into New York because I couldn't tell you. I think it's about ten o'clock even though the flight takes about eight hours. I don't really understand how these time zones work.'

'I wish you weren't going.' This was no time to send coded messages or play emotional games. Raw truths were necessary if he was going to hang on to the girl he thought he was falling in love with.

'I know. I don't *want* to go either but what would *you* do if presented with such an opportunity? I think we both know the answer. Besides, it won't be forever. We will see each other when I get back.'

They arrived at the telephones to find only one cubicle unoccupied. Tom entered it quickly and Emma was not sure what to do. He took the initiative for a change and bundled her into the cramped booth. They were squashed together as Tom picked up the burring, grey receiver and inserted his coins into the slot. He dialled the number, while Emma gave him a squeeze and a girly squeak of anticipated excitement. She could hear his home number ringing as the feedback from the line was quite loud. Tom shot her a knowing look before giving her a quick peck on her lips, ensuring their reconciliation was complete.

At the family home in Consett, Dennis picked-up the tinkling phone in the hallway. As soon as Tom garbled the words, 'I got a first, Dad', his father gave a triumphant fist pump in the air above his head. He was clearly ecstatic at the news. Although Betty must have realised it was good news from her husband's loud reaction, Dennis uncoiled the long lead and walked into the living room with the phone, so she could be told first-hand. Betty was sitting with her bad leg placed at its usual position of rest and started to weep with a mother's joy, when she heard how well her only son had done at University. There followed a great deal of family happiness jammed into three minutes of conversation.

As Tom heard the sound of the pips on the phone, signalling the end of the call, he frantically searched for a two shilling piece in his pocket. Jamming the handset under his chin he rummaged through his clothes, slapping his buttocks and fumbling through his trousers. He looked at Emma, causing the phone to drop and dangle on its cord. He bent down to grab it once more but in a light-hearted attack of panic, his head hit the wall. Emma, standing so close to him burst into hysterical laughter. In the rush to get to a phone, he had failed to check how many coins he had in his pocket before entering the booth. Tom knew it was pointless to leave the kiosk to get more change because a queue of students had already started to gather outside the row of glass doors, waiting to contact their parents. No doubt *they* would have a pile of two-bob bits ready for their important call. As the pips bleeped more quickly to indicate the imminent elapse of the time limit, Tom garbled a farewell message to his parents and promised to ring back later.

He put down the receiver and felt Emma's breath on his face. They looked at each other and started to laugh uncontrollably. Their happiness was propelled by the elation of youth. The couple kissed once again and it felt like the pain of the last two weeks had gone. A promising future awaited and all they had to do was make the right decisions. Their delight was only disturbed by an irritated student tapping a coin on the glass door, reminding Tom that he was not the only one who wanted to phone home that day.

Tom and Emma returned to Trippet Lane together as quickly as possible. He asked her to fill the kettle, while he quickly tidied his bedroom. There was no one else in the flat so they had some quality time to themselves. The environment was not great but that was irrelevant now. Emma went to switch off the boiling kettle in the kitchen and Tom entered the room, unseen. Approaching her from behind, he pulled out the plug. As she turned, he held her and kissed her passionately. There had been a time when he had ignored the opportunity to make love to Emma in his unworthy flat. That time had passed.

In his single bed, Tom held Emma in his arms as they lay under a blanket. Although it was July and warm outside, someone had forgotten to tell his bare cell of a room. Emma tried to talk about recent events but Tom did not want to face his feeble behaviour and acknowledge his weakness. That was for another time. He brought her head under his chin and stroked her hair, enjoying being together again. It was all he could do not to tell her he loved her. Gently and lovingly they were united once more.

The remaining two hours whizzed past and before he knew it, he was waving goodbye to Emma on Platform 1A as she boarded the train for London and headed for her flight. Tom was suddenly overwhelmed with sadness, knowing how much he would miss her. When the train pulled out of the cold station and went out-of-sight along the bend of the tracks, he felt a painful level of grief.

He headed back from the railway station to the University and made his way to Doc's office, on the off-chance that his former tutor would still be around the Faculty building. To his surprise, Tom could hear Doc's familiar voice through the closed door of his office. He was able to tell by the Lecturer's tone that some kind of formal discussion was taking place. Through the frosted panel, Tom discerned a male figure sitting with his back to the office door. He weighed his options but decided to give a quick knock and enter. If he was disrupting anything important, he could return at a more convenient time. Tom felt that his freshly acquired, first-class degree gave him sufficient academic kudos to assert his authority so he tapped on the glass and poked his head around the door.

'Sorry, if I'm interrupting Doctor Herbert. I can come back another time if it's more convenient.' Tom was feeling good. It had been a great day and it was about to get better.

'Aah, Tom. The very man. Come on in. There's somebody here I'd like you to meet... Tom, this is Mr Fitzpatrick. Mr Fitzpatrick, this is Tom Kettlewell who I have just been telling you about.' Doc was always skilled in making professional introductions.

George Fitzpatrick was a well-groomed man in his late forties, who emanated a sense of presence and charisma. He filled his well-cut, expensive suit perfectly. His athletic figure, youthful haircut, exclusive tie with matching shirt and classy shoes, removed a few years from his birth certificate. He spoke with a ubiquitous, trans-Atlantic accent. Extending his arm to shake Tom's hand, his beautiful cuff-links completed the set.

'Pleased to meet you, Tom. Stanley's been telling me all about you. Congratulations on your first class honours, young man.' George was clearly an expert in accepting introductions.

'Thanks.' Tom shot Doc a quick, puzzled look. He was not certain what was going on. It had been that sort of day.

'Sit down, a moment please, Tom,' said Doc. He continued, 'George always pops in when the Department's results are announced. It's become a bit of a tradition; he tries to head-hunt our best students and I try to keep them here to do research for me. He is the Chief Recruitment Officer for the International Computer Company, which you'll know better as ICC. He's very interested in anyone who gets a first-class honours degree in Mathematics and particularly someone who excels in computer programming. I've been telling George about your work developing Pascal and packet-switching. He is very impressed.'

Fitzpatrick took the initiative. 'You see, Tom...' He paused and turned to fix Tom with direct eye-contact. 'ICC is interested in exploring computers to change modern life. We are looking to the future and believe we are about to experience the birth of the next Industrial Revolution – the Information and Communications Technological Revolution. ICC will be in the vanguard of this exciting, innovative phase and we need fresh talent to develop new and exciting ideas, from young bucks like yourself.'

Before Tom had an opportunity to say anything, George continued. 'Of course, we are prepared to pay for that talent. We are the biggest carnivore in the computer jungle and we look after our own. For a young man with your qualifications, we'd be looking at something like a starting salary of *twenty-kay*, with perks, rising further as things go along. What do you say, Tom? You interested?'

'Well I don't really know what to say. I was expecting today to be a big day, but I didn't think it was going to get this big.' Things were happening too quickly for Tom to assimilate. He stood looking straight at George Fitzpatrick, trying not to demonstrate his inner excitement.

'Tell me Tom, how do you see computers developing in the future? Stanley here, has been telling me about what you've been doing on Campus. How do you see things changing?'

Is this some sort of interview? was a thought uppermost in Tom's mind. 'Well, I think variable bitrate data streams will be used to develop protocols for sharing resources, using packet-switching among the nodes. That's an area I've been working on, this year.' Most people in computer sales would have been impressed but 'Fitz' showed no emotion.

'Interesting. We have people working now on transmission control protocols,' he said in a matter-of-fact manner which intimidated Tom, a little.

The verbal jousting continued with Tom becoming more assertive, 'It should be possible to access the data stored on large computers using smaller, more manageable systems, as long as they are communicating in the same language. The smaller, personal computers just need to be programmed to link with the larger ones, and vice versa.' He was baiting the hook.

'So where do you see this leading, Tom?' inquired Fitzpatrick, with real interest. He was definitely beginning to nibble.

'Well I believe mainframe computers will allow big business the opportunity to exercise control. We're seeing this already with the development of the magnetic strip to control finance with credit cards and data storage with floppy disks. I can see a time when smaller computers will be able to time share into the mainframe. These are the protocols I've been trying to improve. I think when it does happen, there will be an explosion in the use of computers and the way they interact with society's needs.' This conclusive landing of the big fish was what Tom was looking for. He demonstrated that he had the vision, determination and the level of ability that any big firm craved.

'Very impressive,' contributed Fitzpatrick, almost under his breath and nodding while he spoke.

Doc rounded the discussion to a conclusion. 'It's a lot to think about, Tom and nobody here expects a response now. You need to go away, collect your thoughts and consider your options. You know I want you to stay here and get your doctorate with us, before you venture into that big ugly world. Anyway, first things first, I'm starving and it's well past my lunchtime. We're going to get something to eat. George, you're paying.' Doc was at the stage of his career where a decent lunch was valued more highly than listening to George Fitzpatrick's sales pitch, especially when his stomach was grumbling about an absence of food.

'Don't listen to him, Tom. If Stanley had his way, you would be covered in cobwebs and smelling of mothballs by the time you're thirty. With ICC you could make your fortune before you get to forty. Here, let me give you my card. When you feel like spreading your wings, give me a ring. If I don't hear anything, *I'll* be chasing *you*.'

Tom gave a polite laugh as they rose from their chairs. After a firm handshake with George Fitzpatrick and a half-hearted wave from Doc, Tom left the two old friends alone in the room.

Tom was beginning to believe that he could have money, *real* money for the first time in his life, working for a large company, with excellent prospects. The day deserved to be acknowledged so he decided to complete the last of his jobs before joining the other students for some hard-core celebrations. This meant getting something to eat and ringing his parents again to inform them of this fresh snippet of good news. After a shower in the dingy bathroom and a change of clothes by the electric fire, he intended to return to the Student Bar, then head into the City and try to forget everything. Adrenalin was charging through his body with every exciting thought.

XV

When Tom entered the Student Bar, a group of newly appointed graduates was already ensconced in a corner of the room. They had started their celebrations early. The brown, *Formica*-topped tables with their mini guard-rails around the edges, were covered with uncollected glasses, empty bottles and half-full pints of beer. Three tables had been shoved together and were encircled by a large tribe of worshipping students, intent on a final hurrah before leaving University. One lad, with shoulder-length, curly hair was resting both arms and elbows on the top of the bench seats and sitting with his corduroyed legs wide apart. Resting on his crotch was an open packet of crisps. Some of the female students were being invited to eat a crisp from the packet, without using their hands.

Young men were shouting and singing obscene invitations to the girls, smiling and pushing each other in loud revelry, while more sober beginners watched with interest. Tom approached to see what was going on and recognised some from the group as geologists. Leaning his head to one side, he queried the point with one of their number who was on his way back from the bar. The newly appointed graduate was skilfully caressing three, full pint glasses in his fingers, while holding half-a-cigarette in the corner of his mouth. The smoke was going into his eyes but he still had the ability to confirm that Tom's assessment was accurate.

Tom was already smiling when he scanned the rest of the Bar, which was beginning to get busy. He was pleased to spot Geoffrey Miller enter through a side-door. It was rare to see his friend in this part of the University. Geoff had made the effort to join Tom when he heard of his brilliant degree result. First-class honours were very rare and Geoff showed his underlying decency by attending the celebrations for his mate. Tom quickly intercepted his progress to the pumps. 'Hi, Geoff. It's good to see you here. When you weren't in the flat this afternoon I thought you must have gone home or something. What can I get you?'

Freddy Miller had not wanted his son, Geoffrey to go to Sheffield University to study Economics. He had wanted him to work in his chain of family grocery shops and prepare to take over the business, when he retired. *'Millers Groceries'* had a mini-hold in the York area and were looking to expand. Geoffrey preferred to swim in a bigger pool. When his dad had failed to top-up his grant, Geoff's student life became a financial struggle, when it need not have been. After a blazing argument with his father, Geoffrey decided to pull-up the emotional drawbridge and had isolated himself from the family.

Tom insisted on buying his friend a pint and knew that despite his principles, Geoff would accept. Given his level of financial plight, Tom was going to look after his flatmate tonight.

'No. I won't be going home this summer, unless my parents change their minds. Anyway, today is not about me. I heard the great news at lunchtime and I've been keeping an eye out for you most of the day. Congratulations mate. I'm really pleased for you. Cheers. I'll have a pint of *Watney's Red*.'

The first of their night's pints were drawn and the level of noise in the Bar began to increase. The cosy chat with one or two noisy groups escalated, while the geologists were not far away from being told to leave and take their noise elsewhere. The buzz in the room soon reached the point where hearing a conversation proved virtually impossible. Singing and backslapping were followed by sighs of relief by the groups of friends. There were also tears of realisation that for most of the young men and women, the experience of university life would soon be over.

At ten-minutes-to eleven, the bell sounding last orders was rung. It was treated with a chorus of boos, followed by the sharp rap of the shutters coming down on the counter. One of the barmen threw his wiping-cloth over his shoulder, rested his arm rigidly against one of the pumps and breathed a deep sigh of relief. The majority of the students wanted the revelry to continue and an anonymous cry of 'Let's go into town,' was greeted with a cheering consensus. Tom was not drunk to the point of finding it difficult to walk but he was aware that his speech was slurring. When invited by others to go into the City to resume the drinking and merriment, he could not think of a reason to say no, although he did find it difficult to say anything at all. Tom's behaviour often changed when he had too much to drink and he sensed some vulnerability.

Once in the cooler night air, his demeanour sobered somewhat. Some students caught the last bus into town, others had a taxi, while one or two loaded into cars and headed off with all windows wide open. Tom was in the minority who walked the mile or so through the City streets to the *Top Rank*. The walk in the fresh air did the trick. His group were sober enough to fool the bouncers, dressed as bingo callers who were manning the doors to supervise the dress code. Tom and his friends were all wearing the required tie – of a sort. Someone had the bright idea of removing a sock and tying it around his collar, while fully buttoning-up his top coat. The rest of the group copied the con trick and from arm's length in the dark, it worked. The socks passed as substitute ties and gave the wearers a sufficiently credible level of smartness to be allowed to enter the night club. Once inside, the 'ties' were removed.

The noise in the *Top Rank* made the University Bar seem like the *Whispering Gallery*. The song *'All Right Now'* by the pop-group *Free* was blasting across the giant room. There was a horrendous queue at the bar, with groups of highly attractive young women standing back in a parallel line. Somehow, Tom found himself with a pint in his hand. He scrutinised the young girls and was sad and angry at the same time for not being able to celebrate his moment of glory with Emma.

Tom was looking around the room for his group of friends, with his left leg anchored to the spot. He could not stop the movement in his right leg as it pushed back and fore. To anyone watching, it looked as if he was dancing. In reality he was simply trying to maintain his balance, while the backwash from his pint glass spilled over the glass, onto his shoes. Suddenly, he felt a tug on his jacket from behind.

It was Felicity.

'Felicity …oh Felicity… hello Felicity! What are you doing here?' said Tom in a state of drunken bravado. He tried desperately to stand still and for a moment, he almost achieved his goal.

Felicity grabbed his arm and pulled him low enough to be able to shout in his ear, such was the noise of the music. 'Never mind what I am doing here. It looks like you should be in bed.' Even now, she was playing games. Tom agreed to take part in the sport and felt free to continue his newly found dancing moves.

'That's the best offer I've had all night!' he said, in a manner he would have never been brave or stupid enough to make, if he had been sober.

'Now, now Tom. What would that lovely little girlfriend of yours think of you talking like that? Where is she, anyway?' Felicity was flirting in a dangerous manner. The only thing missing was the sound of a snake charmer's flute.

Tom should have said nothing but he could not resist himself. Still swaying, he responded. 'She's on a plane, flying to America, whoosh!' He floated his free arm as if it was the wing of an aeroplane. He was risking everything by engaging with Felicity but did not seem to care.

Felicity pulled him down to her level once more. 'It's too noisy here for us. We're going.' A girl suddenly sidled-up to Felicity. 'Tom, this is Sheila.' Tom was aware of another person standing close but he could not focus on her appearance. 'We're just off to a party. Want to come? Bring a pal if you want. We've got room in the car.' This was a tempting but dangerous invitation.

Suddenly, Tom swivelled his head around too quickly and almost fell over. He shouted across to his group of friends. 'Geoff! Geoff! Hoy, Geoffo! Want to go to a party?' It was amazing he was still coherent enough to be understood.

Geoff saw no reason to draw further attention to his flatmate so he simply raised his thumb in the affirmative and made his way across to where the three were standing. Tom attempted an introduction. 'Geoff this is Felicity and her friend, who has a very nice name … that I can't remember.'

'Come on. Let me get him into the car,' ordered Felicity, still taking the lead. The last thing that Tom remembered was getting into Felicity's blue Triumph Herald. Someone wound down a window to let fresh air penetrate the interior. A bonus was allowing Tom to vomit onto the road, without messing the upholstery. After that, everything went black in his world.

Tom woke at about four o'clock in the morning, with a furry tongue, a raging thirst and a bursting bladder. He went to the toilet and on returning to the kitchen, he began to look for a glass. In his drunken state, he was not really sure where he was. After downing two glasses of cold *Adam's ale,'* he wandered back to bed. Within a minute he sunk back into a thick, dreamless sleep.

Three hours later, he awoke once more and suddenly his blood ran cold. Lying next to him was Felicity, naked and still asleep, facing in the opposite direction. Tom turned onto his back and looked at the ceiling, before throwing his hands onto his face in horror, disbelieving what he had done. Under his breath he cursed to himself, like a deceitful traitor, feeling utterly stupid and afraid.

His mind conducted its own appraisal of the situation as he made a rapid assessment of the damage. Thank God, Emma was not in the country ! With a bit of luck, she might never find out that he had risked everything- and for what ? He reached for his underpants and sat on the side of the bed but in the remnants of his drunken clumsiness, he disturbed Felicity, which initiated a verbal spar between them.

'Not leaving me again, are you Tom?'

'Shit, Felicity! How the hell did I get here?'

'You don't remember? That's not much of a compliment, darling.'

'Tell me we didn't …?'

'Didn't what?'

'You know exactly what.'

'A lady never tells, darling. Anyway, you weren't asking me many questions last night.'

'Look Felicity, stop pissing me about and tell me what happened.'

'What's the last thing you remember, *Mr First Class Man*?'

Was she still teasing or was it his worst nightmare? 'I remember being in the *Top Rank* and I remember throwing-up out of the window of your car. After that … nothing.'

'Well I dropped-off Sheila and that friend of yours. What's he called again? … Geoff, that's it. Well they went to the party over at Broomhall but you were totally *incommunicado* darling. Dead to the world. None of us could rouse you or get you out of the car. They were too drunk to care. Probably ended up having sex together, as well.'

'As well as who?'

'Now, Tom don't be bashful.'

'Look, stop teasing me Felicity. I'm not in the mood. I've already got a girlfriend. This is serious – did we have sex or not?'

'Do you mean did we have serious sex?' Felicity could not help herself. Tom was at breaking point. 'If you're going to be like that, I'm going.' He stood and dressed himself as quickly as he could, while Felicity rested her head against her arm on the pillow, crooking it for support.

She watched him, with a huge, smug smile of victory on her face. 'Going to tell that little friend of yours what you did, Tom?… When she gets back from America? That'll take the shine off your first-class degree.' Felicity was hissing venom in every direction.

At this point, Tom became angry. He bent over her, glared directly into Felicity's eyes and threatened her with some bile of his own. 'What I say to Emma is none of your fucking business. And you had better not say anything to her either, or else. Got it!'

With that, Tom turned to leave the room. He slammed the door, thundered down the noisy, carpetless stairs and stormed out of the house. Within an hour of leaving Felicity's flat, he was washed, changed and sitting with a third cup of coffee in Sheffield's Pond Street Bus Station. He did not care that he had a two-hour wait for the next bus back to Consett. He was so angry, sore and ashamed that he just wanted to be at home with the people he loved. It was probably convenient that there was a bit of a wait for the next bus. He was in no fit state to travel. He needed to eat something to line his stomach and take some *Aspirin* to get rid of his headache. When he was finally on the bus, he slept most of the way home.

It did not matter there was no blue Humber Sceptre waiting for him this time. Tom needed to walk home and remove the anger and shame from his core, before he was reunited with his parents. As the front door opened, his Dad was naturally delighted to see his graduate son for the first time and gave him a huge hug of parental pride. After a couple of days of home cooking, adulation and relaxation, he found his feet again.

During the summer months, Tom usually worked part-time in the local Union Offices in Consett High Street. It was mainly form filling and typing accounts, often related to mundane matters. The work was tedious but it kept him occupied during that time of year. His involvement with the Union also reminded his father, that his son shared his left-wing views. After about a week of being at home, the phone rang one evening at about seven o'clock. Tom and his father were doing the dishes as usual, after their evening meal. Dennis had just put the kettle on, when he answered the call and shouted across the hall to the kitchen. It was, 'Some lass, calling person-to-person, from somewhere in America. Will we take the call?'

Tom came rushing out of the kitchen and snatching the receiver from his Dad, declared, 'Of course we'll take the call. Give uz it 'ere. It's got to be for me. … Hello?'

His father lingered longer than was welcome. He stood next to his son, watching his performance. 'Yes it, is. …Yes I will. Thank you operator, you can put her through… Hello. Is that you Emma?… Hi, yes, …it's me, …it's Tom. How are you? … Have you had your results? …How did you get on? …A two-one, that's brilliant. Well done, Emm!' As he turned he could see his father looking at him wearing his familiar, bemused expression. Tom silently shooed him away, gesturing dismissively with his right hand. His Dad was not to be denied and eavesdropped from behind the kitchen door.

'Hi, how's it going? … I can only just hear you. …What time is it there? … Are you enjoying it? … Yes, I miss you too… Good… Good… … Yes, they're fine… They'd like to meet you too…'

Dennis dried his hands on the tea-towel and went into the lounge, closing the door. He began a silent conversation with his wife, who was sitting in her chair, in her usual position. As he approached Betty, Dennis raised his eyebrows and with a smile nodded over towards the hallway. Betty looked at her husband, inquisitively. Dennis hooked his thumb in Tom's direction, before placing one palm against his heart and feigning to wipe his brow with the back of his other hand. Betty silently smacked him with the rolled-up newspaper, before Dennis made a circle with his index finger and thumb, holding it up to his wife, and then planted a kiss on her forehead.

'…ok … ok… same time next week, right… Of course I do… ok… right… bye… bye. And congratulations again – brilliant news.' Tom replaced the receiver and then flowed upstairs to his room. Excitedly, he opened his bedroom door and flopped onto the mattress with a gorgeous inner sigh. He remained in the same supine position for more than half-an-hour, before Dennis called from the bottom of the stairs, 'There's a cup of coffee here for you Tommy. Come and get it while it's hot.'

Twenty minutes later, Tom entered the lounge to see his mother and father silently looking at him as he made his way to the settee. He comforted himself into the luxurious cushions and looked up to notice they were still staring. Fighting back a smile, he waited another ten seconds, before he spoke. 'What?' he asked, defensively, while desperately trying not to laugh.

'So whooz this lass, arm lookin forward to meetin?' inquired Dennis.

'Her name is Emma. Didn't I already tell you that, the last time I was home? Remember …?'

'Oh, it's the same lass as you told uz about at Christmas is it ? Must be serious,' said Tom's Dad defensively.

In an effort to change the direction of the conversation, Betty issued an order. 'Put the kettle on again Dennis. Our Tom's coffee has probably gone cold by now and ah fancy another cup of tea an'all. And open that packet of *Lyons Tarts*.' Wagging her finger in her husband's direction, she added , 'When you bring them in, put them on a plate first, mind.' Dennis obeyed his instructions and scuttled off to re-engage his tea-making prowess, which did not take long. He brought in everything on a tray, eyeing the strawberry tart, before delicately and carefully lowering the ensemble onto the walnut coffee table. He quickly glanced at his wife, hoping for an acknowledgement of approval, which he did not get. As he poured from the white tea-pot, protected by its red cosy, he listened to his son's tale.

Tom decided to tell them everything. Over their cups of tea and coffee, he described how Emma came to be spending the summer in Portland. The phone call was her first opportunity to tell Tom about her degree results and how she was settling to life in the USA. She had gained an Upper Second Class Honours in American Studies. It was clear from his enthusiasm and warmth, this girl was very special. His future seemed to be taking shape and they were excited for him. He mentioned that Emma would ring again in a week's time and his mother suggested that he should invite her to Consett when she returned from America. The three of them were excited at the prospect of a rosy future, all-round.

Several weeks later, mid-way through August, Tom was at home pottering around the house. The Union Office was closed and Tom and his Dad were in the small kitchen, tidying-up once more. Betty was relaxing in the lounge, listening to Radio 2. Dennis gave a gestured wave to his son, beckoning him to come closer. He whispered some important news of his own.

'Arm gontta wait until yer Mam's nodded off and then arm goin' take the car inta Newcastle. It's her birthday next week and I want-a get yer Mam somethin' nice. Will you keep an eye on her, Tommy lad, while arm out?'

'Course I will. I thought it was your anniversary soon, as well? Isn't Mam's birthday just a few days before your anniversary or is it the other way around?' It was unusual for Tom to get his dates wrong.

'Me and yer Mam were married on August 16th 1949. How many years is that, genius?'

'I make it twenty-one, *O Great Master.*'

'Less of the cheek.' Dennis loved it when his son messed him about.

'What are you going to buy her?' asked Tom, with some anxious anticipation in his voice.

'Thought ah might get her some jewellery. She always likes pearls so maybe some ear rings. What do yer think?' Dennis was seeking some reassurance rather than advice.

'Nice.' Tom was genuinely impressed. The gift was thoughtful and expensive, two rare distinctions from his father's normal efforts.

'So you'll be alright with her on yer own?' Tom could tell the origin of his own anxieties and showed some impatience towards his Dad.

'I'll be fine. She's me Mam, not the *Boston Strangler.* Don't worry about her. Just go.'

With that ringing endorsement of approval, Dennis put on his overcoat and shoes and left the house. He opened the car door, sat on the luxury upholstery and pulled away in his pride and joy, feeling pretty good with life. His son had done well, had a bright future ahead and there was something nice to celebrate coming up. Dennis was worried about Betty's health but he was almost used to living with that anxiety. His wife was sleeping more often and her leg did not look good. There were a couple of nasty ulcers developing and he intended to ask the District Nurse to call before her next routine visit. As he pulled out of the street and turned the corner, Dennis did not notice a car pulling-up, outside his house.

There was an authoritative knock on the door and Tom rushed to answer it before his mother was awakened by the noise. He was just about to tell whoever was calling that it was a bad moment, when he was briefly lost for words. It was Felicity.

She had surprised him, once again. Tom was totally bewildered and felt rising anger in his body. 'Felicity? ...What are you doing here?' He had given very little information to his parents about this former girlfriend. She stood on the doorstep, with both hands in the pockets of her blue, full-length coat, her long hair flowing out of the sides of a multi-coloured woollen hat.

'Ok, well I suppose you'd better come in but keep your voice down. My mother is asleep.' Tom took her into the kitchen. He did not want her in the lounge or speaking to his mother and was glad his father had just left. As she entered the house and stood in the hallway, Felicity's eyes were everywhere, scrutinising the family home. Under other circumstances, Tom would have had something to say about her rude behaviour.

'Well? What do you want? I don't appreciate you turning up at my house unannounced. I would not do it to you. So what's so important that you have come all this way to Consett? Just say what you have to say, then go'. His anger had clouded his power to think straight. He was not prepared for the next sentence. It was about to change his life forever. Felicity took a deep sigh and then cruelly, blurted out the reason for her visit to his home.

'Ok then – I'm pregnant and you're the father.' For a brief moment, Felicity enjoyed the power of her disclosure.

'What!' You can't be. ...You can't be. How do you know?' For the first time in his life, Tom felt he wanted to punch a woman.

'The same way any girl knows these days. I was late with my period and went to see the doctor. I handed in a urine test and three days later the results came back. Those results showed I am pregnant.'

'So you're saying it's mine?' This was a desperate, useless attempt to deny responsibility. His emotions were flaying his soul.

Tom's raised voice of panic aroused his mother and a call came in from the other room. 'Tom. Is that you? Is somebody there with you? Bring them in here, it's ok.' Now there was no alternative. He had to think quickly and design a decent plan. He told Felicity to go.

'Go? Go where?' She was as bewildered as Tom.

Tom's sharp mind, racing in panic, instantly came up with a way forward. 'Go over to the Royal County Hotel in the centre of Durham. It's easy to find. I'll meet you there tonight. Say about eight o'clock. We'll talk about it then… *Bloody Hell*! Now just go, please – I'll talk to you tonight'

Betty called-out once more. 'Tom, invite yer friend into the living room… Tom?'

Tom ushered Felicity out of the house and abruptly closed the door. He went into the lounge to ensure his Mam had not been distressed by the sound of raised voices. 'Who was that, you were talking to in the kitchen, Tom? You should have brought them in here.' Betty was confused at being woken so suddenly.

It was nobody, Mam. Don't worry about it. It was nothing.

Tom was wrong… It was everything.

XVI

The early morning stillness was broken by the cockerel's daily call. It was enough to waken Onaedo, who jumped to her knees on her bed. She looked out of the window to try and spot the location of her nemesis but could not see him. He was undoubtedly hiding somewhere in the courtyard. Then the rooster called again, this time stirring the child's mother. Maki rolled over in her bed and her arm flopped onto Dilibe's head. In return, he spooned inwards like a loving husband. Too soon, Maki heard the scampering bare feet on the landing's wooden floorboards that announced the imminent arrival of their daughter, who was guaranteed to disturb anyone's slumber.

Another play day was beginning for Onaedo, while for her mother a special day was hopefully about to blossom. The door burst open, and the child's eyes glared to see who was going to acknowledge her first. It was her *Mama*.

'Good morning my child, how are you this morning? Did you sleep well?' Dilibe was usually the last to stir in the house, although he was always the first to leave.

Maki dragged her limp arm from her husband's head and plumped it onto the bed sheets as an invitation to her little girl. Onaedo took this as her signal to jump in and cuddle with her *Mama*. It was Maki's last gesture at squeezing as much sleep as possible from the day. Eventually, Onaedo's frantic kicking into Dilibe's back met with his resignation as well and he rolled over to look at the ceiling and ponder whether he was still alive. He turned, looked over the Onaedo mound at his wife and sighed. Reluctantly he got out of bed, intending to get to the bathroom first. A giggling Onaedo jumped up and raced to get there before him, followed by her more reluctant mother. Once inside, Maki turned on the tap, while her animated daughter sat on the toilet to release her excitement. Dilibe sat on the edge of the bed, head in hands, admitting defeat.

After ensuring her daughter was washed and dressed, Maki declared the bathroom was now a female-free zone. Dilibe had retired downstairs to organise his day, having got as far as putting on his underpants, trousers and socks. On hearing his wife's declaration that the bathroom was available, he placed his papers into his briefcase and headed for the stairs. Dilibe's main duty while his wife was otherwise occupied this day, was to look after his daughter and press the flesh at the gathering. It was Maki's special occasion after all. Since the Centre would benefit everyone in the Village, Dilibe thought the inconvenience to his own routine was a small price to pay.

Maki set about making breakfast and with the bread in the toaster, the little girl sat quietly, looking around for a source of fascination. While Onaedo was sitting relatively still, her mother began to plait her daughter's hair, standing behind her like an experienced hairdresser. Occasionally Onaedo took a sip of milk from her glass, while her mother busied her skilful hands. When the two plaits were woven, the toaster popped and the bread stuck its head above the parapet just as Dilibe entered the kitchen.

'What are we doing today, *Mama*?' inquired Onaedo. Maki thought how nice it would be to be able to set every daily agenda in the morning, over breakfast. Most of this particular day had been planned for weeks.

'Well, after breakfast, *Papa* will stay at home to look after you, while I go and make sure that everything is set for our special day.'

'Is *Papa* not going to work today?' Her mother shook her head. 'And he'll be staying with us?' A nod. '... Hooray!' After another sip of milk, more questions. 'Where are *you* going today, *Mama*?'

'I have to go to the new Community Centre in a moment my darling and open the doors so that people may enter. I am the only one who has a key so I have to go early. Special people are coming to the Village today. They will arrive by helicopter and it will land in the field.' Onaedo was staring up at her *Mama* with her adorable, innocent eyes and hanging on her every word. 'They will be our very important guests today and I need to make sure the nice food is prepared for them and that everything is set out properly.'

Onaedo listened intently as if she was learning something wonderful. 'Is that going to be our new school, *Mama*?'

'Not just our new school. There are other things there too. There is a medical room, where *Papa* will work when he is in our Village and a library and hall for people to use, when they want to. It is for everyone in Uminwani – in our community. That is why it is called a *Community Centre*.'

At this point, Dilibe joined the world occupied by the rest of his family. 'Enough questions now, little one. Sit and eat your breakfast, like a good girl.' Maki lifted the two fried eggs from the pan and set them onto the two slices of toasted bread on Dilibe's plate. Her husband's eyes shot her a smile of gratitude. Maki sat down at the kitchen table and finally joined her family for breakfast, sipping her hot coffee gently.

Dilibe accepted his wife's instruction to clear away after breakfast as he pushed his empty plate to one side and smacked his belly like a drum. Meanwhile, Onaedo thought about her first opportunity of the day to chase the cockerel. After rinsing her coffee cup under the tap, Maki kissed them both fondly and made her way to the front of the house to collect her papers and other essentials. She left their home, and turned to walk along the sandy brown track. A mile later, the building appeared in front of her. Maki stopped to admire its fresh, modern appearance and reflected on the hard work and ambition that had brought this day to fruition. A new Community Centre would bring the development of the Village forward by at least twenty years. The small school on the other side of town would eventually be knocked down, before it fell down. The new building would not leak, it did not have a roof made from corrugated iron sheets and no chickens or ducks would make their way into the classrooms. It was as bright and stimulating as any school should be and most importantly of all, it was part of the modern world.

It had been Maki's idea to build the small medical unit immediately adjacent to the new school and include some social facilities such as a hall, for Village meetings. The extra money available in the charity funds had facilitated these additional resources. Other communities would envy Uminwani, although she also hoped they would learn about the Village and the suffering of its people.

Maki reached the impressive entrance and peered through the glass front, holding her hand above her eyes to shield the reflected glare. She could see the large reception desk sitting proudly under bright blue signs, indicating where visitors would find their particular service. It felt like she was breaking a champagne bottle over a launching ship as she placed the shiny new key into the freshly greased Yale lock. There was a special sound of newness as the mechanism clicked and she pulled open the heavy, glass door. She entered the empty building, allowing the door to slam behind her. The noise it made on closing echoed along the deserted corridors. In the isolated stillness, the place was eerie and intimidating for a moment. Then Maki gave an enormous smile of satisfaction, before shouting 'Yes!' as loudly as she could. There was a half-response as her voice bounced back from the bare walls. She hoped nothing would go wrong today but she never totally relaxed. Life's experiences had taught her that particular lesson.

PART TWO

PART TWO

I

It was late, yet the plush, modern office floor overlooking the city of London was fully staffed, with computer screens at every desk. The Company's work area, ten stories above the City, spread its orange glow through a wall of glass, into the darkness. Huge sophisticated windows were a testament to the success of the businesses housed in the luxurious block of thickly carpeted offices. The Tower in Canada Square was one of the new buildings in this part of London as were most of the high-rise blocks in Canary Wharf, at the time. The area was quickly becoming a major business node. London looked different on this particular Friday, something special was about to happen. Hundreds of buildings were illuminated, with their lights shining out into the clear sky like mini beacons, calling to the wider world. The giant, London Eye was prepared for action, ready to herald a new millennium.

'Ok, listen-up everybody.' He did not have to wait long for everyone's attention. When he spoke, they listened. It was his company, after all. 'We have half-an-hour to go and I want everyone to be vigilant. I don't want any cock-ups. Make it just as we have practised and rehearsed. Any difficulties, activate the blue light on your desk and I will be over to help you sort it. Any questions? … No? … Right, good luck. Let's earn our money.'

He turned and moved across to his own personal office door, which showed he was the boss. It read *'TDVK Solutions'* with the words *'Chief Executive'* printed in gold upper-case letters, underneath his name. The blinds in the room were pulled high, exposing everything inside his personal domain. More importantly, the greater transparency allowed him to view the floor so he could observe his workforce. The people at their computers comprised thirty of the sharpest minds in their field. There were seven female programmers in the group, the rest were young men in their twenties and early thirties. All were on a monthly contract and all were highly-paid, as the sports cars and personalised number plates evidenced, in the exclusive basement car park at the bottom of the glass tower that housed them all.

He was not anticipating any difficulties. There had been a dry run three months earlier, when similar worries had been expressed about September 9th. That date could also have presented some difficulty on its own, before the big day. When September 9th 1999 was reproduced in a computer programme it was commonly represented by the numerical format 9999. There was an issue because 9999 was frequently used in computer programming to specify an unknown date. Any problem when the date rolled-over, could potentially crash the system on which it was running. Professional pundits were expressing greater concern about the predicted changes on this special evening. As the new deadline approached, media frenzy had been attempting to generate further panic over the 'Millennium Bug'. In thirty minutes time, his firm had the massive responsibility of ensuring the transition went smoothly for a significant number of companies and organisations. This particular Friday was 31st December 1999 and midnight was about to introduce a third millennium to the World.

The majority of programmers and managers only started recognising the possibility of a looming rollover problem in the mid-1990s. Inertia and complacency caused the issue to go unresolved until the last few years of the decade. *TDVK Solutions* had been working on producing a remedial programme for five years. After effective trials, culminating in its success on September 9th 1999, the 'White Dove' algorithm would be applied to address the issue. Its flexibility had been embedded into several computer languages and would ensure a successful transition to the new millennium, as long as it worked. 'White Dove' had been the pet project of *TDVK* since the Company was established in 1986. It was the result of years of experience and expertise, the reward for a proactive approach to problem solving.

The Chief Executive sat in his office pondering the night's potential for excitement. The burden of responsibility was less of a challenge than the thrill of the anticipated adrenalin rush. He had always enjoyed working with computers and as his skill increased over the years so did the enjoyment of watching his programmes succeed. Behind his large, curved glass-topped desk with its three computer screens, he decided to relax for at least twenty of the remaining minutes by looking through some of his recent personal bank statements. Now was not the time to assess the financial progress of the Company but he could indulge in some personal business. It was the current account that was occupying his attention. His sapphire eyes scrutinised the neatly presented text. These days, he needed the help of a pair of rimless spectacles, which fitted snugly against the greying hair on his ageing temples.

There was a healthy, seven-figure balance shown on his statement's end-of-month printout and he could easily afford the private nursing arrangement, the heavy utilities bills and the costly memberships for exclusive clubs. He had even continued to increase the standing orders that he had been paying to *Support an African Child* since his days at University. It now comprised a three-figure monthly sum, which did not scratch the surface of his available funds. In addition to his current account, he had two savings accounts, an investment account as well as money in a German bank. Tom Kettlewell had come a long way and now he was luxuriating in personal wealth.

At eleven-fifty-five, he rose from his black leather, swivel-chair and stood outside the office door to peruse his empire. The level of noise amongst his workforce had subsided and there was hardly any audible banter across the floor. It was almost time to begin their task and his staff were preparing themselves. They would not hear the distant chimes of *Big Ben* at midnight, through their double-glazed armour. This did not matter; their computers were tuned with exact synchronicity to time absolute. They would not be able to observe the fireworks display due to explode in the skies around them. This youthful group were not tourists positioned to admire an aerial spectacle. Workers in *TDVK Solutions* were well-paid but if they made a mistake, they were out. The boss would make sure of that. There were plenty of other young bucks, waiting in the wings to challenge the old bulls. The spoils that came from being at the top were not insignificant.

Everyone in the office watched the large second hand on the wall-clock countdown the final minute of the millennium. While they might be able to hear muffled celebrations from a distant source and fleetingly catch a colourful explosion in the nearby skies by accident, the workforce had to stay focussed. At the magic moment, lines of white text on green backgrounds were wildly appearing on monitors around the room. The screen print was emerging faster than speech. Each computer was counter-punched by a programmer's dancing fingers on a keyboard. The first blue light appeared after five minutes, clearly the default time set on that computer's mainframe for a potential shutdown. The head of *TDVK* walked swiftly across to the point of concern, stared into the meaning on the screen and proceeded to enter two lines of a command that were followed by a rapid scroll of phrases racing down the screen. Finally, after dashing for about two endless minutes, text at the end of the computer monologue simply stated, '*Programme Running*'.

This scenario occurred about eight times during the first three hours, before things settled. Most of the problems were resolved directly by the high achievers. Several of the young specialists sat at their desks, with their arms folded behind their heads, palms massaging or scratching their itchy hair, while they stifled a yawn. At five-thirty in the morning, after the East Coast of America switched on and was running smoothly, the worst was over. He stood in front of the tired eyes staring back at him.

'Ok everybody, the *Bug* appears to have been squashed. Things are working. The City and New York are running and no problems reported. Congratulations and good job, everyone. Phil, Samantha and I will see out the remaining time. The rest of you, go home or celebrate, or do whatever you want to do and catch-up with what you've missed. Happy New Year, or rather Happy New Millennium. See you in two days' time.'

Half-an-hour later, Tom Kettlewell took his grey *Armani* jacket from its stand and while holding a slim-line briefcase in his right hand, he tossed the exclusive coat in the air, allowing it to free-fall over his left arm. Turning to say goodbye to anyone left in the office, he was disappointed to note that everyone had gone. While others had broken away in sub-groups to call into a club or an all-night *yuppie* bar, he was alone. It was not really surprising that his workforce did not want to drink with the boss. They were frightened of him and not without justification. He was a ruthless, autocratic and brilliant individual, who had to be respected.

No one really knew him. Rumours in the Company circulated that he had been married once but the story remained unsubstantiated. For all they knew, he may have still been married. He kept himself to himself. Even Phil and Samantha, who were his best workers and the ones he trusted with most of the Company's secrets, had rarely been to his home. They knew that he lived in Loughton but they had never been invited to any special parties or gatherings, official or unofficial. Tom Kettlewell was an enigma.

He pressed the intercom on his desk to reach the Reception area in the building's suave foyer. A few cleaners were beginning to arrive for work in businesses on the other floors of the glass memorial, even on this special morning. Knowing that someone would be manning the main entrance, he spoke down the line.

'George, this is Mr Kettlewell. I'm on my way to the exit. Have someone bring my car around, please.' He stood alone and vulnerable for a moment, issuing the instruction to one of his subordinates. After ordering the delivery of his car, he flicked the switch on the intercom upwards, changing its colour from green to red. He decided to put on his jacket, it was easier than carrying the damn thing, and after casting one more backward glance into his personal office, he switched off the light, before heading for the main door of his business floor. The red carpet felt reassuringly comfortable under his feet as he pressed the silver, down-arrow on the lift's home wall. The metal doors opened and he stepped in, before pressing the number '0' on the interior panel, still deep in thought. He enjoyed the lonely ride in an empty lift: it gave him a few peaceful, relaxing moments all to himself.

As the smooth lift doors pinged open, Mr Kettlewell stepped out into the lobby. A man in a stylish dark maroon overcoat and top hat, opened the glass door as he approached. The VIP exited the building, and walked swiftly and smoothly into the dark morning, while one or two people glanced in his direction. A young man aged about twenty was standing beside a sparkling, dark green *Alfa Romeo GTV*. His right arm was behind his back and when he bent forward to open the car door with his left hand, it looked like he was grovelling.

'Morning, Mr Kettlewell, sir. Happy New Year, sir.' The young man was not wearing a top-coat, only a grey waistcoat, with black tie, charcoal trousers and ultra-shiny shoes. His hair was neatly greased and parted, razor sharp. He seemed pleasant enough, trying to simper into the business man's world, even at this unholy hour.

'Yes, thank you … er?' There was a momentary delay as he waited for a response. Mr Kettlewell was only mildly interested in the boy's name. Reaching into his right trouser pocket and hoping to locate a couple of pound coins, he walked past the young man, pressing some money into his hand, which closed like a clam's reflex.

'Tom, sir.' Skilfully, the minion looked into the man's eyes without glancing to see how much his fawning was worth.

The boss crouched low and eased himself gently into his treasured automobile, before he remembered to complete his final act. 'Thank you, Tom'

He relaxed into the luxury car seat as the door was caressed into its closed position. Accelerating smoothly out of the drive and into the flow of traffic, he allowed himself a sardonic smile. *'Another Tom,'* he thought. *Earning money on January 1st in the year 2000 instead of recovering from a good night out. That would never have been me during my student days.'*

The drive to Loughton in Essex was surprisingly quick, although he should have realised he was going in the opposite direction to most of the City traffic, at that time of the morning. He was exhausted, almost too tired to drive safely. His tiredness had been a bone of contention at home for quite a while because he was always shattered. After taking the slip road from the M11, the car eased its way around the familiar country road before turning into the private lane on his land. Two minutes later, he reached inside the glove compartment and pressed a red button on the remote control. The impressively huge, electronically controlled double-gates opened and the *Alfa Romeo* pulled into the grounds, its headlights flickering through the darkness.

The car crunched its way over the long, gravel driveway to the main entrance of Tom's home, which he had named *Derwent House*. A roundabout, centred with a spouting fountain, allowed easy turning for any visitor arriving at the white, detached building, half-covered in ivy. The drive was also wide enough to allow his other two cars to be left out in the open, without needing to be housed in the triple garage around the back. A conservatory overlooked the pool and the adjoining building forming an L-shape, was a self-contained domicile. Tom enjoyed lounging on the poolside patio when he had time away from work, looking onto adjacent woodland bordering the six acres of land that was the tree-moat to his privacy. He had a pair of strong binoculars, enabling him to observe the wildlife close-up, especially the birds.

Tom had lived in Loughton for almost ten years. The boom that occurred during the 1980s had seen him prosper. Large corporations running elaborate computer systems needed to be serviced. The increased demand for computers and their commensurate need for reliability meant a boom for companies in the I.T. field. After ten years of working for ICC and increasing the company's wealth, Tom Kettlewell decided to break free and establish his own enterprise. His area of specialism came to fruition in the '*yuppie*' 1980s.

The Thatcher Government's monetarist policies led to a 'survival of the fittest' mentality, that pitted stock prices against workers and local communities. Its outlook meant a small state and a mind-set that led the Prime Minister Thatcher to famously declare, "There is no such thing as society". Dennis Kettlewell's prediction about the Consett Steelworks proved to be accurate. It closed in 1980 with the loss of almost four thousand jobs. Closure was a direct result of Thatcher's policies and was perceived nationally as part of her attack on the unionised working class.

After the closure of the steel works, Tom's home town became one of the worst unemployment black spots in Britain, with 36 percent out of work in 1981, three times the year's national average. The devastation to the community of Consett was apocalyptic. Those people who did not move away, were inevitably placed in financial difficulties. Retailers and service providers in the locality suffered hardship. It had a shattering effect on Dennis Kettlewell, for whom Thatcherism was the total antithesis of everything he believed and represented.

Meanwhile, the opportunities the era offered his son, brought huge rewards. Tom's ambition thrived in a business world where hard work brought unparalleled benefits. The move towards *e-trading* meant Tom's skills and those of his company, *TDVK Solutions,* were constantly in demand. During the mid-1980s, he was sufficiently astute to capture some of the world's best talent in computer programming, maintaining the Company's momentum. When the culture of commerce started to change in the 1990s, with instant communication through email and the development of the Internet, he was ready to take advantage. His prediction about personal computers and a *Third Industrial Revolution* based around computer technology was about to explode exponentially. The *'Millennium Bug'* issue alone, had commanded a sum of almost two million pounds for *TDVK Solutions*. Allowing for overheads, this would bring a bonus of just over one million pounds to his personal wealth and it was not the only major contract he was working on. Tom Kettlewell would soon be at the point where his riches would give him the power he had always wanted.

II

Tom pulled up to the house quietly, parked the car and gently closed the driver's door after switching off the headlights. It was only seven-thirty in the morning and he was anxious not to disturb anyone at home. The all-night light was still shining in the Annex so he decided to call there first. The agency worker, who he had not met, would no doubt still be waiting for Sylvia to arrive; she was due to take-over at eight o'clock. Sylvia had been working for Tom and his father for twelve years. She was almost part of the family, a dumpy, irrepressible atom bomb of care and efficiency, who made a great nurse.

Tom went around the back, conscious that his steps were making too much noise, scrunching across the gravel path. Arriving at the white side-door of the Annex, where his father now lived, he could see through the small window into the light of the room. The agency nurse was sitting on a chair in the corner of the kitchen, wearing her cape, ready to go home. Tom always used the same agency when there was a change in circumstances and neither he nor Sylvia were able to be at the house for the night. This nurse was new to the routine and was drinking what appeared to be her final cup of coffee, before the end of a triple-overtime shift. The unknown employee was in the starting blocks, ready to leave as soon as relief came. Tom entered the bijou, functional kitchen, without waiting for a response to his courteous knock on the door. The Annex was his own place, after all. He had extended onto the main part of *Derwent House* in order to satisfy his Dad's requirements. Dennis Kettlewell had been more than welcome to live in the main house, but he did not get on well with Tom's wife.

'How's he been?' asked Tom, who quickly continued with, 'I'm Tom, his son. You are …?' Tom extended his hand, while the nurse tried to push her heavy uniform up and out of the seat. She offered him a limp, nervous handshake.

'Nurse Atkins... Gaynor Atkins.' She stood and they shook hands politely. 'Pleased to meet you, Mr Kettlewell. Yes, he's been fine. He got a little restless at about five o'clock but soon went back to sleep.'

The light blue uniform was occupied by a smart-looking lady, about sixty-years-old, who had once worked as a Theatre Sister in a London hospital but had signed-up to the Agency in order to supplement her low pension. Her husband Ivor had passed away two years earlier but left very little to support her. Gaynor Atkins' attendance at the Kettlewell residence on New Year's Eve was motivated solely by cash. She would rather have spent the New Year in Shrewsbury with her son and grandchildren but had not been invited.

'Good. That's good. You can go now, er.. Nurse Atkins, if you want. I can wait until Sylvia arrives. She will see to him. He's used to her after all this time.' There was no attempt to resist. With a brief smile, the Nurse hoisted the strap of her heavy medical bag over her shoulder and without looking back, left the Annex. The back door was closed more loudly than it had been opened a few minutes earlier. In the stillness of the twilight, Tom could hear the fading scrunching noise of Gaynor Atkins's footsteps heading dejectedly homeward.

Before sitting down, Tom quietly made his way to his Dad's bedroom. He slowly turned the handle until the mechanism clicked. This allowed him to open the door silently and he almost got as far as entry width when the hinge squeaked, causing him to whisper a curse. The noise was a reminder to put some oil on that joint, something he had been intending to do for weeks. Tom's Dad was fast asleep, lying peacefully with the back of his head resting on the pillow. He seemed almost restrained by the blankets, tucked so tight that they appeared to embalm his skeletal figure. Dennis had always refused a duvet, preferring the extra comfort and security that blankets afforded. He had enjoyed several layers on his bed since the nights of his youth.

Tom looked at his ageing, broken father and stared at the dendritic pattern of mini, red veins on his nose, the tell-tale signs of his ill-health. His hollowed cheeks and blue lips were more specific in their diagnosis. Ever since his heart attack in 1985, Tom had cared for his Dad. It was one of the reasons for setting-up his own business. Although it meant a greater workload and more stress, the extra money and more flexible working conditions enabled him to provide better care for Dennis.

As Tom stood beside the bed in the red, half-light, he stared at the body of his sleeping father. Tom's face showed no emotion as he became lost in memories of when his Dad looked more like himself. It was no wonder Dennis's heart had collapsed under the strain of 1985. The whole of that decade had been cruel to his father.

His anger at the devastation of his home community in Consett during the early 1980s was only the beginning of Dennis's pain. It was three years after the closure of the steelworks and Dennis was returning from a Saturday morning visit to the Reservoir after buying some groceries in the main street. Carrying his plastic bag over one forearm, he turned the key in the Yale lock of his terraced home as he had done many times before. When he entered the hallway, Dennis thought it was just going to be another, ordinary day. Expertly, he removed his cloth cap and scarf, placing the grocery bag under the mirror of the brown wooden stand, above the coat-hooks. 'It's only me!' he called, 'Fancy a *cuppa*?' Without waiting for a response he went into the kitchen and carried on going about his business. The hiss of rushing cold water from the tap echoed in the small room as he filled the kettle and emptied his favourite tartan shopping bag containing potatoes, bread and two tins of tomato soup. Dennis continued his one-sided conversation in a reassuring tone, while placing his spoils onto the kitchen's work-surface.

Wiping his hands on the tea-towel, he entered the living room to double-check if Betty wanted a *cuppa* or not. In his preoccupation to fulfil his routine, he had not heard her response. Soothing orchestral music on Radio 2 was wafting through the doorway and Dennis assumed Betty was asleep. He approached the armchair, intending to plant a gentle kiss on his wife's cheek, while she rested. As he got closer, he knew something was wrong. Her eyes were open but they stared forward without focus. The remnant of a tear stained the right side of her face.

Dennis took her hand and tried to feel for a pulse. Instinctively, he knew it was futile. Her wrist still felt warm and for a moment he dared to hope that she could be saved. He turned and ran quickly to the phone, realising the need to keep his wits about him. After dialling 999 and garbling his message, Dennis lifted the latch on the front door and returned to his wife. He went to say her name but his lips simply pursed and the air exuded from his mouth without a sound. It was an inner, silent scream of pain. He put his hands under Betty's arms and lifted her forward, causing her head to flop onto his shoulder, confirming his worst fears. She was dead.

Dennis Kettlewell held his soulmate in their last, private embrace together, alone as man and wife for a final moment. They had been married for thirty-four years and for sixteen of those years, illness had left her debilitated. Diabetes had ravaged her middle age and their life together was irrevocably changed because of the disease. At first, she had been able to cope, self-administering insulin and maintaining exercise and a semi-healthy diet. As complications developed, her mobility and general health deteriorated. She had borne it all with courage. The condition had included the loss of an increasing numbers of toes, before the amputation of her right leg below her knee. What had started as resting for comfort became a routine of resting for necessity as Betty's leg became more ulcerated. Tom was unaware of many of her hospital visits following his graduation. The incumbent pain and the humiliation of being incapacitated as a wife and mother were kept secret from her son.

Dennis muffled his sobs into his wife's shoulder as he held her tightly one last time. The tears flowed from a man who had already seen life at its worst. Dennis had met Betty Cartwright at a Works Dance in Newcastle during the Christmas celebrations of 1948. Her flaming red-hair and bright green dress had set her apart, as he watched her dance to the sound of Henry Hall's Orchestra playing *"The Way You Look Tonight"*. He defied his friend's jibes and crossed the floor of the *Leccano* to ask her to dance. They waltzed the rest of the night together and he discovered that she was from a mining family in Annfield Plain, about six miles from Consett. After walking her to the last bus and stealing a goodnight kiss that evening, they started courting. Only one month later, they were engaged and subsequently married in August 1949, before Thomas Dennis Victor Kettlewell entered the world at seven pounds three ounces in October. Their life together had been the best thing in her husband's life. Now it was suddenly over.

Dennis was oblivious to the loud noise of the ambulance's siren as it made its way towards his street. Most of the local children playing nearby ran towards its heralding call. Some even moved their fingers to their shirt-necks, reciting the local spell, as they did whenever an ambulance was spotted: *'Touch yer colla, never swalla, never catch a feva'*. The silence generated by the siren being switched off snapped Dennis back into reality. He looked up and saw the flashing blue light outside, through the living room window. There was a loud knock, followed by an authoritative call as the front door was pushed open, 'Hello ... anybody there?'

As Dennis called out in desperation, 'We're in here!' the paramedics entered the room and instantly assumed responsibility for the situation. Dennis was forced to release his embrace and stood back, brushing back his hair with his fingers in anxious frustration. He stood in reverent silence while the main medic tried to find a pulse. Within seconds of the ambulance man's examination, the local doctor called; Dr Tomkinson had been alerted while on a visit to a patient nearby. He took-out his stethoscope and began to examine Betty. After a couple of endless minutes, he turned to her husband and said, 'I'm sorry Dennis. She's gone, I'm afraid. I'm so sorry.'

Dennis turned away and grabbed the window sill as tightly as he could. His body went rigid with grief, before his head bowed and he sobbed. The scene through the net curtains meant nothing to him. The local policeman had just arrived outside the front door and was getting off his motor bike. While hoisting one leg over the petrol tank, the bobby's voice boomed to the scrummaging kids. 'There's nothing to see here. You kids get off home. If I see any of yer after I've counted to ten I'll be visiting your homes. I know where yer all live.' He raised his right arm and extended it fully three times as if he was ushering sheep into a pen. The threat of a policeman's visit was enough to deter the youngsters. They knew that it meant subsequent action from their parents so the curious group dispersed.

The doctor's attention was directed at the distressed husband. 'Is there anyone we can call for you, Dennis ? What about Tom? Where is he at the moment ? Would you like us to contact him for you ?' Dr Tomkinson had known Dennis and his family for many years, even before Betty's diabetes had required regular visits. Although he could be a cold fish at times, the gesture he made by resting his hand on Dennis's shoulder, conveyed more affection than he realised.

It was all Dennis could do not to break down totally. Confused, frightened and distraught, the man who had berated the insensitivity of six-figure-sum bosses, who had laid down the law to local councillors and risen above the integrity of so-called professionals, was now broken. 'No. ... I'll call our Tommy... What happens next ?'

Dr Tomkinson reverted to his professional persona and calmly explained everything to Dennis. 'Because I've seen Mrs Kettlewell in the last week following her mini-stroke and as she has been treated recently for her diabetes, I can sign the Death Certificate here and now, as her GP. I can declare it as an expected death. That means things can go ahead without any complications.' The reality of the phrase, *expected death* almost made Dennis faint. 'You'll be able to call a funeral director straight away. He'll make the necessary arrangements and discuss things with you. Unless you'd like us to get hold of someone to be with you now?' Dennis shook his head.

Within ten minutes the street outside returned to its former routine. The children and passers-by, who had been attracted by the flashing blue lights, had now returned to their business. One of Dennis's immediate neighbours offered to stay and help but she could tell that he wanted to be left on his own.

As Dennis closed the front door on the cruel world, his forehead slumped heavily onto its wooden interior with a loud thud. Returning the latch to its former position, he was able to keep all potential visitors away. His left hand moved slowly down the door's frame and the smoothness of the varnish felt reassuring. It was something normal in his world, which had just been destroyed. How was he going to tell his son the news of his mother's death ? He turned from the door and went into the kitchen. Dennis picked-up the kettle, which was still touch-warm from his earlier effort to make his wife a cup of tea. Was it really just those few minutes ago ? Somehow he made himself a hot drink but stayed in the kitchen to finish it after scooping in three spoons of sugar : he was not yet ready to return to the lounge, where his wife remained in her chair.

After three sips, he placed the cup on the work-surface and went to the hallway in order to telephone his son with the news. Tom was working at ICC's UK Headquarters in Slough, when he took the call from his father. His reaction was a mixture of shock, agony and relief that his mother's suffering was over. He replaced the receiver and sat motionless for about five minutes. The pain was too deep for tears. Tom took his wallet from his inside breast-pocket and opened it slowly. There, behind a small rectangular, clear plastic insert, he gazed at the photograph he always carried. It was taken in 1956 at White City in Whitley Bay, when the three family members had enjoyed a glorious summer day. Standing in the middle, a young Tom in shorts, held a '*Ninety-Nine*' ice cream up to the cameraman, while his laughing parents had their arms around him and held him close. It was one of the few photographs Tom had of his mother, where she looked well. Gently, he removed it from his wallet and lightly rubbed his thumb over his mother's beautiful face, before holding the image to his lips.

Realising he had to snap out of it for his father's sake, he picked up the phone once more and contacted Consett's main Funeral Director, on his Dad's behalf. Terence Ferris and Sons were extremely sympathetic, no doubt being able to fake sincerity through years of practice. Mrs Ferris, who took the call, informed Tom they would visit the home within the hour and Tom should telephone his father to let him know. The Funeral Director would explain everything to Mr Kettlewell on arrival and she would report back to Tom, following the visit.

Delicately and reverently, after contacting his son, Dennis walked from the hall into the open doorway of the lounge. He wiped his mouth with his left hand, drying his flooded eyes with the striped handkerchief that he had ironed only yesterday. Slowly, he crossed the room and approached Betty, whose eyes had been closed by the GP ; she looked at peace. Dennis took her hand and brought it to his cheek before placing a loving kiss on her wedding ring. Then, he stroked her hair and caressed the fading red locks with his fingers. He kissed her forehead before placing his brow on her bosom, as he recalled some treasured memories of their many years together.

The hour passed in seconds and soon he heard a knock at the front door. The purpose of the black van parked outside his house, which he viewed through the living room window, was clear. In the circumstances, Mr Ferris and his son dealt with the matter with minimal pain. Dennis supposed their years of experience had to count for something. He had seen Terry Ferris sometimes in the Club but only knew him in passing, although they were a similar age. Mr Ferris's son advised Dennis to wait in the kitchen, claiming it was best if the Funeral Directors saw to Mrs

Kettlewell on their own. When the body trolley left through the front door, it was the last time that Betty would depart the family home.

Dennis was left in the house alone and distraught. He went upstairs and lay on Betty's side of the bed in a state of stunned grief. Meanwhile, Tom made his way back to Consett in his red *Ford EXP* as fast as he could, to be with his Dad. Tom instructed his staff to cancel all his appointments for the next three days or deal with any issues themselves. Throughout Tom's journey back to Consett he maintained contact with Dennis on his *Nokia* mobile phone, which he kept on the passenger seat, within easy reach. He instructed his Dad to call him at any time during his journey home, for any reason. When he finally arrived at the family home late that evening, Tom was broken-hearted to see his father wracked with the emotional destruction caused by the death of his beloved wife.

Tom stayed longer than expected. It took a week to accommodate his mother's funeral and cremation. Then he knew he had to return South. Although it was not practical for Dennis to live with his son at the time, Tom made the offer which his Dad declined. Dennis did not want to intrude on Tom's personal life. They returned to their separate worlds at opposite ends of the country. In Consett, Dennis suddenly found himself abandoned and at sixty-five years-of-age, it seemed as if his future life would be without direction or purpose.

That changed a year later when Dennis became involved in events surrounding the Miners' Strike. In March 1984, the National Coal Board announced its intention to close twenty coal mines, including some in the North East, with a long-term plan to close seventy pits altogether. A week after the announcement, the President of the National Union of Mineworkers, called for a national strike. Such disruption had been avoided in 1981, when coal stocks were low and the Government did not have the upper-hand. This time around, Prime Minister Thatcher was fully prepared for a confrontation, .

For Dennis Kettlewell, there was suddenly a new-found purpose in his life, during the Miners' Strike. He had seen his own steel industry and town murdered by Thatcher and he was not prepared to stand-by idly and let the same fate befall local coal mining communities. Even though he was passed his prime, Dennis was prepared to give what little fight remained. If it meant taking the battle to the pits and picketing *'scabs'* he was prepared to engage. If it meant 'secondary picketing' of the haulage firms, whether it was legal or not, he was prepared. If it meant joining groups of 'flying pickets' and descending on the homes of politicians, industrial leaders or individual '*scabs*,' then so be it. He was prepared to join rallies, attend hustings and support voluntary groups to ensure victory for his class over a Government that cared more about rewarding individual speculators than it did about communities in its own country. It was important to show that the whole was greater than the sum of its parts. Dennis Kettlewell had a sense of direction, once more.

Most of the mines in the area were in the eastern part of the region, near the coast. For Dennis, picketing meant catching buses from local pick-up points near Consett and joining the throngs of miners on the picket-lines. He spent more time at Easington than anywhere else. Easington Colliery was a thriving mine and its removal from production could have a greater effect of coal reserves than smaller mines. Using his expertise as a former union leader, he organised food distribution for miners' families and galvanised local opinion by speaking at rallies. The fever pitch of screaming abuse at hauliers as they left the mines with lorry loads of coal and throwing missiles at the wire mesh covering their windscreens, did little to help his blood pressure. He found no difficulty in abusing police officers, who he regarded as the System's lackeys.

Tom's view of the Thatcher years was different to his father and he saw no hypocrisy in exploiting the situation to his own advantage. If Thatcher's Government wanted to reward greed, he was prepared to be greedy. If it allowed him to accumulate wealth, he would seize the opportunity. There had once been a time when Tom had a moral conscience over such matters but his views had changed because his life had been scarred. Better to look after number one, these days. Nobility had its place, just not in *his* life any more. The principles in Tom's morality account were stored somewhere in his life's safety deposit box. They had been stowed since 1970 and it was doubtful they would ever see the light of day again.

After a year of bitterness and political upheaval, the coal miners' strike ended in March 1985. It was seen as a major political victory for Thatcher and her Tory Government and a devastating blow for the Trade Union movement. For those with the values held so preciously by Dennis Kettlewell, it was an insurmountable, gut-wrenchingly, bitter defeat.

Two months after the strike ended, Dennis Kettlewell suffered his first heart-attack. He was walking down the main street in his hometown when a searing pain thundered in his chest, accompanied by severe tingling in his left arm. He could not catch his breath and felt overcome with a sense of sickness. Dennis slumped to his knees and was immediately surrounded by a circle of helpers, who ensured assistance came straight away. He spent nearly ten weeks in Dryburn Hospital in Durham and endured two major operations and countless procedures. It took another month in a private convalescent home and extensive physiotherapy, before he was in any fit state to live on his own or become anything like his former self. The financial cost of his recovery was borne by Tom.

At first, Dennis insisted on living in his own home. Tom paid for a package of care support, which saw people visit his Dad on a daily basis. Tom felt it was important that Dennis was allowed to surround himself with familiar things. It was only a question of time before reality kicked-in and it became necessary for Dennis to live with his son. The family home in Consett was sold and Dennis's few possessions were moved into the Annex of the home Tom had recently purchased in Loughton, Essex. It was probably for the best, as witnessing the further deterioration of Consett would have destroyed what remained of his Dad's heart.

In the Annex of *Derwent House*, Tom continued to watch his father's peaceful slumber, while also feeling the need to rest. By this time, he had sat in the chair next to his Dad's bed, fighting sleep. After sitting with his tie undone, resting his *Armani* jacket on his lap for about twenty minutes, he was about to nod-off when his Dad began to stir. Tom was just going to say something, when he heard the main front door to the Annex open after being assaulted by a key turning in the lock. Sylvia burst into the bedroom and instantly assumed command. Acknowledging defeat without making a sound, Tom stood and pressed his Dad's shoulder, leaving him and his carer to carry on with their morning rituals. Holding his jacket as if it was a precious child, Tom acknowledged Sylvia before turning to leave his Dad's bedroom. He needed sleep more than ever and he wanted the remainder of this first new morning in the noughties to consist only of blackness.

Tom decided to take the quick route to the main house, rather than go back outside. He crossed the link-corridor and walked along the plush red carpet. About half-way across the passage, a floorboard squeaked and he wondered why he was trying to keep quiet. He was not even sure if there was anyone else in the main house. Rather than take the risk of upsetting his partner Geraldine, Tom turned in a different direction at the end of the passageway at the top of the stairs and slipped into one of the guest bedrooms. Within seconds he was in state of innocent nothingness once more.

III

The first week of the new millennium marked Dennis Kettlewell's eightieth birthday and Tom knew exactly what to do. He had been planning the occasion for a couple of months, and finally got his hands on what he had been searching for. The morning of the big day arrived; it was a Sunday. Sylvia escorted Dennis into the main kitchen at about eight-thirty, first ensuring he was appropriately washed and dressed. Tom was in the process of making bacon butties. He was grilling the bacon to within an inch of its life, ensuring it was frazzled and crisp, just how his Dad liked it.

Dennis was helped to his seat by Sylvia, who took his arm, as he shuffled across the tiled floor, dragging his slippers over the smooth surface. He sat on one of the wicker-backed seats and his hands dropped onto the glass-topped table with a plop. Dennis surveyed the table and spied fresh orange juice, a jug of milk, a steaming coffee percolator as well as a basket of croissant and fruit, with all the attendant cutlery and crockery.

He turned to observe his son, who was picking the slices of Danish from the grill pan with a pair of large silver tongs. Tom dropped several slices onto the warm crusty bread that he had just opened with a super sharp kitchen knife. 'Who are you expectin' Tommy. The Queen ?'

'No Dad, the King is coming for breakfast today and that's you mate.' Presenting the large, gold rimmed plate on the table, with its two tempting rolls, Tom continued. 'There you are Dad, get that down you and you'll be off to a good start to the day. What would you like with it, fruit juice, milk or coffee or perhaps all three today, your majesty ?'

Dennis watched his son busy himself and fuss over his breakfast service. As he sat with one elbow on the glass-topped kitchen table, he was feeling pretty good about life after being tantalised by one of his favourite breakfast aromas. He was also a little excited about what the day had in store. The details of Tom's plan were unknown but Dennis always enjoyed nice surprises. While Sylvia and Tom scurried about his every whim, he listened to the *Terry Wogan Breakfast Show* on the radio, tapping his fingers on the table to the rhythm of *Blue's* record by singing the chorus, dabadee-dabadeye, dabadee-dabadeye over and over. The tune had clearly got inside his head.

'Happy birthday, old man,' declared Tom, mocking himself more than his father. Tom was bending slightly at the knees, in order to see inside the eye-level grill to make sure it was switched off. The fact that he was wearing a joke apron that made him look like *Mr Universe* from the front, added to the mood in the kitchen. Sylvia was quietly placing anything dirty into the washing up bowl, leaving father and son to their games.

'Thanks, son. This looks champion, ... bacon and fresh rolls ? Must be me birthday.' Dennis raised his arms as if he had just scored a goal. Tom reached across to the radio and adjusted the volume downwards. Looking over to his Dad he raised his thumb before smelling the air and blowing a fake kiss across with his hand, as if to say the meal was ' *Wunderbar.*'

'Just this once with the bacon, mind. You won't be getting it every day', insisted Sylvia, who did not share their jocularity. She was resting against the kitchen sink, arms folded. 'You know your doctor does not like you eating fatty foods.' Sylvia was never off-duty.

This was not a sequence of verbal banter that Dennis was prepared to abandon. 'Yeah, but what's the point of reaching eighty if you're miserable and starving ? Anyway, I bet Dr What's-his-name has never had a bacon butty. Our Tom was brought up on them, in the good old days.' Sylvia nodded upwards, in acceptant defiance.

Tom pulled out the pan containing the burnt rejects sitting on top of the wire insert tray. He banged it down onto the unlit gas cooker hobs making a noise like a dinner gong. 'Christ, that was hot !'

'Don't blaspheme,' reprimanded his father. ' Now, I'd just like a nice cup of that lovely coffee that you make for us, Tommy lad. And a bit quicker on the service, or I'll send you to the Bloody Tower.' Dennis was enjoying the whole scene.

'I'll get it, before his language gets any worse,' interrupted Sylvia, trying to make herself useful. She poured the coffee into Dennis's special mug, with its large double handles. She knew enough to avoid the sugar and the cream. There were such things as going too far, birthday or no birthday.

Dennis looked at his son and raised his eyes to the ceiling. As Tom looked down at his father, he could see a problem through the glass table. Dennis was sitting with his legs wide apart, in a relaxed state. The problem was that his flies were undone and parts of his underpants were sticking out on parade. 'You'd better zip that thing up an'all or I'll be sending you to the guillotine.' Without any embarrassment or fuss he zipped himself back to a level of decency. 'Nobody's ganna be bothered by that, these days, so dinnit fret, lad.'

Changing the subject, Sylvia inquired about Tom's intentions for the day. 'I know he's got an exciting day planned for you, Dennis but I don't want you over-doing it. I remember the last time you two went out together. You were exhausted the next day. Take it easy. You can still enjoy it.' Sylvia wagged her finger, in a semi-serious manner.

Dennis sprayed a few crumbs as he spoke with a mouthful of fresh roll. 'I've got no idea what's happening, bonny lass. I don't even know who's going'. He looked at his son with inquisitive cheekiness and raised his shoulders in a shrug.

'It's just the two of us, if you're asking. And I'll look after him, Sylvia. Don't you worry. We're not going far and we should be back at lunchtime. It'll be getting dark around three o'clock anyway. It doesn't look particularly pleasant outside. It's dull and windy, but at least it's dry.' Tom could not say what he was really thinking. He could not have wished for better weather at that time of year, for his plan to work. 'If you could leave something cold out for us, thanks Sylvia and we'll see to ourselves when we return. Then just go home for the rest of the day. There's no need to wait for us coming back. I can see to my Dad.'

'Well if you're sure. Have a great day then, Dennis. And happy birthday, again my darling boy. I'll come back and make something before you return.' With that, she planted a great big kiss on his forehead, followed by the '*Mwaaa*' sound she tended to make on such occasions. As she withdrew, Dennis's arm flowed down her own until their fingers touched.

'See you tomorrow, Sylv. Be good,' demanded Dennis as she strode across the large kitchen floor. How Dennis wished he had been saying the same thing to Betty. It was becoming more difficult to remember those days and he even wondered for a second if they had ever existed. Sylvia exited through the white door, crossed into the main part of the house and put on her coat. Within a few minutes, she had left.

It was time to get the show on the road so Tom asked his Dad which car he would like to use. 'Let's take the *Lexus GS*, Tommy. That's a lovely car. There's plenty of room to stretch my legs and it's nice and smooth and quiet. Yeah, let's take that one.'

'Ok, we'll take that one. Your wish is my command. You just sit there a few minutes and I'll load the dishwasher and have a bit of a tidy-up. Mrs Watkins will be here in the morning to do most of the cleaning but we need to make some effort, I suppose.' Mrs Watkins was the cleaner who came three times a week. Tom did not expect Sylvia to do everything. As far as he was concerned, her main priority was seeing to his father's needs.

Dennis sat watching in the chair as his son efficiently whisked around the beautifully fitted, modern kitchen, until the place looked tidy, once more. 'Right. I'm just going to bring the car round to the front and then we'll be off. Just wait there and I'll be back in a jiffy.' Tom stood behind Dennis and patted his shoulders.

As good as his word, within ten minutes they were driving out through the main gates, the two men sharing a special occasion together. Dennis loved these times and he enjoyed travelling in the *Lexus*. 'It always smells lovely in here,' he said. 'It's as if you've just brought it back from the dealers on the first day. Takes me back.' Tom smiled.

As they smoothed out of Loughton, Dennis observed the changing scene through the passenger side window and asked about his son's current domestic situation. 'Yeah, work is going well, thanks Dad. The business is thriving and the future is bright. I think we're going to be ahead of the game with something that's happening at the moment. I don't know if you've heard of the Internet ?'

'Sort of, but that's not what I meant. How are things between you and *her*? Has she been treating you any better ?' He pointed his jiggling thumb back towards the house, like an enthusiastic hitch-hiker.

'*She* has a name, Dad.'

'Ok. How are things between you and Geraldine ? I haven't seen her since the day before New Year. Not that I'm complaining, mind. Has she gone off somewhere, again ?'

'She has flown out to Paris for a few days early this morning, with some of her friends. They've gone shopping.'

'Yes. With your money, no doubt.'

'That's between me and Geraldine, Dad. I don't mind about the money.' The tone in his son's voice persuaded Dennis to leave that particular topic of conversation. He turned to puzzle at the view and silently tried to work out where they were heading.

They were gliding down anonymous country lanes, with no indication of a destination until Dennis spotted a broken sign that simply read 'RAF ...' He could not fathom whether they were going to an aerodrome or to a farm and was totally bemused. They pulled up to an old barn of a building that looked like a dilapidated aeroplane hangar. Tom sounded the horn and a young man in overalls came around the corner, smiling as he walked towards them.

'Hello, Tom. Glad you found us ok.' He shook Tom's hand and then turned his attention to Dennis. ' Hello, Mr Kettlewell, happy birthday, sir.' It had been a while since anyone referred to Dennis as *sir*.

'Er, yes, ... thanks. You are ...?' Dennis was confused.

'I'm Harry, Mr Kettlewell. I'm a client of your son. He helped me buy this place. It used to be the site of RAF Loughton. I'm going to develop it, over the next few years, hopefully.' Dennis stood looking at Harry in total bewilderment. Harry then turned to face Tom. 'It's around the side, Tom. It's come out really well.'

'What has ?' asked Dennis, becoming more and more frustrated.

'Come and see, Dad. It's your birthday surprise. Come on, let's take a look at it.' Tom took his father's arm and escorted him the ten yards to the side of the barn. There was a tarpaulin draped over something resembling a car. As Dennis stared in a continued state of confusion, Tom took one end of the sheet, while Harry grabbed the other.

Then suddenly, they lifted the tarpaulin together, revealing the big surprise. 'There you are, Dad. Happy birthday.'

Dennis could not believe what he was looking at. His eyes began to well-up and it felt like he had been taken back in time. The object of his attention appeared to be brand new but clearly that could not be the case. In front of him, there it was again – a bright, shiny blue 1965 Humber Sceptre Mk 3. How could this be? Surely it was not the same car as the one he used to drive around Consett ? Dennis was totally stunned and raising his right arm, he pointed at the car in total unspeakable silence. Eventually, he had to say something.

'It's my car. It's my car... Is it ?'

Tom put his arm around his Dad's shoulders and gave him a squeeze. 'I've been looking for one for a few months, Dad. Eventually I found this Humber advertised in an auction, in Darlington of all places. It needed a bit of work doing to it but that was no problem. The finishing touch was the re-spray. This is the first time I've seen it since it's been painted. They've done a good job on it, as well. Do you like it ?'

'Like it ? Like it ? ... are you crazy ? I bloody love it. Oh, Tommy, lad. You did this for me ? It's fantastic!' Dennis showed signs of breaking down as he looked up into his son's beaming face. Then he was overtaken by a sense of glee and he clapped his hands together and rubbed them in a rush of excitement. He took a step closer and reached out to touch his gift, hardly daring to believe it was real.

'I'm glad you like it, Dad. Harry has been helping me get it here. I knew he had bought the old aerodrome and would have some storage room. He was more than willing to help out. Happy birthday, Dad.'

'Thanks, Tommy. Thanks Harry. Can I get in it ?'

'Course you can. It's your car, after all.'

Dennis opened the car door as if he was opening a beaded curtain in Aladdin's cave. He remembered the familiar clunk from younger days as he engaged the door-handle. With a little help from his son, he sat in the driver's seat and shuffled across the leather with all the excitement of a child. He put both hands on the steering wheel in the twelve o'clock position and then moved each one in the opposite direction, as if caressing a memory. His eyes explored the interior. The walnut dashboard was there, with the Roman numeral clock dividing the pull levers for air conditioning and the heater. It was all in the right place. Tom had sidled alongside into the passenger seat, almost unnoticed.

Then Dennis started to boast about his present. 'Look at that walnut panelling. Quality. Not like your modern rubbish,' declared Dennis.

'Start it up, then,' ordered Tom. It was role reversal as son and father re-played a former childhood Christmas together, when Santa had brought Tommy a new train set.

'What you mean I can turn it over ?' asked Dennis, anxious to receive a positive response.

'No. I mean you can drive it.'

This was a step too far for Dennis. He could not believe what his son was saying. 'But I haven't got a licence. I'm not supposed to drive,' he said defensively.

'Just as well we're on an aerodrome with some disused runways then, isn't it. Why do you think I chose this place ? You can drive it, if you want. That's why we're here. It's your birthday. Come on then, what's the matter ? Forgotten what to do ?'

'Haddaway, lad. It'll be like riding a bike.'

Dennis turned the ignition key and the car started immediately. 'Listen to that. It's music to me ears. I never thought I would ever hear it again.'

'Right, what are we waiting for. Take it away, driver.'

With that final invitation, Dennis mastered the take-off. Stretching in front of them was about two miles of old runway, in a matrix that constituted almost four miles of track. Without having to worry about other cars, pedestrians or the police, Dennis was free to indulge in one of his favourite pleasures once again.

'Oh, Tommy-lad, this is great. What a car. It's just like my old one. Not quite as quiet mind.' He shot his son a quick, impish look, before continuing . 'But it'll do.'

After about twenty minutes of exploring the tarmac wasteland, Dennis's confidence grew and he was manoeuvring the car along like a veteran. Tom observed his father carefully during his imaginary *grand prix* and saw a fire re-ignite in his eyes. The look was something that had been missing since the days of his first heart attack and just for a short while, his Dad was whole again. Tom was pleased he had followed his instincts and bought the car.

From the auction four months earlier, it had been lifted onto a trailer and taken to a specialist workshop in York. The Humber was given a complete overhaul, with re-tuning, parts' replacement and a full valet. When they asked him what colour he wanted to have the car re-sprayed, it was obvious. The look on his Dad's face when the tarpaulin was lifted, was a moment Tom would never forget. The whole business cost about twenty thousand pounds. It was cheap at the price.

Tom could see that the experience was reaching the threshold of his father's concentration capabilities so they pulled alongside the barn and Dennis turned-off the ignition. Once more, his Dad rubbed his hands together with excitement. 'That was great. I can't begin to tell you what that meant to me. I only wish yer Mam could have been in the back, with us.'

'Maybe she was, Dad. Maybe she was.'

Dennis looked across at his son with immense pride. He took Tom's hand in both of his own and rubbed it with affection. Although his body was ravaged, there was still some of the old spirit left.

'Thanks Tommy. That was lovely. I ... I ...'

'It's ok, Dad. ... I know.' Harry approached and opening the driver's door, he helped Dennis to get out of the car, while Tom came around from the passenger's side. 'How was that, Mr Kettlewell ?' asked Harry, with a slither of enthusiasm of his own.

'As they say where I come from, Harry. It was champion'.

'Well, anytime Tom wants to bring you over just give me a ring and we'll set it up for you.'

'You mean I can do it again ?'

'Course you can. It's your car,' repeated Tom. 'Harry will keep it stored inside for us. Anytime we can swing it, we'll come over and you can drive the Humber again. Time is the thing but I'm sure we'll work something out.

'Oh, that'll be great. Thanks Tommy. Thanks Harry. It's been magic.'

'Anytime, Mr K. Anytime at all. I'm glad you enjoyed it.'

Tom approached Harry and shook his hand warmly. 'Thanks Harry. I'll be in touch.'

'Pleasure, Tom. I'm pleased it worked out so well.'

As Tom and his Dad made their way back home to Loughton, Dennis could not stop talking about the car and how it was just a little different to his magnificent original. After five minutes of nodding in agreement and defending his own beautiful automobile, Tom looked across to the passenger seat, where his Dad had fallen asleep. A few more miles later, the noise of driving over the gravel at the Loughton mansion broke Dennis's slumber. The light was fading and Tom helped his father to the living room in his Annex, where Dennis fell into his favourite armchair.

Tom nipped into the kitchen and found two plates of salad covered with cling-film, sitting on a pair of lap –trays : they had been prepared earlier for the duo by Sylvia. It was not far from Tom's kitchen to the part of the building that he had converted for his father.

This would be Dennis's last burst of energy before he would retire for the day, exhausted. The two of them sat in the small, cosy room, sharing the warm comfort together. The television was switched on but neither was watching it with any sense of purpose. The intimacy of their conversation continued. 'Thanks for today, Tommy. I really enjoyed it. It's just a pity that your Mam could not be there.' His son made no attempt at a response this time. 'She would have been really proud at just how successful you have become.' The BBC News was about to end and they were going to give the weather forecast for the South-East. During the lull, Dennis continued his interrogation. 'Are you happy, Tommy. I mean, despite the success, have you got what you have been working for ?'

'I'm ok, Dad, I suppose. What is happiness anyway ? Things between me and Geraldine are not great. She's always moaning about my late routine and how shattered I am when I come home. Trouble is, I can't help falling asleep in the armchair. I'm just knackered all the time. I can understand that if she hasn't seen me all day, she wants a piece of my time. I just don't have the energy. It's all I can do to keep going at work these days. This bloody shoulder of mine doesn't help either. I felt it again today when I closed the boot on the Humber.' He raised his elbow high and attempted a circular motion.

Dennis wanted to spread a little bit of poison. 'Thing is, she's not exactly the homely type is she ? She's hardly ever here and when she is, she doesn't have to do much. Mrs Watkins does all the cleaning and most of the cooking. Sylvia helps out and that bloke, what's his name, who does the gardening – Miller or whatever – he does the other stuff. It's different for you – you work. But her, she never needs to lift a finger.'

'Ok, Dad, that's enough for now. I know you don't like her but don't go running her down. Anyway, we should be thinking about getting you off for some rest. Come on, I'll take you into your bedroom. There's some clean pyjamas on top of the covers. Do you need a hand putting them on ?'

'It'll be a hot day in the Arctic before you will be helping me to get dressed, Tommy lad. I can manage.'

Twenty minutes later, Dennis was in bed, supported by a tailor-made back-pillow. Resting on top of the adjacent chest of drawers there was a book, open and spread-eagled, with its back and front covers showing. 'What's this you're reading ? Anything good ?' asked Tom, as he picked it up for examination.

'Yeah, it's not bad. Sylvia got it for me. It's called *'The Tipping Point'*. It's quite interesting, about how the world can be changed by things spreading like an epidemic.' Dennis regarded reading as a duty. It reminded the ruling class that they could not dictate a man's thoughts.

'Still trying to change the world, eh Dad ?' Tom handed his father the book and then tidied the bed covers, before kissing him on the side of his head and brushing his hand across his Dad's shoulders.

Tom left his Dad in bed and crossed the covered hallway back to the main living quarters, where he entered the lounge and sat on the cream leather sofa, after pouring himself a whisky from the globe-shaped, drinks cabinet. He took a quick sip and retreated to the kitchen where he grabbed some cubes from the ice-maker and dropped them into the crystal glass with two fingers. Returning to his seat, he looked around the lovely room, admiring a couple of original oil paintings and an oak coffee table that matched the various units, with cabinets and porcelain objects perfectly placed around the room. Tom drew the red velvet curtains and switched-on his own white, thirty-two inch *Philips* television, which sat above the tv cassette recorder in the corner of the room. He thought he could hardly tell Dennis that the room, like the rest of the house, had been decorated by Geraldine ; his Dad simply would not understand.

The trouble was that he knew Dennis was right in his assessment about everything. Tom was not happy and had not been content for many years. Success at work was his only satisfaction. As he placed his feet on the coffee table and took another sip of single-malt, he pondered the silence in the house.

Tom had met Geraldine three years earlier, after breaking-up from another girlfriend, whose make of car he could not accurately remember. She was one of many in a string of meaningless relationships at the time. Geraldine had been the P.A. of the Chairman of *Fitzer-Allens*, a trading company originally based in the Stock Exchange Tower. Tom and Geraldine first met when it was necessary to re-locate *Fitzer-Allens* in 1990 as a consequence of the IRA bomb explosion in the Exchange. *TDVK Solutions* was then a young, vibrant company, earning a good reputation with several big contracts in the City. Over meetings with the Chairman, Irving Spencer, there were occasions when Tom found himself discussing mundane matters with his Professional Assistant, referred to as Gerry by her boss. She was a divorced brunette with a stunning figure, perhaps a little too much lipstick but she exuded female charisma and reminded Tom of someone from his youth. They lost touch when business dealings were concluded but Tom had placed her in the 'possibles' category at the time.

They met again in 1995, when the Exchange launched the Alternative Investment Market, which allowed companies to expand their international markets. By the time the Electronic Trading Service was established two years later, they were an item. In 1998, Geraldine (as Tom preferred to call her) moved into his house in Loughton. Dennis did not welcome the move and regarded Tom's new partner as a 'gold digger', especially when she resigned from her job in 1999, supposedly to manage Tom's household and help run his business, although she never did.

His father had even preferred Tom's ex-wife, Felicity to his new partner. Dennis was pleased his son and Geraldine had not married and had chosen to simply live together. Dennis and Geraldine hardly spoke to each other so it was no surprise that she had cleared-off to Paris over the period of his eightieth birthday. It only amazed Dennis that she did not stay around to sabotage the event. Perhaps she considered that particular strategy would have been sailing too close to the wind because she knew how Tom felt about his father.

Whatever was going on, they were the only two people at home that evening. Tom decided to only have the one whisky as his thoughts tended to be maudlin whenever he over-indulged. Perhaps on this special occasion he could allow himself to remember the time which promised so much and he was genuinely happy. After gaining a first-class degree and having lots of choices at his fingertips, his professional and personal lives seemed to be wrapped in gold. It all turned sour because of one stupid event, one ridiculous mistake.

His eyes began to mist as he drifted into the world of what might have been. He slammed the crystal glass onto the coffee table, almost causing some of the ice to trampoline onto the oak surface. Angry at his own weakness, he got up from the leather seat and moved towards the main light-switch panel at the bottom of the stairs. He punched in the code to engage the alarm system and flicked the master switch that turned-off all unnecessary electric appliances in the main house. More swiftly than required, he ran up the stairs and entered the main bedroom. He used the facilities in the en-suite bathroom, before getting into the four-poster bed and lowering himself under the highly-togged duvet. As he lay there, Tom could only think that despite all the luxury, he had not progressed at all.

IV

The second week of the Millennium was a period of reflection for the way *TDVK Solutions* had handled the Y2K bug issue. Reports were collated by Phil Johnston and Samantha Walters, the twin guardians of Tom's empire. The three executives were in the Boss's office discussing the findings and this time the blinds were drawn. There were two plastic cups of half-drunk coffee on the desk, while Tom slowly sipped from his own mug, casually swivelling in the luxurious leather chair and contemplating his next move. The night of December 31st 1999 had been a challenging evening for the Company and just about everyone had performed well.

There was one exception. Three errors all came from the same desk. The radiation monitoring system at Bradness C Nuclear Power Station failed. Although there was no risk to the public, it caused panic to the technicians working at Bradness. In addition, some Sanjo mobile phones deleted new messages rather than old texts. Thirdly, the webpage of one naval military installation displayed the date of the first day of the Millennium as 01/01/19100. None of the mistakes were disastrous but they damaged the reputation of the Company. Even more frustrating was that none of them would have occurred if '*White Dove*' had been deployed correctly. Engagement of the algorithm came five seconds too late in each case. Gerald Finchley's mistakes were about to cost him his job.

'Generally his work is ok but he doesn't set the world on fire,' confided Phil, a thirty-two year-old former programmer. Phil had earned Tom's respect over many successful deals and felt sufficiently relaxed to have one shoe removed, as he scratched an itchy ankle.

'I understand he's had some problems at home recently. I think he's going through a divorce,' added Samantha, another of Tom's confidants. She was more aware of the need to demonstrate the appropriate body language when in a formal meeting with her boss, though she afforded herself a doodle on the notepad resting on her lap.

'Not interested,' insisted Tom, returning his mug to its desk coaster and rising from his chair with a burst of excess energy. He walked over to the window and focussed on the London Eye in the distance. 'Unless you can give me a better reason for keeping him on, he's down the road.'

His colleagues looked at each other briefly, defying the other to say something but they simply shrugged and offered no further defence. 'Ok, give me ten minutes and then send him in.' Phil and Samantha returned to their own area on the office floor. After a toilet visit, Samantha brushed her hair, straightened her skirt and headed towards Gerald Finchley's modern grey desk. He was engrossed in the contents shown on his screen and did not notice her approach. When she told him that Tom wanted a word, he got up and made his way to his office, immediately. Samantha followed unnoticed, until she overtook him at the door.

She ushered Finchley into Tom's office. Gerald was a bushy- haired, thick-spectacled young man, with a pasty complexion. He had gained an upper-second class honours degree in Computer Science from Oxford in 1996. A degree in the area of computers was something unavailable to Tom when he was at University. Computer courses were rarely taught in schools in the late 1960s and programming was mainly restricted to modules within the study of Mathematics. Gerald Finchley had progressed to the University from Leicester Grammar School, gaining the school's seventh scholarship to the dark blues. Gerald regarded himself as a successful programmer. He was from a lower middle-class background, a nice chap with a steely determination that he preferred to keep to himself.

'Sit down please, Gerald. I won't detain you long, ' said Tom, coldly. He neither minded or enjoyed this part of the job. In logical terms, it was simply necessary and more efficient than doing nothing.

'We've just had the reports back from the study of our coverage of the Millennium issue. There were only three errors made throughout the night and they're all yours.' He detailed the miscalculations and then prompted his employee with an icy stare. 'Anything to say ?'

'No, not really. I thought the programmes I ran in parallel to the mainframe problems would have sorted the issue in each case, so I held back *'White Dove'* until I was certain. Then the main programme was recovered and seemed to run ok.' Gerald thought his approach was good enough.

'Well clearly that lack of certainty created a mini-crash on three occasions, when it should not have done. I'm sorry, at *TDVK* we can't afford that kind of mistake. I'm going to have to let you go. Please clear your desk and say your goodbyes. You'll get two months' severance pay and an hour to sort out what you need to do. Then you must leave the building. Please hand in your pass at reception, when you leave.'

Gerald was aghast. His face contorted into a puzzled expression, before anger took over. 'What, just for one mistake ?'

'No, it's not just for one mistake. It's for an unacceptable pattern of mistakes. You've damaged the image of the Company. I'm sorry but you have to go.' Once Tom made up his mind, it was rarely changed.

'The Company? The Company, you bastard ! Is that all you think about ? What about the people who make up this Company ?' Gerald intended to leave on his own terms. He fixed Tom with a stare of his own. At the end of his third question, Finchley got out of his chair and stood on the client's side of Tom's desk, while fixing a threatening look into the eyes of his boss, ready to spit more bile.

It was clear to the programmers working on the floor of *TDVK Solutions* that someone was extremely upset in the *Chief Exec's* office and it was too tempting not to listen. They all stopped punching their keyboards and sat with raised heads, like a stunned band of mongoose. No one had ever stood their ground with Mr Kettlewell before. This was breaking new territory.

Gerald was in full flow and determined 'not to go gentle into that good night.' He was raging against the dying of his light within a firm where he had given good service. 'If I'm going to go, then you can fucking well listen for once you characterless prick. Everyone in your precious *TDVK Solutions* hates you, because they're frightened of you. But not me. Not today. You're a bully and I can't fucking stand you. It's of no consequence to you that I've had some problems at home. Do you care? Do you shit! You've probably had everything you wanted your whole pathetic life.'

At that moment, Tom returned his glare. He could have told him about his upbringing, hard work and broken love life but this was neither the time nor the place. Security arrived, having been alerted by Phil

Johnston. 'Do you want me to remove this chap from your office, Mr Kettlewell?' asked the guard. Tom simply nodded and the body-builder in a blue uniform clamped one of Gerald Finchley's biceps with his left hand and forcibly marched him out of the office. As he got to the door, Gerald made one last gesture of defiance and turned with a final curse, 'I hope you die in agony you twat !' before forcing a feeble spit in Tom's direction.

Everyone on the office floor sat as if the piano player had stopped playing in a Wild West saloon and a feared gunslinger had just entered the room. Phil gestured by lowering both palms, to remind everyone to settle and carry-on working as he returned to Tom's door. 'You ok, Boss ? You certainly upset *him*.' He knew Tom well enough to know he was shaken. 'Don't worry about it. I'll get you a coffee. He's obviously a bit unhinged.'

Phil was right, the incident had shocked Tom but it was not just because one worker was upset at being fired. Tom had dismissed many people in his time at ICC as well as his present workplace. It was the extent of the vitriolic venom directed at him, personally. He knew as the leader of his own company, there would be some who feared the Boss. This was true in any organisation. It was of no consequence that a worker might declare a boss to be a bit of a bastard but this was different. This was heart-felt hatred and if true, it demanded a major re-think about how he projected himself to the workforce. How could people perceive Tom Kettlewell, former member of Sheffield University's Student Communist Party, as a tyrannical megalomaniac ? His self-confidence had taken a mauling. For the rest of the morning he stayed in his office, behind closed blinds. He instructed Samantha to ensure the contents of Gerald Finchley's desk were boxed and left at the main desk downstairs, with strict instructions never to allow the former employee in the building again.

Tom was pleased that he would be out of the country chasing a lucrative contract in San Jose, California the following week. The trip would also help him to develop a feel for the new, international direction of the Internet. He anticipated that the first decade of the new millennium would see an explosion in the demand for personal computers. Silicon Valley was the centre of the *dot.com* industry and he wanted *TDVK Solutions* to be involved. A new software frontier was due to open up for any company that saw a fresh opportunity to expand. Internet firms and web providers could exploit this potential and enter a new 'gold-rush.'

There was a fresh vein of opportunity waiting to be mined and the change of scenery would also do him some good.

Tom arrived home a little earlier than normal, having enjoyed better days at work. Driving through the impressive gates, he could see Geraldine's black Porsche 996 parked outside the house. As he entered, he called to anyone within earshot but no one responded. For a minute, he thought about going straight into the Annex to see his Dad but heard sounds coming from the kitchen. Feeling too tired to care about what was taking place, he went into the main lounge and sat on a comfortable armchair, dangling his legs over its cushioned arm. Within seconds of relaxing, he was asleep, only to be woken by an agitated Geraldine.

'Charming…asleep again ! Every time you come through the door these days, you are shattered. But not apparently at work.' Geraldine rarely cut Tom any slack. What had once been efficiency in her own workplace was now directed at barbed comments in Tom's direction.

Stirring from his mini nap, he tried to respond, 'What, eh …? Sorry Geraldine, I didn't know you were in the house.' Tom moved his legs off the chair-arm and twisted back ninety degrees to a more respectable sitting position. Geraldine's nagging continued.

'Then you must be blind as well as deaf. My car is on the drive and I've been in the kitchen for the last hour, starting the sauces for tonight.' She was a perfectionist and intolerant towards anyone showing her a lack of consideration, especially Tom who was sitting with his arms open, totally bemused by her reaction.

'Tonight ? What's happening tonight?' he asked, frantically trying to recall any previous conversation that could shine some light on the arrangements. He was so tired he could not remember what took place yesterday.

'I told you last night in bed, before you became comatose. The Paterssons and the Micklefields are coming over for dinner.' Geraldine did not remove her eyes from her cornered partner as she stood with one hand on her hip, the other imitating a gun, pointed directly at Tom.

'Oh, shit ! I forgot all about it. You know I don't like the Paterssons. I can't stand that stuck-up prat Miles Patersson. *She* might be ok but he's so far up himself it's a wonder he doesn't come out the other side. And that vamp, Melanie Micklefield – I mean her name is bad enough. If there's a male breathing within sniffing distance, he'd better run for cover. With those nails of hers she'd skin him alive. Do we have to ? Can we not postpone – please ?'

Geraldine turned up the volume. 'No we *cannot* call it off. They are *my* friends. It's not as if you ever invite any of *your* friends here or take me out anywhere these days. I don't even know who your friends are. I have to make my own pleasures. They are coming for dinner tonight so you will just have to be civil and that's the end of it. I've asked Mrs Watkins to come around and see to the vegetables and the meat. The sauces will take another ten minutes and then I'm going to get myself ready. And you can smarten yourself up as well.' Geraldine half-turned towards the kitchen but Tom spoke so she returned to listen, raising her chin as if in a dare.

'Oh come on. Don't do the – *You never take me anywhere* – routine. You'll be coming out with, *I've nothing to wear*, next.' Tom got out of his chair and turned towards the door. ' I'm going to pop in to see if Dad's ok.'

'That's right. See if the old cripple is alright but ignore me.' This raised the tiff onto another level and it was in danger of entering the Richter Scale. She wondered for a second if she had gone too far. She soon found out.

'Don't ever talk about him like that !' shouted Tom, while pointing his finger within range. There were only a few lines drawn in the sand of Tom's life and Geraldine had just crossed one. She turned away and headed towards the kitchen to finish her evening's contribution to the meal. Tom watched her leave the room, feeling exasperated and hollow.

Dennis was watching the television, with a newspaper resting on the arm of his chair, oblivious to what had taken place across the corridor. He glanced over a familiar greeting as Tom entered the room. His son eased into the other chair, where the cushions were less conditioned to a human shape. Tom sat casually, with his right foot on top of his left knee, scratching his crotch. It went unnoticed as Dennis was lost in the documentary programme about sea lions. Realising his Dad was not in the mood for a chat, Tom nipped out of the room to make them both a cup of tea. After a few minutes he returned and placed Dennis's cup on the small table next to his chair. His Dad open and closed the fingers of his right hand in a gesture of thanks but said nothing. He was lost in a learning zone about the extinction of the Japanese sea lion. They were together for about a quarter-of-an-hour, exchanging only a few comments. It made no difference to the intimacy between them. It was the highlight of Tom's day, sitting with someone he could trust. His father had never let him down.

Tom thought he had better make a move if he was to avoid another run-in with Geraldine. He sprung from the chair, clipping his Dad's shoulder with a copy of *The Evening Standard* as he walked past, in a gesture of farewell. After leaving his Dad in front of the television for the evening, he thought he had better get himself ready for the forthcoming pleasures. He returned to the lounge and sat in the same chair as before.

Within seconds of sitting-down, he fell asleep, once again. Tom was finding life to be more physically demanding in his fifties and whenever he had the opportunity to relax, he invariably nodded off. Night times were the worst when he found himself waking in the early hours, soaked in perspiration. He put the behaviour down to his busy, stressful life, although it had been going on even before his confrontation with Gerald Finchley.

Tom's nap was disturbed once again by Geraldine. 'Aren't you ready yet ? They'll be here in the next hour and you haven't even started to get ready. Come on, Tom get a move on.'

Tom suddenly realised that he should already have picked up Mrs Watkins and his heart sank. He bent over to try and locate his shoes as quickly as possible. As he rummaged, he thought he had better pop into the kitchen first. Among the steaming pans and tinkling glasses Tom found Mrs Watkins, who was already beavering away in the kitchen. When Tom had failed to call and pick-up his charge, Ken Watkins had the good sense to run his wife to *Derwent House*, using his own initiative. He attributed Mr Kettlewell's lateness to work commitments, which had happened before. Tom breathed a sigh of relief, grateful to Mr Watkins that he had helped him avoid another argument with Geraldine.

Reluctantly, Tom left the kitchen and ascended the wide, winding staircase that led to the bedrooms upstairs. Geraldine was sitting at the dressing table, in front of three large, rotatable mirrors. She was leaning forward and squinting into the large, central looking-glass as she applied *Lancome EveryLash* with expert care. She had already been to the manicurist the day before, so this saved some preparation time on her clear-line nails.

The mascara was Geraldine's last act of preparation before she glided into her black *Dior* evening dress. Tom went into the shower while some of the war paint was being administered. Naked, except for a white towel around his waist, he soon returned, just as Geraldine was slipping into the silky number. Admiring her stunning figure from the doorway, he felt instantly aroused and knew why they were still together. 'Do me up, Tom,' she instructed, as she stood in front of the full-length mirror.

He moved across the room and started to lift the zip on her dress, before making the mistake of trying to kiss her neck. 'Not now, for God's sake. Where were you when I wanted *you* ? Your timing always was lousy.' Tom recoiled as if he had just touched a piece of hot pumice.

'Sorry, I won't do it again,' was the only response he could offer. They continued to dress in icy silence and left the bedroom separately.

At twenty minutes past eight, Miles and Sally Patersson arrived. They were dutifully escorted into the lounge by Tom, after an appropriate handshake for Miles and one kiss on both cheeks from Sally. Tom, now almost re-charged, clapped his hands together and when his guests had both pecked Geraldine, he inquired about drinks. Miles asked for whisky-on- the-rocks while Sally requested a '*Gin-and-It*'. They wandered over to the large leather sofa, with Sally complimenting Geraldine on one of the landscapes hanging above a small walnut cabinet.

Tom and Geraldine had originally met Miles when buying Geraldine's first Porsche sports car a year earlier. Tom learned they lived close-by and Sally went to the same exclusive Health Club as Geraldine. For the first six months, Sally and Geraldine saw each other casually but after attending the same charity ball, their 'girly' relationship blossomed. They were of similar age, although the Paterssons had two teenage children who attended a private school in Chigwell.

The second group of guests arrived about ten minutes later, just as Miles and Sally were taking their first sips from Tom's best crystal. As she entered, Melanie Micklefield left an imprint of her lipstick on the left cheek of Tom's face, within ten seconds of crossing the threshold. She was wearing an over-the-top fake fur stoll, bright red shoes and a loud floral dress, topped with a matching rouge, trilby hat. Her husband Lionel followed meekly behind almost in camouflage, wearing his favourite brown suit. Lionel Micklefield was an accountant who met Tom during a take-over of one company that his accountancy service had on its books. Having witnessed his guile first-hand, Tom availed himself of Lionel's professional services for some of his own personal accounts. Lionel was a harmless, prematurely balding chap who was extremely efficient at his job. His social life was dictated by his wife's desires. Melanie Micklefield was a one-woman whirlwind who laid flat any cornfields of men in her path. She had been involved in several affairs, only a few of which were known to her husband, who always took her back. Tom preferred to keep Melanie at arm's length and tried never to be alone in her company.

As they all sat together in the lounge, Tom wished he was anywhere else, hoping for an insurmountable problem to arise at work. The banal chat also left him cold, especially as maleficent Miles attempted to regale everyone with the success of his automobile empire. Although Miles was wealthy, Tom could have bought him out, ten times over. Tom did not care about the size of Mile's bank account and was relieved when Mrs Watkins declared that food was almost ready and everyone was welcome to begin the starters already placed on the long, oak table in the dining room. The food consisted of either lamb soup with sour cream, from the tureen on the side-trolley, or smoked salmon and cream cheese roulades on the centre spread. Geraldine invited the guests to her tastefully furnished dining area, which she reserved for special occasions. Tom wanted to sleep in the armchair or better still, to go to bed and leave them alone with his drinks, his food and whatever else they wanted. He did not care.

The redcurrant jelly sauce which Geraldine had prepared for the duck breasts was complemented perfectly by the three bottles of *Dolcetto d'Alba Bric del Salto Sottimano*. The repast culminated in a choice of white chocolate cheesecake or Normandy pear tart, washed down with a final bottle of *Pommeau De Normandie*. Although Tom did not like to admit it, Geraldine had done an admirable job with the meal, in combination with Mrs Watkins. Tom visited the culinary accomplice in the kitchen in order to tell her she could leave for the evening and go home, after pressing a wad of notes into her hand, as extra gratitude for her efforts. Mr Watkins was already on his way to collect his wife. The remnants of the washing-up and clearing-away could wait until tomorrow.

Tom headed back to his guests, who were now returning to the lounge, where it was more comfortable. Conscious of his responsibilities as host, he accelerated to the front of the ambling group and headed for the drinks' cabinet. He lifted the relevant glasses onto a small bar-shelf in anticipation of his guests' requirements. There was brandy for the men and champagne for the ladies. Melanie flopped onto the leather chair with an embarrassing squeak and as she shuffled for comfort, her skirt rose to expose her shapely legs. She made no attempt to adjust her clothing. Lionel looked away, tapping his brandy glass with rolling fingers but Miles sneaked a peek, when he handed her another glass of *champers*. Geraldine and Sally were discussing the new cross-trainer, recently installed in their gym.

While most were locked into the merry stage of an alcohol induced state, Tom stood outside the gathering, simply observing in action people he did not like very much. Chat was more freely offered than accepted and eventually, Tom's head began to spin with excess alcohol. The same was true of the others so it was agreed that no one should drive home and a taxi was ordered for midnight. Miles and Lionel would leave their cars at *Derwent House* and return at some point the following morning to collect them. Finally, after a great deal of kissing and backslapping, topped-off with several repeated handshakes, the evening came to a conclusion and Tom and Geraldine waved goodbye to their friends in the cab as it headed through the double gates.

Without noticing Geraldine's movements, Tom suddenly became aware that she had already retired to the bedroom. He thought he must have done something to annoy her but could not fathom any obvious reason why she might be upset. Sitting alone, he thought he had better make his way to the bedroom and was halfway up the stairs before he realised he had not engaged the alarm system. However, he did not particularly care if they were burgled that night so rather than risk another confrontation with Geraldine, he returned to the lounge to finish his *Camus Cognac Cuvee*. Five minutes later, he was fast asleep in his favourite armchair. At approximately three o'clock in the morning he awoke and finally ascended the staircase before slipping into the bed in the spare room, once more. Avoiding his partner was becoming a habit.

The following morning, Tom arose surprisingly early for work and noticed the bed sheets were soaked in his perspiration. His head ached a bit and he was suddenly overcome with nausea and had to vomit into the bowl of the nearest toilet. The release of his personal detritus from the previous evening's events, allowed him to feel healthy enough to set off for work. While driving, he became extremely sleepy in the car and still did not feel well. The journey to work seemed to pass unnoticed and it was almost as if he was on auto-pilot.

There were two days to go before he was due to fly to San Jose and it was necessary to meet with Samantha and the Head of Human Resources at *TDVK* that morning, in order to sort-out travel arrangements. They had agreed to meet at nine o'clock and Tom wanted to ensure everything would run smoothly while he was out of the country. As Samantha entered his office to begin their discussions, she looked at her employer closely and with some sympathy said, 'Are you alright, Tom ? You look a bit peaky.'

'No, I'm not feeling great either, as it happens.' Tom had not realised he had drunk as much as his body was telling him.

'Why don't you go home ? We can handle things here today. I can drive you home, if you want. If you are not feeling up to it.' Samantha was a highly competent colleague, a trustworthy second-in-command.

'I think I will actually, Samantha but I should be ok to drive, thanks. I need to go back and get my passport anyway. I'd forgotten I would need it today to sort out travel arrangements so I'm going to need to return.' Tom was angry at himself for being less than his usual efficient self.

After a quick cup of strong, black coffee Tom returned to his *Alfa Romeo* and set off home. This time he became conscious of his vulnerability while driving and wished each mile would pass quickly. As he got closer to Loughton he had to fight to keep his eyes open. Before turning down his own lane, he was suddenly aware that he had nodded-off while driving and was woken by the sound of some dead branches scraping the bottom of his car. A mile from his house, he pulled over and fell asleep once more.

Soon, he stirred from his slumber in the car and after brushing his eyes, he started the *Alfa* and drove the remaining short distance quite quickly. He looked at his watch, it was almost eleven o'clock. Sylvia would be attending to his Dad in the Annex, unaware of the previous evening's events. Perhaps Mrs Watkins would have cleared-away everything by now. Hopefully, this was the case because polite conversation was not on his agenda. Tom just wanted to go to bed. Needing some instant fresh air, he left his car in the lane and walked towards the main house, through the side-gate .

The front door of *Derwent House* was a welcome sight and he entered quietly, intending to return to the spare bedroom and sleep a recovery. When he got to the top of the stairs, he became aware of someone talking. Geraldine had to be on the phone. As he opened the main bedroom door to pop his head around and inform her why he was home, he realised the reason she had been upset at him that night. It was not hard to deduce, considering Miles was on top of her, with his back to the door and she was seemingly somewhere else, judging by the expression on her face.

Tom was pleased they did not realise immediately he was in the room, when he spoke with a lifetime of bitterness. 'So this is what you came back for is it, Miles you two-faced bastard ? And you, Geraldine I mean ... really ? With this total wanker !'

Geraldine shielded her face with her hands. Miles jumped out of bed, covering his embarrassment with a pillow. 'Have you any idea how ridiculous you both look, you pathetic pair.' He forced a laugh, more in mockery than levity. 'I've always felt sorry for Sally, until now that is because she is finally going to be able to rid herself of a smug bastard like you. I hope she takes you for everything you've got, including that fucking Bentley of yours, you pretentious twat.'

Tom spun around and marched off as quickly as he could, heading down the staircase and leaving open the front door. Returning to his car through the side-gate, he sat briefly in a state of confused rage. Although he was feeling angry with sickness, he was above letting his emotions win. After a drive to the nearest hotel and booking a room, he flopped onto the bed and fell instantly asleep.

When he awoke, he looked at his mobile phone to check for messages. There had been four attempts by Geraldine to contact him, including one text that simply read 'Sorry.' Samantha had also been trying to get hold of him, so he returned her call. She had been ringing to ensure he got home safely. Tom told her where he was and why he was there. Samantha was taken-aback at his frankness and it made her feel good that the Boss was confiding in her to that extent. Tom stated that he would be unavailable the following day and intended to rest, he might return to the office later in the day, depending on how things unfolded. Samantha also revealed that his passport was with Joyce Bickerstaff in Human Resources and that he had not left it at home, after all. She would ensure the necessary travel arrangements for his visit to California were sorted, unless he had changed his mind about going to San Jose, given the circumstances.

Tom confirmed that the four-day visit to Silicon Valley would go ahead as planned. He would phone his Dad later in the evening to ensure he was ok. At that moment, all he wanted to do was sleep and he collapsed once more onto the neatly barren, hotel room's bed.

For some reason, Tom slept solidly into the morning and was woken only by the purr of the room's internal phone. The hotel's receptionist was inquiring about his breakfast needs but Tom was in too much turmoil to think about food. The conversation was the rallying call needed to spur him into action. After a quick wash and still dressed in the same clothes as the previous day, he returned to the firm's underground car park, leaving behind the *Alfa*. The visit to the States was planned for tomorrow but he realised he had no personal possessions with him and did not want to go back to the house, preferring to send a clear message to Geraldine. Hopefully, she would have the good sense to leave *Derwent House* before he returned.

When he walked across the floor of the Company's base, one or two of the workforce followed up their routine welcome of 'Good morning' with a second-take. Tom did not look good and it was not difficult to spot. He was picked up on Samantha's radar and she was soon in Tom's office, where he was opening a couple of side-drawers in a mini panic, looking for something. She purposefully closed the door, before dropping the blinds for privacy. Taking a seat opposite his desk, the trusted deputy deposited her open note-pad and pen on a vacant chair and made it clear she was ready to listen. Tom repeated the full story to an attentive Samantha, who activated a plan for immediate help, knowing exactly what to do. She insisted he stayed in his office for a moment to take stock of the situation, while she would get him a coffee. Then she went to Human Resources and removed three young women from their routine chores. They were sent, to various tailors, chemists and department stores with a copy of a man's measurements and requirements, believing the items were for a foreign client, whose luggage had been delayed in transit. As

Tom sat sipping his coffee in the isolation of his office, he was grateful that one of the advantages of being rich was not having to worry about the cost of necessities.

Tom also picked up the phone and contacted Lionel Micklefield at his place of work. He wanted to ensure that any attempt by Geraldine to remove any money from his personal accounts would fail. The accountant did not seem as alarmed at the news as Samantha had been. Perhaps he knew something Tom did not. Who knows what he may have seen ? Lionel was able to give all the necessary reassurances. Tom confided that his relationship with Geraldine was over – permanently.

That evening with the emergency plan deployed, Tom stayed at the five star hotel in Heathrow, ready for his flight to San Jose in the morning.

V

Tom boarded Flight HT649 to Houston, pleased he had been able to phone his Dad before leaving for San Jose. Dennis was blissfully unaware of Tom and Geraldine's fiasco. It was going to be a long journey to California and Tom did not need the extra stress that worrying about his father would have caused. He settled into Business Class and before long was enjoying a glass of free champagne and looking through some papers in preparation for his meetings. The flight would take about eight hours and there would be a further three-hour stop-over in Houston before catching a second flight to San Jose International Airport.

Tom had not been entirely honest with his *TDVK Solutions'* colleagues about the nature of his trip. He was certainly going to San Jose on business but this was no ordinary visit. Mitchell Fraunley, the Chairman of *Modcom International* had invited Tom personally to see Silicon Valley and Tom suspected an ulterior motive. Fraunley's company had made millions of dollars during the late 1990s as one of the many *dot.com* industries located in the Santa Clara area. Initially, he had captured the largest share of the national market, selling hardware tools online, when the Internet had begun to take hold of the retail sector in the States. Tom suspected they were looking to diversify further and expand into Europe. *TDVK Solutions* offered the sort of potential Fraunley was looking for : it was a successful firm, internationally renowned in its field, with a young and vibrant workforce of a size ideal for take-over. The idea of being courted professionally for a few days was certainly appealing to Tom, given what had just happened in his personal life.

An hour after take-off, Tom put the papers back into his slim-line briefcase and stowed them into the overhead locker. He was not in the mood for work. For a few hours at least, he could afford himself the luxury of some peace and relaxation. No one could touch him while he was in the air. He was safe. As he looked into the clear sapphire skies underlain by a blanket of cotton wool, he let his mind wander.

Inevitably, Tom began to think of Geraldine. He knew finding her in bed with that creep Miles was the end of their relationship, although he had never envisaged their partnership would last a lifetime. After University, his love-life had taken an unexpected change in direction. Felicity's disclosure of her pregnancy came as a bombshell. It changed all the plans for his future and his hope of finding a soulmate lay vanquished. Initially, he was not convinced that Felicity really was pregnant when he met her that fateful night, in the Royal County Hotel in Durham. Deceiving Tom was the sort of stunt Felicity was capable of pulling and enjoying. After experiencing her cold despair as she detailed the realisation of her pregnancy, he eventually believed it was the truth. At the time, he was also aware it could only mean one thing : he would have to marry Felicity and accept George Fitzpatrick's offer to join ICC. His plans for a doctorate were also abandoned.

The greatest heart-break of all : Emma. He felt sick at the thought, even now. It was one thing following a dutiful path, it was another to side-line your dreams. After her last telephone call to his home from America there had been hope of a great future together. Felicity's declaration of pregnancy was a dream changer. At the time, he did not have the courage to tell Emma in person about his new paternity status. Like a guilty coward, he wrote his news on thin, blue paper and air-mailed a first-class letter to her in Portland. Tom tortured himself with the image of Emma's heartbreak as she would have read his news. Feeling guilty and angry was the least he could do to himself, something he was determined to repeat every time he felt some happiness. He could remember the letter, word for word.

Dear Emma,

It is with a heavy heart that I write to you but there is something I need to confess regarding a recent incident. I had a visit at home the other day from Felicity Stroud who had driven to Consett from her home in London. She told me that she is pregnant and claims that I am the father. It came as a complete shock to me as I have never encouraged a relationship with her, even though she has pressured me on several occasions. She maintains that

*on the night of my degree results we slept together when I was totally drunk.
Although it was only one occasion, it has resulted in her becoming pregnant.
I am so sorry and I realise that this news will hurt you deeply. Please forgive
me.*

*I have discussed everything with my parents who have told me they will
stand by me, whatever I decide to do. There is only one thing I want more
than anything else and that is to spend the rest of my life with you. I know
it is a lot to ask of you to forgive me but I hope you will find it in your heart
to let me try to make this up to you.*

*Please telephone if you want to talk to me again . If you do not call, I will
know that it has been too much to ask.*

I love you,

Tom X

There were no more phone calls from Portland.

Tom reluctantly arrived at the inevitable conclusion of his actions.
Emma wanted nothing more to do with him and he could not blame her.
He did not speak to her again. When he estimated that she had returned
to Lincoln from her summer work experience in Portland, he tried to
phone the family home but was told by her father not to try and contact
his daughter ever again. She would not speak to him on the phone or
anywhere else. If he knew what was good for him, he had better stay away.

Tom married Felicity in Kensington Registry Office at the end of
September 1970, shortly after he accepted George Fitzpatrick's offer to
work for the International Computer Company as a programmer in the
Development Department of the Company's complex in Slough. There were
only ten people at the wedding. Felicity wore a *Laura Ashley* wedding dress
with a white lily in her hair. Tom wore a brown suit with wide lapels, slightly
flared trousers and brogue shoes. There was no wedding cake and the couple
honeymooned for a weekend in Paris, immediately after the ceremony.

It was with a heavy heart that Tom informed Doc of the developments
in his personal life. Tom told him how he felt obligated to marry Felicity
and give his child a decent start in life. In return, Doc said how disappointed
he was that they would no longer have the opportunity of working together
and taking the Department forward into a new phase of opportunity.

Tom and Felicity moved into a flat in Chelsea a few weeks after getting married. Their new home was bought as a wedding present by Mr and Mrs Stroud for their daughter and her husband. Shortly after moving into the flat, Felicity lost the baby. She slipped from a ladder while painting the kitchen, when Tom was working late. By the time Tom arrived home, it was all over and Felicity was recovering in a private hospital nearby. This was the only tangible evidence Tom ever had that his wife had been pregnant. It seemed as if he had sacrificed everything with nothing to show for his actions. He still tortured himself with thoughts about whether Felicity's story was ever true.

Inevitably, when the glue to their relationship was removed, the marriage collapsed. It occurred about a year later. Arguments ensued shortly after Felicity's alleged miscarriage, with guilt and recriminations the principal weapons thrown. Tom felt it ironic that Geraldine's infidelity had been discovered in an almost identical manner to Felicity's adultery. The only difference was that Felicity had orchestrated the events to ensure she would be found in bed with her paramour. Tom had no idea who he was at the time but later discovered Felicity's lover was an interior designer she had met at a fashion show. It did not really matter. He was simply a vehicle being ridden to the divorce court.

Tom subsequently moved into a flat in Slough and buried himself in his work. He heard that Emma had stayed in America to pursue her ambitions in Civil Rights Legislation. No one had any further news on how she was doing. It seemed as if she had cut-off all ties with Britain. Even her parents moved to the States. He had no contact details for her, which was probably just as well. He felt so alone and so desperate that he would have done anything to experience that closeness once more. Tom's parents knew nothing of his disastrous life, other than the obvious incidents known to everyone. Tom did not want to upset them or tarnish his image in their eyes. He was also aware of his mother's failing health and preferred to avoid adding to her woes.

The tannoy system on the plane crackled and the Captain gave passengers an update on the aeroplane's progress. He declared there was one hour to go before they landed in Houston. Tom was glad his daydreaming had been broken. It was all too painful to bear. If there was to be a good offer by *Modcom International*, he would give it serious consideration.

After another three, uneventful hours, Tom's second plane touched down in San Jose International Airport, half-an-hour later than scheduled. He proceeded through Passport Control, collected his baggage and headed for the bright green sign that ordered *Arrivals This Way*. He was tired and not in the mood to be messed around before finding his hotel bed. Tom could see a gauntlet of welcoming relatives and uniformed officials waiting to catch the eye of their prey as passengers left the final exit point. His attention was drawn to a hand-held, illuminated screen about twelve inches square, that scrolled in bright red, electronic letters the message, *'Mr Tom Kettlewell, TDVK Solutions'*. Tom approached the holder of the screen.

'I believe you may be looking for me,' said Tom with a great deal of relief in his voice.

'Mr Kettlewell ? ... How do you do, sir? My name's Scott. I'm from *Modcom International*. I'm here to take you to your hotel. Welcome to San Jose, sir.' After a firm handshake, Scott followed with, 'Please let me take that for you, sir. I have a car to take you to your hotel.'

With clinical efficiency Tom was escorted by his ultra-polite escort to the Fairborough Hotel in the centre of San Jose. Scott was everything Tom expected from a successful, highly skilled American twenty-something, well-up the pecking order in Silicon Valley. He was blonde, blue-eyed with a great tan and wonderful physique. He ran one of the top departments in *Modcom* and was obviously on his way to the top. Scott had earned his money quickly during the booming *dot.com* days of the 1990s. He had the good sense to get out before the devastating *dot.bomb* was dropped in early 2000. Scott had established several successful sports-content websites that had attracted a great deal of venture capital, before selling at the right time. This was a young man not to be ignored.

The drive to the hotel was conducted mainly in silence. Scott attempted to introduce some light discussion about whether Tom had been to the States before, if his flight had been satisfactory and other areas of friendly chat but Tom was too tired to engage in a lengthy, meaningless conversation with anyone. On arrival at the Fairborough, Scott pulled-up outside the large glass double-doors which displayed huge golden handles. Before he got out of the car, a young waist-coated porter was at the kerb-side with a trolley, waiting to escort Tom's suitcases to his room. Scott left the vehicle outside and with Tom, went through the automatic entrance to the reception desk via the marble tiled floor. Tom wondered for a moment about the redundancy of the large, gold handles on the doors but then realised he was in the 'Land of Show', where presentation is everything.

A senior porter was concerned about an expensive car parked outside the main entrance but was placated when Scott called, 'Two minutes!' Tom then turned to his escort, thanked him for his help and was about to continue to process his room registration, when Scott declared that he would return at ten o'clock the following morning to show him around Silicon Valley. They would then proceed to their early evening meeting with Mitchell Fraunley. Tom thanked his host once more and shook his hand for the last time. Twenty-five minutes later, he sank a whisky from the mini-fridge in his room and un-wrapped his night attire from its shop packaging. After putting it on, he glided across pristine, cool sheets and manoeuvred into the luxurious mattress. Less than four more minutes passed before he fell into a deep sleep.

The following morning, Tom took a shower shortly before eight o'clock and enjoyed a hearty breakfast in his room. Following the removal of more plastic wrapping, this time from his brand new, light-blue shirt and stay-pressed trousers, he got dressed. He sat alone, overlooking a cloudless blue vista of high-rise buildings against a backdrop of the snow-capped mountains of the Sierra Nevada. He slid open the wide glass patio doors and stepped onto his balcony on the eighteenth floor. The sound of traffic was more of a distant interest than an intrusive invasion. The City had been awake for at least three hours and Tom was looking forward to his day.

At nine forty-five he went down to the Hotel Reception area, intending to lounge in the luxuriant seats and take a lazy coffee before his escort arrived. However, as he stepped out of the elevator he saw the bright figure that was Scott, looking alert and ready for the day.

'Good morning, sir. I trust everything was to your liking and you slept well?'

'Yes, thanks, Scott. And please call me Tom. I've never really liked Sir or Mr Kettlewell.'

'Ok then Tom. If you are ready to see the sights of Southern California?' Tom nodded to indicate willing and they made their way out of the Hotel.

Tom was not expecting to be sitting in a rust-red *Lincoln Continental*

Convertible, five minutes later. The car oozed style with its white-wall tyres and robotic face-grid. The new boy in town could not help himself, 'If my old man could see me now he would be eaten alive with jealousy'.

'Why's that, Tom?'

'My Dad has always liked cars but this is something else. He would be drooling on the seats by now.'

Scott laughed. 'You and your Dad are close then, I guess? You're a lucky guy. Me and *my* old man, we get along I suppose but we're too much alike. It's been a while since I've seen him.'

'What does he do?' asked Tom. This time, small-talk was top of his agenda and Tom was beginning to enjoy a conversation with someone who was not interested in anything other than pleasing him.

'He runs his own garage business, up-state. He was the one who got me into cars when I was a kid.' As the *Lincoln* glided over the freeway with the morning sun at their backs, Tom tried to discover more about his young host.

'So how long have you been working for *Modcom*, Scott?' It was proving difficult to be heard in the open-top car. Other vehicles quickly disappeared behind them as they were left in the *Lincoln's* wake.

'Just over three years. Sold my online sports business …having made my millions and then came to work for Mr Fraunley. Been in charge of developing various methods of communication. That's where the future's at. That screen I used at the airport? …'

'Yeah, that was clever.'

'You liked it, huh? That was one of mine. Been workin' on it for the last year. Still got some teethin' problems but it won't take me long to crack'em. I reckon in the future that's how most people will be communicatin' with each other, using their own mini, personal computers and stuff.'

'How did you get the job with Mitchell?' Tom was starting to ask more questions than giving answers. He was making the first direct in-road into finding out more about the business hawk who was circling above his sky.

'Got a phone call out of the blue. I was on my beach house porch and my mobile rang. Beats me how he got my number. Anyway, said he'd heard about me and wanted to sign me, then and there. Told me all he needed was my word and that was good enough for him. Smart cookie,

Mr Fraunley. I've never looked back or regretted my decision. Reckon I'll retire at forty and spend the rest of my life just livin' the dream in good old, sunny *Californy'*.

The rest of the journey consisted of Scott pointing out places of interest from the luxury of his open-topped chariot. In the glorious sunshine, they drove along Highway 87, turning off at Gunderson and its intersection with Highway 85 before heading down the Santa Clara Valley, towards the southern edge of San Francisco Bay. After an hour of admiring the view along the 101 they were crossing the Golden Gate Bridge.

'Can't come to San Francisco and not cross the big G.G., Tom. Just look at the view today. No fog this morning. They must have known you were coming. *Yee-haw*!'

Tom liked Scott's raw, youthful energy. He was young and clever but he seemed to know how to enjoy his life and knew where he was going. More importantly, he was relishing taking his time along the way. Scott was not prepared to wait for things to happen; he was in control. After stopping at an all-you-could-eat Asian sea-food diner in downtown San Francisco, they made their way east, through the City to South Beach Harbour. It was approaching five o'clock and Scott brought the conversation back to reality as they crossed the esplanade and made their way towards the car park, where shrubs planted in concrete tubs were making an attempt to be part of rurality.

Tom looked across the mast-laden skyline and could almost smell the money around the marina. There were expensive boats everywhere. Scott escorted him to the centre of the Pier and they made their way down the steps at the water's edge, before getting on a yacht. It was a brilliant white, 50-foot Carver 506 Motor Yacht, a four-berth boat, with a diver board extension at the rear, where the rubber dinghy was attached. It was very impressive and Tom was instantly captivated by its charms.

Scott called-out in mock fashion as they descended the Pier's steps. 'Ahoy there, Captain. Anyone on board?' Clearly he had a special relationship with his multi-billionaire boss. Tom could see a wisp of silver hair ascending the steps from inside the boat, followed by the tall, tanned physique that was Mitchell Fraunley. With all the brash gusto Tom expected, he was firmly shaken by the hand and welcomed onto the yacht.

'Pleased to meet you, Mr Fraunley. Thanks for inviting me.' For the moment, Tom considered it appropriate to become subservient.

'No formalities today, Tom. Call me Mitch or even 'Cap'tn' if you like.' He shot Scott a sideways smile. 'I hope my man, Scott here has been looking after you?'

'Yes indeed. He's been an excellent host. I've seen Silicon Valley and we crossed the Golden Gate, driving back through downtown San Francisco. It's a long way from the likes of my home town.'

'I thought we would cap-off your day with some sea views around the Bay, before Scott takes you back to your hotel for some rest and down-time.' They were on the upper-deck swaying slightly in the protected swell of San Francisco Bay. Tom was looking around at the boat, taking in the scene and enjoying being pampered. He was more than willing to avail himself of his host's hospitality.

'That would be great. It's a lovely boat,' he said, trying to sound polite.

'Oh, this thing is just something I use now and again, when I want to get away from it all and think. Some people work on cars in the garage, or go fishing by a lake. With me it's the sea. I keep my biggest yacht tied-up in Nice Harbour on the Mediterranean. It's a *Classic Benetti* ...a really beautiful vessel. Perhaps you'll get a chance to see it sometime. That's where I'm really at home. I would normally take *Mitzy Surprise* here out onto the Bay myself but Sam is skipper today. Gives us a chance to talk.'

With that half-disguised announcement of an agenda, Fraunley called to Sam that it was now in order to take *Mitzy Surprise* onto open water. Tom could not help wonder how much Mitchell Fraunley was worth. Most high-flying executives would be pleased if this motor cruiser was their plaything, never mind a luxury yacht based in the South of France. They went below and sat on the curved, white leather seats surrounded by shiny, brown wooden work-surfaces. All the activity and decision making about manoeuvring the cruiser took place above them. Scott attended the small bar, almost as a matter of routine. Clearly, many other potential clients had sat in Tom's place, in the past.

'What would you like to drink, Tom?' asked Mitch.

'Thanks. Just a beer, please if that's ok.' He did not want to send signals about hard liquor on their first meeting, nor did he want to indicate that he was not a man's man.

Scott joined the conversation, 'What sort would you like?' Tom avoided the temptation to ask for a pint of *Federation* beer. He was not in Consett Workingmen's Club now. He simply opened his arms to indicate anything would suffice.

As Scott handed Tom his ice cold drink, with two droplets of foam flowing seductively down the condensation of the glass, Mitchell extended the hospitality. 'There are some strawberries, caviar and crackers on the table over there, Tom if you're feeling hungry. Or even if you're not.' All three men laughed politely and after a few minutes of further pleasantries, Mitch got down to business. Tom imagined it was going to be a discussion similar to the one Scott had experienced before he joined the firm. He was not disappointed.

'Well, Tom I'm not going to insult your intelligence about why you're here. If you are as bright as my people say you are, you've probably got a fair idea about what I'm about to say.' He took a sip from his tumbler of gin and tonic, loaded with ice. 'We've been watching the progress of *TDVK Solutions* for quite a while now and we like what we see. All our reports give a favourable picture of the health of your company. More importantly they all point to the reason for the success of the Company – in a nutshell, it's you.'

'Thank you,' interrupted Tom meekly, wondering what his new friend was going to come out with next?

Tom's response was Mitchell's cue to stand and take centre stage. 'Well I'm not here to give compliments. I'm here to do business. *Modcom International* is looking to increase its presence in Europe and *TDVK Solutions* is just what we're looking for. The *dot.com* industries have had their day. We at *Modcom* believe that the future of the computer industries lies in communication. In ten years' time I believe… or rather Scott and I believe' he shot a sideways look in his young colleague's direction ' … that the Internet and computers will impact on business and society in a way like nothing before. Servicing the needs that go with the explosion in communication will be at the fore of what everyone wants. Thing is, I want it more than any other greedy bastard in the commercial jungle and I intend to be at the head of the fucking queue, when it comes to getting the lion's share of the business.

Tom was locked into Fraunley's every word at this point, conscious to be in control of any gesture that would indicate what he was thinking. He was being scrutinised by two of the best. Then he sensed the punchline.

'So the bottom line Tom, is that *Modcom* wants to incorporate *TDVK Solutions* into its business.'

Now we have got there. 'You want to buy me out, essentially?'

'Exactly. ...Now, I know you started the business from scratch and without you, there is no *TDVK Solutions*. So I'm sure your next question is ...?' There was no need to hesitate.

'What is the offer?' Bang – Tom believed he could 'slug it out' with the best of them.

'Precisely... I intend to make you a generous offer for *TDVK*.' After a pause for suspense, he continued. 'My offer is this ...' *Here we go!* ...'first, the name of your company would cease and you would simply become an annex of *Modcom International* but we would significantly increase the range, extent and volume of your business. You could run the sector if you wanted to but I have bigger plans for you, if you're interested?'

'Go on,' ordered Tom, still wearing his best poker face.

'I would like you to work with Scott here on development work. Instinct tells me that's what you're really interested in. Looking into your background I was surprised that you did not focus on research and get a doctorate at University. I understand that it was something to do with your personal life at the time.'

Tom raised his eyebrows in surprise and felt himself becoming prickly at what was being said, before Mitch continued. 'Anyway, I'm not interested in your personal life.' He held out his palm with fingers pointing upwards in anticipation of an objection from Tom. 'Point is, I know you were always one step ahead of the game at University and you took that into your business. I believe you enjoy research and exploiting new horizons. – the 'grass is always greener' syndrome. Something tells me, *that* part of you has never gone away. So I would like to offer you the chance to get stuck into new developments over the next few years. How can we exploit the future of computers for the better, not just in business but in society generally? Scott will do the business side of things, you can take it in any direction you feel appropriate. Of course, you'd run it past me first. '

'Naturally,' responded Tom wearing an acceptable sarcastic grin. Tom was impressed with Mitchell's accurate insight into his character. He had not only done his research, he was very astute in its application.

'You still have not mentioned any figures,' said Tom accusingly. He was aware that the big gun was still loaded and pointed. It was about to go off.

'Ok here it is. Two options: firstly *Modocom International* buys you out, lock and stock. I am prepared to put twenty-five million dollars on the table, with an agreement to keep you running the operation, unless I say otherwise, for ten years on a salary of half-a-million dollars. You get to keep-on the staff you want to retain, up to half of those currently employed.

'And the second option?' inquired Tom without a flicker of a reaction or hesitation.

'Option two is my preferred option and I think it will be yours too. The offer for *TDVK* remains the same: twenty-five million dollars to buy you out but you hand-over the running of that part of our operations to someone else. Instead, you come and work for *Modcom*, researching on new developments alongside young Scott, here. For that we give you a million dollars-a-year on a five year contract with options for extension. In addition we work-out a lucrative shares option package on any of the new developments.'

Tom nodded his head silently, acknowledging he understood the proposal rather than indicating his approval. Nevertheless, his heart was racing.

'I don't expect an answer here and now, Tom. You'll probably need to think about it. We'll have dinner tomorrow night at my favourite restaurant and you can give me your answer then. Now, unless anyone has any questions, I suggest we pop back out onto the upper-deck and enjoy this glorious sunset.' Tom nodded in silent agreement and got up from his seat.

Leading the way, Mitch took the two steps from the boat's lounge area before turning left and ascending three more rungs to the main vantage point, where Captain Sam was steering the boat. The other two followed, drinks in hand, with Scott at the rear. As Tom looked around from the luxurious platform, he almost gasped at the spectacular beauty of the view. They had been discussing business for about an hour and he could have been anywhere. Suddenly, they were faced with nature's beauty as if it had been waiting for them to emerge from their cocoon.

Mitzy Surprise was living up to her name, as they sailed under the busy San Francisco–Oakland Bay Bridge and headed towards Alcatraz Island. Tom could spot the Golden Gate in the distance with a bright orange sun setting in the west and throwing tricks of light towards them, through the red framework of the Bridge. In the beauty of the occasion no-one spoke and they were united in their appreciation of the view.

Tom was lost in a trance as he stared out to sea but his mind was not just far away in the iconic scene he was viewing; it was also focussed on Fraunley's offer. He immediately knew the proposal was a generous one and his head told him that he would have to be crazy to decline the bid. Tom was already a wealthy man but this would make him mega-rich, without the natural stress that accompanies running a self-made business. Option two would also enable him to turn back the clock of time and revert to his first love of exploring his own ideas. He was tempted.

Scott was just about to break the silence and point out something that seemed to be appearing in the water, when his boss prevented him from speaking. Quietly and authoritatively, Mitch ushered Scott below deck. Tom was left on his own to watch Sam manoeuvre the yacht and to consider his options in peace. As they turned around Alactraz Island and headed back to Pier 40, Mitch and Scott re-emerged. They had given Tom enough time and Mitch also wanted to enjoy the scene for himself.

'The beauty of that island at sunset belies its history,' said Mitchell, waving his glass towards the breaking waves.

'What do you mean?' asked Tom, still half-lost in his business thoughts.

'Well the closest most people get to the Rock is when they watch '*The Birdman of Alcatraz*'. Some of them actually think it's where Burt Lancaster lives. The native Indians thought it was cursed. They came back in force in 1969 to protest at how they had been treated by the Government. It's been a garrison, a military prison as well as a penal penitentiary. I prefer it as a spectacular view because of its rawness. I like to think the lighthouse is the Island's way of giving the world the finger and saying '*Despite what you've done to me I'm still beautiful*'.

Sam turned the wheel clockwise as they rounded Alcatraz and headed back to Pier 40. Tom knew the business of the day was complete. Within a short while they were cruising past Treasure Island on the left before passing under Bay Bridge. *Mitzi Surprise* slowed to the Pier and ropes were thrown and caught by the experts, who knew the waters better than anyone else. Just before saying goodbye for the evening, Fraunley laid down his final item on the agenda. 'Scott will pick you up at your hotel at seven tomorrow evening and bring you to *The Parkway*, in Santa Clara. We won't be disturbed there and we can conclude our business. Enjoy the rest of your evening, Tom. It's been good to meet you.'

'Yes, thanks Mitch. Same here,' responded Tom, placing his empty glass on the nearest available flat surface. 'I'll let you know my decision tomorrow.'

After a light supper in his room at the Fairborough, Tom went to bed. Sleep was no problem: he knew what he was going to do.

VI

Maki turned her head and looked towards the entrance as she heard the sound of a vehicle pulling-up outside. It was the small, white van that she had seen many times before. The back doors sprung open and a pair of legs emerged, followed by clothes she recognised. Pouring out of the 'rust bucket' were two of her closest friends, arriving to give a helping hand. Once she had established who it was, her face broke into a smile of excitement. The explosion of colour and giggling laughter that followed, belonged to Adamna and Urunwa, two women who were equally animated by the anticipation of the day. Walking along the side of the van, in order to try and close the rear doors was Ugonna Okeke, a small, stout man who looked like he was a familiar acquaintance of hard work. He was Urunwa's henpecked husband.

Adamna was a nurse Maki had met professionally, when involved in the Government sponsored inoculation programmes. They had worked together on much of the heavy organisation of the community scheme. Ugonna had been approached to do some of the building and planning work and that is how Urunwa became involved. Urunwa was the loudest member of the trio. She was a genuine character within the village of Uminwani. Everyone knew Urunwa and she was a great ally to the project. When the food started to arrive she would organise its distribution. If people needed to be cheered up, Urunwa was the person to raise their spirits. Together, the trio of friends was an unstoppable force.

Once the giggling and hugging had stopped, the group assumed a sense of purpose. Maki gave her instructions, before Urunwa took control. Ugonna kept his own counsel and quietly sneaked unnoticed into the cupboard beside the stage, to start setting out chairs. The ladies began to assemble the collapsible tables, covering them with their brightest linens and best serving utensils.

'We have two hours before the first of our VIPs arrive, ladies.' Turning to look at Ugonna she added 'and gentleman.' He smiled. 'So we must press on. I know the teachers and the pupils have arranged to be here half-an-hour before our main guests. They are practising their songs and readings at the Old School, while we are here. So please, let's get busy.'

Five minutes later, while everyone was engrossed in their own contribution, groups of women and small children from Uminwani started to arrive with food and drink. Urunwa stopped what she was doing and began pointing, carrying and laughing. She told the villagers where to put their contribution of kola nuts, yams, joloff rice, nkwobi and other sweetmeats, along with palm wine and fruit drinks.

Maki went into the main office and pressed zero on the circuit board for an outside line. Running her finger down the page of her notebook, she located the number she was looking for. While she nervously waited for a response to her request for information, she began chewing her thumbnail. She was eventually told that the plane she was expecting would arrive at Enugu Airport on time. It was only a forty-minute helicopter flight from Enugu to Uminwani. Everything was running to schedule. More than anything, she wanted to ensure that her planning was a success for the main guest. If other dignitaries had difficulty arriving on time, nothing would be affected but she wanted to impress her friend. If his flights were late and it meant waiting, the whole Village would wait, without any murmurs of discontent, no matter how long. They owed him that much.

Maki stepped out of the office and crossed the hall to admire the scene. By this time, there was a lot of polishing of surfaces and floor brushing taking place inside the new building. Sideless, marquis sunshades were being erected outside to protect the loaded food tables. These awnings should have been erected first but they were late arriving. The glorious, open tents added to the colourful scene as the warming sun began to illuminate the day in a spectacular manner. Maki moved over to Ugonna and started pointing where she wanted the outside stage blocks and main shades to be assembled. The temporary dais needed to be as close as possible to the commemorative plaque. Maki noticed Urunwa polishing the brass plate with a small velvet cloth. She could just make out the numbers 2005, from where she was standing as it glistened in the sun.

Ugonna was checking the lead from the power point to the microphone, making sure it was long enough. Moving in front of Maki was a mass of women in black and yellow traditional dress. Men and women, dressed in various shades of orange, white and blue, were moving and carrying a miscellany of items to assist the organisers. A pattern was moving before her eyes, resembling a noble animal gliding through a forest. Working with noisy confusion was the way things were done in Uminwani and everyone was enjoying the beginning of their big day.

Adamna spied Maki through the crowd as she perused everything. She approached her with a glass of lemon juice. 'Drink this, my friend. You need something to keep you going. Everything seems to be going well. Are you happy with what you are seeing?'

'Oh, thanks Adamna. Yes, everything is taking shape, thanks to you and the people of our village. I have a lot to thank you for.'

'You are wrong, it is we who must thank you for all you have done. Tell me, do we know if our friend is going to arrive on time? It will be nice to meet him at last. None of this would have been possible without him. Everyone is talking about you both. You must be very excited.'

'I *am* very excited my friend, my heart is racing. I only hope nothing goes wrong today.'

VII

Tom made two phone calls to the UK from his hotel room, after breakfast. The first was to his father who seemed a little confused over what was happening. Tom tried to spell it out for him, highlighting the two key issuses: Geraldine had been unfaithful and his son was out of the country but would return soon. The second call was to Samantha at *TDVK Solutions*. He told her to make arrangements for an off-site meeting between Tom, Samantha and Philip, the day after he returned. Tom knew he would need to bring his two trusty lieutenants up-to-speed as soon as he got back home.

He had some free time in San Jose but events from the previous day had left him feeling tired and a little stale. Leaving the confines of his room, Tom had a look around the hotel, where he noticed the leisure complex and decided to use the gym and relax. The on-site sports shop was having a sale and he subsequently bought some kit, before heading to the residents' multi-gym. A decent work-out and swim would help his painful shoulder and set him up for the evening's meeting with Mitch.

Tom felt like a novice in his brand new outfit as he stood beside the gym's personal trainer. The kit was not particularly comfortable and he looked like a nerd as he caught a glimpse of himself in a full-length mirror. Matthew, a Fitness Instructor from the Hotel, provided assistance to complete a questionnaire for health and safety purposes, before it was necessary to sign a disclaimer. This really was a society prepared for litigation. Once Matthew was happy, Tom entered the circus of metal torture and began his familiar warm-up routine. Following five minutes on the exercise bicycle and a similar stint jogging on the treadmill, he began his stretching regime. Then he started on the weights and using the small 15kg dumbbells in each hand he raised them alternately to shoulder height. One thing Tom had noticed from recent, similar sessions in his own gym in Loughton was causing him some confusion. Whenever he raised the dumbbells, it seemed as if he could raise the one on his left side, higher than the one on his right, even though he was right-handed. It was becoming more noticeable so he abandoned the weights and focussed on running and cycling for the rest of the hour.

The pool was more like a hot bath than a swimming arena and Tom thoroughly enjoyed languishing in the luxurious, indulgent warmth it provided. He also noticed that when swimming, he preferred breast-stroke to front crawl and wondered if subconsciously he was protecting his shoulder. Certainly, his light touch in the pool was preferable to channelling lengths up and down as one hotel resident appeared to be doing in his swimming goggles, black cap and embarrassing *budgie snugglers*: the other guest's short, tight trunks were particularly noticeable when he stood on the side preparing to dive-in, like a purposeful cormorant. Tom mentioned his shoulder problem to the masseur on leaving the pool, before he entered the sauna. This muscular male seemed to enjoy kneading Tom's well-oiled, ageing body and suggested that a steroid injection from his doctor might help the discomfort and improve his flexibility.

A light lunch from the salad section at the Hotel's plush restaurant was enjoyable and he decided to bury his head in a book and recover some jet-lag sleep before his meeting with Mitchell Fraunley. He was just settling into a comfortable armchair in the conservatory, accompanied by a strong *Americano,* when a senior receptionist brought him a white telephone on a silver tray. There was a courtesy call from someone called Scott Mason. After Tom agreed to take the call, the hotel worker plugged the line of the phone into a jack-point adjacent to his seat. Scott was ringing to confirm the arrangements for the evening and Tom was pleased to hear that a lounge suit would suffice for the *Parkway Restaurant*; he did not want to hire a tuxedo unnecessarily.

Scott was predictably on time and collected Tom from the Hotel's lobby with punctual efficiency. In the car, there was some small talk about the Restaurant's Italian menu and the thrill of the veal but discussion about business did not feature. Scott knew better than to inquire about Tom's decision. It was only right that the first indication of his intent should be reserved for the top-dog. Mitch had given Scott strict orders about protocol but he knew better of it, anyway. They entered the restaurant and were greeted by Arturo, the *Maitre d'Hôtel*. Tom nervously straightened his tie as the experienced sycophant went to work. Arturo gestured with a head-nod and a downward forty-five degree arm movement to show the path to their table. As they approached and caught site of Mitchell Fraunley, who was already seated, there were no clues about which way Tom was going to jump.

The restaurant reminded Tom of many he had seen in films shot in the States. It was a modern place with overtones of new money, where the tablecloths of plain white linen were beautifully pressed and immaculately presented. The eating area was just beginning to get busy, while still retaining a definite sense of order. The pleasant ethos was mainly due to its atmosphere of secret intimacy, where tables were positioned in isolated curved alcoves, allowing private meetings and discussions to take place with discretion. No doubt many deals had been previously completed over a dish of *Cappon magro* and an accompanying bottle of *Cinque Terre*. As the waiter escorted Scott and his guest to the table, Mitchell Fraunley rose from his favourite position to greet them. He looked impressive in a royal blue, shiny Errol Ford suit and plain, scarlet tie, worn with a white, tab-collared, silk shirt.

'Welcome to the *Parkway*, Tom. Please have a seat.' Almost simultaneously he nodded an acknowledgement in Scott's direction. No formal greetings were necessary in his case. As they settled into their seats, Mitch continued. 'I've taken the liberty of ordering a bottle of *Trebbiano d'Abruzzo*. Of course, if you would prefer something else, I'm sure Arturo will be only too pleased to get it for you.'

'No, that will be fine, thanks.' Tom did not see the point of seeking-out a confrontation at such an early stage of the meeting, especially about something as trivial as the choice of wine. Better to keep his powder dry. Having ensured that no ambush took place between the entrance and where Mitch was sitting, Arturo returned to the sanctuary of his lectern, at front of house. On his way, he directed a waiter towards their table.

The small group settled into their seats and Mitch began to pour the wine. The waiter accelerated quickly towards them, in the hope of usurping him from the task but Mr Fraunley waived him away with authority. As they took their first sip, Mitch held the glass up to his eyes and admired its glean as if it had come from his own vineyard. 'That's a glorious wine, don't you think Tom?'

'Very nice,' came the almost curt reply. He had not come all this way to fawn over Mitchell Fraunley's passion for Italian wine.

'I think it would be best if we got down to business first. Do you agree?' Tom nodded. 'So Mr Kettlewell, what do you think of my proposal?'

Tom had been rehearsing his opening gambit in the gym, in the pool and while he sat in the conservatory. 'Ok, then. ...' he began in bullish tone. 'You know as well as I do that *TDVK Solutions* is in a very strong position. We have the lean flexibility needed to develop in any growing future market. I agree with you and Scott that the future in our business lies in communication and technological development. I also agree with your decision to try and take-over my company.'

'Try?' queried Fraunley, in a provocative tone. He did not like others holding the cards.

Tom ignored the question and continued. 'Still, I admire your insight into my business. You are correct that on a personal level, I am more interested in development than making money, as nice as that is.' It was now his turn to fire the gun. 'So here it is: I am prepared to agree to your offer on two conditions.'

'Which are?' Mitch was not surprised. His offer was never going to be accepted without conditions.

'Firstly, I believe *TDVK* is worth more than your offer.'

'Thought you might ...and the second?' Mitch was loving every minute. The haggling stage was always more exciting than the kill.

'Secondly, I get to decide who takes over at *TDVK Solutions*. It's my baby and I think I have earned the right to decide who runs it.' Fraunley nodded in silent acknowledgement at this point.

'So you're saying you prefer my second option – with you and Scott working together?' Mitch now realised that he already had something in the bag.

Tom nodded, in strong affirmation. 'I do.'

'Which now brings us back to your first point. How much?' asked Mitch. The smell of the bull was close and Fraunley could sense the *tercio de muerte* was in its final stage.

'I admire *Modcom International* achievements and know where it stands on the global scale. I know the nature of its share profile and the health of its major investors. You see, I also have done my research Mr Fraunley.'

'Go on…'

'*Modcom* is an American company, *TDVK* is UK based. I think it's only right that we keep the same numbers but deal in pounds rather than dollars, don't you?'

This was a bit of surprise to Mitch. The way Tom played his hand made this condition sound like the deal maker or breaker. 'Mmmm …so, you're saying twenty-five million pounds, not dollars for your company with a salary of one million pounds?'

'And I want the new Executive Officer of *TDVK Solutions* to have a wage of five hundred thousand, with half that for her deputy.'

'*Her* deputy, eh? You *have* thought this through. So you like to be a modern man as well as play hardball? I'll need time to consider it,' said Mitch with just enough hesitation to indicate a weakness. Tom's proposal had caught him off-guard.

'Sorry Mitch. This is a once-only offer. We either shake before Arturo brings us the menu or I leave on the next flight back to the UK.' The roles had been reversed and the bull was seemingly about to charge one last time. *What would he do?* Tom wondered if had he pushed the multi-millionaire too far?

After a few seconds of consideration, Mitchell produced the *estocada*. 'You drive a hard bargain, Tom but it's a deal.' With that declaration, the battle was over and the transaction was completed. Mitchell Fraunley held out his right hand, exposing a pure gold Kruggerand cuff-link. As they shook on the deal, the three men stood in recognition of the importance of the moment. Fraunley patted Tom on the back in a paternal manner. Tom then turned and did the same to Scott, who responded, 'Congratulations, Tom. It's going to be great working with you.'

'I'll get in touch with my people tomorrow, Tom. They'll get hold of your lawyers and the deal should be completed in a month, by my reckoning.' After a pause for thought, he added. 'What time do you get back to the UK tomorrow?'

'My flight back to the UK is a late one, so I won't be home until two days' time,' responded Tom, somewhat defensively.

Mitch stroked his chin, contemplating an idea. 'Given what we have just agreed, I think I can do a little better than that. Scott can you contact Jefferson for me and arrange things?'

'Sure thing, Mitch.' Scott was ever the enthusiastic *gofer* when needed.

'Who's Jefferson?' inquired Tom, aware that there was still an inner circle to which he was not yet privy.

'He's the pilot of my private jet. I think in celebration of our new partnership, the least *I* can do is get you home safely. After all, it's now in my best interests.' The three men laughed together and Tom raised a glass, trying hard to believe Mitch had actually accepted his terms. Tom Kettlewell was about to become a very rich man.

VIII

The Cessna Citation X refuelled in New York before crossing the Atlantic and landing at the City of London Airport around nine o'clock in the evening. Tom felt totally relaxed as he luxuriated in the opulence of the event. A sound sleep on-board meant he felt rejuvenated, while Sally, the plane's sole flight attendant, had seen to his every wish during his several indulgences. Suddenly, he thought this might become a routine event, given his new status and earning power. Within a couple of hours of landing, he was proceeding through the electric gates at *Derwent House*, finally home, once more.

After switching-off his headlights and getting out of the car, he quickly scanned the area around the house, looking for any signs of Geraldine. Her vehicle was not parked anywhere to be seen and there were no lights inside. There was a dull glow in the Annex but Geraldine never visited Dennis, whether Tom was home or not. Tom took his suitcase out of the boot and flinched when he closed the hatch. It made him realise he would have to do something about that shoulder.

Geraldine's absence was confirmed when he entered the house. Although the alarm system was not switched on, the eerie silence confirmed his first instincts. Quickly, he flicked-on one of the panel switches to engage the default lighting in the main block and then ran upstairs to check the bedroom. Her wardrobe had been cleared and there was no sign of her presence in the house. His hopes were realised – Geraldine had gone. Tom knew he would have to engage his personal solicitor before news of the takeover became public. Geraldine already had a reputation with his Dad for being a gold-digger and his visit to the States meant he now had more to lose.

Tom went back downstairs to collect his suitcase and returned to the bedroom, where he threw the heavy bag on top of the bed, before looking at himself in the full-length mirror. It was true that he had come a long way since his days in Consett, yet there was still some distance to cover in the chase for personal happiness. Tom examined his reflection for a moment: he had lost a bit of weight, although he did not know how it had happened. Most days he felt too tired for exercise and his appetite was not great. No wonder he had night-time sweats. Dark rings under his eyes were not hard to spot and he thought that a holiday might be in order, once business matters were sorted.

In a tired state of relaxed satisfaction, he made his way to the passage and crossed into the Annex to see how his Dad was doing. They had spoken only twice on the phone during his visit to California, when all mention of Geraldine's behaviour was avoided. As he approached Dennis's bedroom he could see the red glow of the night-light under the door. It was just after eleven o'clock and Sylvia had seemingly already left. During Tom's phone call she had asked if it was in order to leave Dennis on his own, once he fell asleep. Her own husband was ill and she wanted to ensure his needs were also met.

Quietly and gently, Tom opened his Dad's bedroom door and poked his head through the gap, then crept along the redness to approach the bed. He could see that Dennis was in a deep sleep, catching a click in his breathing with each new intake of air. Tom thought that after the four days he had been in the States, his Dad looked worse and gave himself a mental pinch for having left Dennis alone. There was something exciting to tell him at breakfast tomorrow and knew the old man would be pleased with his son's success. As quietly as he had entered, Tom left his Dad asleep and returned to the main living room, where he poured himself a single-malt. Looking around the room, something was not quite right : a couple of oil paintings had been removed and some pieces of expensive porcelain were missing. No doubt Geraldine wanted a little bit of immediate financial assurance. He did not care – as long as she was gone, she was welcome to the items if they meant that much to her. Nevertheless, first thing in the morning he intended to call a locksmith and have new locks fitted throughout the house.

Breakfast was prepared in a light-hearted mood, the following morning. It was just like old times. Sylvia appeared early with fresh bread and Tom indulged in making the three of them his special bacon rolls with brown sauce. 'They can't make them like this in San Jose,' declared Tom boasting openly and light-heartedly. As he set about making the meal, he started to sing loudly and badly, adulterating *Dionne Warwick's* classic, *Burt Bacharach* hit, while maintaining the tune:

'Can they make bacon rolls in San Jose?
I've been away so long and missed them every day'

'Please stop him, Sylvia. He's destroying a classic,' pleaded Dennis.

'You're telling me,' Sylvia responded, enjoying the whole scene. Tom interpreted this as further encouragement for another verse and continued his impromptu, *ad lib* singing,

'Loughton has great big freeway
Put a hundred down and buy a car
In a week, maybe two, they'll make you a star.'

'Help, no more, please no more! I won't be able to eat the bleeding things if you continue with that racket,' pleaded Dennis. 'You're putting me right off.' His Dad had put both index fingers into his ears.

'Someone's happy,' interrupted Sylvia. 'I presume the visit to America went well?' Sylvia was making an observation rather than asking a question. She always tried to avoid prying into Tom's business affairs, where she knew she was out of her depth.

'It did indeed, Sylvia.' Tom grabbed her around the waist and proceeded to try and dance with his Dad's nurse. His foxtrot was worse than his singing.

'Get off, you terrible man,' responded Sylvia with a mock threat, waving a bread-knife a safe distance from his face.

Tom sat at the table beside his Dad as he placed the plate of bacon butties on top of the glass surface. Dennis reached for the bottle of brown sauce, while Sylvia proceeded to tidy-up Tom's mess. Before any bites were taken, Tom declared that he had something important to report. Sylvia put a frying pan onto the draining-board and indicated that she would leave the room, tapping her chest and pointing towards the door. Tom held-up his hand like a traffic policeman. 'Don't go, please Sylvia, this affects you as well. You are part of our family, after all.' Sylvia waved her hand in feigned embarrassment and pulled-up a chair to sit as the third member of their gang.

For a few moments of silence, Dennis and Sylvia looked at Tom, before glancing at each other. Dennis was just about to tell him to spit it out because his rolls were getting cold, when Tom broke the silence. 'There's only one way to say this… I've decided to sell the business.' His Dad and Sylvia glared at each other, not sure what to say. Tom coloured some of the detail. 'I've been able to get a really good deal. The terms of the arrangement mean I will be able to go back to doing the sort of stuff I enjoyed at University. Who knows, perhaps I'll finally get that doctorate after all.' He shot his Dad a knowing look. 'It also means a lot more money, for all of us. And I mean a lot more money!'

Tom proceeded to inform his attentive Dad and his surrogate mother about some of the details of his visit to California. They were impressed when they heard the word *millions*. Sylvia gave him a hug, causing him to stand and he then leaned across to shake his Dad's hand. Tom was too excited to eat, even his best bacon butties were insufficient incentive to stay. Since there was a need to inform colleagues at the Company about the news he decided to leave for the meeting. As he walked backwards to the door, feeling for the handle, he addressed his Dad. 'Fancy taking the blue peril out for another spin tomorrow Dennis? I've got this meeting and I'll need to call into the office afterwards but I could manage some time tomorrow. Fancy it?'

'That would be great Tommy, lad… and less of the *Dennis* if you don't mind.'

Leaving the surprised couple to absorb the implications of his visit to the States, Tom crossed the corridor to his study in the main house and telephoned Samantha Walters to confirm the arrangements for their update on his discussions with *Modcom International*. The plan was to meet at the Savoy for afternoon tea, where he would inform Samantha and Phil about the trip. The information would come as a bombshell as they probably presumed his stay in California was influenced more by what happened with Geraldine, prior to departing, than any firm business offer.

It was guaranteed that Samantha would be pleased with the outcome. Tom's lieutenant was an extremely bright graduate from St Anne's College, Oxford where she had gained a first-class honours degree. She was a short, tight-haired brunette who wore glasses on a chain, while at work. Hours of looking at a computer screen had left their mark on her eyes. However, her slight demeanour masked a will of steel. Samantha was in her early thirties and a promotion to Executive Officer with a good salary would come at the right time for her. Tom was concerned that she was due to be head-hunted by rival firms and he did not want to lose his best asset. She thought exactly like him when making important decisions and was prepared to take calculated risks but always after making a thorough *recce* of the ground. *TDVK Solutions* would not only be in safe hands, it would continue to develop along the lines he had wanted. Samantha had gained the position ahead of Philip Johnston, who was a much more cautious individual. Phil was dependable and would act as her deputy after the handover, making a good, second-in-command. At least, Tom hoped that would happen, the decision belonged to Samantha but he would do everything he could to persuade her that a promotion for Phil was a wise move.

When Tom arrived at the Savoy, Samantha and Phil were already waiting in the comfortable armchairs, with their briefcases dutifully positioned beside them, on the plush carpet. Phil spotted Tom first and he struggled like an old man to rise from the deeply cushioned seat, before indicating his boss's presence to Samantha. Tom shook their hands, which was unusual, before ushering them along to the Hotel's coffee lounge, which he had previously visited several times. The bistro's manager recognised the head of *TDVK* and the group were escorted to a table in the corner. It did not take long to place their order but Tom requested fifteen minutes of uninterrupted privacy before staff delivered their tiffin.

Tom told them everything that had taken place with Mitchell Fraunley and Scott Mason. Samantha and Phil were stunned as they listened, trying to avoid shooting each other too many looks. Then, after drinking *Earl Grey* tea and eating cucumber sandwiches, the meeting was concluded in just under an hour. Samantha was pleased with the outcome of their conference while Phil was relieved; he thought he was going to get the bullet. Tom was still heady with the excitement of the last five days. The next step would be to sit down with the Firm's lawyers and ensure the deal was completed over the next few weeks.

As the three rose from their low leather chairs, they shook hands once again, smiling and offering each other words of congratulations. It was almost six o'clock and Tom decided to return to the office, needing to catch-up on mail items and messages that he had missed during his visit to California.

'See you, tomorrow …' said Samantha '… and thanks for the opportunity. I won't let you down.' She was thrilled in the same way that Tom had been, when George Fitzpatrick first shed light on his own ambitions, thirty years earlier.

'I know you won't. And you don't have to thank me; you've earned it.' Tom turned to Phil, 'See you in the morning Phil. I am pleased that Samantha has chosen you immediately as her number two. It would have been my decision as well. Go and plan how you are going to spend that new salary of yours. Tom then strolled through the impressive revolving glass doors and jumped into a waiting black cab, before proceeding to the office.

The company floor was quiet when he entered, with only a couple of conscientious workers still on their computers. As he walked past, he made polite inquiries into the nature of their tasks, before taking off his jacket and hanging it on its familiar office perch. Twenty minutes later he was engrossed in his messages. Among the voice mails, there were two that stood out; they were from Mitchell Fraunley and Scott Mason. Both were congratulatory in their theme, expressing their pleasure at meeting him and looking forward to the future. Mitchell Fraunley mentioned that he was due to be in Frankfurt within the next two weeks and would probably stop-over in London, 'For a meet.'

Various invoices which he needed to counter-sign, were occupying most of his time and his desk top was beginning to revert to its familiar chaos. The door was open and he did not see Sylvia standing there. Her eyes were red with soak-stained cheeks, where the tracks of her tears had worn an unwanted pattern. She clasped a handkerchief in both hands, raised to her mouth. When he looked at her, his heart sank and he knew what she was going to say.

'Oh, my darling, Tom. Your lovely father has just passed away… I'm so, so sorry.' With that message, she convulsed into uncontrollable grief, while Tom jumped out of his seat and crossed the room with obvious concern. Holding her close, he then ushered her to a chair as her shoulders twitched and she tried to garble an account of what had occurred that afternoon. Dennis had gone for his nap as usual and when she went to give him a cup of tea, she could not wake him. He was already dead by the time the ambulance arrived. The paramedics said it looked like a heart attack had taken him and he had passed away in his sleep, as his wife had done some years earlier.

Sylvia had tried to ring the office while Tom was at the *Savoy* but had not wanted to leave a message. Her son Jonathan had driven her over to *TDVK's* headquarters and was standing out of sight, just around the corner. Jonathan entered without invitation when he overheard their conversation. After offering perfunctory condolences, he indicated he should take his mother home and Tom immediately agreed. Sylvia told Tom that Dennis lay in his bedroom, in the Annex that had become his home.

Within a blinking, Tom's excited joy at his recently acquired status and wealth, was extinguished. Dennis Kettlewell, the man who was more responsible than anyone else for defining Thomas Dennis Victor Kettlewell, was no more. In the silent doom of an empty office floor, Tom perused the scene through the panoramic window of his room in stunned grief. He clasped his head with both hands, while his elbows tried to push through his desk to the centre of the Earth. Tears cascaded through his matted fingers and pooled on the letter in front of him. In that moment, Tom realised he had nothing.

IX

M r Bolton, the undertaker had offered to lay Dennis's body in the Chapel of Rest at the funeral parlour but Tom did not approve. Dennis was laid out in a coffin in his bedroom, with his son sitting in vigil by his side. It was arranged that the funeral would occur five days after Dennis's demise in St Mary's Church, with the cremation following immediately at Forest Park Crematorium. Tom could see no point in delaying things. There were no other immediate, surviving members of the family, who might want to attend the funeral. Dennis's older sister had died a few years previously and so had all of the close relatives from his mother's side of the family. It was not as if they needed to allow time for anyone to travel a long distance to the funeral. Tom phoned the Obituary Section of *The Northern Echo* newspaper, based in Darlington, to include an announcement, ensuring that anyone known to the family who was still in the Consett area would at least have notice of Dennis's death.

Dennis left very few possessions, except for one or two personal items. Tom found some letters in an old shoe box, written during the War between his Dad and Betty. Three photograph albums had occupied much of his father's attention during his last few years. His wardrobe of clothes was now minimal as his body had deteriorated below its size at his prime. A couple of regimental ties, War medals and cuff-links still in their box with suits hanging-up and shirts in cellophane, more or less completed the list. Tom had removed his Dad's wedding ring and a threaded gold chain ensured he could wear it around his neck. He doubted he would ever take off the beloved keepsake. As Tom looked around the room and then directly at his Dad's pale, expressionless face in the coffin, he was sad that Dennis had never been given the opportunity to be a grandfather. He would have adored the role.

It was ironic that on the day of his Dad's death, Tom had more or less already relinquished his position in charge of *TDVK* and handed it to Samantha. She offered to assume her role earlier than officially planned, to remove any unnecessary pressure from Tom. He was confident that the major stages of the move to *Modcom* would proceed smoothly under her stewardship.

On the day of the funeral, Tom's naturally striking eyes had become dimmed by days of crying. The undertaker called to the home with the hearse at ten o'clock, as planned. Tom had hired two cars: one solely for himself, the other for Sylvia and her family. He could not bear to interact with anyone on such a dark day and had made it clear to his employees that he did not want them at the service. Flowers were welcome but inane platitudes would be more than he could tolerate.

Tom's funeral car followed immediately behind the hearse as it made its way into the Church. The coffin was not carried by pall-bearers but guided on a waist-high trolley through the stone archway at the head of the main entrance, a concession to growing health and safety regulations. Dennis would have enjoyed the irony of his internment being influenced by health and safety. Protective legislation for the workplace was something he had fought hard to achieve during his days as a Union representative. The short procession entered the Church, while organ music droned, before the coffin was brought to rest at the altar. Tom looked down at the floor, he had no desire to take-in the view. As they stood motionless for a moment, the principal bearer placed a dozen red roses on top of the closed coffin, Tom's final gift to his Dad.

The vicar seemed oblivious to the absence of a congregation and proceeded to speak in a voice that presumed the church was full. Tom's pew was just in front of the pulpit, which was not used during the service. Directly behind Tom sat Sylvia with her husband Eric. Their son Jonathan was unable to attend, although Tom never expected that he would be present. Funerals were the burden of close friends and family members and Jonathan had never met Dennis. As the Reverend Alan Williams announced the first hymn, *Love Divine*, Tom finally turned around to peruse the Church. There was a man in black garb sitting beside the main door, who he assumed to be the Verger. On the opposite side, sitting at the back was a well-dressed old lady, wearing a black hat with a green feather; she was sitting on her own. He guessed that she was a regular local church goer, who liked attending funerals.

Tom had arranged with the Vicar that no one would give a eulogy. There was no point in delivering his personal thoughts to two people who already knew them. It never crossed his mind that anyone else would be there. The service was completed in less than half-an-hour. Tom was relieved when this part of the torture was over. The undertaker and pall-bearers returned to the altar and nodded reverently at the coffin, before escorting the casket out of the Church. Tom noticed that the old lady had left.

The mini cortege then made its way sedately to Forest Park, six miles away on the edge of Hinault. The modern, spacious layout of the Crematorium emanated tranquillity and modern civility. It was tidily fashioned in the same mould as so many of its type. Tom observed a couple of people laying flowers in the Garden of Remembrance as the cars pulled into the grounds. He followed his Dad's coffin for the final time and as they approached the entrance, he could hear *'The Very Thought of You'* by Nat King Cole, playing clearly through the loudspeakers. It was the song Dennis used to sing to Betty in the family home in Consett, when he was messing about and it brought back some happy memories. Tom pondered why the solemnity at the Church could not also have been alleviated by the song's inclusion at that service. He realised that when it came to religion and protocol, he was a novice.

There were even fewer people at the Crematorium than at St Mary's. Sylvia had told Tom beforehand that she would be at the Church but not the Crematorium. The final farewell would be too hard to bear. As the most loyal servant to Dennis, her last undertaking was to return to Tom's home in Loughton, in order to ensure refreshments were available to anyone who called after the cremation. Tom had wanted to tell her that no one would be returning to the house and her gesture was futile but he said nothing because he understood her motives.

As Tom made his way to the front of the chapel at the Crematorium, he caught sight of a flash of green out of the corner of his eye. It was the same old lady who had been at the Church. Tom was puzzled: even if she was a funeral fanatic, her presence here was a step too far.

The cremation service was very quick. A brief blessing from the Reverend Williams, as Nat faded into *'... my love'* was almost the final act. The conveyor belt mechanism began to move Dennis's coffin towards the purple, velvet curtain and Tom stepped forward. After kissing his fingers, he pressed his hand on the top of the coffin in a final gesture to his beloved father.

Once the oak casket had disappeared from view, Tom looked around, uncertain of what came next. Mr Bolton stepped forward and took the initiative. He knew exactly what to do after years of experience in the business. The Undertaker explained the protocols and Tom headed for the exit to return to the hired vehicle. As he entered the noticeably brighter daylight, he could see the old woman with the green hat-feather walking towards an old, dark-blue Ford Fiesta. She was only about twenty yards in front of him when he called after her.

'Excuse me ... !' She either did not hear him or chose to ignore his call. 'Hello there! Excuse me ...' he repeated. She half-turned and Tom semi-jogged to catch-up with her. His leg was aching and a little stiff, a discomfort he attributed to sitting in the car.

'Yes?' There seemed some reluctance to stop, which Tom did not understand but he was determined to pursue his quarry.

'Ah, hello there. I'm Tom, Dennis's son.' He held-out his hand, optimistically. 'Did you know my Dad?' He was amazed to see her wiping-away a tear.

'Yes, – you probably don't remember me, but I did know your father. It was a long time ago. A friend phoned me to say she had seen his name in the deaths column of the *Northern Echo*. I wanted to come to the funeral, I hope you don't mind.'

There was something strange going on. This woman was claiming to know his father but Tom had never seen her before. He was a little confused and stammered slightly, 'No, no, no ...it's not that. I'm sorry. You're right I don't recognise you. Er, you are ...?'

'My name is Maisie Springfield, Maisie Huddlestone, as was.' She could not have put it more plainly and there was a distinctive tone in her voice. Tom recognised the accent and her surname rang a distant bell. After a brief but intensive scrutiny of her face, he asked 'Are you Jenny Springfield's Mam?'

'Yes, you remember our Jenny, then?' The accent was now freely available and the woman seemed to warm to Tom's approach.

'Of course, of course. I remember Jenny. Yes, of course. We went to the same grammar school. She was dark, like me, wasn't she, if I remember right?' Mrs Springfield nodded. 'So have you driven down from Consett today just for the funeral?' Tom could sense his voice was slipping into its natural vernacular. He was still puzzled as it was a long way to come for someone who had not seen his Dad for so many years. Then the mist cleared.

'No, I live now with our Jenny in Basildon. Have done for the past two years. Her husband Derek works in the City.' It was a matriarchal characteristic of Tom's home town that mothers never passed an opportunity to boast about their children's achievements. Tom was pleased to hear that his new acquaintance had not abandoned the tradition. He almost laughed aloud at this point.

'Well you can't just go back without coming to his home. My Dad would never forgive me. Please, come back to the house and at least have a cup of tea and a bite to eat.' His offer was genuine, although he had no idea where the interaction was heading.

Maisie felt awkward and knew her place. 'No, it's ok, hinny. I dinnet want to impose.'

'Yer winnet.' Tom was suddenly aghast at how he had plummeted into a North Eastern accent so effortlessly. He corrected himself, 'Please, it would be lovely to talk to you and find out about Jenny and about Dad and how you knew him. I've got some old photographs back at the house and you may be able to fill-in a few blanks for me.' The old woman was beginning to relent but she then said something which threw him completely.

'Ok, then Tommy, if you could wait until I get in the car and don't pull-away too quickly, I'll follow on.'

As she started to move away, he realised that without thinking, Maisie had referred to him in the same intimate manner that his father used to do. She was the first person other than his parents, who had called him *Tommy*. He turned away with tears in his eyes and headed to the car.

Within twenty minutes, they were driving into Loughton and through the main gates of *Derwent House*. When he got out of his vehicle, Tom cast a rueful look in the direction of the Annex, while he waited for Maisie's car to pull-up. As he opened the door for her, she could not resist the temptation, 'Eee, is this your place, Tom? It's lovely – really special. You've done well for yourself and no mistake.'

Sylvia was standing by the open front door and gave Tom a hug as he approached. Maisie stood uncomfortably just behind him. 'I've set-up everything in the main room, Mr Kettlewell. I hope the service at the Crematorium went well?' She erred on the side of servile subjugation in her choice of words, not knowing Maisie's position in Tom's social hierarchy.

'Thanks, Sylvia. It went as well as it could have, in the circumstances. This is Maisie, an old friend of my Dad's. You may have seen her at the Church.'

'Ah, yes. Pleased to meet you, I'm sure.' With that, Sylvia stepped back and wafted her left hand to waist height, in the direction of the light refreshments. By the time Tom took his guest's coat and arrived at the cups, Sylvia had overtaken them and was already standing behind the large silver coffee percolator and Royal Porcelain teapot. Silver trays housed several plates of smoked salmon and several other appropriate types of sandwiches, along with plates of gateaux that looked as if they had appeared on the cover of a cookery book. Tom could only admire Sylvia's loyalty and efficiency.

Maisie sat on the edge of a seat and sipped her tea nervously, her eyes scanning the room. She declined any of the cake and sandwiches. Tom thought he had better break the ice, 'So, you knew my Dad from the Consett days, Mrs Springfield?'

'Yes, I knew your father a long time ago. We were very close, once.' Her eyes wanted to continue exploring the expensively adorned room but she knew that would be bad manners. Conscious attempts to control her fidgeting told Tom she was out of her comfort zone. The implications of her final, short phrase took Tom by surprise. He queried the time when Maisie had known his father.

She answered as a simple matter of fact. 'Just after the War. Dennis was my first boyfriend. We used to go out courting together.' Tom was taken aback by the bluntness of her declaration. He supposed that it was a characteristic of getting old. At her age, there was no reason to circumvent courtesies. The truth was the truth, although Tom wondered if perhaps her Consett background helped her to disclose it more readily.

'Really?' This was the best he could offer in the circumstances. He was becoming increasingly perplexed with each verbal interchange.

'Yes, we used to go dancing together, when the War had finished. In fact, we were courting for nigh on two years before we broke-up.'

Tom could not believe it – two years! That was longer than he had been with Felicity or Emma. 'So you were sweethearts, before my mother came along?' said Tom innocently, not wishing to provoke anything controversial.

'Oh, yes. It was Betty who took him from me.' This woman was exploding emotional grenades faster than an *agony aunt*.

Tom was in shock. He wanted more. 'So, really? What happened?'

'Oh, it was nothing dramatic or anything like that. Me and your Dad used to write to each other during the War. He was a gunner so he was out of the country a lot. I used to write to him just to let him know there was someone waiting for him back home, when the War finished. When he did return we used to 'walk out' together and go to dances. Dennis used to like Ted Heath, I remember.'

'What, Ted Heath! My Dad – never!' For a moment Tom thought he had revealed this woman to be delusional liar but was about to be disappointed.

'No, not *that* Ted Heath – Ted Heath the band leader. I can guess what your Dad thought of Ted Heath, the Prime Minister. The Ted Heath Band was very big after the War. We went to see him once at the Winter Gardens in Blackpool – towards the end of the Illuminations, if I remember right. Let's see … that would make it about October 1948. I remember the landlady in our b&b insisted we had single rooms at opposite ends of the corridor. She used to patrol up and down late at night – a proper Blackpool landlady she was and no mistake. But they were happy times, believe it or not. The War was over and there was everything to look forward to. After a couple of years being with me, he met yer Mam and that was it.'

Maisie dismissed the end of the relationship with Dennis and Betty's capture of her man, as simply *'one of those things'*: either that was true or it was too painful for her to talk about, especially to his son. Tom was disarmed; it was an area of his parents' personal life, about which he knew nothing. Maisie's account was a salutary reminder that Betty and Dennis were individuals before they ever became his parents. Tom thought he had better offer some distraction to the way the conversation seemed to be heading.

'I had the house adapted after his heart attack, when he came to live with me. Would you like to see where he lived? It's just across the corridor. He's got some mementos and old photographs that I've had a look through, if you would like to see them. I've still got all his clothes to sort out in his wardrobe. I don't have the heart to throw them out just yet.' After some deliberation, Maisie agreed to accompany Tom to the Annex.

They left the refreshments and made their way to Dennis's quarters. Maisie nodded a polite acknowledgement of thanks in Sylvia's direction, as she walked past. It was the recognition from one matriarch to another. For some unknown reason, Tom and Maisie whispered their conversation while walking across the adjoining corridor, before arriving at the Annex. Tom was glad that he had someone with him, when he entered his Dad's rooms for the first time after the funeral. However, he could never have thought it would be with his father's old girlfriend. Tom took the photograph albums and a couple of shoe boxes containing trinkets and memorabilia from under the bed. They went into the Annex's kitchen, where he had enjoyed so much time with his Dad.

Maisie sat at the glass-topped table while Tom disappeared for a moment, allowing her eyes free reign to explore the walls and décor. He returned carrying the photo albums, which he carefully placed in front of her. She declined his offer of another cup of tea. Tom opened the first book, which was positioned between their line of vision. They saw old photographs that centred mainly on Tom's childhood days. There were a couple of fading pictures containing images of people who Maisie thought she recognised but there was nothing conclusive. While she studied some of the pages, Tom turned to sort through one of the shoeboxes. He started to remove one or two items and place them on the kitchen table. Maisie picked up the small cuff-link box with the perspex cover and almost shrieked.

'Well I never! ... I bought your Dad these cuff-links years ago.' She qualified her declaration in response to Tom's look of surprise. 'I bought them for his twenty-first birthday. I couldn't give them to him at the time because he was stationed overseas but when he came home I did. He must have kept them all this time. It doesn't look as if he has used them. Wonder why he never threw them away.'

One of the old, black and white photographs also caught Maisie's eye. It showed a young couple walking along Blackpool promenade with their hair almost vertical in the wind. They were laughing and seemed carefree, strolling along the seafront, with the unmistakable Tower in the background.

'Well I don't believe it!' exclaimed Maisie, once more. 'That's me and Dennis. Fancy that! That's the time we went to see Ted Heath at the Gardens. Well, blow me down with a feather!'

'You look as if you're enjoying yourselves.' Tom felt the need to say something, no matter how feeble.

'Yes, I remember it was the day after the dance, before we caught the coach home later in the evening. We went for a stroll along the *prom*. It was blowing a gale and a photographer stepped out as we approached Central Pier. By the time we walked to the South Pier and back again, we were one of several snaps on a noticeboard on the promenade. I said to your Dad that they were expensive. They cost a shilling each but he paid for one anyway. I asked him to put it in his pocket but then forgot all about it. He must have kept it. Silly man…silly, sweet man.'

Tom started to feel a little uncomfortable. 'You can keep the photograph and the cuff-links if you want, Maisie. I've never seen them before but clearly they meant a lot to my Dad. Or rather, *you* meant a lot to my Dad.'

'I did at one time. I only wish I'd fought harder for him. About three weeks after we came back from Blackpool, your Dad asked me to go to another dance and I thought I should make a stand. We had been going out together for a long time and a lot of my friends were married by then. My parents told me to let things cool to see if that made a difference. My father was a right stickler for protocol and what other people thought. It was make or break time for me and your Dad. Anyway, Dennis went to the dance regardless and that's where he met your Mum. You can't turn back the clock … Who knows …? if I'd gone to that dance with him, things might have all turned out very differently.'

For a few seconds, Maisie was transported back to that moment of regret. Tom's frame of reference had been skewed by the attendance of the old woman at his Dad's funeral. There seemed to be an episode in

Dennis's life that was an important omission in a son's knowledge of his father.

Maisie spotted something else in the shoebox as she filtered through its contents. It was a collection of about a dozen letters held together by a red elastic band. She picked them out of the box. Tom reached across, as if to take them from her.

'They must be some old letters my Mum wrote to my Dad,' said Tom, defensively. He felt that Maisie had already over-stepped the mark and now she was going too far.

'No, that's my handwriting on the envelopes.' Instinctively, Tom withdrew, while Maisie held the pile of letters in her left hand and flicked through them slowly. 'They're all franked 1942, 1943 or 1944. They must be the letters I wrote to him during the War.' Tom was now focussing an incredulous glare on Maisie's face, while she was lost in the moment. It got worse for him. 'Hang on a minute, this envelope is dated December 1948. It must be the last letter I ever wrote to your Dad. ... He's kept it all this time.' She finally averted her eyes and looked at Tom, who felt a need to say something.

'I've never seen them before. Please take them. I hope they will remind you of my Dad.' Tom thought he should try and change the direction of their discussion but Maisie continued. His mind was in an emotional panic and he wanted this terrible day to end.

'Thanks, pet. It's all taken me a bit by surprise – all this. He was a nice man, your Dad.' Tom did not want to hear her emotional conscience, it was all too much.

After a brief moment of uncomfortable silence, Maisie also recognised the need to change the subject. 'What about you, Tommy? Is there no lass in your life? The last I heard of you was when you were at University. I bumped into your Mum sitting in the car in Consett a few years ago and she said you were courting someone. Was it Lincoln or somewhere, she was from? Your Mum was quite excited by it all. Did you marry her in the end?'

Tom remained silent. He accommodated her comment with a shake of the head and thought that Maisie was beginning to delve into aspects of his life that were none of her business. It was time for her to go.

Tom decided to prompt her departure. He stood and looked directly at Maisie so there was no mistake about his intention. 'Well it's been nice seeing you after all these years Mrs Springfield. Give my best to Jenny, won't you and don't forget to call in, if you're ever this way again. Fancy living so close and my Dad didn't know. What a pity! You could have talked about old times. Hope to see you again.' He was lying.

Maisie gave Tom a handshake and a hug before leaving the Annex by the side door. She looked around for a few moments to get her bearings and then turned back to look at Dennis's home once more. Breathing a deep sigh of uncertainty, she was not sure whether to cry or smile. Finally, Maisie got into her old Fiesta and drove through the large black gates. Tom was not to know that she would return one day, under dramatic circumstances.

Maisie's visit had alarmed Tom and given him thoughts he did not want to contemplate. He roamed through the Annex, touching some items of furniture with fond tenderness, provoking an intimate memory of some of the lovely times he had spent with his father. Then, he went quickly to his bedroom to change out of his funeral uniform. He decided there was only one place he could go and returned to the emotional sanctuary that massaged and distracted his thoughts whenever it was required. Tom went to his office to work.

X

Harry Thompson arrived at *Derwent House* from his business premises at the old RAF Loughton site, closely followed by a workmate in a white, Toyota Hilux pickup. Eamonn Stafford, Harry's mechanic and handyman was having an easy morning. All he had to do for the first hour of the day was shuttle his boss between Loughton and the former aerodrome, to hand-over a Humber Sceptre to its owner. Tom heard the vehicles arrive from inside the house and he opened the front door to greet the men. Half-way down the steps, he was within hearing distance and called to his friend.

'Thanks for doing this, Harry.' The number of additional chores associated with the aftermath of Dennis's death seemed endless.

They shook hands on the gravel driveway, at the bottom of the steps, while Eamonn stayed in the pickup. 'No problem, mate. It should get you there easily. Your Dad was right. It purrs like a minx. What will you do with it, afterwards?' inquired Harry.

Tom nodded an acknowledgement to the man in overalls, who was sitting behind the wheel of the Toyota and responded, 'I'm meeting some bloke in Durham, tomorrow afternoon after I've done what I need to do. He's from the Humber Car Club and agreed to take it and look after it. I've asked him to give some money to charity. I don't want anything for it and I didn't have the heart to scrap it, especially after my old man enjoyed driving it so much. At least this way, it will be cared for. Thanks for everything you did with the car for my Dad, Harry. It's greatly appreciated.'

Tom shook his pal's hand once more, before Harry quickly jumped in the Hilux alongside Eamonn and they roared-off, back to the remnants of RAF Loughton. Almost disconsolately, Tom returned to the main kitchen to finish his coffee. Sylvia was not there this morning, she had reduced her hours after Dennis's death. Tom had offered her generous redundancy terms so she could finish work completely. However, Sylvia was old school and could not give-up on her charge simply because his father had passed. Someone had to watch out for him and she now worked three mornings a week, starting at ten o'clock. No doubt Tom would deliberately leave an untidy kitchen so it would give her something to go-on about. They were both happier in that atmosphere.

There was only one thing left for him to decide before he set off and not everyone would have agreed with what he was going to do. Tom placed the two urns containing the ashes of his parents in the shopping bag his Dad always used. Dennis never trusted polythene carriers and preferred the security of something more substantial. His tartan shopping bag had never worn-out during more than twenty years of visiting Consett High Street. It was the ideal size and the identical rosewood receptacles fitted snugly inside, shoulder-to -shoulder. Tom placed the bag on the passenger seat of the Humber, secured by a safety belt. It was only fitting that the last time he would drive the blue Sceptre, he was taking his parents home.

Harry was right about the Humber, it was a pleasure to drive. As Tom sat in the driver's seat he stroked the leather upholstery on the passenger's side with affection. During the ride, he frequently checked the time by looking at the clock on the walnut panel that had caused his father such glee. The journey back to Consett soon passed :Tom did not want to leave his mother and father in the car so he did not stop on the motorway. In an act of pure sentiment, he took a thermos flask containing coffee, to break-up the journey on the A-roads. He left the A1M at Darlington and headed north-west along the *'Big Dipper'* A68, across the remnant landscape of the exposed North-East coalfield. Familiar road signs featuring places like West Auckland, Crook and Wolsingham gave him a warm glow of nostalgic comfort.

The western part of the coalfield had been the first area of the North East mining region to lose its pits. Those collieries were soon excavated before the devouring miners moved eastward into the concealed coalfield. Eventually they were chased deeper underground, into the North Sea at Easington. It also meant that West Durham was the first area of the coalfield to be reclaimed, where the scars of mining were initially repaired. Tom perused the new rural landscape from the car, now devoid of pit-heaps and was reminded of the natural, rugged beauty of the area where he was raised.

After five hours, he reached the village of Castleside and crossed the junction by the post office before heading along the A692 Consett Road. He now began to feel nervously excited about returning to his birthplace and was less than three miles from Consett. As he entered the Town from the south-west he was shocked by its new image. Where there had once been a vibrant iron and steel works, there now stood a usurping trading estate with a large supermarket and factories. Consett seemed to be dominated by light, modern buildings with glass that reflected a lack of industrial virility. It was as if the community had been castrated. His Dad would have been heartbroken.

Tom drove up the Front Street where he saw some shops closed and shuttered, before driving along the familiar streets which he had known so well as a child. As he turned into the terraced row of his parents' former home he had to stop. It was becoming too much. Once he had regained his composure, he became annoyed at his own weakness. This was not the purpose of his visit and he headed towards his intended destination, without any further detours.

The original blue Humber Sceptre had travelled the journey many times in the past and within half-an-hour of leaving Consett, he had arrived. The spot was the same destination that Tom had enjoyed with his father all those years ago, when they watched the starlings swooping over the trees and Dennis referred to his wartime nightmares. On that occasion, Dennis told his son it was the one place he felt a free man. The area around the Derwent Reservoir, where the three family members had once enjoyed picnics together, would be the final resting place for Dennis and Betty Kettlewell.

Tom walked across the bridge in front of the dam to remind himself of the day his father dropped a coin into the water for luck, before he headed towards Dennis's favourite spot. Carefully, he unscrewed the first casket and took a handful of ashes before throwing them into the wind. The grey-white, sandy dust did not go far at first so Tom threw the next cloud as high as he could. Within a few seconds, Betty had been cast to the elements. As he unscrewed the second container a small flock of birds crossed overhead. Tom wanted to believe they were starlings but he could not see through his tears. He tossed Dennis's ashes into the air and they followed the same pathway as those of his mother. Suddenly, it was over and his final North Eastern farewell was complete.

Tom returned to the car and replaced the empty caskets back into his father's shopping bag. All the items that remained from this private ceremony would be buried in the garden at his home in Loughton. He did not want to look back or ever return to the area, it would be like an acceptance that his parents were no longer with him ; he knew he would always carry their love, wherever he was.

Tom drove to the Royal County Hotel in Durham, intending to stay overnight. It was the place where he had been confronted by a pregnant Felicity more than thirty years earlier so he already had negative feelings about the location. Another one did not matter. The quicker everything was over, the sooner he could leave the car with Cyril Watkinson from the Humber Car Club and catch a train to Kings Cross. Determined never to return, Tom's business with the North East was over – or so he thought.

XI

Maki surveyed the scene. Things were going well and in just under an hour all the important tasks would be finished. It would soon be time to change into her ceremonial clothes. Her thoughts turned to Dilibe and Onaedo, whose arrival was imminent. Dilibe was under strict orders to bring Maki's best dress and matching head-tie. She had not trusted herself to wear them while preparing everything for the official opening. Dilibe was charged with ensuring they remained in their protective cover until the very last minute and Maki intended to change in the main office. It was important to her that she looked her best on this very special day.

Exotic smells wafted across the area from the grills and boiling pots inside the open-sided marquis. Traditional music in the background added to the atmosphere. Lots of people from the Village were now starting to leave their houses and head towards the Community Centre. Only the sick and the very old would remain at home. Everyone wanted to be a part of the celebrations and to have the opportunity to thank their benefactor.

Maki felt a tug on her dress and looked down to see her daughter's adorable, moon-eyes staring back up at her. Onaedo did not speak but half swung around her mother's leg, while holding her dress as if rocking herself for comfort. Onaedo's thumb was receiving some heavy duty sucking and she was unusually shy, no doubt overcome by the noise and the strangeness of the occasion. Holding onto Onaedo's other hand was Dilibe, who had a suit cover containing Maki's dress, casually slung over his shoulder.

Maki picked up her daughter and planted a huge kiss on her cheek, partly to show to everyone that she was pleased the organisation of the event was going well. She turned to receive a kiss from Dilibe, who gave Maki her clothes in exchange for his daughter. As she passed Onaedo into her father's arms, Maki's shoulders rose with excitement and anticipation.

Adamna was standing next to Maki when Dilibe acknowledged her with a self-conscious mini-wave. He was used to seeing Adamna at various clinics in the villages and knew she was a close friend of his wife. Everyone was smiling as Maki rubbed her hands together with gleeful exhilaration.

'I will now go to change and finally wait for our guests to arrive,' said Maki. Dilibe and Onaedo gave her a quick peck on the lips and she started to thread her way back to the main building. Walking through the growing crowd, groups of people nodded across to her, acknowledging her presence. The day was turning out the way she wanted. Surely, nothing could go wrong.

Maki strode past the curtained plaque and through the large doors into the foyer of the Community Centre. Colourful red, green, black and yellow bunting adorned the area and young children had painted a glorious sign of 'Welcome' that hung precariously over the entrance. Ugonna Okeke was hovering in the vicinity to ensure that any last minute hitches were accommodated. Maki approached him and a huge smile exposed his large front teeth, dominating his quiet demeanour. 'Thank you, my friend for helping with everything today. It is very much appreciated. You are a true friend of this Village and we all appreciate what you have done for us.' Ugonna nodded vigorously and shook Maki's hand as if his life depended on it. He said something unintelligible, which she tried to indicate she understood.

Maki then unlocked the main office door and placed her dress cover over the back of a chair before switching on the light and closing the blinds. Secretly and indulgently, she unzipped the cover and removed her purple, silk, full-length dress. Intricate web patterns embroidered in pink, contrasted against the dark plum background, highlighting the wide cuffs and the flowing hem of the dress. The front was covered in a large pink, U-shaped web design that paralleled the neck-line. Maki fashioned the head-tie so the matching pink lines were vertical to make her appearance seem slender. The whole impression of sleek elegance was completed by a black choker-necklace, covered in small, white brachiopod shells. She looked stunning and was pleased with the outcome as she admired herself in a large wall mirror.

Self-consciously, she folded her other clothes and put them into a pile on the chair before secreting them in an adjacent cupboard. Finally, she glided her hands down the front of the dress as far as her waist before giving one deep breath and exiting to face the action. The preparation of the day was over and soon all the planning would come together. There was only half-an-hour to go before the scheduled arrival and it was time to get everyone in their place.

Maki was spotted returning from the building by the whirlwind that was Urunwa Okeke. She spoke with her usual frenetic authority. 'Quickly my friend. The schoolchildren have just arrived and are in place, the Village elders are sitting in their seats and the music is underway. Many people are eating their food so all is well. It is now time to say something to them so they know what will happen. Do you want me to speak to them?' Maki considered discretion to be the best strategy and nodded. 'Good – then I will tell them that the helicopter carrying our special guests will be here soon and they should carry on enjoying themselves until I tell them otherwise. Is that ok with you, my child?' Maki nodded a smile once more and before she had a chance to say anything, Urunwa had turned away and was one stride towards the stage.

Maki approached her husband, who had been scrutinising the entrance to the Community Centre building, waiting for his wife's return. It was clear that he was overcome with pride as he approached his beautiful Maki. Even Onaedo took her thumb from her mouth as she gazed in awe at her beautiful *Mama*. 'You look stunning my darling. Come – let us take a drink and wait for our guests.' Knowing enough not to unsettle his wife's grooming, he made no attempt to kiss her on this occasion and the three members of the Nkowo family made their way to refreshment stalls. As they walked, Maki's eyes focussed on the plateau to the east. She thought she half-heard the sound of rotary blades but dismissed it as her imagination playing tricks. She looked again and noticed that something had disturbed a flock of birds on the horizon. Could this be the arrival the helicopter carrying her special friend?

XII

I t was a strange time and Tom could not help feeling that his life was at a major crossroads, as he sat alone at the kitchen table drinking coffee. Since his Dad's death, things had changed: he had less contact with Sylvia, Geraldine had moved abroad and was no longer in his life and there was the impending sale of *TDVK Solutions*. It seemed as if nothing was the same and he was lonely. A meeting was due that day with his team of lawyers and those from *Modcom International*. Mitchell Fraunley was flying over from Frankfurt and the plan was to have dinner later at the Dorchester Hotel, where he was staying. They would celebrate the merging of the two companies, or at least the take-over of *TDVK Solutions*. Mitch would be travelling on his own, having left Scott to look after business in California, while he was out of the country.

In less than five hours Tom would be very rich, a multi-millionaire; not bad for a boy from a rundown iron and steel town, in the North East of England. He was now in his mid-fifties and although he was excited about working on new schemes and regressing to his University pet-project days, he did wonder if he should just retire. *Modcom International* wanted to buy his company as their first priority. Their attempt to involve him in research was flattering but he felt it was more of an after-thought on Mitch's part, something to sugar the pill, rather than an imperative. He could not imagine Fraunley would put-up much of a fight if he decided to withdraw his personal services.

Tom no longer felt like an energetic young man. The physical malaise that had upset Geraldine so much when they were together, seemed to be a constant. He was fed-up feeling so tired all the time; his shoulder still hurt and now he had developed a limp in his left leg. Perhaps he should tone down on gym time. Tom had promised his Dad he would have his shoulder looked at by a doctor. Once the deal was done, he would do something about it and take a break, before re-engaging with Scott in California. It was time to take stock of his life.

Tom poured another cup of coffee from the percolator and decided to cast a look around the house. Perhaps it could do with some re-decorating. As he sipped his cup on walkabout, he was undecided about whether to call-in the decorators or simply sell and move somewhere more convenient. He would need a base in California and there was some logic in moving to the States permanently. It might offer the best solution. Deep down, he preferred to live in England, although he knew he would look for a second home in California at some point. Tom had made a lot of emotional investment in *Derwent House* and it was convenient for London. He did not know what to do.

Crossing the familiar corridor and entering the Annex, it felt like the right time for a clear-out of his Dad's stuff. A fortnight had passed since returning from the Derwent Reservoir, where he had scattered his parents' ashes. Although his Dad did not have many personal possessions, there were several items in the Annex that charities would value. He decided to offer some of the furniture to the *Cyernians*, which had its headquarters in Newcastle. It seemed appropriate that some of Dennis's possessions would be managed by a charity with its main base in the North East. Everything else would go to *Oxfam*: Tom had supported African aid for many years so he had some link with that part of the world. There was symmetry in supporting these two organisations. Once the day was over, he intended to make contact and invite their representatives to meet him. Anything they wanted, they could take away. Tom thought he might even demolish the Annex altogether. The main house was more than enough for a middle-aged man, living alone.

A date was fixed and the following week, Tom arranged for the charities to arrive at eleven o'clock in the morning. The *Cyrenians* and *Oxfam* were keen to visit as soon as possible. They did not want to risk any other agency usurping them in the pecking order. They were aware that any donations emanating from Loughton meant they would be valuable and were not to be refused. It was a well-known money area.

Tom took the day off work to sort out the disposal of his father's possessions. Although he knew it would be upsetting, he believed it was the only sensible course of action. Soon, he would be a very rich man with other important decisions to make about his future. Once this domestic necessity was removed from his agenda, he could devote his thoughts to more selfish aims.

Sylvia volunteered to be on hand to make tea and coffee for the charities' volunteers. She arrived at the same time as everyone else, on the early side of eleven. Three white vans pulled into the drive simultaneously from the two organisations, the doorbell rang and the overalled helpers began the initial task of familiarising themselves with the layout of the Annex, casting an eye over the items and planning the best way to get them out of the house.

Two tall men in brown coats were miming a method of how to manipulate a large armchair through a narrow passage. There was some disagreement between them and it was bedlam as voices were raised, with other charity workers walking between them. Then the phone rang, while two men carrying the glass table from the kitchen pushed their way past a woman with a clipboard. The front door was open, people were walking in and out and Tom was attempting to speak to someone from his office on his mobile as another minor dispute occurred in front of him. He tried waving his arm in two directions while holding the phone under his chin, in a vain attempt to divert the noise. It was unsuccessful so he went into the hallway for some peace. The doorbell rang once more and the place seemed like the venue for a new pantomime rather than a well organised distribution of assets.

As Tom looked towards the entrance of the house and the open doorway, he could see a young African lady, dressed in a brightly coloured blue and yellow dress with matching head-tie. With mayhem all around, she seemed starkly out of place and at the instant she tried to talk to him, two men carrying a refrigerator walked between them, in an attempt to load one of the vans.

'Hello sir, can you please help me and tell me where I could find Mr Thomas Kettlewell, I'm a ...'

The end of her sentence was lost in the noise and she did not even attempt to go any further. Tom tried to help by finishing her words for her. 'Are you from one of the charities?'

'Well, er ...I suppose so,' she said, somewhat confused.

'Which one? Sorry, hang on a minute...' He turned his attention to the surrounding chaos, 'Take that out of the other door. You'll find it a lot easier.' It was much simpler planning a contract than doing all this, he thought to himself as he tried to address the lady at the door.

'I'm sorry, please come with me into the corridor towards the main house. We might get some peace there. Believe it or not, it's not always like this here. *I'm* Tom Kettlewell, by the way.' Tom escorted the startled woman past Sylvia who was now carrying a plastic tray with mugs of tea and coffee, covering its transfer of the Tower of London: this was not a 'best china' day.

Tom continued, 'Sorry, you were saying you're a .. what? … I missed what you said, sorry'

'I'm Amaka.'

'You're a what? Sorry, I don't understand.'

'I'm Amaka .. my name is Amaka Onyali.…I'm your Amaka. How do you do Mr Thomas. ' She stretched out her hand.

Tom stood in awe, silently stunned. This could not be. Amaka Onyali was the little girl whose painting of a family standing under the sun had tickled him and Emma in his student flat some thirty years earlier, on the day of the Anti-Apartheid demonstration. He had been sending money to the *Support an African Child* since 1967 and never given much thought to how the money from the standing orders was used or where it went. He had simply eased his conscience by trying to help a deprived child gain an education. He had expected to do this anonymously, even though he had received letters over the years from the St Jerome Mission. Sister Mary had informed him about the little girl called Amaka but he had lost touch with the Nun when he moved to Loughton. Tom had maintained and even increased the value of the standing orders as time passed. The last occasion he gave any thought to the payments was at the turn of the millennium, when he had occupied himself with some personal paperwork and *Big Ben* had ticked-down to midnight.

Yet here she was, standing in front of him. He felt a heady mixture of bewilderment and excited joy at seeing the person who was the outcome of his donations over so many years. She was a beautiful woman who seemed to emanate decency and innocence. Tom's mind was racing and he was lost for words. He realised he should have a lot of questions but found speech elusive. Equally, this lady from Nigeria would have a lot to ask of him, to find out as much as she could about the last thirty-odd years. Meanwhile, chaos ensued all around them.

Tom looked into her big, bright, brown eyes, stared at her immaculate smile and was totally gobsmacked. He stepped back and examined her in detail. She was striking in appearance, with a smooth, lustrous black skin and a figure hidden by the extravagant outfit she was wearing, which Tom assumed was some sort of national costume.

'I ... I ... I don't know what to say. What are you doing here? How did you find me?' It was the best line he could come up with after such a surprise.

The woman had her own agenda and had clearly spent a long time practising what she wanted to say at such a meeting. 'It is important to me to thank you for all you have done for me. For you have changed my life Mr Thomas Kettlewell and I want to …'

Tom interrupted her, trying not to be rude. 'But I haven't done anything,' he said, still stunned by the realisation of who was standing in front of him. 'Please Amaka? … sorry is that how you say it ?' She nodded. 'Please Amaka – come through to the main house and sit with me in the lounge. I'm sorry that your arrival has coincided with such turmoil. I don't know if you are aware but my father died recently and a couple of charities have arrived today to collect items which I no longer require.'

'Yes, I am sorry for your loss Mr Thomas. One of the men in the drive told me why he was here, when I asked him if Mr Thomas Kettlewell lives at this house.' Tom remembered once being told by Doc Herbert that 'timing is everything.' He could not help feel the truth behind the saying at that precise moment.

'Please. Just call me Tom. I simply can't believe that you are actually here with me now. After all this time! Wow …we certainly have a lot to talk about. If you would be so kind as to stay here for a moment, I will return to the Annex and try to hurry things along. Don't go away, I'll be right back. Promise me you won't leave.'

'No, I shall remain here and wait for you, Mr Thomas.'

XIII

Tom returned to the lounge in the main house, after he had spoken to Sylvia and left the removal arrangements in her capable hands. He was no longer concerned about what the charities removed from the Annex. There was nothing remaining that he either wanted or needed. On entering, Amaka immediately jumped to her feet, like a startled gazelle.

'Please take a seat,' instructed Tom, sympathetically. Amaka was clearly nervous. After a pregnant pause, he took the initiative. 'Well, this is a remarkable day. I never thought for one minute that I would ever meet the child I started to sponsor all those years ago. It is truly amazing. I'm guessing you have a formidable story to tell...but first ... how did you find me?'

'I am here in Great Britain working for my Government in the London School of Hygiene and Tropical Medicine. I am a doctor involved in medical research for my country. I am researching the causes and prevention of schistosomiasis.'

She had Tom's full attention and interest. 'You're a doctor – wow! So what is schistosomiasis?' Tom was smiling and on the edge of his seat. He was excited in a way that was new to him.

'It is a disease caused by parasites that are released in water by infected snails. It is a big problem in my country, er ... in Nigeria. Some countries have removed it as a disease. I am here to find out how they do it so I can help my people. I graduated five years ago in Enugu at the University of Nigeria. After two years of working around my country, I was invited to work for the Government. They sent me here to London to work on my specialist area, which is parasitology. There is some excellent work currently being undertaken in Great Britain in this area.'

'Wow!' repeated Tom, who was aware that he was saying *wow* too many times, although he genuinely could not respond any other way. He was overwhelmed. 'Congratulations. You have done remarkably well.' The irony of his sponsored child being a doctor was not lost on him, even at this special moment.

'Yes, thank you. ...Of course, I could not come all this way to Great Britain without coming to see you to thank you for what you have done for me. You have changed my life and I thank you for everything you have done for me. Without you, my life would have been very different. Yes, very different indeed.'

'You still haven't told me how you found me? I don't think anyone at the charity knows my address. Certainly, I didn't tell anyone when I moved to Loughton.' Tom was scratching the back of his head.

'Sister Mary Uloma at the St Jerome Mission died last year. You knew of her, I think. I believe she was the person who told you about me when I was a little girl. She was like a mother to me. When she was buried at the Mission I went to her funeral. In her living quarters there were some diaries. I asked the Sisters at St Jerome if I could have them to remember her. I found your name and your address in her writings. You come from a place called Kinsett, I think.'

Tom smiled. 'Consett, yes.'

'Sorry, yes Consett. I telephoned the police station in that town and they told me that you had a business company called, er ...DVTK Solutions, I believe?'

'Yes, TDVK Solutions. How on earth did they know that?' Tom was becoming thoroughly intrigued by the tale.

'I spoke to a man with a funny name. I think his name was Sergeant Puppy or Poppy or something like that.'

'Blimey, that must be Harry Poppy. I went to school with him, years ago. Fancy him knowing that. Well, I never!' Tom's success was well known in Consett. Certainly everyone in the Workingmen's Club had heard Dennis going on about his son Thomas Kettlewell, who ran his own company

'I looked up the name of your Company in the business dictionary in Westminster Reference Library. Eventually I found the address of TDVK Solutions in Canary Wharf. I travelled there on the tube and asked the man in the Reception for your address but he would not give it to me. I went to ask him every day for a week and eventually he gave me this address.

He said I was not to tell anyone who gave it to me but I think now it does not matter.'

'My goodness … you have been very persistent and resourceful.' Clearly, this young woman possessed admirable qualities.

'It was very important for me to find you. I knew this would be the best chance for me. I am in Great Britain for one year only. Then I go back to Nigeria.' Tom had forgotten about time passing as he listened to Amaka tell her story. He slapped himself lightly on the thigh as chastisement for forgetting his manners. He sprung to his feet and rang Sylvia on the internal phone, who soon brought some tea and scones with fresh fruit and ice cream on the best silver tray. It was difficult to see whose eyes were opened wider when she entered the room. Sylvia looked at Tom's new African guest in amazement, while Amaka's eyes were bewildered by the refreshments. Sylvia placed the tray onto the coffee table without saying a word. When she got as far as the door, she turned to take another look at the incongruous duo.

As Tom poured Amaka's tea, he picked up on their conversation. 'So have you had a good life?' he asked, genuinely hoping for a positive response.

'My life has been made possible only because of the money you sent for me. It paid for my food and clothes and then for my education. I knew that if I was to make something of my life, I would need to be educated. So I read every book I could get hold of when I was a little girl. When I was old enough, I gained a scholarship to the University of Enugu, after I finished school. I did not have to work while I was at University because of the money you gave to the Mission. I studied hard so that your money was not wasted. I used to return to St Jerome's when the University was closed for the holidays. Then I would work in the fields to help the nuns and the villagers with the crops or I would walk a few miles to help get water for our village.

Tom was shaking his head incredulously. 'I don't know what to say. You are a remarkable young lady and I feel so, so proud that I have had an influence on your life.' He felt as if his pride would lift him out of his skin. Tom was rapidly beginning to think it was his greatest ever achievement, yet he had known nothing about Amaka's life. He felt ashamed and proud in equal measures.

'Not just an influence. You have saved my life. I hope that through me, you will also save the lives of many other people. That is why I became a doctor.'

With those words, Tom felt something that he had not experienced for a long time. It was the exhilaration he felt on the day he learned of his brilliant A-level results, more than thirty-five years ago. At that time, he had looked forward to a bright future when all was possible and he could not see his own horizon. The feeling was the invigorating glow of hope.

Tom insisted that he take Amaka out to dinner that evening so they could continue their conversation. He needed to return to his office and since Amaka's digs were not far out of his way, she also accepted his offer of a lift. Tom felt alive as he drove his *protégé* into Central London. Their conversation during the journey mainly focussed on what they could see from the car, with Tom feebly trying to point out places of interest and exaggerate his knowledge of the mundane. He felt embarrassed when he compared himself to Scott Mason, whose performance as a guide to San Francisco was infinitely better. Tom told Amaka that he would arrange for a taxi to collect her at eight o'clock to take her to the restaurant. Amaka was impressed. She had never before been treated so regally. Tom waved goodbye through the open car window as Amaka stood on the kerb-side outside her lodgings, pleasantly stunned at the day's turn of events.

After completing his paperwork and changing into his evening suit at the office, Tom drove across the City to the Dorchester Hotel, where he had booked a table for two. He informed the *Maitre-D'hotel* that he intended to leave his car overnight in the Hotel's underground car park as he would be drinking alcohol that evening. He planned to return home to Loughton in a taxi. Tom entered the Dorchester Bar at eight o'clock and ordered two Martinis. Before Amaka arrived, he had almost drunk his cocktail and began to feel a little uneasy about her absence.

Then Tom noticed one of the Hotel staff accompanying a lady to the entrance of the Bar. It was Amaka. She was wearing a simple, bright green, knee-length, shoulder-less dress, with a gold crucifix resting starkly against her ebony skin. The blue and yellow head-tie had gone and for the first time he was able to see her black, shoulder-length hair, which was glistening in the light. It was clear that she had little idea how beautiful she was as she crossed the floor towards the table, where Tom was now standing. Their greeting was clumsy: he did not know whether to shake her hand or kiss her cheek. He did neither but simply gestured for her to take a seat beside him.

Amaka's eyes were everywhere as she lowered herself into her chair. 'This is an extremely beautiful place, Mr Kettlewell. It must be very expensive.' Her reaction came more from a sense of awe rather than any judgement.

'Oh, don't worry about that. I can afford it and please, it's Tom – just Tom.' The claim about his wealth was simply a matter of fact, rather than any conceited attempt to impress. She did not seem to notice in any event as her eyes scanned the room in the same way that she had inspected the lounge in Tom's home.

Tom stirred an olive around the remnants of his drink in the conical glass and pointed to the other. 'I've ordered a Martini for you. I hope you like them. If not I'll order something else.' For the first time in a long while, his obvious joy was being driven by pure relaxation, rather than alcohol.

'I don't know, I've never had one before.' The event was proving to be as exciting for Amaka as it was for Tom.

Amaka took a sip of Martini and her eyes squinted on impact, whilst Tom tried not to laugh. When she raised her glass a second time, they chinked their glasses together and made a silent toast, feeling happy in each other's company. Amaka began to tell Tom about her life at Enugu University, how she had grown-up at the St Jerome Mission after being orphaned in the Civil War in Nigeria, in the region formerly known as Biafra. She revealed how she used to enjoy returning to the Mission during breaks from University. Enugu was busy and noisy with lots of traffic and she felt more at home in the countryside. She did not know many people in Enugu, although she impressed at the University, through her studies. Tom could tell that Amaka only knew how to work hard.

During the holidays Amaka would return to her village, called Uminwani. She used to enjoy the daily rituals, especially visiting the market with Sister Mary. Everyone knew her in the Village and she did not feel threatened. The evenings were the best time, when she would walk into the setting sun and spot the growing numbers of stars. The whisper of the savannah grasses and the smell of yams, cocoa and palm from the fields spoke a friendly language. In the rich reds and oranges of an evening twilight, the countryside painted a beautiful scene compared to her ravaged memories. Eventually, its colours, scents and peaceful silence became the senses of safety. Although Tom was aware that Amaka had been orphaned during the Nigerian Civil War, he did not press her for any details. It was clear that she preferred to talk about her life during its post-childhood phase than to re-visit early traumas. Perhaps if they got to know each other better, it would be an area she would be more willing to talk about.

Tom felt a strong protective sense towards Amaka as he listened to her story. He imagined it was how a father would feel and it was pleasantly unusual for him to think this way. Tom had not felt a sense of love for a long time, except towards his Dad. Listening to how Amaka had overcome her difficulties, Tom felt a little ashamed of his success. Amaka had travelled many miles on a more difficult road to achieve her goals. His journey had been a self-indulgent one. Even the standing orders that he had established to look after a child he did not know, had only ever really been an attempt to sooth his moral conscience.

After finishing their meal, they returned to the Bar, where it was Tom's turn to recount his life story. They sat on the high stools, while the bartender busied himself on the other side of the counter. Amaka listened attentively to his tale of life in Consett, his days at University, a disastrous marriage to Felicity and how he came to set-up his own company and care for his Dad in Loughton. He mentioned the business success he was currently enjoying and told her about the imminent sale of *TDVK Solutions* and the financial consequences it would have on his own personal wealth.

There was one important omission from his life which he almost mentioned at one point. Tom made no reference to Emma, despite having drunk three Martinis and most of a bottle of *Dom Perignon*. In the same way that Amaka found aspects of her childhood experiences too difficult to talk about, Tom could not forget Emma. She had been the love of his life.

Before either of them realised the time, midnight was calling. Tom walked across to the reception desk, leaving Amaka to enjoy her drink and after negotiating with the manager, he booked the last single room available at the Dorchester. She watched Tom through the Bar's glass room-divider as he then moved across to the Doorman and ordered a taxi for his guest. Alone with her thoughts, Amaka pondered how much their meeting had been a revelation to them both.

Tom returned to the Bar and raised himself onto the stool next to Amaka. 'It's been a lovely evening. I would like to see you again,' he said, sounding quite vulnerable. 'Perhaps I could show you around my Company and we could take-in some tourist locations. I don't suppose you've had much chance to see the sights of London.'

She smiled. 'I would like that. Thank you. I too have enjoyed the occasion.' The bartender watched the pair from the end of the counter, swivelling and turning his drying cloth inside a wine glass, before holding it up to the light to ensure the lipstick mark was gone. He moved closer, opening the till as an excuse to eavesdrop on what he thought was a courting couple.

'I'll look forward to it. Take this. It's my card with all my contact details on it, in case you need to get hold of me for any reason.' Then he gave her another card. 'Please write *your* number on the back of this and I will give you a ring soon so we can meet again.' The bartender reached under the counter and found a pen, which he placed next to Tom's card. Amaka smiled a thank you, before the hotel worker moved along to serve another customer. Tom was a little agitated by the barman's uninvited efficiency.

With the arrangements completed, the cherry-coated Doorman at the Hotel approached Tom to inform them the taxi was waiting. They both stood to acknowledge the implications. Quickly and efficiently, the concierge returned with Amaka's coat and with effortless ease, helped her to put it on.

'Until next time?' said Tom, who suddenly felt sad that she was leaving. The bartender approached the two deserted drinks and looked across to the doorway, where the couple were now standing. He seemed uncertain whether to take the two glasses as one still contained some Martini. Deciding not to risk losing a tip, he removed only the empty glass and hoped someone would return to finish the drink.

Amaka surprised Tom when she gave him a warm hug of affection. She looked at him and said '*Dah-loo-nooh, ee-chee-ye.*'

Almost as a reflex, he responded, 'Thank you. What does that mean?'

'It means thank you, in my language. It is the most honour I can give to an elder in my village and a mark of great respect.' Amaka had waited a lifetime to say that to her saviour. Tom was used to receiving professional respect but being acknowledged as a real person was rare. His emotional compass was spinning. It had been a while since anyone made him feel like this. That person was Emma and the emotion was explained simply by one word – love. Tom felt special, something he had not done in years.

After ensuring the cost of the taxi was covered, he waved goodbye to Amaka, who returned the gesture through the taxi's rear window. Tom made his way back to the cocktail bar, where a few couples were left in the room listening to the smooth, dulcet tones of *Matt Monroe*, no doubt making their final arrangements for the climax of their evening. Tom raised his glass and finished the drink in one gulp, without bothering to sit down. Reaching inside his jacket, he removed a five-pound note from his wallet and dropped it onto the Bar. The relieved bartender swooped to claim his tip, before offering 'Good night, sir' as a thank you.

Tom turned towards the direction of the elevator and while standing in the isolation of the lift, his head was stinging with his thoughts about the experiences of the day. When he had got out of bed that morning, he considered everything would be straight forward, ensuring his Dad's remaining unwanted possessions would go to a good cause. The fact that Amaka had never featured on his radar made him feel ashamed. She was a good person and he had played a significant role in her development, albeit in ignorance. Amaka had made something of her life and was determined to change the world, just as he had done once, when he had graduated in 1970.

Pushing the white plastic, monogrammed card into the silver slot under the handle, he heard the mechanism engage. Tom opened the door and walked across the empty room before flopping onto the side of the bed. He removed his shoes and turning his body, lifted both legs on top of the covers, before putting his hands behind his head to explore the patterns on the ceiling. Tom knew that Amaka's influence in his life would be unsettling but he could not have predicted just how significant her friendship was to become in his life. The extra alcohol in his system helped him to fall asleep in a manner he did not deserve.

XIV

Two days after his meeting with Amaka, at seven-thirty on a Tuesday morning, Tom made his way from his Loughton home to Canary Wharf as usual. This day would be different. If things went to plan, it would be a life-changing milestone. The team of lawyers from *Modcom International* was meeting Tom's own legal experts to sign the final papers that would seal the takeover of *TDVK Solutions*. Neither Scott Mason nor Mitchell Fraunley would be at the meeting. Mitch's plans to dine at the Dorchester and celebrate with Tom were a casualty of pressing business needs in Frankfurt. He and Scott had already signed the papers and the process in London would be simply a rubber stamp, confirming not only the transfer of ownership but also the movement of funds into Tom's personal bank accounts. He knew he would never have to work again.

Tom was looking forward to a new chapter in his life and felt rejuvenated at the prospect of working on research projects with Scott. More importantly, Amaka's unannounced presence in his life had given him renewed vigour. It could so easily have been a sexual attraction but it was something else, even though Amaka was an attractively exotic, young woman. The days when Tom was considered physically striking were now behind him but he was still a handsome and successful middle-aged man. Those sapphire eyes were ageless. Amaka's innocence and outward demonstration of respectful deference ensured that the terms of their relationship were clear. Tom was relieved at that thought and enjoyed the special circumstances of their friendship.

He arrived early for the business meeting but was not surprised that Samantha Walters and Phil Johnston were already at the office. It was a big day for them too. Their lives and ambitions would also be enhanced by what was about to happen. Tom felt reassured that his baby would be well cared for and would continue to grow healthily.

At ten o'clock precisely, Tom and his colleagues marched along the corridor to the glass-fronted Conference Room, where the dark-suited, grey-haired lawyers were waiting. Tom followed his colleagues into the room, brushing an imaginary piece of fluff from his tie as he entered. Henry Brubaker, the head lawyer and personal confidant of Mitchell Fraunley stepped forward to introduce himself. He explained that *TDVK Solutions* lawyers had given a final inspection to the papers and they simply had to be signed. Tom glanced at his own legal personnel, who nodded affirmatively. Samantha and Phil signed their areas on the documents first, before Tom was required to write his name eight times at key points on the document. The deal was done quickly and in reverent silence. Someone else now owned *TDVK Solutions*.

There was a small technical issue with Tom's proposed contract working with Scott Mason. This problem was a separate matter to the takeover of the company. The papers relating to the Kettlewell and Mason deal needed to be corrected so Tom suggested he would sign them when he returned from his month's break. It was not a major hitch but there was some question about proposed copyright on projects that Tom would lead. He wanted his lawyers to ensure he would take the major share of any profit when developing his own ideas.

'It's not a problem, Mr Kettlewell. We'll make sure the changes are made for your return,' said Henry Brubaker. Then, in a misguided attempt to retain a congenial atmosphere the business lawyer added, 'What do you intend to do with all your newly acquired wealth, Mr Kettlewell?

Tom resisted the temptation to tell him to mind his own business. 'Not sure. First, I'm going to take that break and then I'll just see how things go. I'm not due to hook-up with Scott Mason at *Modcom* for another month, so I have a bit of time. Deciding to redress the balance of superiority in the circumstances, Tom added, 'And you'll have time to get those papers drawn-up correctly, Mr Brubaker. '

There was nothing left to do but shake hands one last time and depart from the action. Samantha and Phil simply had to return along the corridor to resume work, although Tom would have understood if they wanted to abandon their duties for remainder of the day. As the conscientious workers he knew them to be, they returned to their responsibilities, waiting to celebrate in their own way, at a later time.

Tom decided he should leave the building. No doubt he would return at some other date but he was no longer the boss. He called to see Samantha and Phil who were engaged in intimate conversation, probably ruminating over what had just taken place. Not wishing to interrupt their chat, Tom shook Phil's hand warmly and after a double-cheek kiss with Samantha, he quickly departed.

After revisiting his own office one last time, he called down the intercom for his *Alfa Romeo*. Before he left the room he turned to absorb the scene and it felt like the door was closing on an important chapter in his life. The walk to the familiar lift passed without sentiment and he felt unmoved as its doors pinged open. A different young man was now waiting to open the car door as the ex-boss stepped out of the foyer. He briefly wondered what had happened to young Tom and did not feel like tipping this youngster. Driving through the City, Tom realised that he had not given any real attention to his immediate future. Samantha and Phil would almost certainly prefer not to have him around the office. They would want to establish their own mark on the business, about to be called *Modcom Solutions*, affiliated to *Modcom International*. He sat, waiting in the car near Tower Bridge, pondering his next move before the red traffic light changed to green.

One thing he knew he had to do, was finally address the pain in his shoulder. An appointment had been arranged for Thursday at Hillside Hospital in Wimbledon. Tom would fulfil the promise he made to his Dad and allow the Consultant, Mr Woodicott to examine him. The discomfort was beginning to be a nuisance. Just as he was rubbing his shoulder, a dog ran out into the road and the car in front pulled up sharply. Tom came within a whisker of rear-ending a cheap Volvo Estate.

Soon, the journey home was nearly over and while pulling into the lane he gave some deliberation to Amaka's situation. Friday evening seemed to be the best time to contact her once again. He felt a need to explore ways of helping her reach her goals in life. She would only be in the UK for a year and that time would soon pass. Amaka's emergence had enabled things to matter to him again. Her sudden presence in his life was making him feel that he could change the world. It was almost as if he was a student once more .

XV

Saturday morning dawned and Amaka picked-up the handset from the phone on the wall, in the hallway outside her room. She placed Tom's card on top of the coin box and rotated the dial with her index finger, after two glances at the number, fumbling the strangely shaped, twenty-pence piece into the slot. For some reason Amaka was anxious. Once again, there was no answer from Tom's phone and the call went straight to the answer machine's taped message. She replaced the receiver and tapped the card against her cheek several times, pondering her options. The chair was uncomfortable and prodded the question of what to do next. Surely if there had been a practical problem with meeting up with Tom again, he would have let her know? He did not seem like the sort of person to mislead her but he had promised to be in touch by now. Amaka got out of her chair and headed towards the door but as she went to grab the handle, she paused and returned to her seat. There had to be some rational explanation for Tom's failure to contact her but there was nothing more she could do about it today. She reconciled to phone his office, first thing on Monday morning, unless she heard from Tom over the week-end.

After a worrying Sunday, Amaka eventually spoke to Samantha at five-past-nine the following morning. Amaka explained her predicament but Samantha could not provide any useful information: Tom's private contact details and whereabouts were confidential. Amaka understood Samantha's position and decided to withdraw. Using her last two ten pence pieces, she tried Tom's home number once more and after six rings it went to answer machine, once again. She heard her coins drop into the payment box shortly after she replaced the receiver.

Amaka endured a difficult week and on Friday afternoon, she gave it one last try. If there was no answer this time, she would make her way to his home after she finished work. At least she was certain where he lived. After dialling his number, she was surprised when the phone was picked up after three rings. Sylvia answered. Amaka asked to speak to Tom but Sylvia explained he was not there. Sylvia recognised Amaka's voice; it was not difficult.

In a flustered response, Sylvia suggested that Amaka should give it a few days and then call again. By that time, Sylvia maintained that Tom should have re-surfaced. Sylvia knew Tom's location but she was sworn to secrecy. However, when she next spoke to Tom she would tell him about Amaka's concern. Hopefully he would release her from her commitment of withholding the truth. Either that, or he could phone Amaka himself. For the moment, Amaka would have to wait. Tom's instructions took precedence over someone she hardly knew. A worried Amaka gave Sylvia her phone number and asked her to pass-on a message to Tom, about getting in touch.

Amaka was alarmed. As far as she was concerned, Tom was missing.

PART THREE

I

Tom had never felt happy about paying for medical treatment. It was one of the few remaining glowing embers of his socialist principles. The National Health Service was the jewel in the crown for his parents' generation but when it was a case of looking after his father's health, things had been different. His Dad's well-being was too precious and delicate to allow any ideology to get in the way. Tom was also prepared to abandon his socialist principles for his own treatment. The more he thought about his actions, the more he wondered if he knew himself at all.

An appointment for ten o'clock in the morning at Hillside Hospital had been arranged. There was no trouble being seen by a doctor, he paid more than enough medical insurance. Parking the car in any London hospital was a nightmare and after paying the taxi fare through the driver's window, Tom crossed the road and walked past five patients who were standing outside the main entrance, in their dressing gowns. They were smoking cigarettes surreptitiously and made a pathetic sight. One elderly man was even holding onto a mobile saline drip as he puffed on the weed.

Tom entered the outpatients' area through the automatic glass doors and spotted a blue background sign with white writing, indicating the direction to the X-ray department. On registration at the reception desk, he was directed to a private waiting zone at the end of the corridor. He had to walk past a throng of NHS patients who all had a ten o'clock appointment. At least *he* would not have to wait, thanks to his private insurance.

Before Tom had finished his coffee, a young female in a white jacket and blue trousers approached him. The badge on her lapel indicated that she was Julie Maynard, a Radiographer. 'Sorry to keep you waiting, Mr Kettlewell. This won't take long and you will soon be able to enjoy the rest of your day.' She presented Tom with a sealed polythene bag containing a newly pressed white dressing-gown, accompanying flip-flops and a slipover.

219

When he re-emerged from the changing cubicle feeling vulnerable, Julie had a request. 'I've got a student radiographer with me today, Mr Kettlewell. His name is Stewart. Will it be ok with you if he sits-in on the X-rays? He will only be observing so he will not intervene with any of the normal processes but feel free to say no if you're not happy with him being there.'

'No, that's fine.' Tom was always willing to help someone trying to learn a new skill. He removed his dressing-gown and placed it over a nearby chair before Julie ushered him across to a metal plate, positioned on the wall, in front of the X-ray machine. She told him to remain still for a moment, while she stepped outside the room. Tom heard the whir of the equipment and looked around, half-wondering where she had gone. As soon as the machine stopped, Julie reappeared. Tom was asked to sit and wait while the negatives were examined for clarity. On the hard, plastic chair he bent forward, drumming his fingers and popping his lips, hoping it would not take long.

After about five minutes, Miss Maynard returned and surprised him with more instructions. 'Could you lie down now please, Mr Kettlewell? We're just going to take pictures of your legs as well.' Tom presumed the additional shots were for the benefit of the student radiographer. The tiles on the ceiling became a friend for the next quarter-of-an-hour as he lay still, exploring the blinkered view. Julie then concluded authoritatively, 'That's it done now, Mr Kettlewell. The radiologist will take a further look at the X-rays and report to your doctor. You can return to the changing room and get dressed.'

When he had completed his return to normality, Tom stepped outside the drab changing room and adjusted his collar. While leaving, he saw the radiographer, who was with another patient and about to enter the X-Ray room. 'Thanks again, cheerio,' he called. Tom had been impressed by her efficiency and consideration. She gave him a closely scrutinised farewell.

Tom was glad to leave the Hospital and get into one of the waiting taxis. Soon, he was drinking a single malt in the conservatory at *Derwent House*.

He happened to be in the fruit aisle at the local supermarket the following morning, when his mobile rang. Answering the phone, he tried not to speak too loudly as he half-reached for a punnet of nectarines. Tom had always considered that mobile phones were a necessity rather than a luxury. He hated the pretentiousness that some people seemed to enjoy when responding to a call in public and they spoke louder than necessary. The young boy topping-up the stock of *Golden Delicious* gave a brief but intrusive glance in his direction.

'Good morning, Mr Kettlewell. This is Doctor Thomas from the Medical Practice. I'm calling about the results of your X-rays which we have received this morning. Mr Woodicott, the Consultant Orthopaedic Surgeon would like you to call back to Hillside Hospital this afternoon to discuss things with you.'

Tom was surprised. Everything had seemed to go well, the day before. He had not anticipated any problems. Suddenly, half-a-dozen butterflies fluttered in his stomach. 'Oh … right…er … is there a problem?'

Dr Thomas refused to discuss the matter on the phone, preferring to defer to the Consultant. As Tom listened carefully to the message, he withdrew his hand from its nectarine target and placed it into his rear trouser pocket. His eyes were rolling three-sixty degrees as he pondered the voice on the phone. Suddenly, the conversation was over.

The young 'fruit' boy was now looking at him more intently. Tom wondered if he had been raising his voice during the call: Dr Thomas had unnerved him. He put down the shopping basket and walked out of the main glass door exit, not caring for the inconvenience the abandoned items might cause the supermarket staff. He crossed the road and went to the nearest coffee shop. After ordering an *Espresso* he sat quietly alone, in sombre contemplation. It was another three hours before the appointment. He was concerned about the reason for the urgency of the afternoon timing, only a day after having been X-rayed. It all sounded serious.

Earlier than necessary, Tom returned to the Outpatients Department at Hillside Hospital. For NHS patients, a two o'clock appointment was the afternoon equivalent of its ten o'clock, morning counterpart. Once more, he walked the corridor and could see the packed NHS waiting area. The scene reminded him of a departure lounge on a budget airline flight. Compliant herds were being corralled into a pattern of movement, complaining only to themselves. Tom registered at the appointment's desk and sat in the more sedate surroundings, reserved for those VIPs who had pre-booked airline extras. Within two minutes of taking his seat, his name was called. He walked past a corner of the clinic and felt the burning stare of envious and tired NHS patients, fed-up at already having waited too long. The nurse showed him to an examination cubicle and asked him to take a seat, before drawing back the blue, courtesy curtain.

Tom sat on the edge of the grey inspection table, which had been covered by an extra-wide sheet of paper roll. Just as he started to explore the intimacy of the cell's contents, the curtain was whisked back speedily and Mr Woodicott arrowed into the booth. 'Hello, Mr Kettlewell. I am Mr Woodicott. I am the Senior Orthopaedic Consultant at Hillside Hospital.' He held out his hand and Tom tried to shake it as firmly as he could in the circumstances.

Mr Woodicott was in battle gear, in anticipation of dealing with the many people sitting in the patients' waiting area. He was seeing Tom before his regular, weekly afternoon NHS clinic. The Consultant was a tall, athletic, bespectacled man in his forties, who emanated the kind of professional charisma that Tom had seen in other 'winners' during his own business dealings. The spectacles were for purpose and not vanity. Simon Woodicott had studied medicine at Imperial College, London and followed his qualification with three years biomedical research at the College's Alexander Fleming Building, progressing to specialise in orthopaedics. He was consistently ranked among the top three students throughout his time at the Imperial College School of Medicine. During his younger days he was a top rower and also played badminton for England, just failing to be selected for the team that went to the Seoul Olympics in 1988. His principal leisure activity now was skiing in Cutigliano in Lombardy, where he had a log cabin. Simon inherited his father's love of Italy during his youth, along with his confidence, auburn hair and passion for opera. It was during holidays to Italy that Simon first experienced the slopes of the Piedmont and the exhilarating thrill of freedom, found only by cutting through the fresh, crisp Italian air on *Carradan* skis.

Mr Woodicott was holding X-rays in his left hand and with swift precision he inserted the first one into the clip on the plates' viewer. 'I have your X-rays here Mr Kettlewell. As you can see, there appears to be a problem.' He pointed at the light-and-dark blue picture, while holding his white, cloth cap in his left hand. 'That area you can see there, should be bone but there is a dark shadow over the femur.'

'The femur! That's in the leg, isn't it? But I have a bad shoulder. Is that an X-ray of my leg?' Tom was totally bemused. Was this doctor brilliant or an idiot?

'Yes, that's your left femur. You had it X-rayed yesterday?' Mr Woodicott thought he had better check. Mistakes had been known in the past and private patients were more likely than NHS cases to sue for any incompetence demonstrated by his staff.

'Yes I did. I wondered why they X-rayed my legs and my other shoulder. I thought it was a part of the student radiographer's training, or something.' Tom felt as if he was handing control of the situation to someone he had only just met.

Mr Woodicott was targeting the essential information. 'No, this is not your shoulder. I am more concerned about your leg. The femur is a load-bearing bone and as you can see, yours is very thin indeed. This is not to scale. Your femur bone is really that thin. Have you been experiencing any pain with it?'

Tom cast his mind back to how one or two people had commented on his limp when he had crossed the office floor and he had dismissed it as something trivial. 'Yes but I thought it was an old sports' injury. I've been trying to run it off.'

The Consultant's eyes had not left Tom's face. When he heard this information he became very agitated. 'Dear, dear! If that bone snaps you would have serious problems. Trying to run on it, is just about the worst thing you could do. We need to see to that straight away.' The doctor blew out his cheeks and raised his eyebrows in alarm.

'But what about my shoulder? That's been causing me more problems.' Tom was beginning to flap. His voice was raised in volume and pitch, more from the concern that was being generated than any feeling of annoyance.

'Ah, yes... right.' Mr Woodicott replaced the leg X-ray with the one of Tom's shoulder. 'As you can see, you have a shadow over that area as well. The bone is probably in a worse state but it is not load-bearing so I'm not so concerned at this stage.' The word *shadow* had terrible connotations.

'So what is it?' asked Tom, whose mouth was becoming drier with every word. He felt the discussion was hurtling towards a tragic conclusion.

'I don't know yet. I can only say it looks serious. You can see for yourself. That shadow area should appear lightly as clear bone, like the rest of the leg around it. A shadow on an X-ray like that and of such magnitude is usually indicative of a serious condition. Because the femur is so fragile I want to bring you in straight away and *'nail'* that leg. Then we can take a bone biopsy and find out what the problem is before I nail the shoulder.'

'When you say *nail*? ...' asked Tom, who felt he was beginning to regress into childhood, sounding more like a little boy than a multi-millionaire.

'Yes, I will insert a titanium pin along the femur to take your body's weight. I'll screw it into your hip, run it down the length of the femur and then insert a couple of screws to attach it to your knee.' Mr Woodicott was in full flow, standing within touching distance of his patient. He was directing his hands and arms over Tom's body to explain his intended treatment plan, like an illusionist waving over his assistant before sending her into a trance. 'After that it will be impossible for the bone to snap. I'll then do the same sort of thing with your shoulder. I'll run a pin along the humerus up to the shoulder and insert a sort of hinge that will allow you some movement and flexibility.'

'So how long after you have *nailed* my leg and shoulder will it be before I can return to work?' As Tom was about to realise, this was a naïve question. His moon-eyes were cast upwards towards his doctor, making a plea for some indication of positivity. The hammer came down on his hopes.

'Oh, I'm sorry, Tom. Did I not make myself clear? I will be very surprised if you will ever work again. This is serious – very serious. You are about to embark on a major medical journey. We don't know yet what that entails but I do know you will need every sinew of energy to address what will be invasive and challenging treatment. There will be a long period of recovery after major surgery. This is a major, life-changing event for you I'm afraid. Now – I need to see if I can get a bed for you today. I don't want you to walk out of here, only for that femur to break. If it does, you could lose your leg.'

Tom sat with his head bowed, his hands and arms collapsing into the space between his thighs. There were no tears in his eyes but he was totally flabbergasted by this appalling medical revelation. Anyone would have been traumatised by such devastating news. It was like something in a film or on television, only it was real and it was happening to him.

'I can see you're stunned but don't worry, we will tackle this together. I think it best if I give you some time to absorb what I have just told you, old chap. Would you like me to ask a nurse to be with you, unless you have come with your wife or someone?' Tom shook his head, without saying a word. He could not speak. 'In that case, I'm going to leave you on your own for a couple of minutes to see if I can find you a bed, today. I know my colleague is in the next corridor. I'm going to have a word with her to see if she can chivvy up something for you, now.'

Within ten agonising minutes, Mr Woodicott returned, accompanied by a middle-aged nurse wearing a dark blue top. Tom presumed from her demeanour that she was a Sister. The Consultant broke the news with some gusto, 'Success! I've had a word with my colleague and she has agreed to do a bit of shuffling around with a couple of her patients so I've been able to get you a bed in the Emergency Orthopaedic Ward today. There are no private rooms available I'm afraid but we can't really afford to wait. The Emergency Ward will give us some breathing space before we consider our options. If you go now with Sister into another room, she will sort you out and I'll see you on the Ward, later.'

In keeping with his decency as a compassionate human being, seeing that Tom was devastated with the news, Mr Woodicott added, 'I know this has been a tremendous shock for you and it is obviously a worrying time. My advice is to stay positive. I will guide you through every phase of the treatment programme and please feel free to ask me any question at any time. If there is anything you don't understand and want me to clarify, just tell me. I don't believe it is a good idea to try and mislead patients. My experience is that people want to know the truth. Yes?' Tom nodded.

The man who had made millions and dictated his ambition to the world, was now completely humble. It was all he could do to speak. 'Thank you. You are right, the truth is always best. I honestly thought I must have damaged some tendons or something. It never occurred to me that an injury to a shoulder could have such drastic consequences.' Mr Woodicott offered a final handshake before turning away and heading towards another treatment room. Tom's session was over and he was obliged to follow the nurse to an adjacent corridor, still stunned by the news.

The Sister led Tom into a treatment room, which housed some silver-coloured trays and utensils on a large trolley, next to a mound of wrapped, new syringes. She gestured for him to take a seat. There was only one plastic chair in the room. 'Are you alright?' asked the Sister with genuine compassion in her voice. 'I know you've had some terrible news. Is there anyone you would like to call? I can get you an outside line.' She nodded in the direction of a white phone, beside the sterilisation unit that looked like an empty fish tank.

Tom shook his head. 'No, there's nobody.' The level of pathos in his voice was sufficient for the Sister to offer a sympathetic smile and some words of support.

'Mr Woodicott is good. He's just about the best doctor I've ever worked with. You could not be in better hands.' After a brief moment of reflection she added, 'Now there must be someone you could call to get some personal stuff for you, pyjamas and things. You wouldn't want to wear one of our horrible gowns all the time now would you?'

Tom's thoughts came to the surface. 'Well there's Sylvia I suppose. She's got a key and could bring me some toiletries if I asked her.' The nurse gestured once again towards the phone. All Tom had to do was dial nine for an outside line. As he lifted the receiver, his back was towards the door and he did not notice Sister Withers leave the room.

When she returned, guiding a full cup and semi-wet saucer carefully through the heavily hinged door, Tom was in the process of explaining his afternoon experience to Sylvia. He did not need to ask her twice and having disclosed this most intimate of secrets, he commanded her not to say anything to anyone. With typical efficiency she organised her husband to drive her across to *Derwent House*, where she let herself in through the front door. She was one of only two other people who knew the security code for the alarm system so she switched-off the increasingly frenetic high pitched beep at the white number panel, before going upstairs. Sylvia collected everything Tom requested and gathered a full travel bag containing the items she hoped would suffice.

She then went downstairs and was just about to re-set the alarm, when the phone rang. After three rings, she picked up the handset. It was 'that girl from Africa' who had been trying to get in touch with Tom. There was no alternative but to play ignorant. After fudging the truth , Sylvia replaced the receiver, re-set the numbers on the panel and made her way to Hillside Hospital with a heavy heart. 'That poor man! What he's had to put up with recently. What good is all that money to him now?'

II

Tom was shown into the Ward by Sister Withers and he felt the scrutinising eyes of other patients boring down in his direction. It was not every patient who entered the Ward wearing an expensive suit. As his eyes examined the room that was to become his home for the next couple of days, the reasons for the majority of the patients' incarceration became clear. Pulleys, white plaster of Paris and metal limb structures were on many of the beds. Most people were in the Emergency Orthopaedic Ward because they had suffered some kind of trauma or accident, causing an obvious incapacitating break to a part of their body.

One chap, who was a painter and decorator had fallen from his ladder onto the flat roof of a garage, where he remained undetected and in agony for three hours. Another, who was engaged in a basic call of nature behind a curtain when Tom entered the room, had been involved in a motor cycle accident and had two broken legs. A teenager in the bed opposite had his plastered hand in a stirrup to help the blood flow through his arm. As Tom learned later, the boy was drunk at a family wedding and seeing his girlfriend flirting with his uncle, decided to take out his frustration by foolishly punching a radiator. Metal rods were placed along the length of three shattered fingers in his right hand, inserted at the points where his finger nails had been removed.

After Sister Withers had left Tom to change into his gown, he flumped into the chair beside his bed and threw his gown onto the top sheet. His body folded with total despondency as he looked down at his feet, head in hands. Glyn, a patient confined to the next bed, took responsibility to break the ice.

'Hiya. You look like you've got the world on your shoulders. I'm Glyn.' He gave a polite gesture of an imitated wave.

'Hi, Glyn. I'm Tom. I'd like to say I am pleased to meet you but the circumstances don't seem to be appropriate. How are you doing anyway, you look to be in the middle of some gigantic *Meccano* set. What happened or would you rather not say?' Tom had forgotten there were others like him, who preferred to keep matters to themselves.

'No, it's ok. I've been like this for a month. I was on holiday in Majorca when I jumped-off some rocks into a pool. Unfortunately, the pool wasn't deep enough and I broke my legs. The right one was particularly bad and the bone pierced the skin. I had emergency treatment out there but the insurance company paid for me to be flown home and they put me in here.'

'I thought they only kept people in this ward for a couple of weeks?' Tom had not forgotten that everyone's stay in the Emergency Orthopaedics Ward was supposed to be limited.

'Yeah, that's right. Trouble is I need specialist nursing. These rods are meant to keep the tibia and fibula in place. Only thing is I have to have the wounds cleaned twice a day and it hurts like buggery. There's only a couple of nurses trained to do it. So I have the long service medal for this place. What are you in here for, anyway? We don't see many admitted into this ward that are not on a stretcher, sitting in a wheelchair or on crutches.'

'That's a good question. I haven't got a clue why I'm here. Two hours ago I was expecting to hear that I needed some sort of physiotherapy or a steroid injection or something to help ease the pain in my shoulder. I didn't think they were going to drop the bombshell like they did. They are concerned that my bones are crumbling and that's what's causing the pain in my shoulder and left leg. No one has used the word *cancer* yet but I can't think of anything else that it might be.'

'So what are they going to do?' Glyn had witnessed a few conditions occupy the next bed. He regarded himself of something of a connoisseur of broken bones and was naturally curious.

'Apparently, I need an operation on my leg, more or less straight away. The only way they can tell what it is for sure is to take a biopsy. I've got nothing with me, not a razor, pyjamas nor slippers. I only hope my friend turns up before they start on me or I won't have anything decent to put on.' Tom then turned towards a sound he had never heard before.

A clink of crockery and a chink of cutlery heralded the forthcoming meal. The smell was not the best advertisement for hospital food. A woman in a red overall changed from being a servant into a grand inquisitor as she brought her tea trolley to a halt, opposite Glyn's bed. She also did a supplementary imitation of a court jester.

'Who's this then, Glyn? Got yourself a new friend? He's a bit of alright isn't he? Hey, Jeanie there's a new one over here. Come and see which one of us he wants to take out this Saturday. Hello, sweetheart. I'm Doris and that fat porker over there with the spots is Jeanie. Are you staying here with us tonight at the Salubrious Palace or are you going to leave all this behind and whisk me off to the West End?'

'Don't be stupid, Doris. He wouldn't take you to *Arse* End even if he had a tandem and you did the peddling!'

'Charmed I'm sure.' Turning to Tom, she asked ultra-politely if he would like to partake of a beverage. Tom declined but thanked her anyway. 'Usual for you, Glyn or is your wife going to come in and disturb us?'

'Just a tea, thank you Doris. My wife will give me everything else.' An advantage of being a long-term patient was forming a unique relationship with some of the members of staff. Glyn and Doris had become very familiar over the past few months. They knew where the parameters of acceptable behaviour lay and there was a lot of latitude.

'Suit yourself dearie. You don't know what you're missing.' Doris turned her head to the side in a feigned huff and stroked her hair, before placing a hand on her hip and pushing the trolley to the next patient. She was intent on transporting her cabaret of sexual innuendo elsewhere.

After she had left earshot, Tom turned to Glyn and stated the obvious. 'She's a bit of a card.' It was the first time Tom had smiled that day. He nodded in gratitude as Doris pushed her trolley out of the Ward.

'Heart of gold but a bit of a rough diamond. She's harmless really. You'll get used to her.' That last phrase made Tom's blood run cold. His projected stay in hospital was becoming a reality.

III

A nurse came through the main ward doors and walked straight to Tom, who was sitting on the edge of the bed. He was lost in his thoughts and had not yet changed into the hospital gown. She told him that someone called Sylvia had just arrived, with some of his personal effects. She was waiting for him in the television room, if he wanted to go and see her. Tom pushed himself off the bed and made his way to greet Sylvia, who was standing anxiously by the window as he entered. She broke into tears when she could see how devastated he looked.

Sylvia asked if there was anything further she could do for him but Tom had only one request. 'Please don't let anyone know that I'm in hospital until we know where all this is going. I was due some time off for a while so nobody at work will be concerned if I'm not around for a couple of weeks. With a bit of luck, they may never know anything about this.' Sylvia decided not to say anything about the phone call from Amaka but she did have one surprise for him.

'I've brought your pyjamas and some toiletries along with some of your mail from the House, just in case there's anything important. There's also a letter there from that woman who called after your Dad's funeral, that Maisie something-or-other. She called to the House earlier and wanted to talk to you about something important but she wouldn't tell me what it was. I said you were out of the country. I hope that was ok?'

'Yes, that's fine.' Tom was only half-listening. His eyes were in a distant stare, wishing he was anywhere else.

'Anyway, she left an old letter for you and said it would explain everything. It's in there with the others. She also left her phone number if you want to give her a ring... you know... when you're better.' Sylvia was struggling to find some words of comfort. She dashed away some imaginary dust from Tom's shoulders before they hugged a farewell.

As quickly as she had arrived, Sylvia was gone and Tom felt alone once more. Reluctantly, he returned to the Ward, carrying the small travel bag containing his essentials. He walked silently past Glyn, who was reading a newspaper. Tom drew the curtain around his bed and changed into his own pyjamas and dressing gown, feeling very defenceless. He did not want to draw back the barrier, preferring to occupy his new world in isolation. Suddenly, a nurse arrived and brought him back to reality.

'Mr Woodicott is on the Ward, doing his rounds so he'll be here soon to see you.' She said it with such reverential excitement Tom wondered if Jesus himself was to walk in and lay hands on the sick. Fortunately, Simon Woodicott did not regard himself so loftily. After working his way along the beds, he nodded to Glyn before approaching Tom. This time, the same nurse re-drew the curtains fully around the bed in a ludicrous gesture at privacy. Mr Woodicott was accompanied by two other doctors, who Tom deduced were his Registrar and a young Medical Student as well as the Ward Sister. After a perfunctory renewal of their earlier greeting, the Consultant got straight to the matter-in-hand.

'I would expect that you will be *prepped* for the operation at about five o'clock tomorrow, Mr Kettlewell so you'll have a bit of a wait, I'm afraid. Try not to worry, I've done hundreds of operations exactly like this one. It's pretty standard in orthopaedics. The issue in your case is determining the cause. … Ok? …'

Tom nodded and Mr Woodicott turned swiftly away, mumbling something to his two minions as the trio left the Ward, like troops marching off to battle. Tom stayed behind the drawn curtain that evening. He wanted to rely on his own thoughts and had no time for small-talk. If Glyn was offended by the gesture, then too bad. Within a few days he would probably never see him again, anyway.

The Ward was noisy that night. The clanking of trolleys, the beeping of saline drips warning of imminent depletion and the snoring of patients, produced an idiosyncratic symphony that was new. Tom was nervous and frightened at the position in life he found himself. The constant anguished calls of Mr Dixon, a lonely, blind and frightened old man from a nearby ward, invaded the corridor to add further distress to everyone within earshot. The occasional angry command of 'Shut up Dixon, we're all trying to sleep!' by an irritated patient, interrupted the murmuring chaos.

IV

Eventually morning came, along with a *'Nil by Mouth'* sign above Tom's bed. Doris, the breakfast-trolley-lady, gave a knowing look as she wheeled past. Most of the other patients were washed, fed and bored by nine o'clock. Some were waiting for the morning papers to arrive. Those who could walk or pivot on crutches made their way to the 'Day Room' for no other reason than a change of scenery.

Tom was sitting in the bedside chair, wondering how to get hold of something to read, when a porter called. The middle-aged man in a white coat was pushing an empty wheelchair and invited Tom to take a ride to the MRI Unit. Tom looked at him with scepticism and tried to ignore the instruction, preferring to walk unaided out of the Ward. However, the Hospital's Health and Safety Regulations won the dispute.

The porter nodded and chatted to some of his colleagues as the unlikely pair bobsleighed along the corridors. Tom rested his elbow on the right-hand arm rest and preferred to look down, ignoring the hell around him. After a few minutes of travel, he could see the clear sign at the entrance of the MRI Unit. The porter spun the wheelchair one hundred-and-eighty degrees, then walked backwards and pushed the double doors open by barging the door with his rear.

Tom was pushed into a side-room where he quickly extricated himself from the wheelchair and sat in a hospital seat, like an ordinary person. A young doctor assigned to the Unit explained that he was going to give Tom a small injection. It contained a contrast medium to enhance the definition of the output images. After waiting ten more minutes for the contrast to circulate around his system, he was invited to lay on a gurney. It was positioned inside a long tube to allow his body to slowly pass into an enclosed chamber, where it was extremely claustrophobic and loud. Tom had to consciously remind himself that the procedure was not painful, merely uncomfortable. It lasted about thirty minutes and just before he was getting used to the noise, the process was complete. A nurse returned him to the side-room, where he waited for another porter to take him back to the Ward, in readiness for his operation. On his way back, Tom was finding it difficult to distinguish between reality and a nightmare. Once again, he looked down at the floor, trying to transport his thoughts to somewhere pleasant.

An hour after lunch was served to the other patients, one of the junior doctors examined him for the last time to ensure that he was fit for the operation. Tom pondered what could have deteriorated since his examination the previous day and the MRI scan that morning. Things were happening too quickly and he was being torpedoed out of his comfort zone. The whole experience was life changing.

Twenty minutes after the evening news had started on television, two porters arrived at Tom's bed. 'Right, Mr Kettlewell we're going to take you for your pre-meds and then shortly after that you'll be wheeled into Theatre. Tom lifted himself onto another gurney and was pushed out of the Ward on super-slick wheels. He watched the conveyor belt of ceiling tiles flutter past as he lay on his back, trying not to close his eyes. Tom soon found himself alone in another curtained cubicle waiting for the next stage. A different junior doctor entered and asked if he was wearing any underpants. When he said he *was* wearing underwear, he was required to remove his boxers and place them in a plastic bag. This was another mystery which was never resolved. Why did he have to remove his final piece of dignity? Then came the final, terrifying comment. 'Ok, Mr Kettlewell we are ready for you now so we are going through to Theatre.' The final call saw about half-a-dozen, green-gowned, masked doctors and nurses, most of whom were looking in Tom's direction. It was not a reassuring sight. Another medic stepped forward, with his role printed on a badge-tag : it simply read, *Anaesthetist*, a label that commanded Tom's attention.

In a whispering, seductive voice the doctor said, 'I'm going to give you an injection in your hand, Mr Kettlewell. As I do that, I'd like you to start counting down, from ten. So it's ten, nine, eight and so on.'

At seven, everything went black.

V

Tom awoke in strange surroundings. Although his mouth was extremely dry, his first priority was to find his bearings. A nurse was sitting beside his bed as he recovered consciousness from the operation. 'Hello there, sleepy head. How are you feeling?' Instinctively, Tom scrambled his fingers to the side, as if his hand was a spider. The nurse's soft palm stopped its progress, while he tried desperately to gauge the nature of his new reality. He took a sip through a straw and ice cold water cascaded into his mouth. The drink was more refreshing than anything he had ever tasted and his pumice mouth absorbed the liquid instantly. After a couple of minutes of holding hands, he started to come around.

'What time is it?' inquired Tom, who was overcome with a sense of relief. He had survived. There was no point in trying to explore his surroundings. The most important question was answered. He was not dead.

The nurse gave him a quick examination. Their intimacy was completed when she said, 'Right, you seem to be fine, Tom. I'll arrange for you to go back to the Ward. The porters will come and get you in a couple of minutes'

Lying on the gurney, he was wheeled back to the Ward around mid-evening. Visiting hour had just ended and everyone was returning to their regular evening routine. There was a pervasive mood of calm and orderliness. A couple of the cribs were un-occupied as patients were completing their ablutions, preparing for the night-time's rest. Glyn was in bed reading a car magazine, trying to look across through a chink in the curtain. The nurse had not fully closed the seal around Tom's temporary cocoon.

'Ok Tom. How did it go?' inquired Glyn, in whispered tones, directed through the gap in the drapes and sounding genuinely concerned about the health of his new friend.

Tom struggled to give a coherent response. 'Still a bit ...'

'He's doing well. Everything went fine,' responded the Ward Sister. The big guns were already on patrol; with that frosty response, the blue curtains were once again fully whisked around Tom's bed. He was still a bit groggy from the anaesthetic as the Sister busied herself around him. She ensured the elasticated dressing that stretched from his left hip down to his knee was not too tight, checked his drip was in place and made certain that the monitor lead was securely inserted. He seemed fine.

'This is your morphine clicker, Tom.' She then lifted-up Tom's operating gown, revealing his bare loins. Neither was bothered about his exposed genitalia. Sister Withers had seen more penises than any of the males in the Ward, while Tom could not have cared less about who saw him naked. She pointed at a white, plastic tube that was taped to his groin. The phial was about the size of a toothpaste dispenser. A lead extended from its base, straight into a vein in his thigh. Tom had been totally unaware of its presence.

'Whenever the pain becomes too much, press this clicker and it will release the morphine straight away. If you press too often it may not release any extra morphine. It's programmed to give you the right amount. We don't want to give you too much now do we, just in case you get to like it? I've got another hour before I finish my shift. I'll come back to see how you're doing before I go and the night-nurse takes over. If you need a bottle or anything just press the buzzer. The worst is over for the moment and it's all gone fine. Mr Woodicott or his Registrar may come to see you. He'll certainly be calling on his rounds tomorrow.' As she finished taking his pulse, she stroked back his hair maternally, before writing something on the chart attached to the clipboard that was hanging on the foot of his bed. She then disappeared behind the magic curtain.

Three days into his recovery from the operation, Tom needed some distraction from the pain in his leg. He began to wonder about the letter left by Maisie Springfield and leaning across from his bed, he started rummaging through the drawer in his bedside locker. There was an envelope among the pile left by Sylvia, in the middle of some bills and a couple of bank statements. It was franked with the date December 16th 1948 and was clearly one of Maisie's post-war letters to his father, Dennis.

At first, Tom was nervous about reading the letter although Maisie had clearly wanted him to view its contents. If it was Maisie's last message to his father, it would certainly contain some highly personal information. The letter was written in black ink, using a simple, quill-nib and there was a *2-d,* red stamp neatly positioned in the top, right corner. For a brief moment, Tom admired its archaic honesty compared to the byte-size emails that now dominated his world of instant communication. He unfurled the twin folds to expose its contents.

62, Wiggins Terrace,
Consett,
County Durham
December 15th 1948

Dear Dennis,

It is with great sadness that I am writing this letter. I know you are angry with me for not wanting to go to the Christmas works dance next week. I know that is why you are avoiding me and why you have not called to our house.

There is something that I must tell you. I have been to the doctor and he has told me that I am pregnant. I know this will come as a great shock to you as it has done to me.

I do not want my child to grow up without a father and want us to get married. I feel that I must be married when my child is born. I do not want to tell my parents that I am in the family way. I do not want to risk the chance of being disowned by them. You know what my dad is like.

So, if you do not want to marry me, I will try to marry someone else. Naturally, I want to be married to you but only if you love me.

If you go to the dance next week without me I will have my answer.

Please make the right decision.

Love,

Maisie

This was another missile exploding in Tom's rapidly changing world. As he lay in bed, his mind was racing while he considered the implications of the letter. The dates and timing of everything were confusing. He tried to piece together the calendar of events in the year before his birth. This was seemingly when all the important incidents were taking place in his parents' lives.

Tom was born in early October 1949 and his parents were married in August, that year. He did not have to own a first-class degree in Maths to work out the implications of the time lapse. He always knew the reason why his parents married so soon after getting together. It was a common reason for marriage during a period when contraception in Britain was so primitive and difficult to obtain. If a girl found out she was 'in the family way', a matrimonial service often quickly followed. However, this situation was different. Tom calculated that he must have been conceived in January, just after the dance mentioned in Maisie's letter to his Dad. Could it be that Dennis Kettlewell was responsible for making two women pregnant within such a short space of time?

If it was true and Maisie was pregnant, it also meant that Jenny Springfield was his half-sister, another dramatic revelation. Jenny had attended a different primary school to Tom when growing-up because she lived in another village, a few miles from Consett. However, both he and Jenny were in the same year group at Grace Darling Grammar School. Tom remembered that Jenny was the oldest person in the class because she was born on September 1st, the first birth date of all school year cohorts. At the beginning of school each year, when the details of the class lists were checked, it was often something noticed and commented upon by some of the teachers. The unusual birth date stuck in Tom's memory from his school days – Jennifer Springfield, the oldest girl in the year group.

Tom and Jenny also shared similar physical characteristics : they both had a dark complexion, black hair and a slim physique. If all this was accurate and she *was* his half-sister, had Maisie discussed it already with Jenny? Was he the last to know? There was no point torturing himself, it was all beyond his control.

Another tormenting question was, why did Dennis not do 'the decent thing,' and marry Maisie? Did he doubt Maisie's story about being pregnant and feel he was being coerced into a situation against his wishes? His response to her letter seemed to be out of character. It was unlike him to ignore such an important issue and go to the dance irrespective of Maisie's expectations. He was clearly making some sort of statement. Perhaps he just did not love her and it was as simple as that. Whatever the reason, it would remain a mystery. Tom's view of his Dad was challenged by the incident but he preferred to focus on Jenny, while he lay in bed gazing out of the window, alone with his thoughts.

Each day, he asked whether the results of his bone biopsy were yet known. Each day, the hospital staff had to respond negatively. 'Unlike soft tissue biopsies, it takes time for the bone to break down before an accurate analysis can be made. So, I'm afraid it could be three to four weeks before we know the results,' This was the view offered by Dr Al-Hussain, Mr Woodicott's Registrar, during a routine visit.

One night after a return to a regime of pain, Tom was finding it difficult to sleep. No matter what he did, there was no position that offered relief from the growing agony emanating from his leg. Eventually, he had to call for a nurse to explain his discomfort. She referred the situation to a medical colleague and returned with some good news. 'The doctor says you can have a morphine injection if you want. If it is that bad.'

There was no need to hesitate. Tom wanted the pain to disappear. 'Yes please nurse. This is giving me hell.' The nurse left his bedside briefly, before returning with a small tray containing a morphine syringe. After putting on some dispensable gloves, she plunged the needle into the muscle of his left thigh. The scene was reminiscent of a Marine medic plunging a field-jab into an American soldier during the Vietnam War. The injection brought the same instant relief as any alleviation felt by a warrior in battle and Tom immediately lost consciousness, falling into a deep, black sleep.

It was ten o'clock the following morning when Tom began to stir. He had missed all the early morning rituals. The curtain was drawn around his bed and there was a *Do Not Disturb* sign above his head. It seemed the return of pain had given more concern than he realised. He felt confused with the curtains drawn and was hot in the enclosed, claustrophobic environment. He also had a temperature and was a little delirious, uncertain of where he was or what was happening.

Was it a dream or was it reality? One of the curtains was drawn back and a dark figure seemed to be standing at the foot of his bed. ...It was Amaka.

VI

'How did you find me?' asked Tom, perturbed at being seen in such a vulnerable state.

'When I waited for you to call and no one knew where you were, I decided to investigate for myself. It was not difficult to track down the records of patients in London. I am a doctor, after all. I thought you might have been involved in some sort of accident but when I searched your name, I saw from central records on the computer that you had been admitted here at Hillside Hospital.'

'You should not have come.' Tom felt that he could not possibly have appeared more defenceless to anyone.

Amaka asked her key question, 'What is wrong with you?' A direct question deserved a direct answer.

'They do not know. They think it might be cancer.'

She was completely unaffected by this information. Amaka was an experienced doctor in a poor African village community. She was more than used to life-threatening diagnoses. 'When will you know?' she asked, without flinching.

Tom was struggling to keep his eyes open. He reached for the beaker of water on the bed-tray, just out of his reach. Amaka passed it to him almost as a reflex action. As she gave him the drink, she continued the conversation and did not break stride. 'If it is cancer, you will need treatment and help while you recover. Will your servant help you?'

Tom surmised that Amaka meant Sylvia. 'She's not my servant. She is someone who works for me, who helped me to look after my father when he was alive. She is more like a member of my family than a domestic help. I don't know if Sylvia will be able to look after me. She has her own family. I will probably hire a nurse. There are plenty of agencies and I have money, after all. I might as well put it to good use.'

Once more, Amaka spoke powerfully, almost as an aside. 'I will help you.'
Tom was not sure if he heard her correctly. 'Sorry?'

'I will nurse you, whatever illness you have. I will look after you.'
There was a level of steely cold determination in her claim. 'I am a doctor.
I have nursed many people. Even when I was a little girl, I nursed people
in my country. Who better to look after you than I? It will be my honour
to help the man who helped me to become a doctor.'

He realised she was being serious. 'What? You can't – what about your
work? Your research?'

Amaka pondered the implications of her instinctive reaction. 'I will
speak to my Government. They will understand. I will make them
understand. Yes, I will nurse you.' She stood beside his bed determined
and Tom could tell she meant what she said. This person was clearly an
extremely resourceful young woman. Tom placed his hand to his throat
and coughed, almost in semi-embarrassment. He thought he had better
challenge her offer.

'I could not ask you to abandon your research, your job. That's the
whole reason why you are here in London in the first place.' He expected
her to see sense and relent if he was sufficiently persistent. He was wrong.

'No. You are the reason I am here. Without you I would not be a doctor.
I came here for a reason. Now I know what that reason is. Please let me help
you now. It will be an opportunity to repay the debt I owe you. I can return
another time with my Government's blessing to do my research.' There
was a level of conviction in her voice that Tom had not heard from anyone
in a long time. Where did this commitment of faith come from?

It was clear to Tom that he was not going to win this argument. Amaka
was a single-minded, focussed and able young woman who had fought her
way to success over many years. She had not only survived an appallingly
savage civil war during her childhood but had also proceeded to win a
scholarship to university in order to fulfil her lifelong ambition. She had
waited until the right moment before deciding to find her benefactor to
thank him. Amaka had a generous, kind spirit and was clearly a special
individual with unique qualities. Tom admired her enormously and felt
that perhaps his years of emotional exile were coming to an end. Eventually
there was no reluctance in his decision to allow Amaka to look after him,
only immense gratitude.

From that moment, Amaka began visiting Tom in hospital regularly. Her discussions with Mr Woodicott confirmed that the biopsy results were pending. Amaka understood that a bone lesion biopsy is a highly specialised procedure and a pathologist may need to undertake several tests before obtaining a conclusive result. The length of time being taken in Tom's case was unfortunate but necessary. During her visits she tried to reassure her new patient. She avoided telling him that her superiors in the Government were not happy at the situation. They had threatened to withdraw her funding if she fulfilled her intended course of action but it made no difference to her plans.

A private room became available earlier than planned. An outgoing patient had recovered sufficiently to leave hospital. For the moment at least, Tom was going to be safe from the mob. The new environment was infinitely better than either of the previous wards. He had his own television and radio, both with headsets, a small refrigerator for drinks and an *en suite* bathroom. Sitting reading *The Guardian* in one of the room's two large chairs and enjoying the peace, he did not notice 'Jerry the Physio' enter.

Jerry announced that he was going to tutor his new patient in the use of crutches and if successful, Tom would be able to visit the toilet independently rather than have to rely on bottles and bed-pans. Some limited respectability was returning to his condition. It was now three weeks since the operation and although he continued to ask the duty doctors daily if the results of his biopsy were known, he always received the same negative response. Plans were now being made to address the issue with his shoulder, where the bone damage was even greater than the more vulnerable femur.

The weather outside was very hot and Tom thought he was beginning to go a little 'stir crazy' due to the length of his confinement. Throughout his four-week stay in hospital he had never been able to leave the Hospital and he was desperate for some fresh air. In the confines of his room, Amaka was watching Tom show-off his recently acquired skill, speedily launching his crutches forward and completing improvised laps around a couple of chairs. As he passed the imaginary finishing line, he plopped onto the bed with a sigh, landing on his back and allowing the metal supports to clatter onto the tiled floor. 'Let's make a break for it!' he gasped. Amaka shot him a puzzled look. 'I need some fresh air. Come on, let's go outside. No one will mind.' Amaka smiled but was unsure what to do. Before she had a chance to say anything, Tom lowered his arms from the bed and scooped up the abandoned crutches. In one swift movement he swung his left leg forward and with two lunges, he was ready to leave. With Amaka's help opening doors, he made swift progress out of the Ward, along the corridor to the main entrance. The unlikely duo exited through the automatic doors and stepped outside where Tom gulped the warm air with relish and for a few moments felt human once more. Unfortunately, it was short-lived as his conscientious side-kick ensured he was returned before tiredness took another victim.

The next morning, Tom finished his scrambled eggs on toast and placed the tray on the side-shelf, next to his bed. His leg was feeling a little more sore than usual thanks to his recent exploit. He was resting in a bedside chair, with his dressing gown unkindly wrapped around his waist, wondering if he also needed to slow down with his use of the *Flexicator* machine, which had been used a lot recently to try and improve the level of suppleness in his leg. His pensive daydream was broken when Mr Woodicott appeared at the door. The Consultant held a slim grey file in both hands and spoke the words Tom had been fearing. 'Good morning, Tom. We have received the results of your biopsy.'

Tom scrutinised his doctor carefully, desperately trying to identify some positive signs from the medic's body posture. He swung his legs to the side of the bed and was about to struggle to an upright position, when Mr Woodicott insisted, 'Please don't get up.' Tom was worried. Did this mean it was bad news? He loosened the belt around his striped robe.

Anxiously, Tom stared at his judge and his mouth went dry. This was not the return of a student assignment, it was his final assessment. Mr Woodicott gave the verdict. 'I'm afraid the tests have proved inconclusive, Tom. We still don't know the precise nature of the diagnosis.' The Consultant looked at Tom, whose whole body folded, almost sinking into the bed. All that waiting and anxious anticipation had been to no avail. He was no further forward. Mr Woodicott paused to let Tom assimilate the information, before continuing. 'There could be several reasons for this. The most likely is that the sample was not good enough. I suspect the one we take from your shoulder will be more definite. I intend to operate on that, early next week. Probably Tuesday.'

'What will that involve,' asked Tom feebly. He did not really care at that moment. It was like saying, '*Do what you want with me. Just give me the truth.*' Tom was rocking near the limit of his mental stamina and opened his arms, pleading with the Consultant to be allowed home for the weekend. He argued that he could return on Monday morning, in readiness for the planned operation. Mr Woodicott could see his patient was in need of a boost. There was no medical reason why Tom could not enjoy a little home-time, especially as he was going to be further incapacitated for at least another two weeks, after the operation on his shoulder. The Consultant gave permission for Tom to leave the Hospital for a short break and it was arranged the following day.

At the house, Sylvia was waiting anxiously. She had prepared lunch for him, one of her specials. Tom asked the taxi driver to get as close as possible to the front door to avoid the gravel. The man opened the passenger door to its full extent and Tom managed the steps without help, although he did have an audience ready to catch him if he fell. With his left leg dangling between the crutches, he drew breath and made his way through familiar passages to the back of the house. Eventually he reached the patio and collapsed into his favourite seat, overlooking the countryside. He allowed the crutches to free-fall onto the wooden floor. Tom felt exhausted and the glass of fresh orange juice Sylvia gave him, was a drink well-earned.

Sylvia knew enough not to ask prying questions about Tom's condition. He did tell her about the inconclusive nature of the test results and that the shoulder problem would be addressed after the weekend. Amaka, who was still carrying Tom's light bag, felt very self-conscious about relaxing in an unfamiliar environment. Equally, she was not used to such luxury. Tom brushed back his hair and gestured with his arm towards the neighbouring empty chair. Amaka accurately interpreted this action to be an invitation to sit. Tom repeated the gesture, this time waving above the table lined with food. Amaka ignored the canapés, *petit fours* and quiche and took only a small glass of grapefruit juice. Tom tried to put her at ease.

'I have spoken with Sylvia and she will prepare a room here for you – for when I come out of hospital. It will be much easier if you stay at the house. Is that ok with you?' There was a new level of acceptance in his voice and the offer was made in a tone of indifference. Tom sounded defeated.

'Er … well…yes, thank you, that will be very nice indeed,' replied Amaka meekly. She was surprised at the offer but knew it was the best strategy for everyone.

While in Hospital, Tom had managed successfully to keep his condition a secret. It was now time to inform his business colleagues and the right thing to do. He declared his intentions to the incongruous pair, while he awkwardly pushed himself up from his chair, using his crutches and was really thinking aloud, as he mumbled, 'I must make a phone call to Mitchell Fraunley about my change in circumstances. He thinks I have taken a month off before starting to work for *Modcom* with Scott Mason in California. It's just as well that we delayed the signing of the papers until I was due to return from a month's break. At least they can't sue me for a breach of contract when there is no contract. I'm going into the main house to make the call.'

Sylvia and Amaka looked at each other with some alarm. 'Can you manage?' asked Amaka as Tom began to wrestle with his support system.

'I'll be fine. Please just carry on and enjoy lunch. It would be a pity to let all this lovely food go to waste. It's certainly a damn site better than some of the slop that has been presented to me recently.' Tom swung his way over to the study, occasionally stopping to absorb the reassuring beauty of his home, which he observed with relish. He sat in the desk chair and waited before dialling. It was a normal moment of pleasure before getting down to business.

The phone call to Mitchell Fraunley was received with total shock. Tom's illness was something even Mitch's efficient planning could not have accommodated. As he listened to Fraunley's stunned reaction, Tom picked up and squeezed a glass paper-weight that was resting on his desk, before shuffling it around the polished surface. It's smoothness was a comforting sensation. In the circumstances, Mitch could only be reasonable about Tom's misfortune, even if it was five-thirty in the morning in California. Any other reaction would have seen Tom withdraw altogether from the proposed deal to work for Mitchell's company . This way, the future still offered possibilities for both parties.

Tom pushed the paper-weight beyond his reach and recognised there was also one other, very important call to be made, this time to Maisie Springfield. While he had been alone with his most intimate thoughts in hospital, he had considered all kinds of scenarios regarding his Dad and Mrs Springfield. In the security of his own home, he felt it appropriate to establish the facts, no matter how painful.

Tom turned the index page in his red, leather-bound contact book until he located Maisie's number and had to look in white pages to find the area code. After the sound of the numbers on his phone's dial pad finished beeping, he eventually heard the ringing tone. It was strangely loud. After five rings, the hand-set was lifted and Maisie's voice came through. Tom removed a pencil from a silver tankard positioned beside his in-tray and started to spin it through his fingers. Before Maisie had a chance to say anything, he launched into his own agenda. He told her about his medical circumstances and her sympathetic sighs suggested she was genuinely concerned about his well-being.

The pencil broke between his first and little finger as he proceeded to tell her that he had opened her letter while in hospital. In the circumstances, Maisie's natural sympathy at the nature of Tom's medical plight probably helped her to talk more honestly than she would otherwise have done. She confirmed that Tom's analysis of events about the Christmas period in 1948 was accurate. Tom listened intently, with half-a-broken pencil between his teeth. It was odd to talk about such important personal details on the phone but they both recognised the unfortunate reality of Tom's condition. Maisie told Tom that she felt able to talk about everything only because her husband, Cyril Springfield had died five years ago. He never knew about the circumstances surrounding Jenny and the same was true for everyone else. As far as other people were concerned, Cyril was Jenny's Dad, pure and simple.

It transpired that Cyril and Maisie had no more children due to complications following Jenny's birth. The three of them had lived as a family, on the other side of Durham, where they had no contact with Dennis. Although Dennis must have known about the birth of Maisie's child and that she was his daughter, he acted with ultimate discretion. He never told another soul he was the girl's biological father, least of all his wife, Betty.

Maisie disclosed to Tom that following her letter to Dennis, he went to the Works Dance that Christmas. It was where he first met Betty Cartwright. Dennis and Betty must have 'hit it off' because it was followed by another date in the New Year. Shortly after that, Betty became pregnant and she and Dennis were married the following August. Maisie met Cyril through work, around February of that year. He was a foreman at the factory, where she worked in the office. She married Cyril on Valentine's Day, 1949 after a whirlwind romance and Jenny was born 'a month premature' on September 1st. Only the medical staff knew that Maisie had actually gone 'full term,' enabling the deception to be complete.

The bizarre telephone conversation ended amicably just as Sylvia was walking past the study to ensure Tom was alright. Events between Tom and Maisie were now out in the open. Maisie said she would give serious thought about whether to tell Jenny the truth. There was a lot to consider. She hoped Tom progressed well with his treatment and asked if she could be informed when he left hospital. She would like to see him again. Tom agreed. The experience had made him feel less alone in the world. He replaced the receiver and without thinking picked tiny wooden shards from the broken HB pencil that had become embedded between his two, front teeth.

Tom sat, looking through the window at the main gates, deep in thought. When the voice in the study went silent, Sylvia grew concerned. She was just about the open the door, when she heard the scraping noise of Tom's chair. Quickly, she scarpered back to the patio and he remained unaware of her presence. Tom plodded across the room and made his way mechanically and slowly back to the refreshments. Once seated overlooking the countryside, he retreated into his shell. Sylvia beckoned Amaka towards the kitchen to give him some peace. Tom remained unaware of their movement and continued to examine his favourite views as a distraction but he was not really taking in the scene. He was lost in his thoughts. There was a lot to consider. He had confronted the dire concerns about his family and they had been realised.

Tom Kettlewell had a half-sister by a father who had not married her mother. If Dennis Kettlewell had married Maisie Huddleston, he would not have met Betty Cartwright at the dance and Tom would not have been born. He would never have known his parents love or experienced happiness with Emma. Absent to the reality of the outside world, his memories returned to the two-shilling coin his Dad had dropped in the stream for luck, all those years ago.

VII

The operation on Tom's shoulder went ahead as planned the following Tuesday and he enjoyed once again, the welcome cold-water drink as he regained consciousness in the Recovery Room. At the end of the procedure, Tom's arm was placed in a sling meaning he would be immobile and unable to use crutches. This time he was returned after the operation to his private room, where his blue eyes explored the den that had become his temporary home. How did he find himself in this position? Only four weeks earlier, it seemed that nothing could shake his world. His ambition to become a wealthy man had come true but just at the time when he should have been able to enjoy the rewards of his life's efforts, it seemed as if everything had been taken away.

In his hospital bed recovering, his thoughts roamed among the shadows. He felt angry and frustrated when he considered what was happening. No one was able to give him a clear picture of a way forward. He was extremely worried and his life was in danger. All the signs indicated his condition was serious, albeit unknown. If it was cancer, how would he take it? He wished his parents were still alive, although he did not want them to see him like this, in pain and wracked with anxiety. When he took stock of his life, he wondered what it was all for. The randomness his father had pondered when they stood on the bridge that day, seemed to be taking another victim. He constantly asked himself the question, *'Is this what life is about – simply struggling to survive?'*

There were no visitors to Tom's cell apart from Amaka. He had no one else to interrupt his self-torture as he lay in a state of lonely recovery. Amaka seemed more than willing to help him but he questioned whether her motives were only being driven by her sense of duty. His involvement in Amaka's life seemed to have been a success and he wished he could have played a more active role when she was a child. Incapacitated with pain, and lying in bed trying to find pleasant thoughts, he wondered what had happened to that picture of the bright yellow sun and the people standing beside a house, that he had caught Emma enjoying in his flat, on the day of the demonstration. Inevitably, he also thought about Emma. His eyes were fixed in a meaningless stare at an insignificant stain on the wall of the room as his mind looked for a better place.

Mr Woodicott entered the private hospital room, surrounded by his mini entourage of white coats and blue uniforms and brought him back to reality. 'Hello, Tom. How are you feeling? I expect the anaesthetic is starting to wear off a little?'

'Yes, my shoulder is a bit sore.' It seemed strange that Tom could only move one arm. The right one was fixed firmly into a blue sling.

'We'll give you some *Oramorph* for the pain.' Tom's eyebrows raised and the Consultant responded. 'Those liquid sachets of morphine solution. Did you not have them, when you were recovering with your leg?'

'Oh, yes those things. They taste horrible.' In fact, Tom did not really care how they tasted. Their flavour was just another small piece of vile in his jigsaw of revulsion.

'Just to let you know that the operation went well. There was a lot of deterioration of the bone in your shoulder. It was in a much worse state than your leg. I have removed all the bone damage caused by the lytic lesions. It was a bit like removing pebble-dashing if truth be told.' Tom admired his confidence in giving such a candid analysis.

'It took some doing, but we were able to attach three hingeable mini-rods to the end of the main *nail* that runs from your elbow to the shoulder joint.' He held out the first three fingers of his right hand, while hooking his little finger and thumb behind them. The surgeon then placed his hand opposite the spot where the hinges were located in Tom's shoulder, without touching the painful area. Tom almost expected him to produce the *Ace of Spades* from behind his hand: the man was clearly a magician.

'We have sent-off some bone samples to the Lab for testing. I know you were disappointed with the nature of the analysis on your leg but I am very confident that this time we will get a clear result. Within the next three weeks we should know exactly the nature of the problem. Then hopefully, we will be able to start treating your condition fully.'

It was that word *hopefully*, again that stung Tom. He could not also help ponder the nature of the '*it*', to which Mr Woodicott referred. Circumstances seemed to be hurtling towards an important conclusion. Unfortunately, Tom had no control over the vehicle that was taking him there; it seemed to be running out of control. At least he felt safer with Mr Woodicott behind the wheel.

The darkest day came three days later. Mr Woodicott had asked the Consultant Oncologist at the Hospital to examine Tom. Her name was Dr Simpkinson and Tom took an instant dislike to her. She was overweight, over-bearing and dismissive of others, particularly her support staff. Her brown hair was sculptured into the style of a 'bob'. The fringe was too long and it demanded to be swept constantly away from her eyes. Tom considered this to be a comfort reflex, a distraction to give her more time for thought. He felt like telling her to have it cut properly the next time she visited the hairdresser. Simpkinsons's fingers were podgy and her breath was not fresh, possibly because her teeth had not seen a brush for a long while. She entered Tom's room unexpectedly, while he was lying on his bed, exercising with the leg *Flexicator* .

'Right Mr Kettlewell! My name is Dr Simpkinson , I'm the Principal Oncologist at the hospital. Don't worry about these other two, they're with me.' She was referring to two, junior doctors who were standing at the foot of the bed. They looked terrified as if their senior colleague was going to spring an important question for them to answer at the slightest provocation. 'Mr Woodicott has asked me to take a look at you.' With that curt explanation of who she was and why she was prodding him, she examined his notes and charts. Then she delivered a bombshell that threatened to de-rail Tom's progress.

'Looking at your notes and your X-rays, it's my considered opinion that your shoulder and your leg have secondary tumours. There is almost certainly a primary tumour somewhere in your body. We need to find it and find it quickly. If I'm right, Mr Kettlewell, I'm afraid you must prepare yourself for the worst. Any questions?' Tom was stunned. 'In that case, I'll say good morning to you. No doubt we shall see each other again, soon.'

Tom was left in a state of stunned shock. Effectively, he had just been told by a senior cancer consultant that he was going to die. There was no wriggle room in that interpretation. He was going to die.

Amaka came to visit him earlier than usual that day. She was wearing her doctor's coat with a stethoscope around her neck, feeling more able to legitimately ask questions of the other medical professionals and with greater authority. Tom made a pathetic sight : a deep blue sling caused him to place his right hand on his left shoulder, leaving his right arm at a forty-five degree angle. He looked as if he had just been blasted out of a war trench, missing only an eye patch. Entering the familiar hospital room, she approached the puffy-eyed patient and gave a customary greeting, before gently squeezing his free hand. She could see that he was upset and Tom told her what had happened earlier with Dr Simpkinson. 'The doctor should not have said that,' she declared with surprising anger. 'She does not know that, so she should not have said that. She has no evidence on which to support such a diagnosis. She may be wrong. Please, Tom do not distress yourself. If you would like me to, I will talk to her. She is very wrong to say these things.'

'No, it's ok Amaka, thanks. It is only her opinion but it came as such a shock.' Tom felt at his lowest point since that devastating revelation at Mr Woodicott's first appointment.

Amaka's clear white eyes were flashing with anger. 'We will fight this. We will fight this together. I have fought death before. I will help you. I have seen death many times. As a child growing up in my country, I saw many people die. It is important to fight death. I have seen it happen. It is a beast you must conquer. When I was a child, we lived with death every day in my village.' This was a rallying call from deep within her soul. She had said it before to herself but this was the first time she had said it aloud.

Tom realised that although he had spent a lot of time in Amaka's company, he knew very little about her early life. When he had originally tried to talk to her about her experiences as a child in war-torn Biafra, she never revealed much detail. He had been too wrapped up in his illness to explore her childhood since his diagnosis. When they had been together before his admission to Hospital, their conversation had focussed mainly on her education and how she had overcome the difficulties of her poverty. She had always avoided talking about her life during the Civil War in Nigeria and Tom had not wanted to pursue what he understood to be a painful subject.

All this changed the minute Mr Woodicott showed Tom his X-rays.

Now Amaka was prepared to abandon her lifetime ambition in order to repay a debt. Although Tom did not want to be the recipient of her emotional charity, he knew she was his best option. Apart from Sylvia, who had commitments of her own, there was no one to look after him. He did not mind hiring nursing care staff for his medical needs. In some ways, not knowing the person who was going to administer drugs, give an injection or empty a bed-pan was better than being reliant on a friend. Nurses from an agency would be doing the caring for money, no matter how it was dressed-up. Amaka would be doing the tending for a more generous motive. Tom selfishly thought he may even have earned that generosity by paying so many standing orders to the *Support an African Child* charity over the years.

After three weeks of routine recovery from his shoulder operation, Tom was beginning to become frustrated at the length of time he had spent in hospital. Although he was still in some pain from the operations on his leg and arm, he had become more mobile and wanted some freedom. Tom forced the issue with Mr Woodicott when he entered his private room during a routine visit of the Ward. To make the point about his recovering mobility, Tom was standing by the window without crutches. There was finally a concession. 'Ok, Tom. I think you are right: a change of scenery can only do you good at this stage. There's no need to keep you in hospital any further for the moment. As long as you have someone to look after you at home?' Tom nodded. 'In that case we'll arrange it and I see no reason why you cannot go home tomorrow. As soon as we have your results, we'll send for you. That should be just a few days now, I would think. The operation on your shoulder was definitive. I'm very confident that the tests will reveal a conclusive analysis this time. Meanwhile, go home and relax as best you can. I'll be in touch once I've had a chance to look at the results.'

Mr Woodicott was as good as his word. The following day, Tom was taken home by a Hospital Volunteer in her car and he was never more pleased to hear the crunching sound of his favourite gravel. With some difficulty and a little help from the Volunteer, he manoeuvred his way out of the car. One step at a time, he ascended the steps to the front door, where he was greeted by an anxious Sylvia and her new apprentice, Amaka. Tom was relieved to be surrounded by familiar things. The comfort and reassuring familiarity of his home assumed a fresh perspective.

Three days later, at about five o'clock in the afternoon, Mr Woodicott's secretary telephoned and instantly had Tom's full attention. 'We have the results of your tests, Mr Kettlewell. They have revealed a conclusive analysis. So we now have a diagnosis.'

'What is it?' This was yet another critical period in the whole affair. Was he due to receive the death sentence, would he be set free, or would it be a period in jail? It turned out to be none of these scenarios.

'I'm sorry, Mr Kettlewell but I'm not allowed to discuss it on the phone. Mr Woodicott would like you to attend his Outpatients' Clinic at Hillside Hospital, at ten o'clock tomorrow morning. He will go over everything with you then.'

Tom's pleas for a definitive response were ignored by the experienced secretary and he would have to wait twenty-four hours for the verdict. Unsurprisingly, he could not sleep that night and taunted himself with every worst case scenario possible. Amaka stayed at *Derwent House* rather than return to her lodgings. At least she would be with him in the morning, when all would be revealed.

They made their way to the Hospital the following morning, as instructed. The Orthopaedic Outpatients Department in the NHS area was full to the rafters once more. Tom received the same jealous looks from patients as he had experienced on the occasion of his previous queue-jumping incident. Their envy was misplaced, waiting two hours for routine treatment was preferable to his endurance.

Tom and Amaka waited anxiously in the Examination Room. Suddenly, an adjoining door opened and Mr Woodicott entered with his Registrar. At the same time, the Outpatients' Sister arrived, with some other nurse, who they did not know. The small room was full and instantly there was an awareness of a significant moment.

'Well, Tom, we do have your results…' The Consultant did not hesitate. 'I'm sorry to say I have some bad news and some good news.' Tom thought that this inappropriate opening line sounded more like a television comedian starting to tell a joke. At least he avoided asking which piece of news Tom would like to hear first. He did not give him the option.

'I'm afraid you have plasmacytoma.'

This meant absolutely nothing to Tom, who was trying not to shrug his shoulders or demonstrate any anger at the frustration he was feeling at such a critical moment in his life. All he could do was ask the obvious question. 'What is that?'

'It's an incurable blood cancer, I'm afraid. It's a tumour of your plasma cells.'

'I'm sorry. I don't understand.' Tom felt as if he was beginning to openly perspire. Was this a death sentence or not?

'Well, I'm not a cancer specialist, I'm an orthopaedic consultant – but from my understanding, a plasmacytoma develops when abnormal blood cells gather in the bone marrow and interfere with the production of normal blood cells. The condition can lead to the sort of bone lesions that we saw in your X-rays. It sometimes develops further into a cancer called myeloma and belongs in the same group of blood cancers as lymphoma and leukaemia. I've seen the condition before. It was always a possibility.'

'So I have cancer?'

'Yes, Tom, I'm afraid you do.'

Bang! There it was. Finally a diagnosis. Tom's mind seemed to step outside his body. The Consultant sounded like the narrator in a film, describing how his constituent parts had become disconnected. Tom's intellectual ability over the years had proven to be exceptional. Suddenly he had been told that his body was less than ordinary. In one moment he was reduced to a statistic, another click in the totting up total of cancer victims.

The group paused in silence, waiting for a reaction from the victim. 'And the good news? Now would seem like a good time to hear something good. If there can be anything good after what you've just told me.' As far as Tom was concerned, there were now only two people in the room – Tom and God.

'Well the good news is that it is treatable. We can't cure you but we can treat your cancer.'

'So there is no primary tumour elsewhere in my body? If I've got this right, these *plamsynopses*?..

'Plasmacytomas. Yes ...'

'Sorry, these plasmacytomas ... *they* are the primary tumours.'

'Yes, that is correct.'

'So the oncologist who saw me in hospital was wrong?' Tom could feel anger rising.

'Well, it would seem as if she did not have all the facts at her disposal on that occasion but there is no doubt this time. The results of your bone biopsy are conclusive. We now know what we are fighting. There will obviously be a need to refer you to an oncology specialist. We will take the stitches from your arm and shoulder today and I'll see you in a week's time to discuss how we will progress.' The Consultant continued in a more upbeat mood and rallied his patient. 'This is not the worst news I could have given you today. Really, this diagnosis is the best of a bad case scenario. We know we can treat your condition and that is what you must focus on. Genuinely, this illness is something we can slow down with the right course of treatment.'

'You mean chemotherapy, presumably?'

'An oncologist will discuss everything with you, but yes. It is.'

'Thank you for being straight with me.' *Well if God was not going to be honest, there was no hope.* Within a few seconds, Mr Woodicott had left the room to move on to another patient. Tom was left with Amaka and a Nursing Sister, who he did not know. She was sympathetic to her new patient in this situation.

'Would you like a few moments before I remove your stitches? You've just been given a lot to take in.' The Sister was standing very close to Tom, as if expecting him to faint.

'No, it's ok, thanks Sister. You can take them out. I don't think I will feel a thing, in the circumstances.' It was the declaration of a beaten man. Tom sat on the edge of a treatment table and released the right side of his shirt, after passing his coat to Amaka. The nurse began to comply with Mr Woodicott's instructions and using a long pair of silver tweezers and a scalpel, she removed a total of twelve stitches from Tom's arm and shoulder. As soon as the two wounds were each covered with a large dressing, Tom was told he could leave. The Hospital would be in touch about the next stage of his treatment.

Tom and Amaka trudged out of the Outpatients Department. They had not spoken a word to each other during the nightmare disclosure. As they got to the main exit of the Hospital and headed for their taxi, Amaka took his hand and squeezed it slightly. It was an unusual moment of intimacy between them. The car was silent on their return to Tom's home. The taxi driver, who regularly serviced patients to and from the Hospital, had learned years ago not to initiate any discussions about a customer's treatment. Tom ignored the familiar views from the taxi and with each passing mile, he felt more angry and confused.

Fortunately, Sylvia was not in *Derwent House*, when they settled into the kitchen. Tom was sitting on a stool, leaning against the breakfast bar, when he finally lashed out at the world. 'How can this be? Now of all times. Just when I was about to start something I care about. It's not fair. I've never abused my body and always kept myself fit. Why is this happening to me? I'm rich for Christ's sake. It's just not fair.'

Amaka stood within arm's length and did what she could to try and shed some perspective on the situation, attempting to gain eye contact. 'Life is not fair, Tom. You know that. And if there was ever a time in your life when you should be thankful that you *have* kept yourself fit, is now not that time? You will need to be stronger now than ever before in your life to fight this cancer.'

That night and for the next seven nights before his next appointment, Tom walked the boards in the early hours of threatening blackness. He became frightened to close his eyes in case he would never be able to open them again. Knowing he was going to die, he was unable to feel beyond the word, *cancer*. It seemed like the death sentence he had been dreading.

Amaka was aware that Tom was going through a well-documented phase of trauma. She had seen the *fight-or-flight* response many times before. The threat of immediate death was something she had lived with during her childhood years. Amaka had seen villagers cowering in fear in fields as MIG fighters strafed the area in thunderous aggression. Exploding shells and smoke rising from burning villages were guaranteed to terrify the most resilient of Biafrans. Children's screams and the howling of mothers suddenly receiving the news of a son lost in battle, were also familiar sounds. The primal physiological reflex involved in hyper arousal was frightening to observe. The emotional reaction of anxiety and aggression to the threat involved in *fight-or-flight* has been the subject of many behavioural studies. In Tom's case, the problems with sleeping, the restlessness accompanied by the mood swings between anger and depression were a Westernised version of the outward emotional arm flailing and wailing, of those African war victims. On this occasion, the grief was not for someone else, it was for the loss of his health and the person he used to be.

Time would determine whether Tom's two isolated plasmacytomas would develop into full-blown myeloma. Not everyone suffering from the condition experiences bone damage so Tom was unlucky in this regard. The development of the cancer had been heralded by his periods of intense fatigue, night-time sweats and bone pain. It was natural to attribute the symptoms of the condition to the sort of anxiety and stress associated with a middle-aged man's problems at work. When Geraldine had criticised him for not wanting to socialise after work, there was a genuine reason for not being enthusiastic. As Tom's cancer was rare, it was hardly surprising that he had not realised the seriousness of his condition. It was becoming ever clearer that he had a major fight on his hands.

Mr Woodicott could see the signs of stress and anguish in Tom's demeanour at their final appointment. The pain of the operations, the perceived threat to his life and Tom's lack of restful sleep were beginning to leave their terrible mark. Mr Woodicott informed Tom that he had been referred to Dr Simpkinson , the Hospital's Oncology Consultant. Given her previous erroneous diagnosis of Tom's condition, the news did not generate a great deal of enthusiasm.

Tom knew he owed a lot to Simon Woodicott. As they stood, facing each other to shake hands, the Consultant was expecting only a brief recognition of thanks. However, when Mr Woodicott tried to withdraw his hand, Tom held on tightly as if clinging to a life-saving rope. The Doctor gently patted Tom's arm in a rare gesture of warmth and said, 'Good luck, Tom. Take care,' in a tone similar to the one used by Doc Herbert, years earlier.

Over the ensuing days, the wait for the next medical notification seemed interminable. Amaka was now living full-time in the Annex and her superiors were made aware that she had abandoned her research work. She managed aspects of Tom's medical care team, supervising the work of the agency staff who Tom had employed to look after his daily needs. Amaka had offered to do those chores herself but Tom did not want to impose on her that kind of personal, basic intimacy. Emotional support was needed and Amaka was the specific person charged with the task.

VIII

Amaka answered the door and was surprised to see two startled women, standing at the entrance. One lady was quite old, the other looked like she could be her daughter. When they saw Amaka, they both appeared a little disconcerted. Amaka invited them into the House and escorted them into a courtesy room, just off the hallway, before quickly returning to the lounge to inform Tom that he had visitors. He became animated when he learned their names were Maisie and Jenny.

Amaka was asked to show them into the lounge and while she was out of the room, Tom struggled to his feet. He was standing to attention by the time they entered, wearing an embarrassed smile and conscious of being suddenly nervous. As they approached, he was unsure how to greet them. Maisie and Jenny stopped about six feet in front of him, equally uncertain. It was too early in their relationship to show any tactile affection and somewhat clumsily, he tried to direct them towards the nearby sofa. They did not read the gesture accurately and remained embarrassingly still. Watching this take place in front of her, Amaka felt intrusive and withdrew to the kitchen. She surmised that tea and coffee were almost certainly required.

Tom decided to break the ice. 'Hello, Jenny. It's nice to see you again.' Before Jenny had a chance to speak, Maisie seized the initiative.

'It's ok, Tom. She knows everything.' Jenny walked across to Tom and without saying a word, she embraced her brother.

After what seemed like five minutes, Jenny broke from the clinch and stepped back. With tears in her eyes, she said 'I'm so sorry'.

This caught Tom off-guard. 'Sorry for what?' he responded, defensively. 'You and your Mum have nothing to be sorry for. It was my father whose behaviour was in question. Your parents behaved impeccably.'

'No, I'm sorry that you are ill. Mum tells me, you have cancer.' Tom had not grasped the fact that Jenny was only recently aware of the enormity of his predicament. The disease had been an unwanted companion for several weeks, by this time.

'Oh, that! Well, your Mum's right but unfortunately, it's cancer that has me. I've only just had the diagnosis. They've told me they think it's bone marrow cancer. Don't worry, I'll soon beat that.' Amaka shot Tom a puzzled look as she re-entered the room, carrying a tray of tea and biscuits.

Tom took the opportunity to introduce Amaka, while everyone assumed an uncomfortable posture in the expensive chairs. The group members were sitting closely together and once the refreshments were poured, the tension quickly eased. While Jenny and Tom updated each other on the highlights of their lives since grammar school, Amaka unsuccessfully hovered with a plate of light snacks. Tom and Jenny expressed surprise at the news they were siblings but neither seemed upset or disturbed by the declaration. They were both middle-aged adults, after all. Jenny told Tom that her daughter Sophie only had one month to go before the birth of her firstborn. It had been a difficult pregnancy at first but Maisie had helped her overcome the worst part.

The conversation between them flowed naturally and it felt like they were simply old friends catching up with each other's news. Tom had known Jenny since school so she was not a complete stranger, although they had not kept in touch over the years. Nevertheless, he was finding it difficult to suddenly attach a new level of importance to their relationship. Tom had hoped he would feel something different towards Jenny, now the truth was out. As he scrutinised his sister's features while she chatted, it was a source of disappointment that he did not feel any special bond. He wondered if his capacity for love had vanished, although he also realised developing a connection would take time. They all recognised that fact.

Given the uncertainty surrounding Tom's health, it was agreed to give each other some space, before meeting again. The circle began to break-up when Amaka got to her feet. She had watched the discussion unfold, with a keen observer's interest and once the level of tea in their cups was lower than saucer height, she decided to take the initiative. 'I'm afraid Tom is beginning to look a little tired ladies.' The implication was obvious so Maisie gathered her handbag over her forearm and sprung to her feet at the second attempt. Jenny approached Tom before contributing an affectionate hug and a peck on his cheek. Meanwhile, Amaka approached the open doorway and efficiently escorted the two ladies from the house. Their visit had lasted almost an hour, which was the maximum that Tom's dwindling health could accommodate.

The demands of Tom's illness were now shaping the days and he was sleeping on demand. The hours of the clock were meaningless in his new world. He had entered into a time zone that was dictated by his needs, rather than by social conventions. Although he had been with Amaka for about a month, he realised he knew very little about her early life. Emotional traffic between them had taken place along a one-way street. It was clear that she had a great deal to relate but she was guarded. Others had attempted to unlock the trauma she endured as a child but Amaka had always refused to let them enter her inner secrets. There was a sensitive truce between the two unlikely companions and they were able to discuss anything but their most dark memories. Tom was beginning to believe he could trust Amaka without conditions and needed to hear the same was true of her so he decided to test the water. One night when they were both sitting in the lounge, he was feeling strangled by the claustrophobia of his situation and he challenged Amaka to disclose aspects of her personal life. It was part of the emotional roller-coaster he was riding due to his condition.

He was in an aggressive mood, lashing out at the world and Amaka was in his line of fire. 'Don't try to tell me that I should be reassured by the fact they say they can treat my cancer. I'm going to die. You know it and I know it. You keep telling me that you saw a lot of death in Biafra when you were a child but I'm just supposed simply to believe that. If you want me to believe you, then you had better start telling me who you are behind those big brown, innocent eyes.'

Amaka was hurt by the comments. Fortunately, she was experienced enough to know that it was part of his illness and she tried to placate him. 'I'm sorry if I have offended you in some way.'

His frustration was not abated. 'Of course you haven't offended me. How can you have offended me? All you have done is help me but if I have helped to mould *your* life, I need to know who *you* are. I have come to realise that I do not really know you at all. I have no children and my own family have all gone. You are all I have at this moment in time but I do not know you. I mean, really *know* you.' This was a powerful admission for Tom to make. It was one thing to admit that he had no one meaningful in his life, it was another to maintain that Amaka was all he had. He surprised himself with the confession.

Amaka was confused. 'What is it you want to know from me, Tom?'

'I want you to trust me with *your* life as I am trusting you with mine. I want to know how I have made a *difference* to your life. It is not enough to know that you are here now, that you are a successful doctor on your way to more success. I need to know how *I* made a difference to the direction of *your* life. Do you not see – it is for *me*? I am asking for *me*. I need to know that my life has not just been about making money. I need to know that my life has mattered in some way. Right now, I know only that my life may end someday soon. I have only a little piece of hope left in my life. Please cultivate that small thing for me and give me something to hang on to.' The disease had changed him beyond recognition. He was no longer the person he once was. The question was whether he was still there at all.

Amaka thought she was justified to show some anger of her own. Life had not exactly been easy for her, either and she decided to snap back. 'Hope was something I did not have. You talk about hope but as I look around your life I do not understand you. You want me to tell you about my life. Huh! Sister Mary tried for years to get me to talk about what I had seen. She tried but she could not help me and you expect me to simply open my world to you. It is not that easy.'

Tom stopped and relented. He was annoyed at himself for behaving so badly and he moved to where Amaka was sitting, taking her hand. 'Please, Amaka. I am frightened. I do not want to die like this. I need to know my life has made a difference, somewhere ... to someone. I don't want to think I have existed for no reason.'

He cut a pathetic figure and after looking directly into Tom's anguished eyes for seconds that seemed like minutes, her own brown pools explored his face, searching for an indication of his truth. They were two people alone in the world. Both had overcome huge obstacles to achieve success. Tom's achievements had brought him wealth but Amaka could not talk to anyone about what she had endured. She knew she owed it to Tom to tell him about her life but she was uncertain about her own capacity to find the inner strength that was needed.

After contemplating Tom's plight, she knew there was nothing else she could do. She owed her benefactor a great deal and would be forever in his debt. How could she deny this person the only thing he had ever asked of her? He was too important in her life.

Amaka went to sit beside Tom on the sofa. She took both his hands in her own and looked squarely into his face. Her eyes were darting backward and forward into the blue pools staring back at her. Then, her glazed eyes returned to the past as she looked down at the rich, red carpet. Neither spoke for a several moments, until she finally summoned the strength.

'I will try to tell you. I do not know if I can but I will try.' Tom's failure to interrupt at this point gave Amaka licence to continue.

'My family were Igbo and there were six of us. My mother was a servant in a big house. My father was a craftsman. I think you call him a carpenter. He worked for himself doing jobs where he could find them. I had an elder sister called Ifunanya. My brothers were Onyemaechi and Akubundu. They were both older than me and my sister. My father's name was Mbadiwe. I cannot recall *Mama's* name. To me she was always *Mama*. We lived in a village in Kaduna State called Kakera. It is in the north of my country.

I remember being happy when I was a little girl. Then, things suddenly changed. My first memory is of people shouting and waving things in the streets where I lived. I remember they were very angry and were making a lot of noise. There was a lot of fighting in the streets, I think. I did not understand it. I remember *Mama* and *Papa* talking in our home. They were not happy. I asked what was wrong but they told me not to worry. They said they would look after me. This is one of the first things I remember.

Amaechi (that is what we called my brother Onyemaechi) came home one day covered in blood. He was crying and his clothes were torn. He was about fourteen years old, I think. Some other boys from his school had beaten him. He said they were shouting *'Uhn-thaw-Gi'* at him. This is not a nice thing to say to Igbo. It means 'goat' and they say it to us because many of my people are farmers. Amaechi's clothes were torn and his head was bleeding. *Mama* bandaged him. My father was very angry but he did not go into the streets. *Mama* told me if he had gone into the streets the bad people would have beaten him too. This made me very frightened. I remember this feeling of fear. It was the first time I knew fear. That emotion was to stay with me for many years.'

262

The soothing lilt in Amaka's voice was very calming. As she broke from the stare of her story she noticed that Tom had fallen asleep on the settee. She got up and lowered him into a horizontal position by gently lifting his legs onto the cushion, before placing a blanket over him. He seemed at rest for the first time in a while. Amaka faded from consciousness in an adjacent chair, something that was to become a pattern, whenever Tom's panic attacks overcame his emotional equilibrium.

IX

Following two hours of radiation treatment at the Ivy Hospital, Tom was accompanied home in a taxi by Amaka and was feeling thoroughly tested by this chapter of his cancer care. The more he thought about his predicament, the more he could only conclude that he was being punished in some way for something he had done wrong. As they sat in the lounge at *Derwent House* one evening, Amaka challenged him on this interpretation of his illness. 'Do you think God is vindictive, Tom?' she asked.

Tom removed his feet from the pouffe and sat upright, struggling to get comfortable. He became agitated and looked directly at Amaka. 'I don't know what kind of God would visit this disaster on my life. I have tried to fathom what I have done wrong that would cause Him to bring this down on me.'

Amaka was aware that Tom was not thinking straight. 'I am sorry to tell you that bad things happen to good people and good things happen to bad people.'

'You sound like my Dad. He always said that life was random, without rhyme or reason and we simply had to get on with it. He did not believe in a God, Christian or otherwise.'

She was not prepared to let Tom's cynicism go unchallenged and she also edged forward in her seat. 'Oh, I am not saying that life does not have a reason. I am simply saying that we are not always given to understand that reason so there is no point in trying. My God is a loving God. I believe he loves you and he will help you in your treatment. Perhaps that is why he sent me to you. To show you hope. I believe you will find hope by fighting this disease. You asked me to tell you about my childhood life. Do you remember I told you about my brother Amaechi?'

Tom felt embarrassed at having fallen asleep during Amaka's intimate account of her early childhood. He hoped she would understand that the drugs had knocked him sideways and nodded in response to her question.

Once again, Amaka moved to sit beside him. She stroked a cushion as a comfort distraction, before hugging it close.

'A week after the attack on my brother, there were more riots in the streets around our home. We lived in a village where many Igbo people lived. One day, my sister Ifunanya did not come home from school so Amaechi went to look for her. Even though he had been beaten in the streets a short time before, he was not afraid. He found 'Ifu' in one of the narrow lanes near our home; she was hiding behind a wall. She was crying and very upset. He tried to lead her back to our home but men with sticks and machetes saw them. They started to beat my brother and tried to undress my sister. They were going to rape her; she was only twelve years old. Amaechi tried to fight them off but it was no use.

A neighbour of ours called Onwuatuegwu Enwonwu, saw what was happening. He went to help my brother and my sister and started to fight off the men who were attacking them. The gang then turned on him and in the confusion, Amaechi took Ifu by the hand and ran away as quickly as he could. They killed our neighbour. They butchered him with their machetes just because he was Igbo. Amaechi said that he could not forget the screams of Onwuatuegwu Enwonwu or the fear he felt that day.'

Amaka returned the cushion that she had been caressing, to the corner of the sofa. While her attention was momentarily diverted, Tom raised his eyes to the ceiling and started mumbling to himself, checking his fingers. Finally, he worked out the year. 'I make that about 1966. I was studying for my A-levels in 1966 and England won the World Cup that year. And all that time you were living in fear in your own country.'

'The riots in our streets were the beginning of what became the pogroms of the Igbo people in Nigeria. Many people were killed just because they were Igbo. You may know about that part of our country's history?' asked Amaka, hoping for a positive response.

'I'm ashamed to tell you that I don't.' Although Tom had supported an African charity and had protested against Apartheid in his student days, there were significant knowledge gaps in his historical awareness of what happened in Nigeria during the 1960s.

'They tried to kill us all. Many of our neighbours were shot, hung or struck down by machetes. My brother's friend Somadina, who was in the same class as Amaechi, had his hand cut-off. On that same day, *Papa* told us we were leaving and we should pack only what we could carry .We loaded his van and all got into the back so no one would know we were in there. Then he drove us away from the North and we went to stay with my Uncle Belonwu in Asaba. This was a journey of about five hundred kilometres.

We got as far as a place called Kubwa when *Papa's* car broke down: he could not fix it so we left some of our things in the van and carried what we could. A convoy of six big lorries was passing on the road. The trucks were full of Igbo returning to their homelands. *Papa* stood in the middle of the road and waved with both his arms, like a bird; the first lorry stopped. He spoke to the man and we got into two of the wagons, with *Papa* and my brothers climbing into the last one. We travelled the final fifty kilometres like this. It was a terrible journey. The truck was full of people ...so many people; there was not even room for our cases. All our possessions were left by the side of the road.

Everyone was trying to get away from the North of Nigeria and return to their homelands in the South East. Many people were badly injured. I saw one girl I knew, called Mgborie, who was with her parents. Her father was covered in bandages because he had been caught up in the street riots. One man had wrestled him to the floor and while he sat on top of him, he took out a knife and gauged out his eyes. This poor man was now sitting on a seat opposite me, while I sat on my *Mama's* knee. When I saw him I started to shake and turned my head into my *Mama's* bosom.'

Tom did not know what to say. There was a long period of silence between them. It was the silence that can only be experienced between close friends who trust each other. Their tranquillity was broken by a ringing telephone. It was Jenny, calling to inform Tom that her daughter Sophie had given birth to a little girl. They had named the new baby Sarah, in memory of Maisie's mother. Although it was good news, Tom struggled to offer his congratulations. Amaka's story had left him feeling like he was emerging from an emotional wilderness.

X

Tom's nights continued to be long, quiet periods of self-torture. Every time he reached critical panic, Amaka was only a few steps behind him. He never called her during the night but she always seemed to know instinctively when he was awake. In fact, during the period of radiation treatment, Tom only achieved two nights with more than four hours of continuous sleep. When he did nod-off, it was usually the consequence of total exhaustion. During one clear, dark, cloudless night, Tom was in his study looking out of the window and gazing at the stars, in the early hours. Amaka approached from behind and asked him what had caught his attention.

Tom stood motionless and seemed to have been transported to a distant planet. 'I'm just amazed at how many stars there are out there. It's incredible to think that some people believe the Universe and everything in nature is divine. They believe God is that Universe. So we could be looking at God every time we look at the stars. When I look out there, I wonder what is *between* the stars. Why is the space between the stars not just as important as all the stars and planets?'

Amaka was not sure where Tom was going with these thoughts. She tried to jolt him out of his morose mood. 'But that is nothing, it is just empty space.'

Unfortunately, Tom's depression was coming to the fore and his darkest thoughts were flying from his mind's deepest cave. 'Exactly – so when we die, do we not just become that empty space? I think death is simply the obliteration of our consciousness and then we become nothing once more. Why is it, that when you die, you will not simply return to the same state that you had before you were born?'

Amaka could not let him get away with this self-torture. It was something she had also endured during her own bleakest days and the mood was destructive. 'Because that would mean life would have been for nothing. Living would have no point.'

'So what do you believe, Amaka? That we will all go to heaven and be looked after by a man who lives in the sky? You know as well as I do that no one ever beats this insidious disease. I may live for a few years and fight off this myeloma for a while but then it will come back and claim me. Or do you believe in miracles?'

'I do believe that miracles happen but not in the way you seem to think. In every life there are miracles. We just do not always see them.' With that, Amaka turned away and returned to the Annex. She knew that when Tom became emotionally aggressive, there was nothing she could say to placate his anxiety. All she could do was hope that events proved her correct.

After his final session of radiation therapy, Tom received some good news. The next stage of his treatment had been referred to the Consultant of Haematology, Dr El-al-Karim and his case would no longer be considered by the Oncology Department. More importantly, Dr Simpkinson would no longer be in his life. As one of the three main blood cancers, myeloma is handled by the same group of specialists as leukaemia and lymphoma. Within the British medical world of haematology, Dr Karim was regarded as a leader in the field. Clearly a man of principle, he did not treat patients privately. Tom's recent medical history ensured an early appointment but from that point onwards, he would be treated the same as anyone else in the NHS system. Tom already had admiration for the man, even before he met him.

A week passed before Tom was notified of his appointment with Dr El-al-Karim. This time as an NHS patient, his ten o'clock appointment did not see him jump the queue. The corridors and waiting areas were full of patients who had conditions similar to his own. He was in a bad state and his GP had prescribed drugs to help him cope with depression. Compounded by the lack of sleep, his failure to eat properly and the legacy of radiation treatment meant he was in danger of collapse.

Dr El-al-Karim was a doctor with a brilliant reputation. He was an Iranian who had emigrated to the UK during the late seventies in order to avoid the impending religious and economic problems in the country of his birth. He was a small, bespectacled, gentle man with a calm bedside manner. The most striking physical characteristic that immediately struck Tom when he shook the doctor's hand was his high forehead. Dark hair cushioned the sides of Dr Karim's temples but the bald, shining pate that divided the two sides was disproportionately large. Like many others before him Tom was soon impressed by the medic's charisma. In their first meeting together, Dr Karim gave a direct diagnosis to Tom. The Doctor showed him the results of his bone scan. There were four images of his skeleton and Tom was shocked at the exposure of his vulnerability.

'You can see clearly from this film where the problems are.' In his consultation room, Dr Karim held the large transparency up to the light and pointed with a pen to the areas of concern. 'The very dark images on your skeleton are the hotspots we were looking for. As you can see, the one in your shoulder is completely black showing the bone damage to be more extensive than your femur. There also seems to be the possibility of another area on one of your ribs, although this could be an issue associated with the scan. Have you been having any pain in your ribs?' Tom shook his head.

Dr Karim summarised Tom's position. 'There is a lot of progress being made in the treatment of blood cancers at the moment. As we sit here today, I would like to be able to say to you that a cure for your myeloma is just around the corner but unfortunately, I cannot. Perhaps in ten years' time there may be a breakthrough but until then, all I can say to you is that we can only treat your condition and give you as much time as we can. We will fight the disease together and I will keep you informed at every stage.'

After collecting the drugs from the hospital pharmacy, Amaka and Tom returned to *Derwent House*, where he sat in his favourite conservatory chair and waited for the first cycle of his chemotherapy to begin, like an expectant diner in a restaurant. It was a shock when Amaka entered the room and presented the first instalment of pills on a tray. There was a dose of eighteen tablets of cyclophosphamide, twenty five tablets of dexamethasone and five of thalidomide. 'Jesus! Do I have to take this many tablets every day?' he asked with some justifiable anxiety as he moved forward to examine the dietary supplements.

'More or less, I'm afraid. The full thalidomide dosage is taken every three days but the number of the other tablets is to be taken daily.'

Tom swallowed the tablets with some ice cold water, taking about five minutes to complete the task. The greatest difficulty involved the steroids. Although they were small, the cyclophosphamide pills were dry like pumice and several stuck to the back of his throat, when he tried to swallow them in groups of three. Each one tasted vile.

He sat back into the chair, waiting for his body to react to the drugs. It did not take long. In addition to feeling incredibly nauseous, his face flushed bright red and he felt light-headed. When he tried to stand he had to hold onto something, feeling like a marionette being controlled by someone else. Perhaps the most sinister response was emotional. The power of the drugs was a reminder of his precarious state and his serious battle against a potent illness.

Over the next few days, fatigue wracked his body. Even the most basic of personal tasks left him exhausted. Whereas at first, he dressed when getting out of bed, now he preferred simply to slip-on his dressing gown and rest in one of his favourite chairs. All he could think about when resting was that he was dying. He did not want to close his eyes and tried to fight sleep at every waking opportunity. The thought that filled his mind was that if he entered the darkness, he may never return to the light.

He was becoming a fixture in his conservatory, resting and looking longingly through the patio doors at the garden and the countryside beyond. The weather was rainy and cold and Amaka was opposite him with her back to the glass frontage, quietly reading some medical journals and trying to reconcile her own professional responsibilities. Although she was no longer working on her research project, she needed to ensure she would be ready to return as effectively as possible, when the situation allowed. She did not know when this would be and never spoke to Tom about how much difficulty his medical condition was causing her own life.

There was a lull in conversation, the only sound was the patter of light rain on the glass. Tom decided to continue his pursuit of Amaka's childhood. A rabbit raced across a field and disappeared under a hedgerow and the sight was enough to break his daydream and stir him into action. 'So when you arrived at Asaba, what was it like for you? Were you safe there?' he asked.

After a few moments to decide whether to continue with her story or not, Amaka re-visited their previous conversation in her mind as she looked directly into his eyes. She decided she was no longer prepared to fight to hold on to her past. Their earlier interaction had enabled a catharsis to take place and helped to release some of her own inner demons. 'It is not easy for me to talk about Asaba. It was the first time I heard *Papa* use the word War. I did not know the meaning of the word and I thought we had just moved to stay with my Uncle to get away from the bad people who were in our other home.'

'What was it like, with your Uncle Belonwu?' There was a tone of casual familiarity in his question.

'He had a small house made of a tin roof and earth bricks; it was close to the mighty River Niger. My Uncle worked on the ferry that transported people across to Onitsha. He was able to find work for my father there and things were good for a while. There was plenty of garri and kokor to eat. My Uncle grew cassava and yams in a small plot of land by the river bank. Me and my sisters slept in one room with my girl cousins and *Mama*. My brothers slept in another room with *Papa*. They used to weed the crops and fetch water to wash from the River and try to help the best way they could. *Mama* did most of the cooking. My Uncle's wife had died the year before we arrived so he was glad to have someone to prepare his food.

Then it all changed. It was October 1967. Many troops and Igbo soldiers returned from fighting and tried to cross the river at the ferry. Federal soldiers were chasing them. There were many lorries with wounded soldiers in the back. There was so, so many of them. Shells exploded nearby and aeroplanes were in the sky. We were very frightened.

Suddenly there was a lot of gunfire and lots of soldiers in dark green clothes everywhere. Federal troops were shouting 'One Nigeria' and beating those who were not shouting it too. *Papa* told me that my country was called Biafra and my people were Igbo people. He said Igbo people were fighting the Nigerian Government for their freedom. After two days of the sound of shooting and the smell of gunshots in the air, something bad happened.'

'What was it?' It was an obvious question to ask but a more difficult one to answer. Amaka continued.

'There was a big explosion. The Biafran soldiers blew-up the bridge so the Federal troops could not follow them across the river. When the soldiers from the North came into Asaba, they did many bad things to Igbo people.

The troops came into people's houses with guns and machetes. They came into my Uncle's house and his daughters were screaming. We were all screaming. I did not know where all the men were at this time. Families were ordered out onto the streets and made to shout things. There were lots of people and guns firing everywhere. It was very loud and very frightening.

Then we were told to go to a big square in Ogawa Village, where all the people were shouting and wailing. A soldier was standing on the back of an open lorry with a megaphone. He was ordering the soldiers to drag people away and the soldiers were beating those who did not go freely. *Papa*, my Uncle Belonwu and my brother Amaechi were among those men taken away by the soldiers. My brother Akubundu was only eleven so he stayed with my *Mama*, me and my sister, Ifu. We were watching what was happening. All the men were rounded-up and made to stand in line. All the women and young children were taken to the opposite side of the square and told to watch. We did not know what was going to happen.'

'What did happen?' Tom's question seemed like an intrusion.

'Suddenly the soldier on the lorry shouted in a very loud voice and the sheets that were over some of the trucks were dragged-off. The covers were hiding machine guns and soldiers were already in the trucks waiting to fire. The guns were pointed at all the men and young boys. When the officer shouted *Fire* they started to shoot at all the men. It was a noise I will never forget. The rat-a-tat of the guns, the smell of the gun smoke, the screams of fear from the boys and the wailing of grief from the women terrified me in a way I cannot describe to you. The smell of death and the stench from the smoke of the guns made me feel sick and very scared.

You tell me that you are frightened of dying. I too was frightened of dying in that moment. It was the moment I saw my *Papa* fall as a bullet ripped open his head. It was the moment I also lost a brother and an Uncle who had cared for us and two of my cousins who had played with us. The firing of the guns lasted for only a few minutes but it felt like they went on for hours. I could not believe what I was seeing. I did not speak for a long time after that.

We could not even bury our dead brothers, fathers and uncles. The soldiers threw the bodies onto the back of their lorries and drove them away. *Mama* tried to push through the crowd of soldiers holding her back but one of them hit her with the end of his rifle. She fell to the ground.

Akubundu and I tried to stop people from tramping on her because everyone was panicking. *Mama's* head was bleeding.'

'What did you do next?' This reality was truly a nightmare more horrendous than any cancer.

'I cannot remember all of it. I remember *Mama* taking us to the river when we got away from the square. There was panic and chaos everywhere and small boats were crossing the river. People were shouting to go to the East where it was safe. We were on one of the boats and I remember a big man with a blue shirt, holding a long pole helping all the women and children. The boat was very crowded and the water was high on the side. The man took us across the river by pushing with the long pole and then returned for others. I do not know how many times he did this but the Federal soldiers were killing anyone who stood in their way. I remember shots were fired at the boats and small splashes of water jumped as the bullets fizzed into the river.'

'Where did you go?'

'We walked for three days through the bush, eating berries and anything we could find. We drank out of streams that we came across. *Mama* had a cousin who lived in a village called Uminwani. We had nowhere else to go so we headed for that village. We were all very frightened.'

'I don't understand how you were able to keep your faith in such Godless conditions.'

'We would pray to God to win the war. *Mama* taught us that if we were good and asked God to help us, we would win our freedom.'

'I still don't understand.' The reality of Amaka's story and Tom's awareness of its brutality was challenging everything he believed. He felt that he was coming to an inevitable truth about Amaka and recognised he was privileged.

'That is because this is your first experience of fear and your own death. For us it was all around. We lived with it, we challenged it. We did not give in.'

'I think you are marvellous to have overcome those problems and made a life for yourself.' It would have been difficult to mask admiration for Amaka's resolve.

Although she listened to Tom's expression of respect, Amaka did not disclose the worst of her experiences. That was still to come. If her benefactor was having difficulty understanding these early incidents, he would not be able to comprehend what happened towards the end of the War.

XI

For three further weeks, Tom continued to battle against the overwhelming feeling of sickness and fatigue caused by the chemotherapy. Although it was autumn, he was surprised there were so many spiders in the house. At least, that is how it appeared. Every time he walked through an exposed entrance, a fine web seemed to brush across his face. As he scratched his head, bemused at the turn of events, he realised what was happening. It was not a spider's web he could feel on his face but the fall of his own hair. Whenever he moved through an open doorway, the slight draft was enough to dislodge some fine strands and once he scratched his head, the locks started to come out in clumps. Rather than wait until he left a trail throughout the house, Tom decided to take the initiative and remove the problem. Some electric hair clippers were ordered from the Internet for next day delivery and Amaka performed her barber impersonation. Looking at himself in the hallway mirror, he now recognised the complete cancer set being reflected back: emaciated body, dark-rimmed eyes, sickly appearance and totally bald head.

Throughout the chemotherapy treatment, Amaka managed the situation, ensuring that each morning Tom had a bowl of tablets to accompany his orange juice and banana sandwich. The thick, unpleasant coating on his tongue was a discouragement from certain foods. Only the refreshing taste of fruit seemed to offer any appeal. A banana sandwich was a legacy from his childhood, a cheap, quick way employed by his mother to stave off the pangs of hunger before a main meal. Eating the snack in these circumstances was also a reminder of happier times.

Half-way through his second cycle of chemotherapy, Tom started to feel unwell in the early hours of the morning. He called on the internal phone to Amaka, who was asleep in the Annex. Within a few minutes she was at his bedside with her medical case. She felt his brow and carefully put a thermometer under his tongue. The reading indicated a high temperature and she could see that his face was flushed. Rather than send for an ambulance, Amaka gave him an injection containing a strong antibiotic and decided to monitor his progress. For a couple of days she did not leave his bedside while the intensive medication did its work. Soon, Tom's condition stabilised and he was allowed out of bed once more, although he was still feeling weak. Amaka helped him shuffle to and from the stair-lift by supporting his arm. On reaching the lounge, he slumped into his favourite chair with a deep sigh. 'I never want to go through that again,' he said, with a meaningful portion of relief.

However, Amaka brought him a measure of reality. 'In cases of myeloma, this sort of thing is common. I told you before, we might never know why this disease flares and threatens. You can only take it one day at a time and live your life in hope.'

Tom was not in the mood for platitudes. 'But what's the point? Surely, unfulfilled hope is destructive. We both know I'm fighting a losing battle.'

Amaka did not let the matter drop. 'It is true that the opposite of hope is despair but why focus on something that is destructive? Is it not better for the human spirit to be driven by the wish for something better? At least if that happens, the result is a positive one. Simply abandoning hope will bring about the inevitable result of nothingness. Hope is part of being human – to want something better.

You said that you want to know about my life and I have told you about the death of my father, brother, uncle and cousins when they were shot by the soldiers in Asaba. Do you want to know what happened to us when we escaped to the village of Uminwani?'

'Of course …but surely you cannot have been subjected to more suffering? I cannot imagine that life could be so cruel at such a young age.'

Amaka faced the palm of her hand towards Tom, indicating she was not ready to begin. She left him on the sofa and went into the kitchen to make a light snack. By this time, she knew her way around *Derwent House* as well as anyone. She was not hungry but simply wanted some breathing space, before re-visiting her nightmare. Amaka filled the kettle and leaned against the work surface, supporting her weight with a straight arm.

Her mind left for another place, casting itself back in time. The switch's automatic click from the boiling, silver container broke her trance. After placing a scoop of instant coffee and a drop of milk into two red mugs, she returned to the lounge with a semi-laden tray. The sandwiches were absent. No one was hungry and biscuits would have to suffice.

Tom took the closest mug and went to take a sip just as Amaka broke the silence. Lowering herself onto one of the armchairs, her memories reverted to those distant childhood days. 'For a year we lived in the village of Uminwani. All the villages in that part of the country were overcrowded. Many Igbo people fled from the North and other parts of the country to escape to our homelands. We were safer there, although everyone talked of war and our brave soldiers. Many young men only returned to the Village at night time. They did not want to be taken to be conscripted by the Biafran Army so they took refuge in the Bush during the day.

The Biafran Army would sometimes swoop on the villages without notice, looking for young men to conscript. There was chaos when they suddenly descended, with screaming mothers haranguing soldiers to release their sons ... but they never did. The girls would take turns to look out for the trucks coming into their village to warn everyone. In the evening, the boys would return to the compound as the sun began to set. They would sleep with their families at night because the Bush was no longer safe in the darkness.

One day, an old man called Madueke told the soldiers where some young boys were hiding. The soldiers found three of them and took them away in a lorry. One of the boys was Aku's friend. His name was Jamuike. He was only fourteen years old. After they took him, I never saw him again. No one in the village ever spoke to Madueke after that day or to anyone in his family. My sister Ifu would throw stones at him and call him names. She was very angry that he did this thing. We were all very angry at him and my *Mama* spat at his feet and shouted in his face because of what he had done. But Madueke did not regret what he had done. He said that people in Biafra must fight. If that meant losing the lives of some young men then it had to be that way. No war was ever fought without someone losing their life. His own son had been killed in a battle at the beginning of the War. Madueke left the village. I do not know what happened to him.'

Tom could see that despite the obvious heartache, there were no tears in Amaka's eyes. She was recounting her story as if it had happened to someone else. He supposed that the only way she could cope with her heartache was through detachment. The sorrow was so deep that it had removed her ability to outwardly grieve.

'For the rest of us in Uminwani, life was becoming more difficult. *Mama* was finding it harder to get food for me and my sisters. We relied on Aku to look after us and worked in any way we could to help. Death was all around us. Every day we could hear shells exploding, the noise of jets in the sky and the cries of distraught mothers who had learned of the deaths of their sons.

To get water, *Mama* and Ifu used to walk three miles to a stream, while I stayed in the Village. I was about five years old. This is the way we lived in Uminwani. Everybody was sad and frightened. The stories that reached us from the battles told us that we were going to lose the War. We just wanted the fighting to be over. But I will never forget that day.'

Tom did not want to press Amaka. He felt she was going too far. This was dangerous and unchartered territory. He could see the coffee in her red mug was untouched. 'Please, Amaka you don't have to tell me any more if you don't want to.'

'I need to tell you so you will understand. The only other person who knows what happened to me is Sister Mary and she is dead. It is important that someone with influence like you, understands so that nobody forgets what happened in this war.

On that morning, that terrible morning, *Mama* and Ifu went to get water from the stream once more. They walked along the dusty road with others from the Village. *Mama* used to carry a pitcher on her head like all the women. On their way to the stream *Mama* and Ifu would see mothers with their children from nearby villages going to collect their water also. The noise from the guns was getting closer to our Village each day. With every shell explosion or loud noise, someone would scream in fear. The aeroplanes were beginning to shriek over the area and fire their guns into the countryside. Every time a jet flew overhead we would cheer when it was followed by anti-aircraft fire. It gave us hope that we could still win the War.

But it was not to be. The first jet flew past the line of women and children and fired its guns at the hillside where the soldiers had their big guns. Everyone ran off the road and into the Bush for safety but nowhere was safe. The second jet started to fire at the road and everyone was screaming and running in panic. *Mama* was hit first as she cradled Ifu in her arms. She had been running for her life and suddenly her life was over. Ifu was struck by the third MIG before it disappeared into the distance. My sister and my *Mama* were killed in the time it took for a jet to fly overhead. They were collecting water for their families not shooting at soldiers. That day there were three others from my Village who were killed also.

Their bodies were brought back to our homes in the Village. I can remember seeing a cart being pulled along the road. At first, I thought it was carrying clothes but it was not; it was carrying bodies. The bodies of my *Mama* and my Ifu. All the women were wailing and beating their chests in pain. There was a lot of crying and shouting. I cannot recall what I did but I remember when Aku came into the village at night-time with the other boys, he was crying.

The next day a priest came to our Village. His name was Father Donovan. He said prayers for my *Mama* and my sister and they were buried that day. I do not know if I was crying or not but I was very sad. My cousin told Father Donovan there was not enough food for us and he had to take us with him. This he did. I went with Aku to a camp run by the Red Cross. It was in a place called Kukaru about ten miles away from Uminwani. There were many people there. It was a terrible place but we did have some food to eat.

I saw many bad things in that Camp. I used to stand by the hospital tent hoping to see someone I knew. All I saw were many bodies, injured and screaming. People would arrive on stretchers bleeding or sick. The smell is something I can never forget. There was so much crying and screaming in that Camp. Doctors and nurses were busy all of the time, running and shouting to try and keep people alive. Little children looked like walking skeletons and were dying every day. So much death, everywhere.' Amaka stared into her painful recollection of her past, seemingly distant from the safe reality of the present.

She observed Tom with tormented eyes and decided to go no further. He looked tired. Once more, their discussion had finished without a conclusion. Tom was helped to his bed, where he was soon in a rare, sound sleep, driven by fatigue, no longer able to keep the darkness at bay.

XII

There had been another telephone call from Jenny that week. It was a pleasant enough conversation under the circumstances but Tom still felt emotionally detached from his new relative. He wanted to experience more passion but it was just like talking to an old friend, rather than a close member of his immediate family. Perhaps too much had occurred, before the truth was revealed. The new association with his sister Jenny, was a disappointment.

The thought slipped from Tom's mind as Doctor Karim shook his hand and invited him to sit in the chair beside the desk. Amaka stood anonymously in the corner of the room, listening intently. While scrutinising the computer screen, Dr Karim got straight to the point of the consultation. 'Looking at the current readings of your blood counts, I now think we are at the stage of going ahead with a stem cell transplant.'

'What is that?' Tom felt assured that he was about to learn more than he had from the Internet.

'Well, we give you a growth factor that stimulates the bone marrow in your body to produce more blood cells, called *HSCs*. We then remove these stem cells from your blood and put them into deep freeze for storage. Once we have done this, we will give you one final, very powerful dose of chemotherapy that completely destroys your immunity system but also destroys any remaining malignant cancer cells. Then we re-introduce the stored cells into your body to replace damaged tissue. Normal blood cell production resumes and this will hopefully slow down the cancer. If you think of your body as being a computer, it's a bit like re-booting its immunity system. As you may recall, I said at our first meeting that unfortunately we cannot cure the cancer but we can give it a good run for its money. A stem cell transplant is our major weapon against myeloma.'

Tom was slumping into the seat with every depressing thought. He looked at his hand resting on the table and it was shaking as if he had palsy. The situation demanded a response but his lips merely pursed and he could only blow air in an attempt to speak. Amaka took the initiative and moved across to his aid. Placing her hand on Tom's shoulder, she asked, 'When will this happen Doctor? Will it be before or after Christmas?'

Dr Karim looked up at Amaka and waggled his pen under his chin. 'I think after Christmas is best, all things considered. It will probably be the first or second week of the New Year. We'll let you know as soon as possible.' Turning to address Tom he added 'You'll be able to enjoy Christmas at home, at least, Tom.' It was said in a tone reminiscent of a patronising carer talking to a deaf old man, although the patient was unable to interpret any potential insult. Tom felt defeated and sat as if waiting for the final blow of execution before Amaka helped him to his feet and they left the room, nodding thanks to Dr Karim on the way.

Tom was admitted to the Cancer Ward at the Ivy Hospital for his final stage of treatment in the first week of January. The plan was to undergo three weeks of intensive chemotherapy followed by a challenging stem cell transplant. The latter would take a further ten days, while his total recovery time was estimated to be approximately three months. After that, his future would be determined, one way or the other. The final stage was now taking place and Tom's life was in the balance.

Most days, Amaka would read to Tom during the relative tranquillity of the Hospital's evening routine. The intimacy of the private room ensured they had no unwanted visitors. There were no set visiting times for Amaka because of her professional medical status. They were forming a close, loving friendship. Tom was lying in bed, half-propped up by pillows, while Amaka was sitting in the bedside chair facing him, reading aloud a chapter from *Treasure Island*. Her gentle voice was soothingly warm and the story of Jim Hawkins was a reassuring reminder to Tom of his youth. Amaka was engrossed in the tale, unaware that Tom's focus was on her and not the cabin boy. It was the situation he found comforting, not the book. He watched Amaka, outside himself for a moment, admiring her beauty. She was a striking, intelligent young woman with an attractive, warm personality. Tom hoped that she would meet someone who would love her and care for her in a manner she deserved.

Conversation between them in this private world was natural and unstilted. They exchanged intimate stories of growing up and would often laugh at some of the differences in their daily, childhood routines. Every time Amaka spoke about her early upbringing, Tom wondered if there was more drama to unfold. He suspected that despite telling him about the deaths of her family members, she had suffered even more heartache. While Amaka spoke of *Long John Silver,* Tom drifted peacefully towards sleep.

With each day of his powerful drug regime, Tom's strength faded. He was now restricted to his bed and even too tired to get up and use the toilet in the room. Forced to rely on bed-bottles and bed-pans to complete nature's basic tasks, even the chirpiness of the woman delivering the daily confectionary and newspaper trolley was now lost on him as he began to lose his sense of reality. The climax to his treatment was only three days away.

Amaka had reassured Tom that the stem cell transplant was a painless procedure but she had neglected to inform him of the level of danger it could impose if complications arose. He was transferred to a two-bed isolation room at the end of the main Cancer Ward and told the procedure would take place the following day. Tom had listened intently as Dr Karim informed him that the transplant would totally destroy his immunity to infection. This vulnerability would require isolation for about two weeks. The highly restrictive cleanliness regime that existed in the segregated room would be critical to his treatment.

The restricted area had special air filters and he would be allowed only one visitor – Amaka. She was required to wash her hands thoroughly, wear protective overalls and a mask when visiting. Tom would have access to his own nurse at all times, while in isolation. There would be one of two carers at his disposal, depending on the time of day – Nurse Suvindra (*Suvvy*) and Nurse Mai Lee (*Mai*). In addition to managing his drugs, taking blood samples and dealing with most things medical, they would also prepare his meals; he was allowed to eat anything from a personalised menu.

Three days later it was time for the transplant and Tom was very nervous. The drama of the unfolding scene did little to alleviate his anxiety. The doctor and specialist nurse entered the isolation room wearing masks and protective coats. They brought with them Tom's frozen stem cells, contained in what looked like a mobile, global drinks' cabinet, except its outside cover was devoid of any cartographic outlines. An aquarium of hot water was introduced on another trolley. The top half of the globe was lifted open, using a pair of surgical tongs and causing a hissing noise. Tom expected an alien to suddenly appear and zoom around the room. Once removed from the reservoir of preservation fluid, the plastic bag containing the frozen cells was defrosted. This involved immersing the bag into the aquarium of hot water, which caused steam to rise and fill half of the room. The stem cells were then introduced into Tom's body through his Hickman Line catheter, in a manner similar to a blood infusion.

This was the key moment, the pinnacle of months of preparation, anxiety and pain. Slowly, the life enhancing transplant fluid containing Tom's own stem cells, flowed down the tube and into his veins. The doctor monitored the patient carefully, trying to gauge any signs of a physical reaction. The amber-glowing numbers changed quickly on the black pad attached to the drip. Flickering orange and green lights looked like a computerised space machine in an amusement arcade, while the rapidly changing numbers were significant only to the scrutinising doctor, who watched with keen interest. There was an unexpected beeping sound as if a large lorry was reversing in the room. Tom felt his brow with the back of his hand and sensed the sweat develop under his arms. He looked at the medical staff and made a conscientious effort not to panic, aware of the procedure's significance to his fight against the cancer. As he looked down at his feet, his vision started to close as if he was entering a tunnel. Desperately he tried to retain an even keel. Then suddenly, the flickering numbers stopped changing and the beeping noise became more regular. Gradually, he felt more comfortable as his temperature dropped and his sense of claustrophobia diminished. Finally, his full vision returned and he could see his toes once again. He had just experienced the longest fifteen minutes of his life.

Tom had been told that immediately after the procedure, the number of his red and white blood cells would be at their lowest. He had been advised by the specialist nurse that the best way to handle the impending feeling of overwhelming illness was to sleep. This was not really a problem as he felt terrible and sleep offered an escape. It was too much effort to speak and he wrestled with demon thoughts, drifting in and out of consciousness. The ride was an emotional roller-coaster and it was difficult to retain a sense of perspective, feeling so desperately sick. Even the periods of sleep were dominated by constant, irrational hallucinations. When Amaka saw him at this critical time, there was nothing she could do: he was in his own, surrealistic world. Although Tom sensed someone was in the room, he could not gauge who it was or even if it was all in his imagination.

After five days of struggle, there was the beginning of some interaction with the world beyond his bed as his body started to produce bone marrow once more, thanks to the infused stem cells. During this early period of his return from the impact of the transplant, Tom was feeling emotionally raw and angry. It was a side-effect of the treatment and he let rip at Amaka's expense. 'If this is supposed to be doing me good, I don't want it,' he maintained. 'I am tired of feeling so ill. I have been this way for six months now and I can't stand it anymore. I have never abused my body yet I am being singled out by this lousy disease. I just feel awful and I have had enough.' This was the most critical phase of treatment ; Tom had climbed to the top of the volcano and was now staring into the crater's abyss below.

'You were told it would not be easy, Tom. A stem cell transplant is challenging.' Amaka sensed he was experiencing a loss of perspective and was trying to stamp reality into his awareness.

'Yes but they never told me I would feel like this for so long. It's not fair so don't give me any more of your banalities. I am sick of hearing them. If you are going to talk to me, then make some sense out of all of this. If you can't say anything useful, just go away and leave me alone.' Tom was lashing out and felt there was nothing left to hang on to. It seemed that he was prepared to cast himself adrift.

Amaka remained silent, collected her handbag and meekly left Tom in the room alone. When he heard the door close, he felt annoyed at himself for losing his temper. Perhaps it was the medication or a judgement on his own life that had caused him to lose self-control. In any event, the world of sleep presented some relief and after a short nap, he stirred to find Amaka sitting in the chair next to his bed. Before she had a chance to take the emotional initiative, Tom apologised.

'I'm sorry, Amaka. I don't know what I am saying. Please, forgive me.'

This was a time for compassion and friendship not confrontation and recrimination.

'Forgive you? Forgive you? You must understand that there is nothing to forgive. It is *you* who have saved *me*. You have saved my life. There is nothing for me to forgive. While you were asleep I was thinking about what you asked me so I am going to tell you something now that I did not even tell Sister Mary. It is something I have never told anyone before.'

'Please, not if you don't want to. You don't have to confide in me.'

'I am going to tell you this because I think it may help you to recover something you have lost. I want it to give you hope and for you to feel and believe in hope. Amaka leaned across and lifted Tom's fringe before placing a gentle kiss on his forehead. Then, she held his hand as she slid back into her seat, beside his bed.

'Towards the end of the War, I was in the Camp. It was a terrible place, full of Igbo refugees who had fled from other parts of the country. There was nowhere left for me to go. This was the final piece of our land that we could call Biafra. Food was impossible to find. In the villages, school compounds were converted into living quarters for refugees but for children like me there was only a Camp. We had stopped praying to win the War. We were praying for the War to end. Then, the end of the War came. Finally, it was over but we did not see any difference, at first.

For the refugees, a Camp was the worst place of all. Refugees had no land and had to rely on foreign aid. There were many camps. Robbery was everywhere. It was generated by hunger. People would uproot un-ripened crops from the fields just to get something to eat. If someone who was not a refugee did this, his treatment would be very hard indeed. People who had always lived in that area had some land of their own to grow yams, cocoyam or cassava. To take crops from someone else's land would be a bad thing. The people would beat him or even kill him. If he was a refugee they would be more understanding and just send him away. He would be forgiven because he did not have land. What else was he supposed to do if he was dying of starvation?

There was disease in the Camp; many diseases. It was in this place where I saw schistosomiasis. People were so hungry they would look for snails to eat in streams or anywhere with water. But parasites living on the snails contaminate the water. Anyone in the water or drinking it will catch schistosomiasis. It causes many bad things to the body.

But it was not the only disease in the Camp. The main disease was kwashiorkor. It is so simple to stop but the aid that countries were sending to my people could not get through. There was a blockade around Biafra. Supplies could only get in by aeroplane. The Federal soldiers stopped the supplies getting through to try and starve my people into surrender. The only thing the children needed to stop kwashiorkor was more protein to eat but we did not have enough. Towards the end of the War, kwashiorkor had increased a great deal. Many children looked like walking skeletons, with eyeballs sunk deep into their cavities, sitting on the ground with swollen bellies. It is the image that most people have of children suffering in Biafra during the Nigerian Civil War. Kwashiorkor killed many little children.

I too was very weak from kwashiorkor. There was no food. Aku took me to the nearest village, away from the Camp, to ask the people to help us. Igbo soldiers had started to return to their villages and the War was over. If the Federal soldiers came into the villages they would shout '*One Nigeria!*' and if the people in the villages did not shout with them, they were badly beaten. There were many reprisal killings by the occupying Federal troops after the War.

One family in the village helped us and said they would look after me. I do not know their names. Aku went into the bush where it was safer for him, even though the War was now over. He did what he used to do when hiding from the Biafran soldiers: he returned at night-time and slept in the compound with us. One evening when Aku returned, Federal soldiers came into the village. They were shouting and singing and firing their guns in the air. They had won the War and made us do things for them as if we were their slaves. One of them saw Aku running away in the dark and grabbed him as he tried to escape into the Bush. The soldier held Aku by the shoulders and screamed at him.

'Come on boy, sing *One Nigeria* and I will let you go.' Aku did not respond. 'Come on, boy. Do you not want me to let you go? Hey, Lieutenant I have caught a boy here and he does not know if he wants me to let him go! What should I do with him? Should I shoot him?' Aku looked at him, terrified.

I was too weak to run so I hid behind a tree and watched the soldiers with Aku. The Officer marched across to my brother. His big, heavy boots made a loud noise as he stomped over the dusty ground. He went right up to Aku and started to shout at him. He sounded just like the officer at Asaba on that terrible day when *Papa* and Amaechi were shot. I do not know if it was the same soldier. The Officer bellowed at my brother.

'How old are you boy?'

'I am fourteen years old, sir.'

'Did you fight in the War.?'

'No sir.'

The soldier slapped Aku. *'You are a liar. I saw you fight. Say you are a liar, boy.'* Aku said nothing.

The Officer took over the interrogation. *'Is that right? Did you fight against me and my men in the War, boy?'* Aku remained silent. *'So if you do not deny it, it must be true.'* Aku was still standing upright, almost to attention. He made the mistake of looking at the Officer directly into his eyes, in an act of defiance. *'If it is not true then you must sing One Nigeria with us. If you do not sing this, you are my enemy and I will order this soldier to shoot you.* Aku remained mute. *'Shoot this boy, soldier!'*

There was the loud noise of a gunshot as the soldier lowered his pistol and fired.

He shot Aku in the foot. It was clearly an act of terror which these soldiers had carried out before, in other villages. Aku screamed in pain and hopped around violently but he did not fall to the ground. He refused to show that he was going to be beaten by his oppressors. I watched in terror from my hiding place, not daring to make a sound. The Officer seemed impressed by Aku's defiance.

'So you are a man and not a boy, after all. Well done, soldier. Well done.' The officer beckoned another subordinate to where they were standing. Aku was now hovering on one leg, hanging on to the branch of a nearby tree, with his injured foot held off the ground. He must have wanted to scream in pain but he would not give the soldiers the satisfaction. The Officer gave his orders.

'Soldier, watch over this man. We are going to make camp here tonight and continue in the morning.' He then turned directly towards Aku and standing within breath-tasting distance of him, looked at my brother. He spat out his final order. *'Soldier, I have ordered this man to stand. If he falls over during the*

night or tries to sit on the ground, your orders are to shoot him dead. If he remains standing all night without falling over, we will let him go in the morning.

Young man, you heard what I said. I am giving you an order. If you follow my order to stand it will show that you are a good soldier. If you are still standing here in the morning when I return, you will be released.'

Without waiting for a response or a reaction, the Officer turned away, got into a jeep and was driven into another part of the village. I huddled into the base of the tree. That night, I watched Aku as he stood in silent, defiant pain, still hanging on to the branch. I prayed and prayed with all my might that Aku would not fall to the ground. Each time I awoke, my eyes dashed across to look for Aku. Each time I did so, he was still standing. He was resting his injured foot on top of the other one, using a dead branch as a crutch, for support, while the guard slept beside his rifle. Aku stood like a flamingo, trying not to show his pain. It would have been easier if he simply fell and was removed from his agony by a bullet but he did not give in. He never gave in, even though he was in so much distress.

After many hours I wished for the sun to rise. I prayed that he would last those final hours. Still, he stood defiant. He was determined to return, to look after me. All I could do was watch and hope. Then, first light came and the soldier was sitting on the ground, resting against his rifle, while Aku was still standing, still awake, still leaning against the branch. I could not see if his foot was bleeding but he must have been weak from the loss of blood. I heard the roar of engines and could see the jeep followed by a truck, coming around the corner. The guard jumped to his feet and stood to attention. The Officer was sitting beside the driver in the jeep as it pulled up alongside Aku.

'Well soldier, did this young man obey my standing order?'

'He did, sir.'

'Well done, well done young man. Your country is proud of you. Soldier, you may return to your unit. I will see to this young man's release.' As the guard marched towards the back of the lorry containing the other soldiers, the Officer got out of the jeep and walked behind Aku. *'Right soldier, you may sit.'* As Aku lowered himself gently to the soil, the Officer produced his hand from behind his back. It contained his revolver. Without a second thought or any compassion, he shot Aku in the head, as if putting an animal out of its suffering. I called out with a scream, 'No, no! Aku, my brother!' The

Officer heard my screams and looked over to the tree where I was hiding. He walked over to me and pointed his gun. I thought he was going to shoot me but he did not. He simply turned and got back into the jeep. With a wave of his arm he gestured forward and the lorry followed. They were gone and my brother was lying on the ground.

People came out of their houses and everyone could see that Aku was dead. A man put some branches and leaves over his body. Then some of the women from the village took him away. I did not cry. I was too weak. I turned away without saying any words. No one tried to stop me, even though I was ill and starving.

I started to walk out of the village. I think I was trying to return to the Camp. As I was walking, a jeep with a white circle and red cross on the front stopped beside me. A young man got out and said something but I just looked at him. He gently picked me up and lifted me into the jeep. I remember an aeroplane was flying in the sky and boxes with parachutes were falling into the fields beside us. They took me to a different place. It was to the Mission where I first met Sister Mary Uloma. A priest approached the jeep and he carried me into the Mission. He laid me on a bed. Then Sister Mary came and spoke to me.

'It is alright now my child,' she said, gently. Sister Mary could see that I too was close to death. I do not remember what happened next but slowly and surely, I began to recover. Despite everything that had happened to me, I still had hope for something good.'

Tom sat, silently stunned at what he had heard. 'Amaka – I don't know what to say. I feel humbled that you have told me your story. I do not understand how you have been able to keep going after such a horrific life of misfortune.' He felt embarrassed and ashamed.

'It was not all misfortune, Tom. That is my point. The money that you sent for me, it saved me. It gave me a chance for an education and a better life for myself. I took that chance and the only thing I ask from you is that you take your chance too.

I know you feel very ill at the moment and that is because you are fighting a terrible disease. The only thing I will ever ask of you is that you take hope from my story. The doctors are pleased at the way you are recovering. I have spoken to Dr Karim and he says that your progress is very good. What you are going through at the moment, it will pass.

You will get better and even if you do not beat the illness forever, you will still have a life worth living. Please, have it in your mind to *make* it worth living. None of us knows what the future will bring. It is part of our condition as human beings. But you must reach inside yourself, deep inside yourself and you will find hope. That is all I ask.'

Tom reached out his hand across the top sheet of his bed and wiggled his fingers, which Amaka took and clasped to her bosom. She leaned forward and kissed him on his forehead once more and said, 'Thank you, for *you* have saved me.'

Tom pulled her close and held his friend in a loving embrace.

XIII

Two weeks after the stem cell transplant, Tom received a visit from Dr Karim on the Ward. This was unusual as the duty doctor was nearly always the Registrar, Dr Hemmings. It was good news.

'How are you feeling today, Tom?' asked the Consultant in the familiar manner that had become the norm.

'I believe the expression is *as well as can be expected*, Doctor.'

'Well actually, I think it's a bit better than that. You have made a very good recovery. The fact that you had maintained a level of fitness through a healthy lifestyle has clearly helped. Your strength has allowed us to take you closer to the brink than we would normally have been able to do, with that final dose of chemotherapy. This means the re-introduction of the stem cells has had a more powerful effect when fighting the malignant cells. As a result your recovery has been good.'

Tom patted his chest, catching one of the catheter tubes with his pyjama button and tweaking a pinch of discomfort. 'In that case, I doff my hat to those poor souls who have suffered more than me and survived. I thought that my recovery was bad enough. To have endured worse must have been Hell.'

'Well drinkers and smokers have other issues to deal with. You did not have those difficulties to obstruct your recovery. In fact, I have been looking at the pattern of your blood counts in the last week. They are encouraging. I think we can let you go home tomorrow, if you want to?'

'If I want to? Much as how I love you Doctor, I would rather be in my own home.' There was a hint of optimism in Tom's voice. Amaka would have been proud of that sentence.

When the following day arrived, it was an emotional moment. Tom was able to dress in daytime clothes for the first time in a long while. He needed to wear an extra-large sport shirt as he still had in place the

Hickman Line, which was a minor inconvenience. Nurse Suvvy was on duty that morning and before she addressed her daily routine of chores, she was able to say goodbye to Tom. He was sitting on the edge of the bed with his back to the doorway, looking out of the window with one arm resting on top of a travel bag. The clothes looked too big for his emaciated body and he appeared like a lost little boy.

'So you are leaving me?' she teased.

'Ah, well – you know. They said it wouldn't last but we had four great weeks together. And we'll always have *Plaster of Paris*.' Suvvy came around the bed with a puzzled look.

She looked him squarely in the face. *'Plaster of Paris?'*

'You've never seen *Casablanca*?' asked Tom, trying to stifle a painful laugh.

'With Humphrey Crosby?' inquired Suvvy, innocently.

'Humphrey *Bogart*. Never mind. I'll get the film for you so you know what I'm talking about.' Suvvy gave Tom a sympathetic goodbye hug. He stifled a pathetic response of gratitude. 'I'll always remember your kindness.' Suvvy simply smiled and left the room, making her way to the next patient. Within a few moments Amaka appeared.

Tom was too weak to walk quickly out of the Ward and while Amaka carried his travel bag, he slowly shuffled down the corridor towards the Reception Desk. A couple of people in their beds waved jealously as Tom walked past the large window in their alcove. The Sister and a couple of Auxiliaries were near the Ward's exit doors, completing some forms and discussing a potential work roster for the coming week.

'Cheerio Tom,' said the Sister in a tone she had done many times before to other patients. 'See you in a month's time.' Initial outpatient appointments at the Day Unit following release, were normally on a monthly basis. If Tom's blood counts continued to be satisfactory, the period between appointments would be lengthened to two months, then six months. However, there were many bridges to be crossed first.

As Tom and Amaka exited the lift and made their way to the Main Hospital Entrance, he gulped and exaggerated his first intake of fresh air in a while. It was a cold, blustery February day which made its sting even more enjoyable.

'Where's that taxi?' asked Tom, sounding annoyed.

'It's over there,' responded Amaka, suppressing a smile.

'Where? I don't see anything.'

'Wait here a moment.' She ensured Tom was sitting safely on a bench in the covered waiting area, adjacent to the Entrance. 'I'll be right back.'

Within a couple of minutes a car pulled-up to where Tom was sitting. He could not believe his eyes. Getting out of the driver's side was Amaka, who was wearing a huge grin as she started to giggle in girly good humour. 'This is your taxi,' she said.

'Is this your way of telling me that you can drive now?'

'Well I could not simply read medical books all day, when I was not with you at the Hospital. So I decided to try and pass the British Driving Test and I have been having lessons during a lot of the mornings. Last week I passed my test. I used some of the money you have been giving me. I know I won't get a lot of opportunity to drive here because it won't be long before I have to return to Nigeria. Still, I hope you don't mind?'

'Mind!' You have to be kidding. I think it's great. Well done, you! And well done for keeping it a secret. I think it is amazing.' Tom could not believe Amaka. She was continually a source of surprise. He did not know how she was able to persistently challenge herself after everything she had endured. Compared to her problems, his own were less significant.

On their way back to Loughton, Tom's mind was suddenly occupied by thoughts of what Amaka had said about returning to her home country. It was always something he knew he would have to accept at some point but suddenly it was becoming a reality. He did not attempt to speak to her while she was concentrating on driving but he tried to distract his own anxieties by focussing on absorbing the normality of the views from the car. It did not work. Tom did not want to face the inevitability of losing Amaka.

As they approached the lane leading to *Derwent House,* Tom noticed a little boy standing with his father. They were both watching a mechanical digger tear up the tarmac to access a drain. The youngster was pretending to operate the machine and no doubt would repeat the exercise with his own toys at home, as Tom used to do, many years ago. He was brought back to reality by the familiar sound of his own driveway. The thud of car doors slamming brought Sylvia to the front of the house. She walked quickly to Tom and squeezed him a little too tightly in her welcoming embrace.

'Ow! Careful, Sylvia I'm a lot more delicate than I used to be.'

'Oh Gosh, sorry Tom. Are you alright?' asked a startled Sylvia.

'It's ok, I'm only kidding. It's great to be home.' At least he still had the semblance of a sense of humour.

While Sylvia took his coat and hung it on a peg in the entrance hall, Tom made his way to the lounge. Stopping at the bottom of the stairs and staring at the mountain face before him, he wondered if there would ever again be an expedition involving such a climb. He could only appreciate his decision to install a stair-lift when he had first become ill. Using the automated chair might make him feel like an old man but it was better than moving into the Annex. This way, sleep would take place in his own bed. Feeling exhausted, Tom declined Sylvia's offer to make him something to eat and slowly headed for slumber.

During convalescence and with time running out, the conversations between Tom and Amaka became even closer. They both possessed intimate knowledge about each other's lives that no one else knew. Tom confided in Amaka about Emma, the lost love from his youth. In exchange, she told him about her recovery and the time Sister Mary nursed her back to health.

'Sister Mary cared for me, like *Mama* had done. She was with me every day, looking after me, feeding me and changing me. Most children were taken into care homes when they were well enough but I was allowed to stay at the Mission. I could do this because of your money. I was allowed to live in a big room with some other children who were also being helped by charities from other countries. I do not know what would have happened to me if I had to leave the Mission. All my family were dead. The War had killed them all.

It was Sister Mary who taught me to read. She also made it possible for me to trust again. It was her love that allowed me to eventually speak once more. Before that, I did not want to talk to anyone. People had killed everyone I loved and taken away everything that was important to me. She showed me the authority of love and it made me whole.

I enjoyed reading. I loved to read. There was a small library at the

Mission and I read many books. I was taught by two of the nuns and a priest at the Mission until I was old enough to go to school. Then, when I was twelve I went to the big school in Emweniguku. Every morning I walked two miles to the bus which took me to school and I walked back to the Mission at the end of the day. I did not mind this. I was free and safe from shooting and death. There were no planes in the sky, no shells exploding around me and no smells of death in the air. Walking back to the Mission every day in the setting sun, reminded me of those happy days when I was with my family and *Mama* and *Papa*. It was like they were with me.'

Tom was sitting in his favourite chair, drinking a glass of milk and listening intently. He did not mean to interrupt but was naturally curious about Amaka's past. 'What happened when you were old enough to leave school?'

'I realised that I was clever when the Headteacher in Emweniguku told me that my exam results were the best in the School. He said he would to try to get me a place in university. First, I had to sit an exam to get a scholarship. I did this and I passed the exam. When I was eighteen, I went to University in Enugu and eventually gained a degree in Biology.

The generous standing orders that you sent to the Mission were used to pay for me while I was at University. I did not know this until I graduated as a doctor of medicine. I worked for the Government and travelled around the South East Region of Nigeria, mainly in the States of Enugu, Imo, Abia and Adamawa. I visited the villages and established clinics to inoculate children, examine them and give medicine where it was needed. I specialised in the treatment of children with schistosomiasis. I have seen too many children with this disease. It is a terrible thing in my country. When I was in the villages I spoke to groups of children to show them how to look for the danger signs.

If we had more fresh water in our country the problem would not exist. In the village of Uminwani, women still walk to the stream where *Mama* was killed. There has been no progress since the War. If we had enough money we could have water pumped from under the ground and it would be safe to drink. The Government do not see this but I will continue to fight so the children are safe. That is what brought me to Great Britain.

My work in Nigeria became known to the Government. I spoke with the Minister of Health for my country and told him about the work being carried out on some drugs in your country. I persuaded him to allow me to come and research here.'

'And then you gave it all up, for me,' commented Tom trying to convey as much appreciation as he could.

'It will mean only a delay in my work. I will have to leave the country soon before my visa expires but I will return. I will convince my Government of this. It is an odd coincidence that education gave us both opportunities, don't you think ?'

'Not so strange, really. We share many things and are alike in lots of ways. We are both determined and single-minded. We knew where we wanted to take our lives, once we became adults and we both came from loving families.'

Each day, Amaka accompanied Tom during his exercise regime as he set about re-building his physical strength. At first, the activity comprised nothing more than walking to the main gates at the entrance to his house, when he would lean heavily on his human crutch. Then, his exercise programme developed into a walk around the outside of the house, which he eventually managed on his own. Gradually and slowly, the length of each walk was extended and his independence returned. Amaka began to drive Tom to areas where he wanted to visit and they would walk arm-in-arm together.

Tom's hair returned. His appearance made him laugh when he looked at himself in a mirror because his grey hair had grown thick and frizzy at the back. He had never been curly in his life yet here it was. Dr Karim informed him that sometimes it was an unusual quirk after chemotherapy for hair to return differently to its original consistency. Tom was also assured that the state of his hair would not be permanent and eventually its former growth pattern would be restored.

It was soon time to revisit the Hospital's Day Unit in order to remove Tom's Hickman Line. The disconnection of the catheter was further physical proof of his progress. Amaka drove to the Hospital and when they arrived, she dropped him off by the main entrance to the Wards and the Unit, while she looked for a space in the carpark. Tom sat by the entrance to the lift, next to a confectionary kiosk and waited for Amaka to return. While he was waiting, he suddenly felt unwell and thought he was going to faint. At that moment Amaka re-appeared from the car park and immediately she could see his distress.

'Are you alright, Tom?' He did not answer and appeared to be unfocussed on Amaka's question. Amaka looked around but there was no obvious sign of support. Tom removed his woollen hat and vomited into it before crumbling to the floor. Amaka shouted towards the lady serving in the kiosk.

'Do you have a phone?'

'Yes.'

'Then call for assistance, quickly!'

Amaka checked his racing pulse and placed her hand inside his shirt, pressing against his chest. His pupils were dilated and he was losing consciousness. Within a couple of minutes, several other doctors arrived, along with a pair of porters pushing a gurney. Amaka took the initiative. 'Can we please take him to the Day Unit? They can take a better look at him there.'

Tom regained consciousness while on the stretcher and arrived horizontally for what should have been his routine appointment. This caused a mixture of concern and amusement among the medical staff in the Day Unit. The loss of equilibrium was attributed to a problem with blood pressure, although no specific diagnosis was provided. Despite the hiatus, the Unit's doctor decided to remove his Hickman Line and a couple of stitches were inserted at the point where the catheter had previously exited his chest. The procedure was less painful than when the tube was fitted. Although Tom's faint was not as serious as first thought, it was a reminder that his convalescence still had some way to go. It affected his confidence a little and when they returned to his house, his morale was shaken. 'I don't know, it's like two steps forward and three steps back. Every time I fight against it, something else happens.'

'That is the nature of the illness, I'm afraid. You've just got to keep fighting.'

'I'll try,' replied Tom, not meaning to give any false sense of determination.

'That's more like it. I have to say that I admire the way you have fought this illness. You have accepted every procedure they have thrown at you and taken it all in your stride.'

In that special moment between them, Amaka smiled to herself. She knew exactly what needed to be done before she returned to Nigeria and decided to set in motion something that would change the rest of Tom's life.

XIV

Amaka had been in Great Britain for ten months and was aware that soon she would need to give some attention to returning home. Time was running out and choosing the right moment to reveal her final secret was going to be difficult. Their long walks together had become enjoyable and Amaka estimated that Tom had regained approximately eighty percent of his strength. However, myeloma possesses the ability to return at any time and can suddenly flare into active mode, without warning. Full remission is very rare and living with the potent disease means being permanently aware of the state of human frailty. The unpredictability of myeloma means that chances at happiness should be taken, once they arise. This was the thought that had influenced Amaka. Today would be the day.

Amaka made breakfast that morning as she knew Sylvia would not be coming over to *Derwent House*. Tom was taking a shower upstairs, before he got dressed. Breakfast was not a big meal and did not take a lot of effort. A fruit salad on cornflakes, with orange juice, toast and freshly-made coffee had been prepared in the main kitchen before Amaka was due to take it on a tray into the conservatory, at the back of the building. The fresh, spring sun was shining on that side of the house and Amaka felt that brightness would help lighten the mood. She was not sure how well Tom would accept her revelations but chances had to be seized at this stage of his life.

It seemed like a normal breakfast : Tom wiped the side of his mouth with a blue napkin as the brown toast was finally devoured. He lifted his cup of coffee and sighed with satisfaction, gazing across the open countryside. 'That was nice. Thanks, Amaka.'

'I am pleased you are feeling good because I have something important to tell you.' This immediately grabbed Tom's attention as he looked at Amaka's determined expression. He had almost come to fear her disclosures. Amaka continued. 'I know there is no need for me to tell you anything about the Internet but I have been exploring the Web on your computer, while you have been resting or in hospital. I find it fascinating.'

This was not what Tom was expecting and with some disappointment he shot her a perplexed look. He felt he should say something profound. 'I believe it is the future and people's use of the Internet will explode over the next fifteen to twenty years. It was one area I intended to exploit before this illness struck me down.'

'Have you heard of a website called, *Friends Reunited*?' Amaka began laying her trap.

'No, I don't think I have.' He had been out of the game for a few months so he reassured himself after declaring his lack of knowledge.

'That's a pity because I think you would admire the enterprise of the people who have set it up. It developed two years ago from an idea in someone's bedroom and now has boomed, with over two million users. All it takes is seven pounds to join.' Tom turned his head from side-to-side and opened his palms as if to say, *'So what?'*

'It brings together people who have lost touch with each other. Old friends and acquaintances are brought together. ... Literally former friends are re-united.'

It sounded like a cute idea and Tom showed a polite flicker of interest. 'So what groups do these *friends* belong to?'

'They are mainly old school friends and former work colleagues. They simply add their names to a list of people who were at a place during a specific year and others can see the list and then get in touch by sending them an email. They receive the email even though they may not have signed up to *Friends Reunited*. If they want to respond to their friends' emails and get in touch, they must join as well. It's quite clever, really.'

Tom resumed his state of neutral interest. 'Doesn't sound like my cup of tea? I'm not really interested in finding out what people I went to school with forty years ago are doing now. I've had my share of that recently.'

Amaka decided to dangle the fly a little. 'It also lists people who went to the same university. For example, it lists all the people who graduated from Sheffield University in 1970.' The tone of Amaka's voice was deliberate. She said the sentence with rising poignancy in her voice. Tom bit hard onto the hook. She definitely had his interest.

'But my name is not on that list? I haven't joined *Friends Reunited.*' He wriggled in his seat as if trying to withdraw.

'No, but there is one name on their website list that caught my attention: that name is Emma Lawson. You have told me about the role she has played in your life – remember?'

'Yes...I remember. I wonder what Emma is doing now. It must be thirty years since I last saw her.' He tried to downplay his interest at the mention of Emma's name but he had taken the bait.

Amaka was not distracted by the reaction. She knew she almost had him landed. 'It was thirty one years ago and she is still living in America.' Amaka said it with such authority that Tom pushed himself to his feet, surprising himself at his own strength. The next two minutes were about to change his life.

'What! ...How do you know that?'

'Because I have been in contact with her. I sent her an email.'

'What! You had no right to do that.'

'Oh, I think I do. As someone who cares for you, I do not like to see you like this. Please don't be angry with me.'

If he had more mobility Tom would have stormed out of the room but he was glad he had an excuse to stay. 'What did she say?'

'She responded to my email.'

'What! Are you telling me that you have been in touch with Emma Lawson?'

'Yes. That is what I am telling you.'

'Good God!' Tom stared out into the distance. A fox was running across an adjacent field but at that moment, he was not interested in the wildlife.

'So what did she say? More importantly, what did *you* say?'

'I asked her if she was the same Emma Lawson who was at Sheffield University with Tom Kettlewell.'

'And?'

'She said she was, except her surname is no longer Lawson. Her name is now King but she and her husband divorced five years ago.'

'So what is she doing these days?' He was out of the water and wriggling in the air.

'She told me that she has her own law firm in Richmond, Virginia. She specialises in Civil Rights cases.'

'When you said, she *told* you, what do you mean by that exactly?'

'I have spoken to her.'

'What! Jesus Christ, Amaka. I can't believe what you are telling me. How the Hell did you manage to speak to her?'

'We spoke on the telephone. When I sent her a second email, she returned my message and her email included her phone number so I called her.'

Tom was speechless, excited and dumbfounded in equal measures.

'What did you say in the second email that made her give you her phone number?'

'I told her about me and why I was getting in touch with her.'

'Which was?'

'It was to tell her about you. To tell her how ill you are and to see if she wanted to contact you.'

Tom was now floundering on the deck of Amaka's boat. 'And does she?'

'Yes. She said that it was the time to put things right.'

'I have printed the emails. I have copies if you want to read them?' Her question was superfluous.

Amaka half-stood out of her seat and crouched over the coffee table. She lifted the morning newspaper to reveal a few A4 sheets underneath. Then, she gave Tom two printed emails with their corresponding replies as she stood to face him. He almost snatched them from her hands and was no longer focussed on Amaka's face. He was glaring at the printed emails. The first one was simply the contact and response message that Amaka had reported. The second contained more information.

Dear Amaka,

Thank you for your email and for telling me about Tom's illness. I do remember seeing the picture you drew for Tom. He was very pleased to receive it and it was a very sweet drawing. I recall that there was a big yellow sun, with some people standing beside a house.

Please tell Tom that I hope he has a full and speedy recovery and that I am sorry for what has happened to him.

A lot has happened in the time since I last saw Tom. I think it is probably

time to put the past behind us and talk about the present, while we are able.
There are many things I would like to say but they are too important to
communicate in an email. If you are able to telephone me, please do so. My
number is 804-604-7574963
Thank you for getting in touch with me.
Emma

'So when was the last time you spoke to her?'

'It was last week. Do you want me to get her for you on the telephone?'

'No, please – don't… at least not just yet. Not out of the blue like that.
It's all too sudden. What did she say to you?'

'She asked if you and Felicity were still together.'

'And you told her …?'

'I said you were divorced many years ago.'

'What did she say then?'

'She said that perhaps now might be the time to get in touch and put
things right … and then she went on to say something else.'

'What was it she said?' Tom could not believe the tale was getting
deeper.

'I asked her about her life in America and if she has any family.'

'And… ?'

'She has a son. …His name is Tommy …Tommy Lawson… '

'Tommy Lawson?'

'He is thirty years old.'

'Thirty years old?' repeated Tom, incredulously.

There was a period of a few agonising minutes of silence as Tom
engaged his *chemo-brain*. Eventually, a bead of truth dropped.

'That means … Jesus Christ. It can't be… he could be my son!… Oh
my God, if he is thirty years old, he *must* be my son…The dates fit ! … I
can't believe it !'

Tom slumped back into his seat in a state of dazed silence, stunned
and unable to speak. The shock of the realisation of this news was as
traumatic as any bereavement. He had already grieved for the loss of
his health. This was another loss, a greater cost: it was the reality of the
forfeit of the life he could have had with Emma. Tom's deepest thoughts
came to the surface.

'When she was working in Portland that summer, she must have realised she was pregnant. Why did she not tell me? I knew that she did not return to Britain. I heard that she stayed in Portland. A few months after we broke up, her family moved from Lincoln to be with her in America. That must have been why – no wonder they didn't want to talk to me. Jesus – what a mess!'

Amaka's tone changed as she listened with sympathy to her friend's distress. She had not anticipated it would be such a devastating blow. She crouched in front of him, placing her hands on his lap and tried to provide some reassurance. 'That analysis of events would make sense. She did not try to get in touch with you to tell you because she thought you were going to marry someone else – Felicity. She must have decided to bring up the baby on her own in the USA, with the help of her family.'

'But I had a right to know about my son.' There were tears in his eyes as Tom sounded like a little boy who had been treated unfairly.

Amaka tried to suggest a way forward. 'Emma would have been angry and upset. Who knows the way she was thinking at that time? But now, you must get in touch with her – to find out the truth.'

'He has to be my son. The time frame fits. There is no other explanation…oh, my God, forgive me. Poor Emma, what did I do to you?' Tom clasped his hands in front of his face, to hide his sense of shame.

Amaka pulled his hands apart and exposed his tears, even though there was some resistance. 'She was very sad to discover that you were very ill. That is why she wants to contact you. She thinks now is the time to get in touch.'

Tom finally broke down. 'My God. Oh, my good God!' There was nothing Amaka could do except allow Tom's outpouring to run its course.

While Tom sobbed uncontrollably, Amaka talked over the sound of his grief. 'Yes, indeed – God is good. If it had not been for your illness, you may have never known that you have might have a son.' She took his hands and shook his arms, trying to jolt away his anguish. 'You see, there is still some hope for you. Never abandon hope.' Tom returned her gaze before turning his head and staring into the distance, viewing without focus, except in his own inner world.

It seemed to work as Tom's weeping abated. 'Thank you, Amaka. Thank you, for bringing my world back to me and for all you have done for me. You may yet have saved me.'

Amaka retained her steely resilience. 'You do not have to thank me. I am pleased that you think this news has saved you but perhaps what has happened is that we have saved each other.' Tom nodded, before he leaned forward to embrace his friend.

XV

The day that Tom had been dreading was now confronting him. There had been enough to think about during his recovery without having to face the painful inevitability of time passing. Now, he had no choice. Amaka was due to return to Nigeria, as there were only two days left on her visa. Her bags were packed and waiting by the front door of *Derwent House,* while she and Tom were in the kitchen, trying to drink one last coffee together. A loud blast from outside indicated their car had arrived to take them both to the airport. Tom's mouth was dry and he was desperately trying to hold himself together. Neither spoke as the chauffeur loaded the boot and eventually started the blue Bentley, before heading off towards Heathrow Airport. Sitting quietly in the back, Amaka and Tom held hands.

As they approached the Airport Terminal, they both felt anxious about having to say goodbye. Their relationship since Tom's first diagnosis was now a loving friendship. Tom thought his heart was going to break with sadness at Amaka's departure. Then he looked at her infectious smile and something good stirred within. He knew they would never lose contact with each other and this was a wonderfully reassuring thought. Their first sighting of the *Departures* sign was the trigger to a break in the silence. 'I have upgraded your flight,' Tom told her as the car began to slow down. 'You can collect your first-class tickets from the desk, when you check in.'

'I am travelling first-class?' asked Amaka, trying to sound positive in such dire circumstances.

'Indeed you are. That means you can wait in the Executive Lounge while your baggage is processed. There is free champagne on the flight and I expect you to drink at least one glass. I have arranged for someone to meet us here to take your bags.' Just as he finished speaking, they pulled up to the Terminal's *Departures* doorway and a young man in a blue uniform stepped forward, after being beckoned by the chauffeur.

The kerbside collection of the luggage was organised while Amaka helped Tom out of the vehicle. Free to link arms, the two made their way through the Terminal while the driver headed off to the waiting area. The busy Airport was loud and overwhelming. Tom was gazing upward above the crowd of travellers and quickly spotted the sign for the *Executive Departure Lounge*. They both knew it was the moment they had to say goodbye. The swish, automatic smoked-glass doors were the final barrier to all non-passengers.

Tom stopped and turned to look into Amaka's glorious brown eyes. He held her arms as they faced each other and spoke forcefully, determined to keep emotion at bay. 'So… this is goodbye?'

Amaka did her best to lighten the mood. 'For the moment, yes. But I shall see you when I return next year to complete my research and I will expect another glass of champagne when we meet.'

Before they embraced, Tom held out one hand towards Amaka and reached inside his jacket breast-pocket with the other. He pulled out an envelope and gave it to Amaka, 'Before you go, this is for you – I hope it will also help others. Don't open it until you get on the plane. Everything has been organised by my lawyers so don't worry about anything.'

Amaka's surprised expression indicated that she had not expected any exchange of tokens between them. It was not necessary. 'Thank you. I don't know what for – but thank you.'

With that, she stepped forward and as they hugged their final farewell, Amaka started to cry. It was the first time since her childhood days before the Civil War that she had been able to shed a tear. Their locked embrace lasted for a full minute, with neither willing to break the bond between them. Eventually, when she stood back, Tom could see Amaka had been crying. He gave her his handkerchief and lightly mocked her, 'Real tears? I didn't think I would ever see the day.'

Through her sobs, Amaka made herself heard. 'You did this to me.'

Tom made an apology, almost as a plea. 'I'm sorry. I did not mean to upset you. I would not do that for the world.'

Her response surprised him. 'No this is a good thing. It is good to cry. I had forgotten what it is like to cry. Goodbye, Tom and thank you.'

'Goodbye – *God is Everything*.' He looked directly into Amaka's eyes when he said these words, causing her to burst into laughter because the phrase was the English translation of her Igbo name.

Her face was a picture of joyous shock. 'How did you know this is what my name means – *God is Everything?* This is what Amaka means in my language.'

'The Internet can be a wonderful place. I cannot think of a more apt name for such a beautiful person. Don't forget to get in touch with me as soon as you get back home.' Tom gave one last flurry. 'And hurry back to Britain.'

'I will. Goodbye, my darling friend.'

Too soon, Amaka crossed the threshold and disappeared through the first set of double doors leading into the Executive Lounge. When finally out of sight, Tom gave an enormous sigh of sadness and returned to his waiting car.

Two hours later, Amaka settled into her comfortable seat on the aeroplane. She thought she would wait until she was airborne before she opened Tom's envelope. Within twenty minutes of take-off, the beep on the overhead console indicated that it was safe for passengers to remove their seat-belts. Amaka made herself comfortable and accepted the Air Stewardess's offer of a free glass of champagne. She reached into her handbag and removed the envelope. It had something written on the front, in Tom's shaky handwriting: *'This is only the beginning.'* Her fingers fumbled with excitement as she struggled to open the folded A4 letter inside. It read,

> *Dearest Amaka,*
> *As you can see from the wording on the cheque, I have started a charity in your name.*
> *Please use the money to help the children of your Village.*
> *With love and gratitude,*
> *Tom*

Inside was a cheque:

Pay*: The Amaka Onyali Foundation*
Amount*: One million pounds only.*
Signed*: TDV Kettlewell*

She let out an enormous scream of excitement which made her fellow passengers turn alarmingly in her direction. A stewardess quickly approached her seat.

'Is everything alright, madam?'

'Oh yes, everything is very alright indeed. It is very fine, thank you.'

Amaka re-adjusted herself and took a gulp of champagne, her mind racing. As she looked out of the window at the infinite stretch of blueness, she had only good thoughts for the first time in her life. Instantly, she decided to allocate the funds in her mind. Some of the money would go towards providing a source of fresh water for her village. The rest could contribute to the building of a school or even a Community Centre. Tom was right. It was a new beginning. Amaka settled back into her seat, closed her eyes and looked forward to a new challenge. A few minutes later, she stirred from her semi-doze. It was no good trying to switch off, her mind was battling with exciting thoughts and she could not sleep. Despite all the slumbering around her by the other tired passengers, relaxation was out of the question.

Her excited state of mind did her body no favours and after almost sixteen hours in the aeroplane with very little sleep, Amaka was exhausted. Travelling first class certainly helped but it had still been a long flight. On landing at Akanu Ibiam International Airport in Enugu, Amaka descended the steps and made her way to passport control before proceeding to collect her luggage. Standing silently in front of the baggage carousel, she was finding it difficult to stay awake. The repetitive humming noise of the circular conveyor belt, on which anonymous cases were disappearing in front her, had a hypnotic effect. Gradually, all the cases were removed from the carousel and the last passengers headed towards the *Arrivals Exit*. Amaka was left bewildered, wondering what had happened to *her* suitcase. She was accompanied by one other person, a Nigerian man of similar age. When they both realised there was a problem, they looked at each other. The man smiled before declaring, 'It looks like we shall be going home without our luggage. I suppose we had better go to the *Help Desk*.'

Amaka sighed with the kind of resignation that can only be placated by having a cheque for one million pounds in your purse. At that moment, a lost suitcase was not important. She nodded in agreement before confirming the young man's assessment of the situation. 'I suppose so.'

'The Desk is over there in the corner. Thank goodness it seems to be open.' The man escorted Amaka to the counter and took the initiative with the attendant on duty. He gave the assistant the luggage receipts and waited while the green-uniformed official picked up the phone and proceeded to contact someone. After a couple of fast-talking minutes, the attendant replaced the receiver.

'We have located the two cases sir, ...' he turned to face Amaka '... and madam... There are two blue cases. The names on the tickets indicate they belong to a Dr Dilibe Nkowo...? ' He looked at the young man, who nodded. ' ..The writing on other one is not very clear but it suggests a ... Dr Mmm..aki Nali?'

This was too much for a tired Amaka, whose day was getting more absurd with each passing hour. She burst into an embarrassing fit of laughter, fuelled by travel fatigue and the champagne. Her accomplice took a step back in surprise at her sudden outbreak of the giggles. The attendant bowed his head in subjugation and attempted to avert his eyes elsewhere. Then he turned away to collect some forms, no doubt as an excuse to remove himself from the situation.

A stunned Dilibe Nkowo punctured Amaka's balloon. 'Remind me never to call you Maki,' he said, with a smile. When the attendant returned, Amaka apologised for her behaviour. 'Sorry about that, my friend. It has been a very tiring journey.' The official nodded a silent acceptance of her apology. After a further five minutes of waiting by the *Help Desk*, they heard the carousel begin to move once more on the opposite site of the baggage area. Two blue suitcases appeared through the entry flaps and entered a circular race on Belt 3. Once the bags were opposite the two weary travellers, they were dutifully snatched from the moving conveyor belt by the young man, who thumped them down onto two luggage trolleys. The couple then made their way to the *Arrivals* lobby.

As they pushed their trolleys together, side-by-side, Dr Nkowo felt sufficiently confident to engage in conversation. 'Got far to go ... *Maki* ?' he asked, with an impish grin. He felt like pushing the boundary of this new relationship a little further.

Amaka shot him a look of mock aggression. 'Yes, about another six hours by bus. I think I may stay at a hotel tonight, before I continue my journey. I am heading for my home village, Uminwani. It is about a hundred miles south-east of here.'

'I know it. I too am going that way. I am heading for Uzukwu. It is only twenty miles from Uminwani and I have a hire-car waiting for me. I work for *Amstil Oil* and the Company have paid for a car so it will not cost me anything to take you to Uminwani – if you would like me to? I can take you there with no difficulty – If you trust me, that is. I know we have just met but honestly, you will be safe with me.'

Somehow, Amaka did feel safe with this young Igbo man, who called himself Dilibe.

After sorting out the paper-work at the Car Hire desk, Dilibe Nkowo left her to guard the two trolleys. He soon returned from the car pound and pulled into the lay-by outside *Arrivals,* sitting behind the driver's wheel of a clean, white Nissan Pathfinder. Dilibe opened the passenger door and a tired Amaka flopped into the seat. Once Dilibe had stored the cases and closed the boot, she felt her eyes begin to close. In a state of drowsiness, she let the warmth embrace her. Not only did it seem that she suddenly had the beginning of a new life, she appeared to have a new name. The more she thought about it, the more she liked the sound of 'Maki'.

XVI

Tom was sitting in the Airport Restaurant drinking coffee and watching the letters flick audibly on the overhead screen like a waterfall of illegible scrabble. Although he was not yet strictly strong enough to travel on his own, Amaka had taught him that opportunities had to be taken when they are presented and he was following her advice. It had been three days since Amaka had left for Nigeria and Tom was in the Executive Departure Lounge at Heathrow, waiting for his flight to Richmond International Airport. There had been no contact with Emma on the telephone, despite his promise to Amaka. He had always bitterly regretted not speaking directly to Emma about Felicity. It had been a coward's path, only writing a letter , back in 1970 and he was not going to make the same mistake again. Tom was now a different person to the immature undergraduate he had once been. Time had moved on and he had changed.

Tom was going to Richmond to seek out the truth, face-to-face. It was the very least Emma deserved. He felt he had also earned that right over the last twelve months, having stared death in the face and won a temporary victory, thanks to Amaka's help. No one knew how long the remission from the cancer would last so he was going to make the most of the time he had left.

Tom picked up his newspaper and then put it down again, just as quickly. Drumming the table with his fingers, he asked a passing waitress for another cup of coffee, before checking his watch. There was still an hour to wait before his flight. He blew his cheeks and turned to explore the area. A fat, bald man in a light grey suit was dozing three seats away from where Tom was sitting, his silver briefcase by his side. As the attendant brought the order, she spilt some of the coffee into his saucer. Tom did not notice the small pool under his cup because an attractive young blonde in a green trouser-suit had distracted him, calling after her partner. When he took a sip, a drop splashed into the reservoir, causing some of the coffee to land on the cuff of his new cream shirt. Tom shook his wrist vigorously and inwardly cursed as he took a napkin and began to wipe himself. Suddenly he was caught by a distant thought and began to laugh aloud. He wished Emma was there, giggling opposite him as she had once done in his flat, that day of the Anti-Apartheid protest march, when he spilled coffee over his hand. He did not know what the future would bring but for the first time in a long while, Tom had hope in his heart. Hope had been Amaka's greatest gift to her friend. Perhaps he might even try to reconcile his affections towards Jenny, one day and build a new relationship. The more he thought about his sister, the more he liked the idea.

Tom was a new man.

XVII

M aki was right. It *was* the sound of the helicopter in the distance she could hear. Others around her also heard the unusual noise and soon, excitement spread through the villagers. Children began screaming with enthusiasm and anticipation. A round of applause was somehow started by the adults but it was difficult to hear over the increasing noise of the approaching engines. There was a rumbling blare as the vibrations echoed around the surrounding plateau. The visitors were here. They were coming.

Urunwa raced to the stage and took the microphone. She gave an announcement with authoritative enthusiasm. 'Listen, please everyone. As you can see, our visitors are coming. Please take your positions. Everyone to their places now please.'

The whirring noise became louder and louder. Birds and animals in nearby fields were scurrying for safety as the sound became deafening. The outline of the pilot's uniform could be discerned through the smoked glass of the windscreen. Then, the helicopter hovered overhead in a circling motion, about fifty feet from the ground, before being slowly manipulated towards the field next to the Community Centre. Ugonna had cordoned-off the area with a long rope for safety and had cut a huge, white letter 'H' into the grass at the centre of the field as a landing guide.

The din of the engines became deafening; children put their hands over their ears to protect themselves, while smiling and cheering. Several risked one ear as they chanced a wave in the direction of the laughing pilot. Slowly, the helicopter lowered onto the 'H' while the down-draught created waves of rolling amber grass around the field. On touching the ground, music from the stage began in earnest and the musicians played for their lives.

The rotary blades decreased their circular speed to create a chirping noise, distinctive of all deflating helicopters until eventually, they stopped spinning. A hand could be seen waving through a small window. A cheer greeted the opening of the main door hatch and there was a thud as the steps were unfolded, creating their own landing ritual. Then the guests appeared.

Amaka could barely contain her joy as she waved vigorously through clouded eyes. She wanted to rush forward and put her arms around her friend but she had to set an example of decorum to those around her. At the bottom of the five steps, a slightly older Tom Kettlewell turned to help his wife Emma descend safely from the helicopter. Still holding her hand, he raised his right arm above his eyes to protect them from the sun. He perused the fantastic scene of colour and festival around him before he recognised a lady dressed in purple waving in his direction. It was his beautiful friend Amaka.

Tom was pleased to be in Nigeria to officially open the Uminwani Community Centre built by money raised through the Amaka Onyali Foundation. In the four years since the inception of the Foundation, the equivalent of five-and-a-half million pounds had been raised. The Charity had flourished under the leadership of its founder.

Tom and Emma Kettlewell moved away from the steps and were soon followed by a young man, who Amaka had not seen before. As he stepped down from the helicopter she could see he was strikingly handsome. He was wearing a light blue suit with a sparklingly bright, white shirt. The clothes highlighted his distinctive, sparkling sapphire eyes. It could only be one person.

It was Tommy.